MW01200495

To request permissions, contact the publisher at
ScharaReevesPress@gmail.com

ISBN: 978-1-7362987-3-2

First paperback edition October 2022.

Edited by Alyson Montione
Proofread by ScribeCat (ScribeCat.ca)
Cover art, interior art by Rebecca Schmid

Schara Reeves Press

ScharaReevesPress.com

Acknowledgments

Content Editor:

Alyson Montione

Proofreader:

ScribeCat (ScribeCat.ca)

General Support:

Jesus Christ
Psalm 27:13 Ministries
Family
Friends
Schoharie Library Writing Club

Beta readers:

Rebecca Rowling
Emma Panzera
Niamh Schmid
Jubilee Schmid

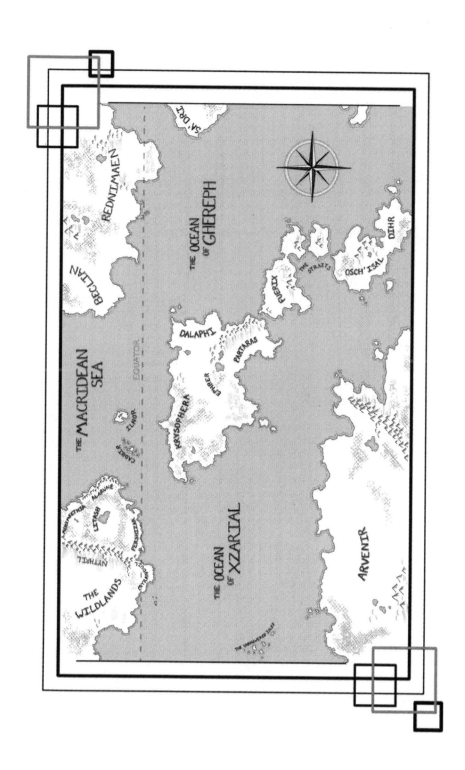

Pronunciations

Ajhal: J pronounced like *ge* in "beige" (ah-JAHL)
Ameri: (uh-MAYR-ee)
Arhys Saen: (ARE-iss SANE)
Arvenir: (ARE-ven-eer)

Beclian: (BEC-lee-un)

Cadbir: (CAD-beer)
Cithan: (SIGH-than)

Destrin: (DES-trin)
Dolsni: (DOLS-nee)

Eatris: (EE-tris)
Elescar: (el-eh-SCAR)
Ethian: (EETH-ee-uhn)
Euracia: (yur-uh-KAI-uh)

Faelie: (FAY-lee)
Fuerix: (FWAIR-ix)

Grand Va' Kied: (VA KYED)

Ilske: (ILSK)
Iruscaed: (eer-uh-SKADE)
Ithynian Gasper: (EYE-thin-ee-uhn GAS-pur)
Iveros Kstoren: (EYE-vur-ose KSTOR-en)

Judican: (JOO-dih-can)

Karansuur: (ka-ran-SOOR)
Kassander Knyte: (CAS-and-dur NIGHT)
Krysophera: (kris-OFF-er-uh)

Litash: (lih-TASH)

Mikaud Lenstativ: (mih-CAUD LEN-stah-teev)
Myrandi: (mih-RAHN-dee)
Myranduil: (mih-RAHN-doo-ill)

Oskoristiv: (auh-SCOR-his-steev)
Ovok: (OH-vok)

Perras: (PEYR-iss)
Pershizar: (PER-shih-zar)

Rheritarus: (rur-ih-TAR-us)

Silbyr: (SILL-beer)
Sohlv: (SOULV)
Solus: (SOUL-us)
Svarik Ihail: (SVAR-ik ee-HAIL)

Tahra, Elaris: (TAR-ah eh-LAR-iss)
Tirzah: (TEER-zah)
Treiset: (TRY-set)
Tskecz: (TSKEZH)
Tulstead: (TULL-sted)

Udeneran Talsk: (yoo-DEN-uhr-en TALLSK)

Verzaer: (ver-ZAYR)

Xyridcylduin: (zy-rill-SILL-doo-inn)
Xzarial: (ZAR-ee-uhl)

To Niamh,

My best friend and the only

reason I ever finished this book.

TALES OF REDEMERÉ: BOOK I

ASKEFISE

REBECCA SCHMID

PART I

PERSHIZAR

CHAPTER I

Rhioa

"Is he dead?"

I nudge him with the toe of my boot. "I don't think so. We wouldn't be hearing his Gifting if he was."

But I understand why Tirzah is dubious. The stranger is very thin. His sullen skin and the dark circles beneath his closed eyes tell me he is dehydrated. His coat has a large gash and, where his breeches are torn, I can see dried blood. A sword is belted at each side and I can make out the shape of a dagger hidden in the folds of his tunic. It's hard to tell his age between all this and the mud he's caked with. I would guess that he has only recently entered adulthood.

Tirzah sighs. "Well, now what?"

I shift my weight from one foot to the other, skirt rustling across the leaves with the slight motion. "I don't know," I murmur, trying to think.

I know what's going through Tirzah's head: Helping him is a risk. But if we leave him, he won't make it until morning—much less all the way to civilization.

"We could just leave him food and water," Tirzah reasons, voice betraying her impatience.

"Yes, and attract some Forest animal that would eat him before he even woke up," I reply dryly.

Tirzah huffs. "We don't have time to be playing nursemaids to someone who could turn around and ruin our cover."

I look him over, noticing the worn patches on his shoulders that indicate he'd been carrying a pack. But I don't see any belongings besides what he's wearing. How did he lose them? Did he wander too far into the Forest of Riddles? Or...is it possible that he was coming out of it?

"We could just drop him at the closest settlement," I hear myself argue. I draw my sword in precaution and nudge him with one foot. No reaction.

Tirzah's terse sigh and following silence says what she does not: She has given up trying to reason with me.

I adjust my grip on my blade and use a little more force as I cautiously nudge the young man again. This time he jolts into consciousness with a rapidity that startles both of us. His reflexes are impressive: He manages to turn from his side and on to his back, scuttling away from me in the same motion. He stops the instant my sword touches his neck.

"Who are you?" I demand with stern calm. I hear Tirzah draw a dagger from behind me.

The stranger cocks his head and messy black hair, complete with bits of leaves, slips down over one eye. "What?" he asks in the trade language.

I switch to it. "Who are you?" I repeat.

"I...." He looks suddenly quite lost as he notices his surroundings for the first time. In an accent I don't recognize, he goes on in a raspy voice. "My name is Tyron. I'm nobody. Just a traveler." Under his breath he adds something about being a very bad one.

Everyone who has ever described themselves as 'nobody' has always had something to hide. I share a quick glance with Tirzah.

"Where are you traveling from and to?" I keep the sword at his neck. At least he's bright enough to keep his hands still and within my sight.

"I am from Litash," Tyron replies. "I'm not really traveling anywhere in particular; just away from Litash."

Litash? If it wasn't for the hum of his Gifting, I would call the man a liar. "How did you get across the Forest?" I question, skeptical.

Tyron blinks at me a moment, looks down at his torn and splattered clothing, then looks back up with an odd, nearly mystified smile. "I'm across? Thank goodness...." His voice trails off and his brow furrows. "My apologies, what did you ask?"

The sluggishness of his movements and voice tells me that his adrenaline is wearing off, and the effects of dehydration and mild starvation are setting in. "When did you last eat?"

"I guess that depends on how long I was asleep," he says, looking around as if his surroundings might help him recall.

I suppress a sigh. I finally withdraw my blade and slide it into the half sheath at my hip. Tyron watches but makes no move. I turn and cross the few feet to Tirzah. With a look of stoic resignation, she pulls off her pack and opens the flap, keeping the young man in the corner of her eye. I note how he watches us with equal attention.

What he really needs is some kind of mild broth. Since such a thing is impractical for travel, we have none nor any way of making it. The mildest thing Tirzah and I have is bread. While she pulls that out, I take out my water skin.

"If I give this to you, will you be able to keep from guzzling it all at once?" I have no wish to care for a vomiting stranger.

Tyron's eyes immediately fasten on the skin. He hesitates, then nods.

So I give it to him. True to his word, he takes only small sips at intervals as he continues to watch me. I have to give him credit for his self-control. Tirzah slices off a small hunk of bread and hands it to me. In turn, I hold out my hand to Tyron for my water skin.

There is a slight delay, and I see his lips press together, yet he gives it back easily enough. I squeeze out just enough water to soak the bread and then give the latter to him.

Tyron takes it gingerly, hands nearly trembling. His eyes meet mine. "Thank you."

I don't reply. I re-cork my skin and let him eat as I puzzle over what to do with him. Tirzah is right: We can't just take him with us. What would keep him from running his mouth? Besides, we don't have enough supplies to walk the whole way—especially with another person. Even if we were better stocked, we can't abide that much delay. But the issue of supplies also means we can't just give him what we have and point him towards a city.

I watch him, still sitting there, very slowly eating the bit of bread. Even I would feel bad to have woken him just to abandon him to the fate he would have otherwise entered peacefully. His bright green eyes flick between me and Tirzah every few seconds, and I know he is evaluating us just as we evaluate him. I set my pack on the ground and sit down across from him.

"What is your name?" he asks, voice quiet and scratchy.

I consider lying, but opt for seeing how he reacts instead. "Rhioa."

"That is a lovely name," he says with strange sincerity. "It is good to meet you, Rhioa." He looks up at Tirzah. "And you?"

Tirzah doesn't reply, only looking at me with one eyebrow raised.

"This is my sister, Tirzah," I answer for her.

"It is good to meet you, too, Tirzah," he says with the same earnestness.

Tirzah scoffs under her breath.

Tyron goes back to his bread. I can't help but think how oddly polite he is for someone who is starving. Or perhaps it is the starvation that causes it. Surely he realizes he won't survive without our help.

With his current condition, it is clear we won't be able to get any further today. So I begin to clear a spot in the dry leaves, gathering twigs for tinder. Without a word, Tirzah sets her pack near me and begins to gather bigger pieces for fuel.

"What are you doing?" Tyron asks.

"Seeing as you're unfit for travel, I'm going to build a fire." My reply is taut. "You'll stay here and rest while we hunt. We can't afford to lose any more than a day so you'll have to get up and walk by tomorrow."

He dips his head in acknowledgment. "Alright. Thank you."

The thanks strikes me curiously but I make no comment. I leave my pack next to Tirzah's and go to join her. I can feel Tyron's green eyes follow me all the way out of sight.

Between the two of us working silently, we gather the wood in short order and return to the spot where we'd left him. I catch the scent of smoke and see Tyron sitting by the pile of tinder I'd made. He must have gotten a flame going. Remembering that he has no pack or notable supplies, I quickly guess that he used Gifting to do so.

While I have no plans to reveal my race, the last thing I need is him using Gifting for everything. So I drop the wood next to the little fire, kneel down to begin adding pieces, and address the man without even looking up.

"I don't like Gifting," I say bluntly. "So if you want to travel with us, don't use any. Is that clear?"

There is a brief pause, then, "Very clear." His tone remains mild-mannered despite my brusque countenance.

"Good." The word leaves no room for further conversation.

Now sure that the wood I brought will catch, I turn to the packs and slice off another piece of bread. I water it down, give it to Tyron, and toss my water skin beside him.

"Eat," I order. "Then sleep if you can. We may be gone a few hours to hunt, but don't leave this spot until we return. The campfire will be enough to keep away any animals." I mentally review the contents of our packs, making sure there's nothing that could give us away if he decides to rummage through.

Again, I receive a sluggish nod and a, "Thank you."

I say nothing. There will be plenty of time to question him after he wakes up. For now, Tirzah and I have work to do if all of us are going to eat. I nod to my sister and turn from the fire, aware of him watching us go.

As soon as we're out of earshot, I brace for what is undoubtedly coming.

"Your kindness is going to cost us," Tirzah says, each word clear cut and cold.

I keep walking. "Perhaps a few days. It's no matter. We've kept contacts waiting for longer."

"That's not what I'm talking about." I hear Tirzah stop as she asks, "What if he talks? What if he finds anything out? Will you be the one to silence him?"

I turn to face her, chin lifting ever so slightly. "We'll deal with it if it comes to it."

Tirzah tilts her head and narrows her eyes. "*We*? I think you mean *I* will. I'm a little tired of doing the dirty work, Rhy, and I don't feel like taking on extra."

"What would you have me do? Leave him to die?" I snap. "I'd be no better than Mother."

Her countenance settles back into stone and I receive no reply.

I turn away and keep walking as I ignore the lump in my throat. We have too much work to do to be arguing. "The trees are close here. It will be easier for me to drive prey to you."

Tirzah gives only a grunt in acknowledgment.

So I shift, feeling myself grow and lengthen as I dig my claws into the tree-tangled earth. I keep my wings folded close to keep from hitting branches as I shake thoroughly. The motion helps me settle back into the feeling of this second skin. I swing my head around to check on Tirzah, and just in time to watch her accidentally take out a sapling with her tail. Her Dragon form always has been larger than mine. She gives a low growl to tell me she's ready and I dart off through the trees.

Time to hunt.

Tyron

I'm cold, dizzy, thirsty, hungry, and an absolute *idiot*. I sit by the new fire and try to limit myself to small, occasional sips from the water skin. It takes more self-control than I care to admit, but not even that draws my mind away from the face I had woken up to. I make myself refocus on the fire and keeping it going while my rescuers are gone. Each motion revives the stinging sensation that wraps up and down my legs, reminding me of the fall I'd taken a few days ago. I'll have to clean the cuts if I want to avoid infection.

My gaze is tugged towards the two packs that sit across the fire. I don't dare touch anything. My mind might be fogged with fatigue, but not so much that I don't instantly recognize the signs: the specialized weaponry, the close-fitting clothing that still allows for easy movement, the supplies that allow for quick travel, and the clear evaluation of my condition. These women are lethal if they choose to be. And they are traveling with intention. *And I can't get her brown eyes out of my head....*

"You sap," I mutter, reminding myself that I am much too spent to trust my own judgment. *You are going to wake up and laugh at yourself for being such an infatuated fool.*

I tell myself that a little food and a little rest and I will be back to rights. For now, I need to start with the cuts on my legs. I reluctantly set the water skin aside and roll up my pant leg. I run one hand gingerly over my shin, trying to loosen some of the caked dirt and dried blood. None of the cuts feel very deep. I'm very lucky to have fallen from so high up in that tree and suffered nothing more than a few scratches. Well, and a massively bruised shoulder. I suppose climbing a tree to try and get a sense of my direction wasn't exactly my brightest idea.

I glance towards the woods and don't catch any sight or sound of my rescuers. I know she had been adamant about not using Gifting, but I can't risk infection. I take the water skin and dampen my hand, wiping away more of the grime. Then

I reach for my Gift. I use it to feel out the cuts in a way my fingers and throbbing leg cannot. Only two of the cuts are deep enough for concern, so those are the ones I focus on. I have to block out the accompanying burning feeling as I weave together muscle and skin until the openings are sealed.

I repeat the process on my other leg, then again for the one cut around my rib cage. It's not very much work—certainly much less than other healings I have done—and yet it leaves me drained. So after a little more water, I pull my ragged coat more closely around me and lie down as close to the fire as I dare. But when I shut my eyes, I still see a figure with golden hair and hunter green skirts, glancing over her shoulder one more time before disappearing into the trees.

You are an idiot.

"Wake up."

Something prods my shoulder and I jerk backward and into a sitting position. *Ow.*

"He's still alive, then?" Another voice asks as I sit up, dazed.

It takes me several long seconds to remember where I am and how I came to be here.

"So it would seem," replies the woman who woke me. Rhioa.

I am dismayed to find that she is just as stunning as she was when she first found me.

"Are you hungry?" Rhioa asks, peering at me oddly.

I realize I haven't said a thing after bolting upright. I try to gather my thoughts as I nod.

Rhioa crosses to her sister on the other side of the fire, skirts whispering over the leaves as she walks. That's when the scent of roasting meat hits me and my stomach groans in response. Tirzah is kneeling by the fire, hanging thin strips of red meat above the glowing bed of coals. I notice the carcass of a small, unfamiliar type of deer hanging from a tree several yards away and wonder how they brought it down. I hadn't noticed any hunting implements....

"Here," The word snaps me back to attention. "If this settles well, we'll see about trying something more." Rhioa holds out another piece of bread and her water skin.

I accept both, noticing the latter has been refilled. "Thank you."

Rhioa returns to her sister's side, sitting down cross-legged and pulling out a small knife. She takes what appears to be an edible sort of root and pares both ends. Then, with slender fingers, she sets it to cook on a flat rock beside the coals.

I watch, still chewing the bread slowly. They must not have had enough food to accommodate an extra traveler. "Is there anything I can do to help?" I ask.

I catch the way Tirzah's gaze flicks towards me, but I can't read her reaction.

"Rest while you can," Rhioa answers without looking up. "You'll have to walk by afternoon."

Afternoon? I hadn't realized I'd slept into the next day. In that case, I am glad that I healed all the cuts on my legs yesterday. Travel will be hard enough as it is. "Alright."

Rhioa and Tirzah continue their work, cutting, cooking, and packing in unspoken coordination.

"Is this your first time outside of Litash?" Rhioa asks, using twigs to pull a cooked root away from the coals to cool.

"Yes," I nod, taking another sip of water. I notice idly that, though they wear no other jewelry, the sisters each have a ring on their right hand.

Rhioa picks up another root, her gold-blonde braid slipping over her shoulder with the movement. "So how do you speak the trade language so well?"

"Is that what they call it here?" I nearly laugh as I set the water skin down. "Where I come from, they call it Litashian. Though claiming a language as their own does seem an appropriately arrogant thing for Litash to do."

Rhioa lifts an eyebrow but gives no comment. She slices the ends off the root then holds the paring knife out to her sister. Tirzah trims another switch to hang meat from and then hands the knife back.

"Why did you leave?" Again, it is Rhioa who asks.

I've never seen someone look so graceful while doing something so mundane. "There was nothing there for me." I shrug and tear my eyes away from her. I wonder what Judican's reaction was when my guards returned to the capitol without me. "I decided that left me with nothing to lose to the Forest."

"Except for your belongings," Rhioa comments.

"Except for those," I acknowledge wryly. Not that I had brought much of value. I am thankful that I'd thought ahead well enough to keep all of that directly on my person: my swords, my dagger, and my savings.

"So, in essence, you walked into the Forest of Riddles with no plan or motivation besides disliking your native country?" Now Rhioa looks up at me, brown eyes sharp and searching.

The full story is much longer, but I'm guessing neither of them have any interest in a full synopsis of my life. "I suppose that's an accurate summary."

The look the sisters exchange is very clear: They think me either a liar or a halfwit.

I am definitely the latter.

"We are traveling to the port city of Ajhal," Rhioa finally says, brushing a paring scrap from her skirts. "We will take you that far. From there, your fate is your own."

"I understand. Thank you for your aid—I will do my best to not slow you down," I reply.

The way Tirzah huffs quietly tells me that this has already been a point of contention.

Rhioa's lack of reaction towards her sister is equally telling. But just as before, she gives no response to my thanks. Instead she pauses, then turns her paring knife and offers me the handle. "Finish paring these. I will go refill the water skins."

I take it obediently and reach for one of the roots. My hands feel clumsy, reminding me of how sore I still am. But I peel the hardened tips off and set it down to cook with the others. I reach for another one and try not to watch Rhioa walk off into the woods.

She hasn't been gone for even a minute before Tirzah speaks.

"If you so much as look at her wrong, I will kill you. And no one will ever find your body. Do you understand?"

I pick up my head, meeting her stone-faced gaze. She said it so simply—a statement of pure fact. I know that she means every word.

"I understand," I reply.

"Good."

We both go back to our work.

CHAPTER 2

Rhioa

I look over my shoulder, checking again to make sure he's still walking. He had started limping by the time we'd stopped yesterday evening. But Tyron has yet to complain. He manages one foot after another, his tattered coat catching on branches and bushes as he goes.

"What's the plan for crossing the outcroppings?" Tirzah asks.

I adjust my satchel. "The Karam Basin. We'll need the water."

Tirzah frowns and glances back at our tag-along. "You really think that's a good idea?"

"What's so bad about a basin?" Tyron asks, apparently listening in.

I level a look at Tirzah. She should have at least asked in Pershizarian; We really don't need Tyron asking questions. But I suppose this one is harmless enough. "This one is the only place with water on the western dunes of Pershizar. It is also incidentally on the way to the black-market port of Salzor, making it a popular stop for all the Dune Pillagers."

"I see." He sounds nearly winded as he presses on. "This does not deter you?"

"Anyone can make it through easily enough if they know where to avoid," I reply as I push a tree branch out of the way. "Tirzah and I have made it through before."

"You two travel often?"

I narrow my eyes at Tirzah. This is her fault.

She gives me a look in return, as if to chide me for answering him in the first place.

"Often enough," I answer with a shrug. Then I turn it around before the questions can continue. "What about yourself? I've never met a Litashian."

He gives a sort of chuckle. "Often enough."

The way he mirrors my answer irritates me.

"But this is my first time beyond the border," Tyron goes on. "I'm not sure if others have made it across before. Either they never make it through, they never make it back, or they like it out here far better."

The benign continuation makes it easy to drop the whole matter, which makes me wonder why he offered it. Either way, I don't reply.

That doesn't stop Tyron. "Have you heard of others from my country before?"

I shake my head. "Why? Do you know someone else who crossed the Forest?" Maybe this is his motive—maybe he's looking for them.

I hear Tyron's coat rustle as he shakes his head. "No. As far as I know, I am alone."

He says it simply enough, and yet I wonder if there is more meaning behind the admission. Why can't I figure out what it is? And for that matter, why would he tell us and thus admit his vulnerability?

"What about you? Where are you two from?"

And we're back to this. "We've lived in many places." It's easier to be vague than to lie. But just to cover my tracks—"I think my favorite was Ilnor. They have lovely skies there, always clean and blue."

"Ilnor..." Tyron says the word slowly. "It is one of the isles in the Macridean Sea, correct?"

Surprised, I look back at him. "Yes. How do you know that?"

Tyron gives a tired sort of shrug. "We still have old maps and history books. I'm sure much of it is outdated, but some study it all the same."

So he was either a scholar or nobility. Who else would study such things? But few scholars are in the habit of carrying swords, and fewer nobles would leave their title behind. Perhaps he was the son of some lesser lord. It would explain the plain attire yet polished manners.

Up ahead, Tirzah stops and pulls off her pack. I squint up at the still thick foliage and wonder again how she's always able to tell time so well.

"Sit and rest," I tell Tyron.

He sinks down against the base of a tree and leans back against it.

Normally we don't stop while traveling, but Tirzah and I had agreed the occasional respite would be easier than wearing Tyron out entirely. As slow as walking is, carrying him across Pershizar would be even worse.

I take out my water skin and drink what I need before passing it to Tyron. Then while Tirzah pulls out some dried meat, I cut bread for Tyron and count out cooked neri roots.

I give the bread and a small piece of meat to Tyron. "Don't eat too quickly," I warn.

He nods, thanks me, and begins to eat.

"*You are talking to him too much,*" Tirzah murmurs in Pershizarian.

"*It's the only way to make sure he's no threat,*" I counter, watching Tyron from the corner of my eye.

Either he doesn't know the language or he is talented enough an actor to suppress any sort of reaction. He stays where he is, leaning back against the tree with his eyes half-closed and chewing slowly.

Tirzah scoffs under her breath. "*He's too worn out to be a physical threat. But any fool can spread a story; make sure you don't give him any means to do so.*"

"*I hadn't realized that you think me so loose-tongued,*" I say with some sharpness.

"*No, I think you're still too **nice**,*" Tirzah shoots back. "*We agreed to helping him, not learning his life story. The less you know, the better off you are.*"

I bite my tongue. I wish she wouldn't always put me first—it would make it easier to argue. But no, Tirzah has always been the protector. And I have always been the weak one.

The rest of the midday meal passes in silence until Tyron passes the water skin back with a quiet, "Thank you." Then we're up and walking again.

"How far south does the Forest extend?" Tyron asks from behind us.

I bite my tongue again. "Depends on where you are." I keep my tone as short as my answer.

"Is it common to travel in it?"

I turn around. "I'm not sure what things are like where you come from, but here we don't tend to reward the kindness of others by prying them with constant questions."

Tyron wears his surprise openly. His green eyes turn towards Tirzah then back to me. "My apologies." He bows his head. "Please forgive my curiosity—I did not mean to be rude."

I turn back and begin walking again. "Your breath is better saved for the journey."

He doesn't say a word until the very end of the day. And then it is only when I give him the water again and he says, "Thank you."

I give no reply.

I hold a hand up to my brow to block out the sun. Heat makes the horizon shimmer. It's barely mid-morning, but already the day is warm out here on the outcroppings. I turn around as Tirzah and Tyron step out of the woods.

Tirzah takes one look at the barren expanse and sighs. Neither of us travel Pershizar on foot when we can.

When Tyron sees it, on the other hand, his eyes go wide.

He hasn't asked any questions in the three days since I snapped at him, but his curiosity has shown through all the same. Several times, I've spotted him pausing to pluck a leaf or plant stalk, examining it, and rolling it around in his fingers as we walk. Yet one would think that, being in the poor condition that he is, he would be less enamored by the sight of the arid plain ahead of us. Perhaps it hasn't occurred to him that he will have to cross it.

"Ajhal is only about three days from here—four at most," I say, though I suppose this all depends on Tyron. He still lags behind by the end of the day.

"Is all of Pershizar like this?"

I abide the one question. "If you mean baking hot, then yes." I take off my pack and pull out a light headscarf. Tirzah is already doing the same.

Of course, Tyron is not prepared at all for the heat. His tunic and breeches are both of heavy material, and his boots of thick leather. His ragged coat is warm enough that he has carried it for the last few days through the Forest

"Untuck your tunic and unbutton your sleeve cuffs," I order, irritated as I take a blade to my scarf. It slices through the sheer fabric easily and I hand him half of the material. "Keep your face and head covered. The sun is unforgiving here."

Tyron does as he's told, giving his usual quiet thanks.

"*What happens if the heat proves too much for him?*" Tirzah asks, again in Pershizarian.

"*Well, I suppose if he goes unconscious, there's no reason not to shift and carry him,*" I answer.

Tirzah raises an eyebrow. "*If you'd told me that when we found him, I would have just knocked him out for you.*"

Now it's my turn to look unimpressed. "*Maybe that's why I didn't tell you.*" We both know that it wasn't a feasible option—as tempted as Tirzah might be. We ran out of sleeping draught on our last mission and we have no way to ensure steady unconsciousness without it.

My attention shifts back to Tyron and I survey him quickly. "I suppose that will have to do," I say of his attire. "But hold on to that coat; you'll need it once the sun is gone."

"The nights are that cold?" he asks as he scoops the sorry piece of leather up.

"As cold as the days are hot," I reply as I tie what's left of my headscarf in place. "And we won't have the warmth of a fire—even if we had the fuel, a flame here can be visible from miles away."

Instead of looking disheartened, Tyron looks fascinated. He opens his mouth only to snap it shut. It's nearly amusing to watch him try to swallow all of his own inquisitiveness. In place of whatever it was he wanted to ask, he gives a nod and a simple, "Alright."

Then I notice the dark marks that run across his left arm. "How did you get those?"

"Hm?" He follows my gaze to his arm and twists it around to look, revealing what has to be large teeth marks dotted in a half circle across his entire forearm. "Oh, yes, that." He shakes his head. "I'd tell you what did it, but I have no idea what it's called. Whatever the animal was, it apparently hunts it pairs."

I glance at Tirzah. Animals aren't the only ones.

I turn around and lead the way into the rocky desert.

Tyron

I shiver, pulling my coat more closely around me. The dried grass we'd gathered as insulation from the sand shifts and crackles beneath me. Yet I barely notice the cold and the poking of the grasses. I am too drawn in by the stunning array overhead.

I've spent many nights camping on the open plains of western Litash, staring up at the stars. I don't know if it's a result of the air, or the open dunes, or the positioning of the moons to Pershizar, but the skies here put Litash to shame. The clusters of light are so bright that it never fully grows dark, and they're so clear that it seems one could simply reach out and snatch them. They paint the heavens in bands of soft colors: deep, velvety purple; dark blue; and even borders of pink. Some of the constellations are familiar—I can trace Fiondyn's Sword, pointing north for all lost travelers. But other stars and groups are completely foreign and I can't help but wonder what they are named.

I could look at them all night. I'd caught glimpses while we crossed the stony outcroppings, but only ever at the edges of the clouds. Last night, when we'd finally reached the dunes, both moons had still hovered at the horizon and cast too much light. Not tonight. Tonight, the sky belongs to the stars.

My gaze is drawn a little lower to where a dark silhouette sits atop the nearby dune. Rhioa is almost perfectly still, only moving her head now and then to scan the perimeter. Between these searches, I notice the way her head tilts back ever so slightly. She, too, is watching the stars. *Except you're being a besotted dimwit and watching her.* My cheeks burn in embarrassment and it makes me glad that it's too dark for her or Tirzah to see me.

Why her? Why, after so many years of turning so many away, should I suddenly fall for a woman I've known for mere days? More than that, a woman who is so clearly unattainable. And here I'd thought I'd turned down ladies and noblewomen because I'd wanted something deeper! I let out a long breath, mentally calling myself a fool and every other synonym for the word that I can think of.

But it does nothing to lessen that draw. *Why? Surely not her beauty. Oh please, don't let me be shallow **and** a fool.* I reassure myself with the reminder that her sister is also quite fair, but I feel no such draw there. No, no, it's something more; there is something beneath that hardened exterior. I just can't tell what. She is clearly afraid of something, though I can't tell what it is. Perhaps it is whatever has caused her such hurt—the same hurt she carries around like a shield. I have not missed how Tirzah protects her sister by remaining physically between us at all times, nor how Rhioa seems to protect Tirzah in return by deflecting attention away from her.

Which makes me wonder all the more about why they brought me with them. Why aid someone they seem to think might be a threat? I'm not exactly sure what language they keep reverting to, but I do remember studying something similar. At first, the words only brought up fond memories of studying in the library with Master Feld, or sitting at the Verzaer's family table while Ameri read aloud and I scribbled notes on pronunciation. Now after several days of listening to Rhioa and Tirzah argue in undertones, I am beginning to catch more meaning.

The word that keeps coming up is "risk." How am I a risk to them? Certainly not physically—I can barely keep pace with them as we walk. Besides, if they are what I suspect they are, they could overpower me even at full health. The only kind of people I could think of that would travel such dangerous territory with only rations, a few hidden weapons, and two waterskins would be spies, thieves, or assassins. If they are any of those three, then I am a risk simply because I know them. So why would they rescue me? Why would they spare limited rations and water? *And why would you fall head over heels for one of them?*

I sigh to myself. All these thoughts and more continue to roll around in my head as I gaze up at the stars...and up at the other person who sits watching them. Suddenly, something shifts. Rhioa's outline stiffens, then crouches, until she is nearly laying down on top of the dune. Scarce seconds pass in strained silence before she half slides, half runs back down towards the little camp.

I sit up as she reaches Tirzah's side. Rhioa lays one hand on her sister's shoulder, putting a finger to her lips as soon as the latter stirs. Rhioa then points towards the dune where she had been keeping watch and makes a few sharp gestures. Tirzah immediately begins to tie up the packs and scatter the grass beds.

I get to my feet, staying low as I pull on my coat. I copy Tirzah and spread sand over the some of the grass so it appears to have been there some time. When both packs are secure, Rhioa motions quickly and I follow her and Tirzah to the other dune. They both crouch against the small rise as if using it for cover. I do the same.

Breathless, I listen for whatever it is that has both sisters at the ready. It takes me a moment, but then I hear it: the faint jingling of metal. And it's growing closer. Another minute ticks slowly by and an animal lows. In response, a whip cracks and a voice shouts something indistinguishable. More and more sounds emerge as we wait: the muted padding of large feet, the quiet conversations of deep voices, the snorting of horses, and the dulled clatter of armor.

As softly as I can, I whisper, "How strict is your rule against Gifting?"

Rhioa looks at me, furrowed brow showing her bewilderment.

"I can hide us," I explain even as I strain to listen. "Or Gift us elsewhere if it comes to it."

Rhioa starts to shake her head. "Gifting harms us—"

She cuts herself off when another voice calls out. This one is much closer than any of the others.

My fingers wrap around the handles of both of my swords.

Whoever it is whistles to themselves as they walk the ridge of the very dune we are pressed against. I can hear sand spraying and tumbling with each step.

Then the whistling stops.

Tirzah moves first, darting up with unnatural speed. There is the thud of someone hitting the ground and a muffled cry. Tirzah pulls the thrashing man down on our side of the dune, one arm locked around his neck and the other hand clamped down over his mouth. I move to help but his flailing has already slowed. He goes limp and Tirzah lets go.

"Jotta? Jotta!"

I don't need to know the language to know that this man's disappearance has already been noticed.

"Scout," I mutter as Tirzah searches the unconscious pillager.

She tears a fabric patch from his cloak, tossing it to Rhioa.

"Saheer Tribe," Rhioa says under her breath. The look on her face tells me that this is a bad thing.

"Let me help," I whisper.

"*No Gifting*," she hisses back.

"Jotta!" The voices now sound in an echoing chorus, indicating that they've spread out in search of their missing comrade.

Tirzah cuts in, looking straight at Rhioa. "Anyone who sees will have to be kept silent."

Rhioa purses her lips.

A shrill whistle erupts from the top of the dune and all our heads snap towards the sound. But the rider who had crested the ridge has already disappeared, his cracking whip giving evidence to his haste.

Rhioa turns on me, sword in one hand and dagger in the other. "If you must use Gifting, keep it small, and keep it away from us. It will harm us otherwise," she tells me tersely. "And watch out for their spears—they're poisoned."

It's strange to feel so much adrenaline pulsing through my veins while taking orders from someone who seems more annoyed than scared. I nod as a I draw both blades.

The shouts have turned to raw-throated cries, accompanied by the pounding of hoof beats.

"Hurry."

In quick steps, I follow Rhioa and Tirzah to where the crest of the dune falls. We stay low and just out of sight.

"They'll come around this edge." Rhioa's voice is even as she pulls off her pack and tosses it next to her sister's. "Tirzah, you take the first rider. I'll bring the second to you. Tyron, try and get clear of us and then Gift yourself over the next ridge."

"I'm not lea—"

I don't get to finish. Another hair-raising cry comes screaming from our right and Tirzah is on her feet, running. She leaps forward just as the raider comes riding around the corner. He doesn't even have time to duck before she collides with him, wrapping both arms around him and twisting so that she lands on top of him. The rider's loose horse cuts off any more visual.

Rhioa wastes no time. She is down the rise, swinging herself onto the mount before any other raiders can round the corner. Her face twists in the manner of an animal baring its teeth as she sends the horse into a gallop. She keeps her sword drawn and low, held out at an angle as she rides straight towards the two mounted spearmen. I'm not sure I've ever seen someone look so lethal.

For a moment, I am paralyzed. What do I do? My Gifting instinctively reaches as if to try and stop her while the racing of adrenaline urges my feet forward to help. My rational mind puts a stop to both and, in doing so, leaves me stranded. I do nothing but watch as Rhioa slides down on the horse's side, ducking the first spear. Then she's up and arcing her sword towards the second. She bats away the shaft and carries through to bring her blade down against the raider's helmet. He falls forward onto the neck of his horse.

The crack of a whip jolts me back to my senses and I spin around to see three raiders skidding down from the top of the dune. Two are on foot, but the third is on a creature unlike any I've ever seen. It is twice the height of a horse with a large hump on its back. Six knobby legs carrying it forward at an amble. It tosses its head and its long neck sways as it lets out a bray.

It takes me half a second to assess my opponents. Then I dart up the ridge to meet the first raider head on. He wields one curved blade, raised high as he lets out a war cry. I lift my right sword and parry the blow. Either I am even weaker than I realized, or this man is stronger: I am barely able to deflect the force of the attack and send his blade away from me. I bring my left sword up as I sidestep and try to get behind him. The raider recovers too quickly, blocking my left swing and trying to cut towards my center.

The motion puts him off balance. So I bring my swords together into an X and press forward. As soon as his blade meets mine, I take one foot and sweep his legs out from under him. He gives a yelp as he goes crashing down the dune.

I immediately turn towards my next assailant, yet I'm already aware that the first one took too long. I have to dive out of the way of the strange beast to avoid being trampled. I roll twice and regain my footing, both swords ready. And just in time, for the other grounded raider is charging towards me. He comes in with a crescent cut, I parry with the left, then come around with my right towards his exposed middle.

My blow never lands. Pain sears around my ankle as a loud crack fills my ears. Then the whip goes taut and my foot is pulled out from beneath me. I fall hard, rolling just enough to keep from landing on my swords. It's all I can do to hold on to them as I'm dragged across the dune.

As the spray of sand leaves me blind and gagging, I swing as far as I can reach in a desperate attempt to cut the line without damaging my own leg. The blow bounces off and I fight to keep my grip. I try again. This time, I feel the tension give out and I go tumbling. My left sword catches on something and is wrenched from my hand before I can stop it. I scramble upright, nearly falling again when I try to put weight on my injured foot. *That's not good.* Especially not when my dropped sword is somehow several yards away. The mounted raider has already spun around: I won't make it to the weapon in time.

So I adjust my grip on my remaining sword and shift my weight to my one stable foot. The man raises his whip to strike again even as his horned beast gives a deafening bray. But this time, I'm prepared: I lift my right arm to eye level and let the whip wrap around my heavy leather sleeve. As soon as the line begins to go taut, I brace with both feet, lean back, and pull with all my might. I can't bite back my yelp of pain. But it works—the raider is torn from his saddle.

Before he can regain his bearings, I disentangle myself from the whip and cast it aside. But now I have other problems—and by problems, I mean opponents. Four more raiders, all of which are mounted, have crested the dune and now surround me. To add to all this, my right leg is now throbbing so badly that I can barely keep my balance. I don't even know if I'll be able to withstand a blow.

As I sink into a lopsided fighting stance, I try to spot Tirzah and Rhioa. Are they far enough away for me to use Gifting? What happens if they aren't? I have a feeling that I'm going to have to find out.

CHAPTER 3

Rhioa

The butt of my borrowed spear strikes the raider's chest with a resounding crack and he howls as he falls. I wheel the horse around to finish him off but hear a piercing whistle. *Tirzah.* I duck as far forward as I can just as two shafts go hissing over my head. I twist in the saddle and throw my short spear, hitting the first karansuur rider in the shoulder. In his frantic attempt to stay mounted, he grabs at his reins and sends his karansuur swerving. The six-legged camel bellows its protest as it crashes into the other mount. Both riders and animals fall.

I turn back, spotting the de-horsed raider half way up the other dune and running away. I let him. I steer my mount back towards Tirzah, still on foot and now dealing with three of the pillagers. The first comes at her with a sword and she steps to the side. In one deft motion, she grabs his wrist, wrenches it around, and kneels. The raider is thrown over Tirzah's shoulder and into his companion.

The third man tries to attack while Tirzah is down, but she swings around and pincers her legs around his. With a twist, she sends him to the ground. She pulls a knife and plunges it down in between his shoulder blades.

"Tirzah!"

As she looks up, I stretch out a hand. She starts running in the same direction as my galloping horse. When I'm about to pass her, she grabs my hand and vaults up behind me. I bring the horse around to face the rest of the pillagers only to find that they haven't followed me. They've veered off towards the top of the dune.

That's when I see him. He's standing there, sword in hand, completely surrounded by Saheer pillagers. Even in the low lighting, I can see that some injury has left him dangerously unbalanced. *Imbecile!* Why didn't he run? I had told him to Gift himself away!

I dig my heels into my mount as the first raider rushes him. Tyron blocks and gives a swing of his sword, which the raider parries effortlessly. Tyron staggers as he blocks again and then tries to spin around as another pillager attacks from behind. He dodges, deflects, and then buckles and falls to his knees.

He's not going to make it. We're not close enough. *Use Gifting, you idiot!*

"Take the reins," I call, letting them drop onto the horse's neck. I grab the horn of the saddle, pull my feet up, and jump clear of the running animal.

I've shifted before I even touch the ground. A bound and a leap and I spread my wings, filling them with air and lurching upwards. I use the momentum and dive down at an angle. With a roar, I grab the first raider in my talons and pull him from his karansuur. I slam him into the ground and grab the pillager nearest Tyron in my teeth. I fling him off to the side and turn to let out a stream of acid at the remaining riders. Their animals panic and take off with the raiders in tow. I see a pair of pale wings go after them and know that Tirzah has them covered.

So I shift back, keeping my sword drawn as I kneel next to Tyron.

"Thank you," he pants, pushing himself upright. His head turns as a shriek erupts in the distance. "Is Tirzah al—"

"She's fine," I interrupt. "Are you?"

Tyron looks down at his leg, one hand prodding at his ankle. He grimaces. "It will need attending, but it can wait."

I have to suppress the sudden urge to scream at him. Instead, I settle for growling, "Why didn't you Gift yourself away like I told you to?"

"You said it could harm you. And how could I just leave you in the middle of all these...." His sentence trails off as he looks around at all the pillagers strewn around the sand. "...Though it does not seem to have mattered."

Too angry for words, I don't bother replying. I begin checking all the fallen raiders, making sure that any of the ones who saw me shift are dead. I know that these are Saheer tribe—criminals and outcasts who have turned to pillaging their own people. But even with that knowledge, and even with the hundreds of times I've done this before, it's still hard to swallow the bile that rises in the back of my throat with each kill I confirm.

When the cries in the distance cease, I know that Tirzah has silenced them. I finish my check just as silver wings glimmer in the moonlight, flitting towards us. She lands with a muted thud and shifts as she steps forward.

As always, she checks me over before asking, "Everyone quiet?"

"Everyone who saw," I nod. Well, except for one....

She looks to Tyron. "Still alive, I see," she mutters.

Tyron, now on his feet, limps over and picks up his second sword. He brushes the sand from the metal and sheathes it. "That is only thanks to you both. Again."

"Keep your thanks for later—we need to get moving," I say. Then I spot a horse milling around near the base of the dune, reins dragging on the ground. I turn towards Tyron. "Can you ride?"

I see him look down at his foot, testing his ankle. He gives a lopsided shrug. "I can manage."

We ride until mid-morning. Then between the heat, the tired horses, and the fact that Tyron has not even been able to get his bad foot in a stirrup, I give the call to stop. Thankfully, we're near enough to Ajhal now that we're able to find a crag of rock big enough to act as shade. Tyron slides off almost immediately and practically collapses against the rock face. Tirzah sets to hobbling the horses—her way of saying she already knows we'll be here a while.

I dig through the pillagers' saddlebags, taking stock of what they had. Not much in the way of food—that was likely on the karansuurs—but plenty of water. I find an assortment of weaponry, some spare clothing, flint and steel, and then finally the small box I was looking for. I pluck this out, then grab my pack, and carry it all to join Tyron.

He has his boot peeled off and is rolling up the leg of his breeches. He glances up as I draw closer.

"Is there any water to spare?" he asks.

I nod, setting everything down and pulling out my water skin. I take out the spare bandaging, too, cutting a section off with my dagger and dampening it before handing it to Tyron. He thanks me and starts to wipe off the dried blood.

Tirzah finishes the hobbling and joins us in the shade. She takes one look at Tyron's ankle and asks, "Whip?"

"Mhmm," he nods, wincing as he works.

With his ankle a little cleaner, it's easier to see the laceration that runs around it in a spiral. The skin around it is red and swollen and the cut itself is alarmingly inflamed. It must have been deeper than I realized.

"Got dragged for a few yards," he murmurs, sounding nearly embarrassed. Then he rolls his sleeve up more and continues cleaning. A black-and-purple bruise wraps around his forearm.

"We have needle and thread for stitches," I offer as he sets the now bloodied cloth aside.

Tyron frowns at his ankle and begins to shake his head. "No, I think it's too swollen. I'll have to bandage it and just keep from using it for a few days." He seems entirely unworried.

Either this happens often, or he has medical experience. "We don't have much to keep it clean with. How will you avoid infection?"

"I can use Gifting if it comes to it," he says, grimacing as he shifts his leg around to get a better look at the wound. "Wouldn't take much. Besides the cut, it's merely a mild sprain."

"You are a healer?" I ask in surprise.

"Among other things," Tyron smiles faintly—almost fondly. He looks up and glances from Tirzah to me. "If it wouldn't be too much trouble, I'll put some distance between us and see if I can at least get it closed up."

I share a look with Tirzah. "You say it wouldn't take much?"

"Correct."

"Tirzah and I will wait on top of the ridge, then," I stand up and brush myself off. "Make sure you drink one of the vials from that box. If there was any poison on the whip, that will neutralize it."

"Thank you," he says again, reaching for the box.

But there's one more thing. "Tyron."

He looks up.

"What you saw.... No one can know." I lock eyes with him. "Do you understand?"

Tyron does not look away. "I understand," he replies, voice quiet and level.

Time will tell if he means it. I turn around, saying, "Call up when you're done," as I fall in alongside Tirzah.

We hike the short distance to the edge of rock face and then up around it so that we will be well removed yet still in hearing distance. We both sit down in the sand and I wait for the scolding I'm sure Tirzah has been mulling over for hours. I know she's worried about Tyron seeing us shift. Am I a fool for letting him walk away? Perhaps. He might end up like all the others we've tried to spare. But I can't help but hope that this time will be different.

As if sensing my turmoil, Tirzah says nothing. We sit in silence, swatting at the occasional insect and squinting out over the sun-burnt dunes. The quiet and heat make me drowsy and remind me that I have been awake since yesterday morning.

A sensation somewhat like sound wafts through the air. The feeling is like that of seeing something hum with vibration and, despite being too far to hear it, having that perception of sound. It's as if it is appealing to some tactile sense that I lack. Which, I suppose, is true. For I know the sensation well enough to place it and know equally well that I do not contain any: Gifting. It was the same feeling that drew Tirzah and I to Tyron in the Forest of Riddles. But where the hum is usually low and subtle, it now grows until it is nearly uncomfortable.

The phenomenon persists for several minutes, swelling and receding at random. Finally, it stops completely. A minute more and I hear the call, "All set."

By the time Tirzah and I rejoin Tyron at the base of the rocky outcropping, he is putting an empty vial back in the wooden box I'd left for him. He holds it out to me and I notice his ankle. It is still red, but the deep cut is now a dark line covered by shiny, new skin. The previously blackened bruising has faded to various shades of green and yellow, and the swelling is nearly gone. It looks like it has healed for five days—not five minutes.

I take the box and return it to the saddlebags where I found it. I notice one of the water skins and grab it before returning to the others and sitting down against the rock face. Thanks to the shade, the stone is almost cool compared to the heat of the day. I push my headscarf back and uncork the water skin. Instead of water I find a thick, white liquid: karansuur milk.

After a sniff and a slight test to make sure it is still fresh, I take a swig and pass the skin to Tirzah. The sweet, smoky taste is a welcome break from days of dried venison and bland neri roots. Tirzah drinks and then, unexpectedly, passes it to Tyron. He accepts it.

"So," I ask as he drinks. "What are you then, if not Human?"

He corks the skin and hands it back to Tirzah with quiet thanks. "Oh, I'm Human," he replied. "There are several of us with Gifting in Litash."

"And your Gift is healing?" I reiterate.

Tyron rocks his head back and forth. "Not specifically. I'm not sure how Gifting functions out here, but where I come from, most Humans tend to have a broader range of ability. They may be more disposed towards one skill or another, but that also depends on what they practice most." Idly, he begins rolling up his other sleeve. "My parents were both healers, so it may be that I inherited that disposition."

I notice his use of past tense when referring to his parents. I pause in my questioning as Tirzah passes the karansuur milk back to me.

"What about you two?" To my annoyance, Tyron uses the chance to turn the question around. "I presume you are not Bandilarian if you are affected by Gifting."

I take a long draught to buy myself time. He must not know what Myrandi are if he has not guessed us yet. As I cap the skin and set it by Tirzah, I ask, "Bandilarians? That's a word I've not heard in a while. Do you know so many that that's your first guess?" I've never met any of the shape-shifters, though I've long envied their ability to change into any form they desire.

"They are the predominant race of Litash. I know more Bandilarians than I do Humans," Tyron answers, though I get the feeling he knows I'm deflecting his question.

"What happened to the Elves, then?" I ask, hoping his usual scholarly tendencies will lead him further away.

He leans forward ever so slightly, looking at me with those bright green eyes. Then he leans back and looks out over the desert. "There are still enough to fill Cithan Citadel, but few can swallow their pride enough to wander beyond their gates. The only one I ever met was a rarity: She had not only left but had married a Human."

I know enough of my history to know of the Elves and their ancient war to eradicate Humans. And while I know that times change, I have not met many people or races who do change with them. So perhaps my curiosity is a little too genuine when I repeat, "Married? An Elf and a Human?" Such a thing has not happened since the days of Astinian.

Next to me, Tirzah picks up the skin of milk and uncorks it.

Tyron nods. Some recollection makes him smile when he says, "They are a bit of a strange couple, but both very kind. Their son is as quiet as his father and as tall as his mother."

Their son? They had a child? I lean back and ponder the strange thought. The idea that two such opposite factions could come together in something as close as a family is a marvel.

I give no reply and Tyron no further exposition. We sit in comfortable silence as we wait out the afternoon heat.

Tyron

I think it is safe to presume that these two are not mere thieves. Not after the way they handled the pillagers. With such skills as theirs, I would almost guess at them being mercenaries. Yet they lack the armor and full weaponry for that field. Besides, for the rest of the day and the subsequent morning, I keep thinking of how Rhioa went from raider to raider to check that any man who'd seen her shift was dead. Her face had been twisted up in so much anger. At first, I had thought it had been at me or perhaps at their attackers. But then when Tirzah had asked if everyone was dead, Rhioa had seemed unhappy to confirm it. As if she wished it was not so.

And so my suspicion begins to grow: Could it be they are forced to do this? Is that why they are worried about helping me—not because I could pass on information, but because they are not allowed to let me live? I have seen both of them in Dragon form and yet they are letting—no, *helping*—me walk away. I think of the look on Rhioa's face when she gave me that order: *No one can know.* They have no guarantee of my silence beyond my word. So was it an order, or was it a warning?

It all makes me wonder what they are, and why knowing they can shift is such a problem. Are shifters outlawed outside of Litash? By the way they mentioned Bandilarians, it didn't seem so. Is it just their race that is persecuted? Is that how they are being forced to do whatever mission they've been sent on? I have no way of knowing. The way Rhioa had deflected my question on the subject told me that it was off limits. Just like everything else.

So how do I offer to help with something that I'm not allowed to speak of? How can I assure them that they are safe to tell me? I don't even know what is being leveraged against them, much less their full situation. Perhaps the dilemma is a moot point: With skills as practiced as theirs, what help could I offer? Even on the dunes, I had been nothing but a liability. I doubt either of them would have needed to shift if I hadn't let myself get surrounded.

With all these thoughts spinning around in my head, the day seems to pass much too quickly. I know that, on our borrowed horses, we should reach Ajhal by nightfall. Each rise we crest, each outcropping we come around, I find myself bracing for what may lay beyond it. *Well, that's a little dramatic, isn't it?* As much as I try to mock myself for it, that deep-rooted feeling refuses to be deterred. I don't understand it. And I can't seem to quiet it.

Just as I notice the sky beginning to color and the air starting to cool, Rhioa pulls her horse to a stop at the top of stony ridge we'd been slowly climbing. What is it? It's too early for me to hope she's stopping for the night. She doesn't seem alarmed. If anything, her posture makes me think of that night on the dunes when she had been watching the stars.

I nudge my mount into a trot until I reach her. Then I pull up short, stunned by the view on the horizon.

"Woah," I hear myself breathe.

I had never imagined it to be so...boundless. From the shore at its edges, it seems to stretch into eternity itself—as if it joins with the sky rather than ends at it.

"Never seen the ocean before?" I hear Rhioa ask.

I shake my head, savoring the lungfuls of fresh salt air. "No, never." I'd been on the Sea of Triscri—a glorified lake, really—but this is somehow completely different.

"Hm." She gives a soft chuckle.

I have to tear my eyes from the sea to look at Rhioa but, once I do, I can't look away. She is gazing out into the distance, her expression and posture more relaxed than I've ever seen. It's as if she's so caught up in the beauty of the landscape that she's forgotten we're here. The smile that edges her lips takes my breath away.

You're an idiot. You're an absolute, infatuated—

"And there's Ajhal," Tirzah breaks in.

I follow her pointing finger down the coastline to where a city sprawls between the cliffs and the shore. My heart sinks.

"Just in time," Rhioa says as she raises a hand to shield against the heavy afternoon sun. Her smile is gone and that relaxed openness with it. "I was nearly worried we'd have to spend the night out here."

With that, we leave the cliffs behind and carefully pick our way down.

Seeing it at such a distance, the city of Ajhal appears to grow right out of the red sandstone cliffs. It's as if the inhabitants carved the walls from the rock rather than built them on top of it. Where the ramparts reach the sea, they rise into tall parapets that stand like twin watchmen over the harbor. The ships sailing in and out between them come in more shapes and sizes than I can count.

We reach the main road and join in the long line of travelers. Carts, wagons, horses, and those creatures Rhioa had called karansuurs—all of them form a strange sort of caravan up to the city gates. Most of the people are dressed in similar fashion to the raiders we'd faced on the dunes, though with comfort more in mind than combat. Longer, looser tunics and robes prevail. Nearly everyone has some sort of head covering and many wear open sandals instead of covered shoes.

The slow procession ushers us through the wide gates and into a crowded street. All of us who had shared the open road are now funneled through channels of plaster buildings, already lined with vendors and people on foot. Bright colors, strong and unfamiliar smells, chatter in a tongue I don't understand, all clamor for my attention. One woman even tries to grab my horse's reins in attempt to stop me long enough to see her wares. I brush her off and ride more closely to Rhioa and Tirzah.

Strange how, after so many years of studying the outside world, I should reach it and be nearly disinterested. I know that it has nothing to do with my surroundings and everything to do with the woman riding ahead of me. How long until they send me away? I'd half-feared they would part ways right at the gate.

We push and press and make our way forward, though I know not where. The street opens up suddenly into a large plaza and I am greeted by the sound of a thousand conversations at once. Some of it must be in the trade language, for I catch snatches of words here and there. But the sheer amount of it all, combined with the calls of animals and clattering of carts, makes it nothing more than cacophony.

The way Rhioa and Tirzah ride through the chaos makes them stand out merely by their calmness. The one time a vendor tries to approach Tirzah, she gives him such a venomous look that he falters and steps back. They navigate through the chaos of the marketplace and down a quieter side street. I follow until they stop at the base of a multi-story building and dismount. Judging by the symmetrical rows of windows, the smell of food, and the people coming in and out, this must be an inn. I dismount as well, dreading what comes next.

Rhioa looks back over her shoulder, purses her lips, and says something to Tirzah that I don't catch. Then she gives her reins to her sister and walks towards me.

This is my last chance. I have to say something, anything—

"Tirzah and I will secure the rooms," Rhioa tells me, pulling something from her pockets. "In Pershizar, if you leave them unattended, the innkeeper will let them to someone else."

Wait, rooms? I look down and realize Rhioa is pressing a coin into my palm.

"But I don't feel like eating stewed tashka in a room with twice as many people as it was built to hold," Rhioa goes on dryly. "Go back to the market and find something more edible. Tirzah likes anything with meat, and I haven't had anything fresh in two weeks. Get whatever you want for yourself."

Apparently, I wear my bewilderment more openly than I intend, for Rhioa raises an eyebrow. "We're staying here for a day or two. With it being so close to evening, we thought we'd at least put you up for the night. You can make your own way tomorrow."

I won't argue with extra time. I bow my head and give a very sincere, "Thank you."

Per usual, she says nothing. She holds a hand out for my reins and I give them over.

I feel somewhere between numb and light-headed as I turn around and walk back towards the crowded plaza. I still have a bit of a limp, making it harder to weave back through the mixture of people, animals, and wide straw mats that are scattered with wares. It doesn't help when a man waves a string of beads in my face, or a woman shoves some kind of live fowl towards me. But I brush past them and press on.

I dodge an oncoming donkey cart and nearly collide with a woman carrying an entire basket of fruit on her head. She gives me a scowl as I apologize—neither of us pausing to do so. Then, realizing she'd probably just come from the food section of the market, I veer right to follow her trajectory.

I'm soon rewarded with the rich scents of roasting meat and sweet spices. I wander up and down a little while, not exactly sure what any of it is. Even their bread looks unfamiliar, shaped in flat, dense loaves and often covered with seeds. I settle on a mixture of fruit and grains with a side of fish for Rhioa, and two skewers of seared meat and vegetables for Tirzah. I try to find something simpler for myself since I'd been limited to bread until about three days ago.

I purchase some kind of roasted grain with broth and head for the inn. My trip back through the bustling plaza is much more precarious now that I am balancing three different meals. The woven dishes of thin reeds don't help my cause. I'm nearly proud that I make it back to the side street where the inn is without spilling anything.

I am almost there when a shriek erupts further up the road. Instinctively, my gaze snaps upwards and towards the source of the sound.

"Please! No, no, stop!" A woman cries.

I see the door of a nearby house burst open and three uniformed men exit.

A child's scream makes my heart drop. "Mama!"

I see him now, the little boy that the men drag between them. A woman in hysterics comes running out of the house only to be held back by two of the men.

Though the street is full of people, no one moves to help. Many glance towards the commotion before shuffling on their way. Others avert their gaze entirely.

Another man, in long robes instead of a uniform, steps out of the woman's house. "You may consider your debt fulfilled," he informs her with unruffled calm, ignoring her desperation as he scribbles something on a piece of parchment.

My purchases are forgotten as I thread my way through passersby.

"No!" The mother cries again, struggling in vain against her captors. "Please! I will pay, I will pay—I promise!"

A man is tying rope around the little boy's wrist. When the child resists, the man cuffs him so hard that he sends him to the ground.

"Enough!" I am in between the man and the little boy before I even realize it. "What is the meaning of this?!"

CHAPTER 4

Rhioa

After I take Tyron's mount to Tirzah, I leave her to haggle the stable price with the horse master. I enter the inn, scanning the crowded dining area that takes up the entire bottom floor. The traditional sash catches my eye and I quickly spot the innkeeper off to the right. I wait briefly while he finishes helping another patron, then step forward as he clasps his hand to his chest in greeting.

"I am looking for someone named Solus," I say before he can even ask my business. "I believe they're letting a room here."

The innkeeper frowns in thought and starts to pull one of the many scrolls from his sash, only to stop and raise a finger in recollection. "Ah, yes, he said he was expecting a guest. He is in the third room to the left on the second floor."

So it's a 'he.' All of us use the code 'Solus,' so I rarely know who to expect during these meetings.

I give a perfunctory, "Thank you," and head for the stairs.

I climb to the second floor and stop at the third door down. After my patterned knock, I hear, "Come in."

I open the door to find Elescar sitting in a chair, looking out the edge of the window screen at the red stone street below. My throat goes tight and I wonder how long he's been there. I mentally calculate whether or not he would have been able to see us arrive.

"Is Tirzah here?" Elescar asks, not even looking at me.

The question, if sincere, means he did not see us. "Does she need to be?" I ask, keeping my tone even. "I left her in the stables."

Elescar turns his head, appraising me with a look that is both unconvinced and uncaring. I have always loathed the feeling of his gaze sliding over me. I raise my chin ever so slightly—the biggest show of defiance I dare give.

"I suppose not," Elescar gets to his feet and reaches into the folds of his overcoat. He extends a piece of tightly rolled parchment to me. "You're headed to Arvenir. The Grand Va' Kied's aspirations are beginning to encroach on Ovok's plans. He wants you to depose him and set up his younger cousin, the Count Ihail, in his stead."

I take the parchment and unroll it, skimming through the usual lists.

"Rhioa," I hate the way Elescar says my name.

I refuse to look up. "Mm?" I unwind more of the parchment and read on.

"Ovok doesn't care what it takes," he says smoothly. I imagine that if serpents could speak, they would sound like him. "But he does want it done thoroughly. No loose ends this time, or I'll be talking to Tirzah instead of you."

It takes every ounce of my willpower to keep my hands from going rigid and tearing the parchment to shreds. I keep my face blank just so that my hatred doesn't show through. Of all the people who serve Ovok, the ones who enjoy it are the most vile.

"Understood," I say coolly. "After all, you know all about loose ends, don't you, Elescar? That's why Ovok keeps you so close, isn't it?"

I draw satisfaction from the way his eyes just barely narrow. "Be careful," he says, descending to a sort of hiss. "I have a feeling you would not enjoy my role. But continue in the way you have, and maybe we'll get the chance to find out."

I bite my tongue until it hurts.

Elescar adjusts his overcoat, inclines his head in a brief parting gesture, and leaves without another word.

As soon as the door shuts behind him, I find myself taking huge gulps of air. Something about Elescar always makes me hold my breath. I force myself to breathe more deeply, knowing that Tirzah could be up any moment now. I need to at least get my hands to stop shaking or she might notice.

With the list still in one hand, I sit down in the seat by the window and pull back the screen to let in the cooling evening air. I close my eyes and try to ignore the fact that I am already tallying the list and all that will need to be done. I pretend that I am able to just sit and enjoy the salt-scented breeze as I listen to the murmur of people in the street below. I wonder what it is like to live in such simplicity, in such blissful ignorance....

My daydreaming is cut off by a shriek and I open my eyes. When it comes again, I stand and look out the window. There, down near the corner, I spot a woman being held back. Then I see the little boy and the man in lender's robes coming out of the nearby house. It's a debt collection. My stomach churns, a reminder of how much I despise Pershizar's slave dealings. I reach for the window screen.

That's when I see him. *Oh no.*

I rush from the room, down the stairs, and out of the inn, but I'm too late: Tyron has already put himself between the little boy and the hired soldiers. I step out of the way of an oncoming cart and rush past a cluster of pedestrians, trying to scan for Elescar at the same time. This is made more difficult by the small crowd Tyron's interference has garnered.

"Is this enough?" His voice is barely recognizable.

I elbow my way past the onlookers and step to the front of the crowd. Tyron is holding out a large gold coin which the lender examines with interest. He takes it in one hand, letting it settle as if checking the weight. Then he tests it between his teeth. He pockets it hastily and waves to his men.

"Let her go; we're done here."

The hired men release the mother, who immediately falls to her knees and wraps her child in a tight embrace. Tyron, after making sure the men are indeed leaving, kneels next to them both.

The spectators begin to wander off now that the drama has subsided. But my irritation has not done the same. I step forward to get Tyron's attention only to freeze in my tracks. There, in the midst of the churning of the city streets, stands a solitary, still figure. I feel very cold. Elescar raises an eyebrow and a smirk touches his lips. He turns and disappears into the stream of people.

Tyron is helping the mother back into her home. She stops in the doorway, thanking him profusely as tears run down her face. Her child hides behind her skirts. I don't catch what Tyron says, but I do see him press something into her hand. He catches sight of me then and, with some last word to the woman, walks towards me. *Oh for goodness' sake—he still has the limp!*

I say nothing when he reaches me. I turn and we walk back to the inn in silence. We are about to step in when I grab his arm and pull him into the alleyway.

"What were you *thinking*?" I force the words out from between my teeth.

"What was *I* thinking?" Tyron's voice matches mine in its heat, catching me by surprise. "Those men were about to drag a child off for money—*money*! They were going to sell him!"

"Keep your voice down," I growl, glancing out at the still busy street then back at him. "You have no idea how much trouble you've just caused me."

Tyron's voice drops, yet somehow holds more vehemence than before. "I'm sure I don't have a clue. But what I do know is that anyone who lays a hand to a child deserves to have it removed; I do not regret my actions."

For what is likely the first time in years, I don't even know what to say. I stare right at him and he meets my gaze head on. I give up with a shake of my head and stalk back towards the front of the inn. I hear him follow me.

Tirzah is inside, waiting on a bench at the front of the room. She stands when she sees me. I see her look from me to Tyron before she falls in behind me.

"Is the room across from Solus still vacant?" I ask the innkeeper before he can greet me again.

He nods, exchanging a key for the copper coin I hold out.

Then it's up the stairs and to the third set of doors down. I unlock the new room, step aside, and motion for Tyron to enter. He does so. I stand in the doorway and hold out his key.

"If you know what is good for you, do not leave this room," I say in an undertone. "Don't so much as look out the window, do you hear me?"

He looks strangely different when he's angry; his whole face seems darker, his presence more dangerous. He takes the key, gives a terse nod, and closes the door.

As soon as Tirzah and I are safely in our room, she grumbles, "I take it he lost our dinners."

My paranoia gets the better of me and I cross to the window so I can scan the street below. I disregard her complaint and get straight to the problem: "Elescar was here."

"Did he see?"

I clench my teeth together and force myself to nod as I close the shutter.

I hear Tirzah exhale. "Rhy...."

"No." The word comes from the back of my throat.

"It would be kinder if we did it ourselves," Tirzah reasons. "You know how Elescar is."

"We dragged him across the desert for a week just to try and keep him alive and now you want to kill him? That's hardly kind." I turn away from the window.

Tirzah's expression does not waver as she sets the packs down on the bed. "You're right—letting him starve would have been kinder than leaving him behind for Elescar."

My nails dig into my palms. "Then we bring him with."

"What?" Tirzah's tone is colored in disbelief. "Rhy, have you lost it? We can't just—"

I cut her off with a wave, sitting down in the nearby chair. "We're bound for Arvenir, which is too far to fly. If we go by boat, we'll doubtless make several stops on the way. We can drop him off on one of those."

Tirzah looks dubious. "What will keep Elescar from tracking him there? And what if he just comes back before we can leave?"

"He won't," I say, but now one hand grips the arm of my chair. "He is on a tight leash after what happened in Nythril; He'll have to report to Ovok before he does anything. That will be plenty of time for Tyron to disappear."

Visibly thinking this through, Tirzah sits down on the bed. "It could work."

It will have to. I can think of no other way that won't simply draw Father's attention more.

"Should we find a different inn in the meantime?" The question tells me that she has accepted the plan.

I shake my head. "No. If Elescar follows the rules, he has to go back to Ovok to report and receive new orders. If he breaks the rules and tries to come after us, he wouldn't expect us to stay here. This is the safest place for tonight."

Tirzah appears to see the sense in this. "So what are we doing in Arvenir?" she asks, shifting the conversation.

I am thankful for the distraction. I would much rather run over plans than think about Elescar. So I pull the parchment from my belt and begin laying down the basic framework. False names, background stories, letters of introduction, attire, entourage—anything to keep my mind busy. Anything to keep me away from the window.

Anything to help me escape the feeling of being watched.

Tyron

I adjust my pack and try to keep up with Rhioa and Tirzah. After the incident in the street yesterday evening, I'd been sure that I'd blown my chance and would wake to find them gone. Instead, they'd woken me up, handed me a pack, and told me to follow them. Rhioa had given me quite the lecture: I was not to mention that she and Tirzah could shift, I was not to speak of Litash, I was not to tell anyone of or use any Gifting, and no more "going around and saving people."

I haven't been given any chance to ask where we are going or why they suddenly want me to go with them. Are they simply sending me off somewhere so I can't make another scene? Possible. I have no way of telling. All I can do is try to limp after them as they move through the bustling city streets.

Wherever we're headed, I start to notice more heavy carts and cargo passing by. Strangely, I also notice more birds. Sleek, white gulls that call back and forth as they swoop overhead. That's when I spot the masts. They rise above the many faces that crowd my view, as thick as a forest. They hold sails instead of leaves and are draped with ropes instead of ivy. Their swaying is from the water, not the wind.

Beneath our feet, the natural red sandstone changes to quarried blocks and I realize that we are now on a walkway leading out into the sea. I catch glimpses of wooden docks jutting off from both sides. Ships rest at these like giant horses left tethered to rest. The further out on the walkway we go, the greater the size of the vessels and the thinner the traffic.

Rhioa comes to a stop, surveying a ship with three masts and layered decks.

"Wait here," she says.

When Tirzah makes a face, she rolls her eyes. "I'll be fine." She leaves her pack at our feet and walks off down the dock.

Tirzah and I do as we're told. For a while, I'm content to simply look around. We're far enough out that I can see the twin watchtowers that I'd noted yesterday.

Yesterday.... The thought brings me back to Rhioa reaming me out in the alleyway. I'd been frustrated with her scolding, but I knew it wasn't the deed that drew her ire so much as its publicity. What I don't understand is why she seemed so scared. Was it a threat to her cover, or did it compromise whatever situation they're caught in?

I glance at Tirzah and weigh the question out in my mind. I think better of it, asking instead, "So which one of you is older?"

Tirzah doesn't move. It's as if she hadn't even heard me. Just when I think she won't answer, she says, "We're twins."

Ah, that makes sense.

"But she has always enjoyed reminding me that she's ten minutes older." Tirzah's mouth tips in a wry expression even though she is still looking down the dock. "Not that it should matter at our age."

The way she says the last bit gives me pause. I nearly open my mouth to ask, but too many years of etiquette lessons—combined with the small shred of common sense I have left—keeps me quiet.

I see Tirzah glance sideways at me and she gives something like a smirk.

She's taunting me, isn't she? In that case—"Alright, you've got me," I give in. "I promise that I was taught never to ask a lady her age, but now I have to know: How old are you?"

Tirzah looks back at the dock with victory in her smile. "Two hundred and four," she replies.

I blink at her. "Come again?"

"You heard me." Her amusement grows.

Two hundred and four. *Two hundred and four. You dolt. You've fallen for the oldest woman you've ever met.* That teaches me for asking.

"What about you?"

Tirzah's question catches me off guard and it takes me a moment to realize she's asking my age in return.

"Uh," I scratch the back of my head somewhat sheepishly as I admit, "Twenty."

Tirzah chuckles, shaking her head. "You're barely more than an infant."

I have a feeling she's not quite joking and it does little to make me feel better. It doesn't help that I've messed up nearly everything I've put my hand to since they found me.

"Well, considering that I don't expect to live to two hundred and four, I am hoping I will mature a little faster than you two," I say, making an effort to keep my tone humorous. I wonder again what race they are that they would live so long without a trace of age. Even Elves, the longest lived in Litash, rarely make it beyond two hundred years.

I'm not quite sure if Tirzah was going to say anything more, but Rhioa comes into view and Tirzah leans to pick up her bag. She starts down the dock to meet her and I follow.

"They'll take us," Rhioa calls as she gets closer. "And they leave this afternoon." She reaches us and takes her pack from Tirzah. "They are predominantly cargo, so our room will be small." Her gaze shifts to me. "You will have to sleep in the cabin with the rest of the crew."

"Alright." I have camped out with a company of soldiers often enough to be used to sharing my space. "How much do I owe you for the fare?"

Rhioa raises an eyebrow. "How much money do you have?" she asks, voice in between curiosity and skepticism. "First you ransom a slave, and now you're offering to pay a ship's fare?"

"I brought everything I had saved." I shrug. "I guessed that the metals might still be of value out here." And thankfully I'd been correct.

Rhioa gives me an odd look and simply turns around, walking back towards the ship without further comment.

I look to Tirzah. She gives a vague wave of the hand and walks off after her sister.

Her two-hundred-and-four–year-old sister.

With a sigh, I adjust my satchel and follow them both.

After four days on the ship, I have earned the nickname 'Lygaidr.' When I finally ask one of the men what it means, he laughs and says, "Big Eyes." Another sailor, an Alarunian fluent in the trade language, explains that it's a term mothers often use for their young children—especially ones who ask too many questions.

I suppose I deserve it. But I can't quite help myself. The biggest vessels I'd ever seen were the modest cargo barges that ran across the Sea of Triscri. This? This is a marvel of mechanics, a garrison with sails that cuts through great waves as if it barely notices them. The men that sail it do with the utmost efficiency and years of familiarity. They scamper up the rigging and across the masts without so much as a glance downwards. The swaying decks and confined quarters do nothing to constrict their movements. And it becomes an endless source of amusement to them to watch me adjust.

I have, at least, convinced them to give me something to do. By the second day, when my sea legs were a little stronger, I'd tired of simply getting in everyone's way and had asked if there was any way I might be of help. Many of them had not been able to fathom that a paying customer would have any desire to work. The rest laughed, knowing my inexperience. Finally, the ship cook had given me a bucket of tubers to peel and cut. He'd seemed surprised when I actually did them all.

From there, word got around and I'd received all sorts of odd jobs: mopping floors, cleaning the cooking stove, hauling water, mending hammocks, and so on. I find that I am still much weaker than I used to be thanks to the rigors of the Forest and the attack on the dunes, but I am beginning to regain my strength. I've even lost that irritating limp. Today, the boatswain has set me to work on some old line that they'd just replaced from the rigging. I am to cut the weak sections out and toss them over board, then coil the remainders for storage. They will pull these out if they ever need to repair mast nets or hammocks.

I sit in a corner of the deck, humming to myself as I saw through the heavy rope with a borrowed knife. The warm day and fresh breeze make me glad to be above decks.

"What are you doing?"

The voice startles me so that I nearly cut myself. I look up to see Rhioa regarding me with a raised eyebrow.

"Um," I haven't seen her since the second day on the ship when she'd checked on me. "Paring old lines for storage and reuse."

Rhioa's quizzical gaze falls to the yards of rope that lay around my feet. "So I see," she says dryly. "Perhaps I should be more specific: *Why* are you doing it?"

I am embarrassingly distracted by the realization that I've never seen her with her hair down. The wind tugs golden strands around her face and she brushes them out of the way.

"Well, I have nothing better to do—I might as well be of use," I answer.

Her mystified expression does not change.

The silence draws long enough to be awkward and I try to come up with some further explanation. Of course, every thought vanishes the moment I try to grab onto it. I usually have no problem speaking—why must I turn into a stuttering halfwit around the one woman I wish to talk to?

Rhioa sits down across from me, folding her skirts around herself as she does so. She takes up the short sections of rope that I've already trimmed and begins to coil them in the exact fashion the boatswain had shown me.

"You seem to be fitting right in with the sailors," she remarks, nearly amused.

I have to remind myself to continue my work as I try to figure out some reply. "They are a decent lot." Perhaps rather rough around the edges, but all decent at heart. They remind me of the men I'd led. "I seem to provide more entertainment than aid."

This nearly makes her smile. "Oh?" she queries, even though she seems to know exactly what I'm talking about. She reaches for more rope.

I have yet to truly see her smile and now I am determined—even if I must be the subject of the joke. "Yes, they have all gotten a good laugh from watching me stagger around the deck. One of them suggested setting up obstacles and seeing how fast I could get through them."

"If they do that, they should do it below decks," Rhioa comments. I see her press her lips into a line to keep them from curving. "Then you'd have the added challenge of the low ceilings."

"Oh, don't give them any ideas. I've hit my head on those beams enough as it is," I say, shaking my head for emphasis. "Between that and my propensity for questions, I've made quite a name for myself."

Rhioa knots the end of her rope coil. "Mm, it sounds rather deserved."

"It is," I admit. "But still, 'Lygaidr' seems a bit much."

The entrancing sound that follows takes me a moment to register: Rhioa is laughing. "Lygaidr?" She laughs again. "Tirzah is going to love that one."

I can't help but smile in return. "At least if she starts calling me that, I have the assurance that she knows my real name. I'm not so sure I can say the same of these sailors."

Features still lit up with humor, Rhioa adds another set of rope to her pile. "Well, in three days, we should be off the ship and you won't have to worry about it anymore."

"Speaking of," As much as I enjoy seeing her smile, I don't want to miss this opportunity to ask: "Where exactly are we headed?"

"Krysophera," Rhioa answers, hands folded in her lap as she waits for me to finish cutting the next piece. "It lays southeast of Pershizar, bordering both the Macridean Sea and the Ocean of Xzarial." Her answer is perfectly even, yet somehow different from her former openness.

I turn the name 'Krysophera' over in my mind until it matches something from my studies. I can recall its place on a map, but nothing about its lay or culture. "So, if I may ask—"

"—you may ask, but that does not mean I will answer," Rhioa interrupts.

"Fair enough," I say with a bow of my head. I finish my cut and hand her the length of usable rope, tossing the rest over the deck rail to my right. "Is slavery common practice outside of Litash?"

Rhioa sets to work, head tilting back and forth as she replies, "Yes and no— it depends on where you are. In Pershizar, many detest the trade. But the established ruler uses it to fund her place in power. Other trade centers such as Cadbir do not permit enslavement of their peoples but still happily buy and sell others." Her tone dips towards cynicism. "Other places, such as Fuerix and Arvenir, simply give it a nicer name. 'Indentured servant,' 'bondsman,' 'serf'— take your pick."

It's hard to swallow the sour taste in my mouth. "And no one will put a stop to it?"

The way Rhioa looks at me is reminiscent to the day in the alley, as if I have somehow said something entirely unintelligible. She regathers herself and answers my question with another: "If the ones who allow it are the ones in authority, what can anyone do?"

"There is always something," I counter. "Perhaps it just goes further than anyone is willing to go."

Rhioa shakes her head and sets her coiled rope on the pile with the rest. "Things must be very different where you come from," comes her dry comment.

If only they were. Then I wouldn't have left in the first place. Yet, I suppose I have proved my own point: Even I would not go as far as was needed to bring change.

I resume my work and turn the conversation. "Did any of this have to do with why you brought me with instead of parting ways in Ajhal?"

By the set of her shoulders and her singular focus on the pile of rope, I begin to think I've landed in the 'no answer' category she mentioned earlier. But she looks up and asks, "You paid the debt collector with a coin from your native country, did you not?"

I nod.

"That would have drawn attention soon enough," she says, looking back down. "Especially combined with the display that was made of giving it over."

Her tone is enough to tell me that being found out would be bad, but it does not tell me why. "Is my heritage such a dangerous thing?"

Rhioa glances side to side before answering in an undertone. "It depends on the country. In Pershizar, yes. And in Alarune, where the majority of these sailors are from, also yes. The wars that preceded Litash's isolation have left many fearful of Gifting even centuries later."

Something about her answer feels incomplete, as if she is omitting a piece. But I have pressed my luck in asking this far—especially on the deck where we might be overheard. So all I say is, "Then thank you. And I apologize for the added inconvenience of dragging me along." ...Again.... I toss another trimmed piece over the rail and hand her the rest.

"But not for the scene that caused it?" Rhioa's question is more of a statement. She eyes me even as her hands work the thick rope into deft coils.

"No, I'm afraid I am not sorry for that," I confirm quietly. "I cannot be sorry for helping someone in need." The memory of the desperate, helpless mother plays again and I am glad of my interference. Even if it meant getting rebuked in an alleyway.

Rhioa's expression is inscrutable.

I suddenly wish that this conversation had happened elsewhere—somewhere more private. Then, perhaps, I could have asked how I could help her.

"Well, I should go check what Tirzah is up to," Rhioa says, adding the coil in her hands to her pile and getting to her feet. "Think you can handle the rest?" She gestures to the remainder of rope still around my feet.

Swallowing my disappointment, I nod and clear my throat. "Yes, thank you for your help."

With that, I sit and watch her walk away. And then I'm back to my work...and my wishing. I know, *I know:* She is beyond me. I recall Tirzah's words, *'You're barely more than an infant.'* I have no hopes of catching her attention, much less her affections. But that does not mean that I cannot help her escape whatever it is she's so entrenched in—her and Tirzah both. After all, isn't love the willingness to put someone else before one's self? Even if the other will never return the favor?

You sound like a bad philosopher, I chide myself. *A foolish, lovesick one at that.* With that self-admonishment, I leave the soliloquies alone and return to trimming rope.

CHAPTER 5

Rhioa

I don't know why, but Tyron's words echo in my head for the rest of the day. *"I cannot be sorry for helping someone in need."* Why should that sentence bother me so much? Maybe it was the way he looked at me as he spoke. I fear that he was no longer speaking about the event in Ajhal.

I refuse to let myself dwell on the matter. This is made somewhat easier by the poor weather that moves in overnight, giving me an excuse to stay below decks the next day. Tirzah and I remain in our room and discuss plans and backup plans for Arvenir. But there's only so much we can do until we have gathered more information. And the darkening clouds outside our small window keep making me wonder if Tyron has been wise enough to remain below decks, too.

"On another note," I change the subject around. "Have you mentioned to Tyron that he will be the only one getting off in Krysophera?"

Tirzah, laying in her bunk across the room, turns her head to look at me. "No, why?"

I tap my fingers idly on the little corner table that someone had bolted to the floor. "Perhaps it is best not to tell him."

"You mean," Tirzah sits up. "You want to just drop him on the docks, tell him we'll be right there, and then sail away while he stands waiting?"

I hadn't expected her to argue. Her sudden spurt of conscience only irritates me. "We've seen his type before: moral to a fault. Now that he clearly suspects we are on some sort of mission, he will likely offer to help or to at least escort us. If we say no, he may endeavor to 'help' anyway—he could easily find out where we're going from the sailors. If he thinks we're all going ashore, he'll likely wait to ask us then and then it will be too late for him to find out anything."

I can see in Tirzah's frown that she knows I'm right. She lays back down as she says, "Fine. We do it your way. But you're wrong about one thing—we've never seen his type before."

"Oh? Really?" Part of me wishes to temper the cruel words, but I let them loose anyway. "Have you forgotten Kassander Knyte so quickly?"

Tirzah stills. Her voice is low when she says, "So *that's* what this is all about. You think Tyron might offer us a way out and you're too afraid to take it."

"I'm more afraid that he'll get himself killed like the last one did," I bite back, fingernails now digging into the wooden table. "He's not nearly as formidable as Kassander was."

"But he's not the simpleton you like to pretend he is." Tirzah's refusal to look at me is grating.

"Yet not even you would have left him to face Elescar," I immediately point out. "And Elescar is nothing compared to Ovok."

Tirzah's voice is bitter. "So what, then? We do this until I succumb to the Dragon and you turn into Mother?"

The words are like a slap to the face. "Might I remind you that Mother was also the dragon half of her set?"

I regret the sentence the moment it leaves my lips. Tirzah's face contorts in a rare show of pain, hurting me more than her pointed words ever could have.

"I...I'm sorry. I shouldn't have said that. That was...."

"Just leave it be, Rhy," Tirzah murmurs.

I sit there, choking on my guilt.

With a sigh, Tirzah sits up again. "This has to end someday, you know. Either we leave, or one day we fail and one of us loses a form." She shakes her head. "Or Ovok finally gets whatever it is he wants. I'm no strategist, but I have a feeling that that's just as bad for us as losing a form would be."

I know she's right. Her saying it all aloud only makes me feel more trapped than ever. "We'll find a way," I say, throat still tight. "We will. I just," I swallow. "I don't want to bring anyone else down in the process."

Tirzah holds my gaze. "Alright. Then we don't tell him."

Any reply I might have given is delayed by the sound of footsteps. I had meant to wait until they passed by, but they come to a stop outside our door. A knock follows.

I glance back to Tirzah, wondering if she has any idea who it is, but she shrugs.

I get to my feet and open the door to find a cabin boy standing in the corridor.

"Sorry, miss," he sputters. "The captain has asked if you and your sister could join him in his quarters. He said it was somethin' about your friend."

What now? I look to Tirzah and give a jerk of my head towards the door. The look on her face tells me that she's thinking the same thing I am: I have a feeling that this is going to be just like Ajhal.

Ten minutes later, I am sitting across from the captain with my suspicions confirmed.

"Now, he has already sworn that you ladies had no inkling of his Gifting," the captain says, hands folded and resting on the desk between us. "So if this revelation leaves you uneasy about traveling any further with him, we'll leave him in the brig until we reach land and discharge him there."

The brig? Really? "He is down there now?" I ask.

The captain nods. "Yes."

"Just so I have this straight," I catch Tirzah's warning look but am too far gone. "He saved the life of one of your men, and you've thrown him behind bars for it?"

Displeasure marks the captain's brow. "With Gifting," he adds as if I had missed the most important part. "I do not know where you ladies are from, but in Alarune, we have nothing to do with such unnatural arts."

Why do I feel like the captain's position would be different if *he* was the one Tyron had healed? "Unnatural or not, Gifting is hardly a punishable crime."

"But it makes the men uneasy." The captain crosses his arms and adopts a nearly patronizing tone. "I realize that seafaring and the men who practice it are a little outside the realm of such genteel women as yourselves..."

Oh, I could wring your neck.

"...but I need you to understand how much it takes to run an efficient crew. Sailors are a superstitious and distrustful lot as it is. After today," the captain shakes his head. "Letting your friend walk around freely would not be good for anyone."

The near threat only adds to my ire. I give no reply, letting the small-minded captain rethink his words—assuming he has the brains for such an endeavor.

The captain lets out a frustrated huff. "Look, I am out of passenger room and I really can't put him back in the cabin with all the men." He leans back in his chair, scratching his bearded chin. "I suppose there is a storage closet adjacent to your room. Maybe we could clear that out and put him in there."

A closet. *How gracious.*

"But I don't have enough men to have one wait on him or any such thing," the captain adds. "You two would have to bring him his meals."

"We will manage," I say, giving a terse smile and standing up sharply. I know that I shouldn't make an enemy of a man whom I will be sailing with for three weeks yet, so I'd better leave before I say anything else I'm thinking. "Unless there's anything else you need, my sister and I will go lend a hand in clearing out that closet."

The captain gets to his feet. "That was all," he says, oblivious to the ice in my tone. "I will have the men bring him up. But please, do not feel obligated to take this upon yourselves. Should either of you feel unsafe, you need only let me know."

I think of how he would react if he knew I could turn into a Dragon. It adds a little more warmth to my voice when I say, "Of course. Thank you."

I fume all the way back to my shared quarters. Neither Tirzah nor I say anything. Not until we get back and find that the described 'storage closet' is little more than a broom cupboard. Tirzah and I pull out a few mops and pails and sponges out, which are in turn toted off by the cabin boy who had summoned us to the captain. Then I stand and survey the space: It is narrow, windowless, with only enough room to lie down in one direction. It makes my blood boil.

Footsteps come from down the corridor and I see Tyron, closely followed by the boatswain. It's not until Tyron raises a hand in sheepish greeting that I realize he's wearing manacles. *Really?*

They stop in front of Tirzah and I and the boatswain produces a key. I nearly scoff at the iron cuffs. Those don't even do anything to suppress Gifting—they would need red-bronze for that.

"I'll have someone fetch your things for you," the boatswain says, unlocking the cuffs.

Tyron rubs his wrists. "Thank you."

The boatswain frowns. "Just remember, you aren't to leave these rooms."

"Understood," Tyron nods.

The boatswain looks as if he is going to say more but apparently thinks better of it. He nods to me, then Tirzah, then walks away.

Tyron steps into the emptied broom closet and turns full circle. "Cozy," is his only remark.

I stare at him, baffled. How is he not angry? If anything, he seems embarrassed, as though being led around in chains was a mere social faux pas.

"This is ridiculous," I find myself saying aloud. "You can't just sit in a cupboard for two days straight."

Tyron waves the matter away. "I'll be alright," he says. "I've had worse; trust me."

Why does his calm demeanor only annoy me further? "I don't care what they say—come sit with us."

He seems surprised by the offer. I see him look towards Tirzah before replying, "As long as I won't be in the way." He follows us into the next room.

Tirzah takes up her usual seat on the bottom bunk, leaning back against the bed post. I motion towards one of the chairs but Tyron lifts a hand. "I'm alright, thank you."

I sit down.

Tyron goes to the window, looking out with apparent interest.

Silence descends.

Tirzah sits; Tyron looks out the window; I fold my hands and let them rest on my lap.

Tyron draws a breath. "I feel like I ought to apologize...."

"How did it start?" I cut in.

He sighs, raking a hand through his hair. "I was helping one of the sailors draw and haul water for the cook," he begins as he turns back towards us. "But with the rougher weather," he shakes his head. "The boat must have hit a breaking wave because it jolted pretty hard—sent us both tumbling. But then a line snapped and a water barrel got loose and crushed the sailor's leg before he could move."

"I warned you about using Gifting," I say, my voice much calmer than the thoughts inside my head.

"I know." Tyron's hand returns to his side. He locks eyes with me. "But the barrel completely crushed his leg, Rhioa—completely. It sent a piece of bone through an artery. By the time I got the barrel off of him, he had less than a minute left before he would have bled to death. What choice did I have?"

I clench my teeth together and look away. He knew that he would be punished for the act, and yet he did it anyway. It only makes the captain's mistreatment of him more infuriating.

There's a knock at the door and, for a moment, none of us move. Then Tirzah gets up to answer it.

"Some bedding and his things," a disembodied voice says.

Tirzah shuts the door and turns around with a blanket, a pack, and that half-shredded coat Tyron had been wearing when we found him.

"Good thing you left your swords with us," Tirzah mutters as she sets everything down in the corner. "They might not have given those back."

I scoff under my breath.

Tirzah sits back down and Tyron returns to looking out the window.

"Well," he comments. "At least we've only a day and a half left to Krysophera."

From across the room, I see Tirzah look at me. But this whole debacle has only proven my point: We cannot tell him. So I return her gaze, she looks away, and neither of us say a word.

Tyron

The next day, the three of us are sitting in the little cabin as it sways back and forth to the rhythm of the waves. The remains of breakfast still sit on a tray on the table, breadcrumbs and fruit peels sliding to and fro on the emptied plates.

This pretty much sums up all that we've done for the entire morning and the day prior. It seems that neither Rhioa nor Tirzah have brought anything with them to keep them occupied. At least, nothing they want me to see. Still, I wonder how they have kept busy this past week. Do they have any interests? Or past times?

I know they dislike my questioning, but I dislike this stale boredom. Especially after an entire day of it. Besides, Rhioa seems to have calmed down some since yesterday....

"So," I clear my throat. "What is Krysophera like?"

I catch the subtle look that Tirzah gives her sister and it strikes me as odd.

"Depends on where you are," Rhioa answers, shifting in her seat and crossing her legs. "It extends a fair ways south and can be quite cold at this time of year. But the northern coast is the closest landmass to the Cadbir Isles and remains rather temperate."

I mentally visualize a map of the Macridean Sea and recall Krysophera bordering its southern edge. "What language do they speak there?"

Rhioa leans back slightly, one hand toying with the ring she wears on her right hand. "On the coast, most everyone knows the trade language. Further north, and they even speak Ilnorian. But further inland and it's predominantly Krysopheran."

"And what of the people? What are they like?" I ask.

"Like any other people, I suppose," Rhioa gives a vague hand motion, telling me that I'm trying her already worn patience. "Busy with their own lives and not much time for anyone else's."

The openly jaded answer surprises me. I pause, trying to decide whether or not to pursue the subject. Perhaps with the trouble I caused yesterday, I should try another route. Something that interests her more.

So, after a long enough pause, I ask, "May I ask about the rings you both wear?"

Rhioa arches one brow. Then she sets her shoulders and lets out a quiet breath. "They are our tokens. Among our people, twins such as ourselves are a rarity. More than that, they are considered two halves of a greater whole. So we are given tokens to remind us of that." She slips off the ring and it falls to pieces.

I realize that it is not one band, but several bands woven together. A puzzle, of sorts.

"If you put our rings together properly, you can make a single pendant," Rhioa finishes. With sure, practiced motions, she slides the bands until they click into place and the ring is whole once more.

The concept is fascinating. I look at Tirzah and spot a nearly identical band on her hand. "May I ask, then, who your people are?"

"No," Rhioa says sharply, putting her ring back on.

I accept the brusque answer. "Alright."

"What about you?" Tirzah asks from her place on the bottom bunk.

The show of initiative and the question itself surprises me. "Hm? I thought I'd told you before, I'm just a Human."

"I mean Litashians," Tirzah looks at me now. "Are they all, you know, like you?"

I'm not really sure what that's supposed to mean. I glance at Rhioa and find her lips pressed in visible annoyance. "If you are referring to being full of incessant questions, you'll be relieved to hear that the answer is no."

Tirzah rolls her eyes. "No, I mean are they all so...." Her hand traces circles in the air as if reeling in her forgotten word. She apparently gives up. "Take yesterday: You knew that you would get in trouble for helping that sailor, and you knew you wouldn't gain anything from it, so why help? Is everyone in your country like that?"

If only they were. "Not entirely," I say slowly, noting Rhioa's narrowed eyes in her sister's direction. What am I missing? "Litash is like most countries, I suppose, full of people both good and bad. It all depends on the individual."

"So what makes you so kind, then?" Tirzah persists, ignoring Rhioa.

I feel suddenly caught between them. "While I'm flattered that you think of me as such, I suppose that has more to do with my parents than any virtue of my own."

The tension in the tiny room seems to freeze, as if it will explode or vanish in the next instant.

"What about them?" Tirzah asks.

"They have always been my example," I explain. "They gave themselves up to help those around them; how could I do any less?"

The silence that follows feels subdued. Neither sister speaks, but both of them have their eyes on me.

So I go on. "They were both Human, and both healers. They met through their work, actually, married and then had me a few years later. I'm told that both of them were very skilled, very knowledgeable, and very generous. So when a plague swept through the city, they did all they could." I find myself running my hand through my hair. "They saved so many people—I've had strangers come up to me and thank me. But by expending so much energy, they left themselves susceptible: Both took ill and died within a few hours of each other."

"Do you remember them?" This time, it is Rhioa who asks.

"No," I shake my head. "I was not even two years of age when they passed. I was taken in by one of the families that they saved." I shrug slightly. "But I've been told that I look very much like my father."

The only sound is the creaking of the ship around us and the muted movement of water outside the window.

The thought of my parents has always been bittersweet. I've always had that close-held wish to meet them, to know them, to know if they would be proud of who I've become. But the one thing I've never doubted is that they loved me. If they had so much love for strangers that they would lay down their very lives, how could they not love me—their own son?

"So yes, I've always strived to live up to their example. It's not a matter of guilt so much as it is a wish to honor what they were." My mouth runs on without me really thinking of it. "I want to carry on their legacy."

The quiet comes again and with it, both sisters return to their former positions: Tirzah sitting back against the bed post and Rhioa looking off into nothing.

An urgency fills me, an instinct telling me that the moment is passing and may never come again. I have to take this chance while I still can.

"Rhioa, Tirzah," I begin softly, leaning forward slightly. *Oh, just get it over with.* "I don't know what it is that you're caught up in, or who is keeping you in it, but there has to be a way out. There always is." I don't let myself stop, not even for breath. "Perhaps it doesn't mean much, and perhaps I don't have much to offer, but I am willing to help you in whatever way I can."

Nothing. Neither of them even moves.

"Rhy," Tirzah exhales.

Rhioa stand up abruptly. "Let's just get to Krysophera," she says. "We can discuss things further there, alright?" She meets my gaze.

"Alright," I bow my head.

"Speaking of," she turns to her sister. "I want to go check with the captain to make sure that this spell of bad weather hasn't delayed us. Would you be so kind as to take our breakfast tray back down to the galley? Lunch should be nearly ready."

Tirzah's jaw is taut. She says nothing, getting to her feet and swiping the tray from the table. She marches off through the door that Rhioa holds open for her.

I also get to my feet, but Rhioa tells me in a thin voice, "You're fine. Seeing as you aren't allowed anywhere else in the ship, I think I can trust you not to run off our things."

And then they're gone.

For a moment, I just sit there and replay the conversation. What went wrong? No, not wrong.... What went on beforehand? Something that left them so at odds with each other. Something they disagree upon. Something about Krysophera....

I have a feeling—just an inkling—but what can I do? I look around the room. I hesitate, stand, then cross to Rhioa's bunk. Very carefully, I mark how her pack is laying on the bed. I open the top flap and study how everything is arranged. Gingerly, I begin to extract each item one at a time.

Ten minutes later, everything is exactly how I found it and I am standing at the window. *Deep breaths. No nervousness.*

Rhioa enters first, announcing, "The delay is a slight one; we should arrive by tomorrow morning."

I turn from the window and the view as Tirzah comes in behind her with the tray of our lunch.

"Oh, allow me to help you," I step forward.

She sets the tray down and I pick up the plates, noticing from the corner of my eye how Rhioa scans the room.

"How much fish do you want, Rhioa?" I ask.

Tirzah pauses, serving fork midair.

"Oh," Rhioa turns from the bunks. "Not too much."

I try not to show my relief as I hold the plate up for Tirzah. "'Not too much,' coming right up."

I wake up early the next morning to shouting above deck. Still groggy, I sit up in alarm and reach for my swords. Panic swells when I can't find them and then ebbs as I listen more closely. The calls are various docking orders going back and forth; we must have made it to port. I lie back down for a moment, trying to reorganize my thoughts. But I give up when the swaying of the boat keeps jostling me against the narrow walls of my 'room.' It was the same reason I'd gotten so little sleep. Well, half the reason, anyway.

I sit up and lean back against the wall, watching the dim lantern light flicker through the crack beneath the closet door. This feels like Litash all over again. And here I'd thought I'd left that behind when I made it through the Forest of Riddles. What am I going to do? More accurately, what *can* I do? Rhioa and Tirzah obviously intend to leave me behind in Krysophera. The knowledge stings and I let out a long breath, trying to let my frustration out with it. I know that they're not doing this because I annoy them or any such thing. If that were the case, they would have told me as much and threatened me for good measure. Instead, they are trying to do it without having to say a word. They are trying to spare me.

Why? What from? What has them running scared? I can only begin to guess. All I know for certain is that they are so frightened of it that any attempt at persistence will only make them less likely to listen. So what is left for me to do? Walk away? I've never been good at that. Yet forced help is no help at all; Rhioa and Tirzah must make their own decisions. Perhaps the only thing left for me to do is to somehow leave the offer open. To give them another chance if they change their minds. Now, how I can do that while they leave me an ocean away is another question....

I get up, fold my bedding, and leave it in the corner. Then I straighten my clothes and run a hand through my raggedly long hair. But having no comb, no razor, no water, and no clean change of clothes, that is the most I can do to ready myself for the day. I step out into the hall and glance both ways. There are no windows or port holes to tell me what time it is, so I knock very softly on Rhioa and Tirzah's door—just in case they are still asleep.

"Come in." The voice is muted through the sturdy wood, and yet no less lovely.

I suppress a sigh as I enter.

"Perfect timing," Rhioa says, looking up from where she is folding a blouse. The window behind her gleams with the pink of early morning sun. "We've just pulled into port."

"So I gathered," I glance up towards the sound of stomping feet across the deck.

Rhioa stows the blouse in her pack. "I have a favor to ask you."

The statement stirs both hope and suspicion. The latter grows when I notice Tirzah won't look my way.

"Tirzah and I have to finish our packing, and then settle our account with the captain," Rhioa goes on. "It shouldn't take us long but, depending on how much cargo they are offloading, there could be a delay. Could you go ashore now to find us a room at an inn?"

My suspicion is confirmed: They still plan to leave me here. "An inn? So early in the day?" I ask, letting only curiosity show.

Rhioa nods. "We have a lot of supplies to purchase before we head further inland and will need a place to keep them throughout the day." She gives a wry sort of smile. "Thankfully, this isn't Pershizar: One can leave their room without having it cleaned out in their absence."

She's very good—if I hadn't already known, the touch of humor would have been the perfect way to throw me off. But how do I reply? No matter how much I'd thought over this, my decision is so much harder to abide by now that I'm facing her.

"Is everything alright?" I wish that the concern on Rhioa's face is for me and not for the integrity of her plan.

"Oh, yes, sorry," I clear my throat. "Got distracted. Of course, I can go reserve a room at an inn. Did you have one in mind?"

Rhioa shakes her head and picks up a skirt to fold. "Just the one nearest the docks so that we know where to find you."

"Alright."

I stoop to pick up my swords, strapping one to each side before tucking my dagger in my belt. Then I pull on my coat and pick up the pack that I'd taken from the dune pillager's horse.

I pause. "Would one of you mind walking with me up to the deck?" I ask as if embarrassed. "Just in case some of the sailors decide to make a fuss."

Rhioa seems to think this through a moment. She shares a look with Tirzah, then says, "Good idea. Give me just one moment."

She finishes folding the skirt, lays it on the bed next to her pack, and then goes digging for something else. She pulls out a few coins and crosses the room to me. "Here. This should cover the cost of both rooms."

I accept the coins, stowing both in my pocket. Then I turn and hold the door for Rhioa. "I'll see you on drier ground," I say to Tirzah.

She makes brief eye contact before looking away with a terse nod.

I nearly say something more but think better of it. I follow Rhioa out and close the door behind us.

Thankfully, with the crew being so busy with their cargo, I receive nothing more than a few wary glances on my way up to the deck. I don't think that adding a fistfight to my departure would curry much favor with Rhioa.

Rhioa. I walk a few steps behind her, aching with the idea of letting her go. Not that she is mine by any means, but.... Oh, I don't know. I have just never looked at another person, and had them look back at me, and felt like they saw me. *Never.* I had given up the hope of ever being truly known. Then, though I don't know why, I was so sure that Rhioa could from the moment I first saw her. And I knew with nearly equal conviction that it could never be.

Yet it is not simply my own desires that make me so reluctant to let go. I think of Rhioa watching the stars, of the way she described the skies of Ilnor, of the way she looked out over the sea when we first reached it. *That* is what Rhioa wants. Peace. Freedom. Not the death we saw on the dunes, or the fear that left her scolding me in Ajhal. But, until she chooses to make her own way, there is nothing I can do. And that's why I have to let her choose now...even if it means she chooses to leave me behind.

We reach the top deck and I take a deep breath of the cool air. Though it is tinged with the scent of brine and fish, it is better than the stuffy little closet. We wait as two sailors walk by with a long crate balanced between them, then skirt another pair heading towards the hold with a barrel of fresh water. We stop at the top of the gangplank.

"Here you are," Rhioa turns to me. "Go ahead and stay at the inn until we come. It shouldn't be more than an hour. Just be sure that the keeper is expecting us."

I nod and she starts back towards the companionway.

"Rhioa—"

She stops, looking at me quizzically.

This is my last chance. "About what I said yesterday."

Her expression darkens.

"I just want you to know that I meant every word," I finish quietly.

For a fleeting, hopeful moment, Rhioa says nothing. Then she swallows and says, "Alright. We'll talk when we're all ashore."

And then she walks away.

It is the worst thing in the world that I have to let her. It is worse still that I have to do the same.

I wait at the inn for three days. Rhioa never comes.

PART II

ARVENIR

CHAPTER 6

Rhioa

Three Months Later

I watch the glittering landscape slide by from behind the frost-edged window. Despite the insulated walls of the covered sleigh, my long coat and warm gloves, and the coal warmers tucked beneath our seats, I still feel cold. Why did I recall Arvenir as being a lovely place? The past two months of acquiring information, of building fake reputations, of procuring proper trappings—it has been nothing but miserable. I would trade these snowy forests for the dunes of Pershizar in a heartbeat. I keep finding myself thinking of the vivid night sky, of sitting beneath it and just watching the stars.

I blame these silly daydreams for my newfound irritability. Even Tirzah has not been herself; she hasn't put more than three words together at once since we left Krysophera. But I know why. *We'll find our own way out*, I keep saying. *There has to be a way.* She sighs and nods and we both go on, knowing the words mean very little. It's at such times that I am taunted by the thought: What would have happened if I had said yes? Could Tyron have really helped us? Did sparing him condemn myself and my sister?

I shut the thought down before it can go further. Shifting in my seat, I look to Tirzah. She is looking out the other window at the snow laden pines.

"We should be there soon," I comment.

No reaction.

"We shouldn't have to stay long," I go on, looking away so I can pretend she's paying attention. "Having to convince someone that they want power never takes much time."

I hear Tirzah adjust her position. "What did they say was wrong with him again?" she asks in monotone.

I look back at her. "Either no one quite knew, or no one was willing to say. Some sort of deformity, I'd presume."

"Are we sure he's even *able* to take up a new role?" Tirzah rests her head on one hand.

"Well, he is a count. So if he is unfit for leadership or the public eye, then surely someone else is already doing all the work behind the scenes," I reply. I'd already thought on this. "That person would become our main target."

Tirzah accepts this without a word.

And back we go to staring out windows.

"I wonder if he's gotten himself into trouble yet," Tirzah wonders aloud.

"Hm?" I act as if I don't know who she speaks of even while I steal a glance in her direction.

The way she rolls her eyes tells me that she doesn't buy it. "Tyron. I wonder if he's already managed to get himself in trouble yet. Never seems to take him long."

I shrug, annoyed and wishing she'd drop the subject. "I'm sure he's fine. Krysophera is more open to Gifting than most places."

"I suppose."

Tirzah lets the matter go. My mind refuses to do the same. It mulls over the same thoughts and comes to the same conclusion: Tyron is a fool. He has no idea what I would give to be in his place—to have nothing, to be no one, to come and go without turning a single head. Yet he throws it all to the wind with his insistence on being so...so...*good.* I have seen enough of life to know that it is the good and the upright who suffer most. And the wicked, while spared this grief, find their work never ends. Thus the only alternative is to be neither—to be no one of consequence at all.

I gather myself and my thoughts as we begin to pass buildings. The various clusters of houses and barns are nearly lost in the deep, white drifts. It is the tell-tale smoke from half-buried chimneys that gives the little dwellings away.

Villagers, bundled well in colorful clothing, raise a hand to wave as they go on their way. Yet I note how we don't pass anything other than homes and a shop or two. It seems the village of Tulstead is as small as everyone described. Between its size and its distance from the capital, it makes the perfect place to keep a nobleman out of the way.

The sleigh leaves the village and enters another patch of forest. I find myself drumming my fingers on the windowsill from sheer impatience, leaning forward in a vain attempt to see ahead of us. Then I feel the sleigh turn and a manor comes into view. The stone walls seem to grow up from the ground as if they are another part of the rugged landscape around them. Indeed, the turrets and sloped roofs that run down to flying buttresses and colonettes give the manor the shape of a mountain peak, complete with layers of snow.

We approach the gates and I feel the sleigh stop as our driver converses with the guards. Then I hear the creaking of iron hinges and the whole cabin jolts. We slide past the gates, their guardhouses, and out into an open courtyard. It seems a trial to wait for the sleigh to stop and the footman to come around. But when he opens the door and the wave of cold air hits, I reconsider my previous restlessness.

I buckle my coat back up at the throat and step out into the snow. At the closer distance, I realize how small the manor is compared to the ostentatious estates Tirzah and I have pretended to be servants at during these past two months. It also lacks the usual showy colors that so many Arvenish buildings favor, using plain stone instead of painted panels.

"Greetings," a voice calls and I turn to face it. A man in a long, woolen coat is descending the front steps. "I am Elgraf Morsiv, Chamberlain of Tulstead Manor and the Count Ihail. Whom might I have the pleasure to address?"

As the footman helps Tirzah from the carriage, I tilt my head slightly as if caught off guard. "Greetings," I return. "I am Lady Arhys from the Beclian house of Saen, touring Arvenir at the behest of my father, Lord Saen. And this is my companion and escort, the Honorable Tahra of House Elaris." I trail off. "Though, I suppose this would be no news to you if my herald was here.... Did you receive no messenger?"

Elgraf stops a few paces from me, looking from me to the carriage with puzzlement. "No, we have not."

"Oh. Oh dear." I assume a worried tone and bite my lip. "How dreadfully awkward." I glance back towards the road that winds out from the gates. "I do hope the man is alright. He should have arrived a week ago to inform you of my coming." I shiver just enough for him to see.

"Hm. Hopefully he simply took a wrong turn somewhere. But come, there is no need to discuss this out in the cold; do come in." Elgraf waves up a few servants who have since filtered out of the manor. "See to their horses and get the footmen a hot meal."

Tirzah falls in beside me as I follow the chamberlain up the front steps. He holds open the heavy wooden door, covered in swirls of wrought iron. I step into a roomy vestibule and a maid steps out to greet me.

"Might I take your coat for you, my lady?" she asks.

"Yes, thank you," I pull off my gloves and unbuckle the heavy garment.

Tirzah does the same, waiting until I've passed mine to the servant before handing off her own.

"Anva, have tea put on and brought to the parlor." Elgraf comes up from behind us. "And send someone to get a fire going."

The maid, now laden with coats and gloves, manages a curtsy. "Yes, Master Elgraf."

The chamberlain looks to us. "Right this way."

Elgraf leads us down a nearby hallway. The whole corridor is paneled with dark, glossy wood. Carved patterns and intricate moldings give it a graceful, albeit austere, air. Instead of the usual portraits or paintings, I notice several small alcoves containing busts and statuettes.

The chamberlain ushers us into a small parlor and gestures towards the elegant sofas that line one wall. "Please, make yourself at home," he says. "Tea should be in shortly to help warm you up."

A serving boy sidles past him and kneels at the already prepared hearth, striking flint and steel together.

"Do you have any letters of introduction you wish for me to take up to the count?" the chamberlain asks.

I nod and provide him with several papers, some forged and some...acquired.

"Thank you." Elgraf takes them. "I will go and inform the count of your arrival."

He bows his head and Tirzah and I nod in acknowledgement. Then he exits, the serving boy not far behind him.

"I hate these dresses," Tirzah mutters as soon as the door is closed. "How do you stand this all the time?" She sits down on one of the sofas.

I cross to the set of windows and look out over what must be a garden. I can make out the shapes of hedges and a fountain beneath the snow. "By not wearing wool or velvet," I reply idly. "It's the weight that makes them so cumbersome." That and the tight waistline, and the full skirts, and.... "Just wait until we're wearing court dresses. Then you'll miss these."

Tirzah sighs.

I step away from the windows and to the hearth, warming my hands over the new fire as I survey the parlor. The touch of dust on the drapes, the stiffness of the furniture, and the nearly sparing decoration tells me that this room does not get much use.

The door opens and several maids enter bearing trays. These are set on the low table in the center of the room. In no time at all, porcelain saucers and cups are set out next to painted dishes of sugar and syrups. A tiered tray of sweet rolls and candied fruits stands in their midst. A maid pours steaming water from a kettle and then holds a tin box out to me. I select a tea and she fills an infuser, leaving it to steep before repeating the process for Tirzah.

Soon we are alone again. Tirzah and I sit, sipping our tea in mutual silence. We have long since learned to enjoy these small reprieves from our work. They do not come often during missions.

Five minutes pass before I hear footsteps coming down the hall, accompanied by a soft tapping. I lock eyes with Tirzah before resuming a more placid expression. When the door opens, we set our cups down and rise to curtsy.

"Oh, please, do not trouble yourselves," a deep voice says. "Do sit down."

The tapping I heard in the hallway resumes and I realize the young man is using a thin cane. He has it extended out in front of himself as he walks, letting it slide back and forth across the floor. It knocks against the leg of one of the chairs and he reaches out with his other hand. He sits down and leans the cane against one leg. It's only then that I notice his eyes: They are cloudy, unfocused, staring past me and into nothingness.

"Do you care for some tea, Your Excellency?" Elgraf asks.

"No, thank you," the count replies, head turning slightly. "I am all set here. You may be dismissed."

"Very well, Your Excellency." The door clicks as the chamberlain leaves.

"So who may I have the pleasure of welcoming to Tulstead Manor?" The count asks.

I catch Tirzah glancing my way. "Lady Arhys," I reply, smoothing over any of my surprise. "Daughter of the Lord Saen, the head of the House of Saen. I have traveled from Beclian with my companion, the Honorable Tahra of House Elaris."

"It is good to meet you, Lady Arhys," he bows his head. "I am Count Svarik Ihail, Count of the Far East County of Arvenir. I am also, so I hear, woefully unprepared for such esteemed guests as yourselves."

"I fear that the lapse is on my account," I say. I try to refocus on evaluating this new target. "It seems that the herald I sent on ahead of us never reached your lovely manor." I note that his attire, though still orderly, is a touch plain for someone of his station.

The count frowns in thought. "Hm. Perhaps he ran into last week's blizzard and was driven off course. It is possible that he took up lodging with the Baron Urik, my nearest neighbor. If you would like, I can send someone over to inquire."

"I would be very grateful." I try to keep a touch of earnestness in my tone. It is surprisingly off-putting to know he can't see me; I have only my voice to sell my act. "In the meantime, I would hate to prevail upon you when you were not expecting us. Is there any suitable lodging nearby that you could recommend us to?"

"Oh, please don't fret over such matters," the count waves one hand. "You are no trouble at all. So long as you can pardon the hour or so it will take my staff to make up your room, you are more than welcome here."

I dip my head before remembering he cannot see it. "Thank you. You are too kind."

The count smiles politely. "If I was, I would not have left you waiting so long in this chilly little parlor." He gets to his feet. "Why don't you join me in my study until your rooms are ready? It is much warmer in that room and my other guest is already comfortable there."

Other guest? Who would be visiting a disgraced noble in such a frigid season? This could make things difficult.... "That sounds delightful," I reply, setting my cup down.

The count holds the door for us and then takes the lead, cane sliding and tapping as he goes. "So what brings you all the way out here, if you can pardon my inquiry?"

"My father has newly come into his place as the head of House Saen," I explain, wondering if I should warn him of the approaching stairwell. "He wished to make better connections for our House and so has sent me to tour Cadbir,

Krysophera, and Arvenir. Madam Tahra has accompanied me in order to gain experience in diplomacy, as well as to establish connections for her own house."

His cane hits the stair post and he reaches out, hand sliding along the rail as he climbs the stairs. "I'm afraid that Arvenir is not as quite as pleasant as Cadbir this time of year," he says with polite humor.

I gather my skirts as I follow. "Yes, I suppose my timing could have been better." I agree. "Such is the downfall of any touring foreigner, I suppose."

My mind is still on this guest. If they are here during such heavy snow, they are likely to remain for some time. They could be a hindrance...or perhaps a help. I guess the Count Ihail to be in his mid-to-late twenties. Men of such age tend to keep friends who are in a similar stage of life: young enough to be influenced, but old enough to feel entitled to that which they have not yet earned.

"Here we are," the count announces as we reach the first door at the top of the stair.

To my surprise, the study is nearly twice the size of the parlor and lined almost entirely by bookshelves. A variety of small sculptures rest along the shelves, along with what I take to be musical instruments. The light comes from a large window at one end and a blazing hearth at the other.

That's when I notice the other figure in the room, sitting in a padded chair facing the fireplace. He closes his book and stands up as the count enters behind us.

And then he turns around.

For a moment, I don't even recognize him. Gone are the hollow cheeks and the gaunt frame. This man is tall and well-built, wearing an air of nobility that is reinforced by perfectly tailored clothes and neatly trimmed hair. But those green eyes are exactly the same.

"Lady Arhys of House Saen, Honorable Tahra of house Elaris," the count steps up. "Allow me to introduce you to Prince Tyron of Litash."

Tyron

Well, well, it seems I've actually managed to surprise her. Or so I gather by Rhioa's slack-jawed stare. Tirzah, on the other hand, wears a near smile as she slowly shakes her head.

"So good to see you again, Lady Arhys, Madam Tahra," I greet them both in Arvenish as I tuck my book under one arm and give a half-bow. "I'm glad to see you have had safe travels."

"Oh, you three are already acquainted?" Svarik asks.

Rhioa has recovered enough from her shock to cut in with an answer. "Yes, we met while touring Krysophera." Her tone is sweet—a sharp contrast to the glare she's now giving me.

Krysophera, eh? I raise an eyebrow but play along. "And it was a lovely time. You are very fortunate to have such a guest, Svarik. If you thought I had stories for you, just wait until you get Arhys going."

Svarik looks almost relieved. I'd seen how worried he'd become when Elgraf had come in to announce the unexpected guest. I think he'd been fearing either a fellow Arvener, or another touring noble who would treat Tulstead Manor and its count as a circus spectacle.

"In that case," Svarik says. "I will let you all catch up while I go inquire about some tea. The ladies were just finishing theirs when I came in and it has put me in the mood. I hope you won't mind another round of it."

"Not at all." Rhioa is still glaring at me.

"Then it's settled. I'll be right back." Svarik is already half way out the door, calling back, "Do make yourselves comfortable," just before the latch clicks behind him.

For a moment, we all stand perfectly still, listening to Svarik's receding footsteps and the occasional tap of his cane. Then there is silence, immediately followed by....

"What in the worlds are you doing here?!" Rhioa's whisper is vehement. "Better yet, *how* did you get here?"

Tirzah doesn't seem particularly concerned, plopping down on a nearby settee.

"That's a long and irrelevant story," I wave a hand, setting my book down on the arm of my chair. "I have more pressing questions. First of all, you're not here to kill him, are you?"

Rhioa's expression scrunches up. "What? No—"

"Good. Then you're here to make him king? Or Va' Kied, I think they call it."

"Who told you all this?" Rhioa turns her glare on her sister.

"It wasn't Tirzah," I say, shaking my head. "But I'll take that as a yes on the making him king. Which is perfect; he'll be much better than that Talsk fellow. We'll have some work to do to get him there, but he'll make it."

Rhioa is staring at me again. "*We*? There is no *we*—you are *not* staying here." She stays where she is, a waving finger adding emphasis to her words. "All I have to do is expose you and you'll be tossed out on your ear."

"Expose me as what, exactly?" I ask and nearly laugh aloud.

Tirzah apparently gets bored of the settee and gets up to peer out the window.

Rhioa barely notices. "Oh, please, you've practically set yourself up for it, masquerading as a prince. If you'd had half a brain, you would have gone as some baron's son or—"

I hold up my left hand so she can see my signet ring.

She sputters off mid-sentence. "Where did you get that?"

Tirzah turns around, glancing towards my hand.

"From my father," I explain patiently.

"You said your parents were healers," Rhioa objects.

"And that I was taken in by a couple whom my parents had saved," I remind her. I let my hand drop as I shrug. "That happened to be King Otrian and Queen Casidia, heads of the Ethian Council and Rulers of the country of Litash."

Tirzah sits back down with the appearance of being mildly interested.

"But you weren't wearing that when we found you." The argument is a little weaker, telling me that Rhioa is beginning to connect the dots.

I adjust the sleeve cuffs of my new jacket. "It was sewn into the lining of my old coat, along with all my coins." Much of which had been used up purchasing my attire, but oh well.... "But if it makes you feel any better, I am merely the lower prince; I am not in line to the throne."

Whatever Rhioa is going to say is interrupted by footsteps outside. Very quietly, both of us take a seat as the door opens and Svarik steps in.

"I have come with reinforcements," he announces, stepping out of the way and holding the door for Anva and another servant. Both carry trays which they set on the side table.

Soon the servants are gone and everyone is sipping a nice cup of tea—except Rhioa, who is still glaring at me.

"So how long have you been on the road, Lady Arhys?" Svarik asks, leaning back in his favorite chair.

Rhioa tears her narrowed eyes from me, then seems to remember that she doesn't have to. Her face softens to match her tone as she replies, "Quite a while. How long would you say, Tahra? It has to be nearly thirteen months by now."

I look towards Tirzah and she rolls her eyes.

"That's a long time to be away from home," Svarik comments.

"It is," Rhioa admits. "But at the same time, it all seems to have gone by so fast. I suppose that comes with being so busy. We've stopped in so many places and met so many people."

And left some of them at foreign seaports. I sip my tea quietly.

Svarik returns his cup to his saucer as he says, "To be quite forthright, I'm a little curious why my little manor has been included on such a great tour."

"Curiosity was exactly the cause," Rhioa casts another dark look my way. She's wondering how I knew to come here. "I'd heard so much of the salt peaks and the ever-green forests that I decided to come see for myself."

"Ah, I see," Svarik's chin dips down slightly, usually indicating he's thinking something through. "We have plenty of those around Tulstead, though I'm afraid I cannot say much on any of the views."

Rhioa looks embarrassed, floundering for some graceful reply and apparently finding none.

This strikes me as odd. I would not have expected her to be so thrown off by Svarik's blindness. One would think that, at such an advanced age as hers, she would have interacted with people whose perception was different from her own. "Svarik, why don't we ride out towards one of the near peaks? Arhys and Tahra are both splendid riders."

Svarik hesitates, taking another sip of tea. I know he's right to be reluctant around others, but he'll have to let that go some day. It makes me glad when he finally nods. "That's a good idea. We could go out on the morrow if the ladies are up to it. I wouldn't want to have them out and about too soon if they're still tired from their travels."

"Oh," Rhioa's discomfort has not yet ebbed. "I am sure we will be quite ready to stretch our legs by then. What say you, Tahra?"

Tirzah gives an unenthusiastic shrug.

"Tahra is a bit shy, but she would also enjoy the fresh air," Rhioa says.

I suppose that is their way out of having to make Tirzah speak. The fewer people spinning the tale, the less likely they are to put knots in it.

"Perfect. Then I will have the grooms prepare the horses for a mid-morning ride. Shall we meet at, say, the eleventh hour?" Svarik asks.

Rhioa nods, catches herself, and answers, "That would be lovely."

"Now to hope that the weather holds," Svarik says with a shake of his head. He is now comfortably back in his element as count: polite, a touch aloof, and armed with every conceivable form of small talk. "So tell me, Lady Arhys, Madam Tahra, how are you finding Arvenir thus far? I hope the weather has not been too cold for you."

"I must confess that I've never seen so much snow. Certainly never so much that people would use sleighs instead of carriages," Rhioa gives the sort of laugh that any polite noblewoman would give. "But it has its own charm. I've certainly never seen such buildings as you have here, with all their colors and spires."

I notice how Svarik seems to hold in a sigh. "If you are an admirer of architecture, I do hope that your travels will take you by the capital. The palace at Ilske is the crown jewel of Arvenir." He reaches to set his cup and saucer on the table, not releasing until there is the faint sound of porcelain against wood. His voice is quite prim when he adds, "Though I suppose I have not been there in several years and cannot vouch for its current state."

His frustration is evident in his posture and I know that Rhioa sees it. But I don't want her to try and explore it further. Not so soon. So I break in with, "Lady Arhys is also a lover of nature, particularly of the stars."

"Oh, really?" Svarik's head turns.

Rhioa is back to glaring at me while replying in a demure voice, "I'm no astronomer, but I do take an interest."

"Then I shall have to see if we can get the snow off of the upper spire," Svarik goes on, frustration temporarily pushed aside. "The roof is made of glass for stargazing. Tyron used it a few times before the blizzard visited us and put an end to that. Not before he dragged me up there, of course."

With a brittle smile my way, Rhioa says, "That does sound like him. As I recall, he earned himself the nickname 'Big Eyes' whilst traveling in Krysophera."

This elicits a chuckle from Svarik. "I think 'Big Words' might be a little more applicable."

"Either is better than 'Small Mind,'" I raise my tea cup in toast to their attempted insults.

"A fair point," Svarik returns. "And I think we can safely say that none will ever accuse you of that."

The conversation ends with a knock at the door. When Svarik bids them enter, it's Elgraf who steps in.

"The ladies' bedrooms have been prepared," he announces with a bow. "Their trunks have already been brought up and set. Anva has remained in case they should need any help with the unpacking."

Rhioa is on her feet with Tirzah behind her. "Oh, thank you, but that won't be necessary. Tahra and I are old hands at this by now."

"Very well," Elgraf steps to the side to let them pass through the doorway.

"Actually, Elgraf, would you allow me to show them to their rooms?" I set my cup and saucer down. Might as well get this little interrogation over with. "I believe I'm familiar with the guest wing by now." I turn my head. "So long as you don't mind, Svarik."

Svarik is also getting up. "Not at all. I was planning to go up to the studio, anyway."

I follow Rhioa and Tirzah out into the hall. With Elgraf around, Rhioa is no longer glaring.

"They'll be in the two adjacent rooms at the very end of the hall," the chamberlain tells me.

I thank him then motion to Rhioa and Tirzah. "Follow me."

CHAPTER 7

Rhioa

As soon as I have dismissed the maid from our room, I do a quick scan. Then I shut the door, lock it, and stalk towards Tyron.

"You have a lot of explaining to do," I hiss in a low voice. I push him up against the wall, noticing again how much stronger he is than last time I saw him.

He lets me shove him anyway. "Not as much as you might think," he says with amusement.

"How did you follow us here?" I press harder.

"Perhaps you're not as hard to read as you think." Tyron takes my wrist and pulls it away.

I let my hand drop.

Behind me, Tirzah gives something like a chuckle. "You went through our things, didn't you?"

Tyron's mouth tips in a wry smile. "I went through your things," he admits.

Oh, I could throttle him. Especially when Tirzah chuckles again.

"How dare you." The words come from the back of my throat.

But Tyron only regards me evenly. "I knew that you planned to leave me behind. What else could I do?"

"Walk away!" My answer is louder than intended. "That was the whole point of leaving you in the first place. We told you right from the beginning that we would take you as far as civilization and no further; you have no right to meddle in our business."

"Is that what has you angry? 'Business'?" Tyron lets out a breath as he shakes his head. "We both know that ditching me in Krysophera had less to do with me walking away and more with you running. Otherwise you would have just told me."

My teeth clench together. "Or maybe I was worried you would follow us anyway—like you already have."

"You could have asked me to leave and I would have done so," he replies softly.

I narrow my eyes. "Then leave."

Tyron's smile is nearly sad. "I'm afraid it's too late, now." He regathers himself. "I'm here to help Svarik just as much as I am to help you. I plan on seeing this through."

I am too irritated by him to be near him any longer. I turn around and cross to the divan that sits beneath the window, sitting down and smoothing my skirts. I tilt my head, allowing the full of my cynicism to show as I ask, "And how, *pray tell*, do you plan to help? Maybe get yourself surrounded by raiders again? Oh, or maybe get thrown in jail—that'd do the trick."

"Rhy," Tirzah manages to turn my name into a protest.

"What?" I snap. "Am I wrong? Why are you suddenly on his side? You didn't even want to rescue him when we found him half dead in the woods."

Her expression closes off.

"Don't go after her when I'm the one you're mad at," Tyron cuts in. "Your point is true enough: I wasn't much help before. But expecting skilled combat from a yet malnourished Human is hardly fair. And besides, what Svarik needs right now is not a warrior—and certainly not more trickery. What he needs is a friend."

I raise a brow. "Friend?" I repeat, incredulous. No one could possibly be this naive....

Tyron nods and then frowns in thought. "Well, I suppose just someone who believes in him. Someone who will support him. He's spent his whole life pushed off to the side by a society that belittles him. His father was the only exception and he died when Svarik was seventeen. That's when his cousin, the current Va' Kied, stepped in and turned him out." He shakes his head again. "He has all the training, the morals, and the motivation—all he needs is the chance."

"And how do you plan to bring about such a chance?" I ask.

He's back to smiling. I've never found the expression so grating as I do now. "I don't. That will be Svarik's doing."

"Oh, please, he's been hiding here in this little hole ever since they threw him out of Ilske," I roll my eyes. "If he hasn't acted in ten years, the next ten aren't likely to change that."

"Which is where the support comes in. It's not that he's never been presented with opportunities before," Tyron looks from me to Tirzah, finishing: "It's that he never felt he had the means to take them."

I dislike where this conversation is going. "I don't think you quite understand how Tirzah and I work," I reply, lifting my chin just enough to be noticeable.

"On the contrary," He folds his hands behind his back. "I am quite aware. And I'm telling you that it won't be effective. Not in the long term. If Svarik does not make this choice for himself—if he does not take his fate into his own hands—he won't last as Va' Kied for more than a month."

I purse my lips, mentally reviewing all the information I've gathered on this count as well as my brief introduction to him. It only irritates me further that I've already suspected this very dilemma.

"What if we try it?" Tirzah asks from where she sits on the bed. "I mean, what would we lose?"

I grit my teeth. "Time, for one. We have two months left to get this done."

Tirzah shrugs. "So we give Tyron a month to see if he can talk the count into it. If he can't, we have a backup plan ready."

I try to think of an argument, but Tirzah uses the pause to keep going.

"Who knows? If it works, it would be cleaner than just taking out Talsk and trying to wade through the power struggle that follows. And if it doesn't pan out, we'll have better information and more platform than before."

If I didn't still feel guilty for snapping at her a moment ago, then I likely would do so again. But I feel suddenly drained and my anger has cooled to something more like annoyance. "Fine. We try it your way." I gesture loosely to

Tyron. "But I don't have a month to squander on things like making friends: You have two weeks. If the count hasn't taken significant action by then, we do this my way."

"Two weeks, it is," Tyron accepts immediately, bowing his head.

His graciousness rubs raw. I quickly add on, "And if you do something stupid and manage to blow our cover, I can assure you that you'll wish you stayed in Krysophera. Not even running back there will save you from what will come after you." My mind dredges up the image of Elescar, standing in the streets of Ajhal, that knowing smirk on his lips.

"Understood," is the simple reply. He pauses, brow slightly furrowed as if trying to decide something. Then he straightens his shoulders and says, "In that vein, I suppose I should take my leave before the servants begin to gossip. As long as there was nothing else?"

I give a terse shake of my head.

Another bow of his head and he reaches for the door latch. He opens it only to stop and turn in the doorway. "It is good to see you again," he says quietly. He smiles and looks at Tirzah. "Both of you."

Then he pulls the door shut and is gone.

I get up from the divan, crossing to the trunks and not even looking at Tirzah when I say, "Not a word."

Tirzah joins me. But the smug look on her face proves that, as usual, Tirzah does not need words to make herself clear.

I stand on the steps of the manor, adjusting my gloves as servants lead horses into the courtyard. The bite of the cold morning air has put the animals in high spirits. They arch their necks and prance in impatience, ears flicking every which way. The chill has quite the opposite effect for me. Despite the woolen layers of my split skirt and riding jacket, my felted boots and gloves, and my cap, I'm already freezing. I think of the warm hearth back in my borrowed bedroom and grumble inwardly at Tyron for suggesting this whole thing.

"Good morning," a cheery voice rings across the snow-dusted courtyard.

Speaking of....

I turn and look past Tirzah to where Tyron has just stepped out, the Count Ihail right behind him. Tyron waits for the count to catch up and then walks beside him. Both are dressed in long coats and tall riding boots.

"Good morning, Prince Tyron, Count Ihail," I bow my head only because I know the servants are watching.

Tyron's expression does little to hide his amusement.

"Good morning, Lady Arhys," the count replies. His thin cane slides back and forth across the stone landing as he walks, leaving a trail in the scant layer of snow. It dips over the edge of the first step and he comes to a stop. "I do hope the accommodations are suitable for you and your companion. Was breakfast to your satisfaction?"

"Quite," I reply, mirroring his courteous air. "Tulstead is truly as charming as I have heard."

Count Ihail's laugh has an edge to it. "Charming, yes. I suppose that is a fitting word." He shakes his head and takes a breath, letting go of whatever else he had clearly wanted to say. His smile seems forced as he says, "Well, hopefully the countryside will be equally to your liking."

With that, he turns his grip on his cane so that it hovers out across the stairs as he descends. It doesn't make contact with anything until he reaches the bottom.

"Come, Tyron, I want you to meet Eriskatur," the count calls back. A stable hand leads the biggest of the four horses up and trades the reins for Count Ihail's cane.

"What a beautiful animal," Tyron says in appreciation as he joins the count.

"The finest in Arvenir," Count Ihail replies, stroking the horse's neck.

The claim is not out of the realm of possibility. Besides being huge, the horse is well built and even better kept. Even the gloss of its gleaming leather tack is nothing to the shine of its coat. From its shapely muzzle to its long, thick tail, it is ebony black. Only when I get closer do I catch the few flecks of grey on its nose and around its eyes.

"My father gave him to me on my sixteenth birthday," the count says, smiling as the stallion tosses his head. "And he has been a good friend ever since."

A servant brings over a wooden mounting block and the count steps up. For all the horse's earlier pawing and prancing, I notice how quietly he waits for his master. Count Ihail mounts easily.

The next horse is brought up and the stable hand says, "Which of you would like to ride Tirett?" The long-legged chestnut mare pins her ears and the stable hand snaps the reins.

"She's more polite once your mounted," Count Ihail calls back as he adjusts his stirrup. "But do watch out while you're on the ground—she's been known to bite."

Tyron grins and looks my way. "Maybe you two would get along."

I glare at him while Tirzah gives a rather unladylike snort from beside me.

Unrepentant, Tyron steps forward and takes the reins. He thanks the stable hand and mounts up.

I wish the mare had bitten him.

Tyron

With everyone mounted, we pass under the stone archway while the metal gates creak with the cold behind us. The scent of wood smoke fades and the strong scent of ever-green takes its place as the road winds into the forest.

"Do you ride often, Count Ihail?" Rhioa asks in a polite sort of tone.

It's strange to watch her play such a different role. She's an excellent actress— I knew that even before seeing here in Arvenir. But seeing her act out a personality so far from the one I saw in Pershizar only drives the point home.

"I do enjoy it," Svarik answers from the front. "Though I have not done as much of it as of late. The snow makes it difficult. Tyron has been trying to talk me into it since he arrived."

Yes, yes, I had. I'd noticed all the sculptures of horses around the manor and guessed that Svarik must have a love for the animals.

"And how long ago was that?" Rhioa is looking at me.

I shrug and adjust the hood of my coat. "What would you say, Svarik? A week? A week and a half?"

"That sounds about right."

Rhioa raises an eyebrow but keeps any further comments to herself.

We round a bend and the forest falls away on our left, opening up to a wide, empty plain. The snow here is untouched, a perfect veneer over the landscape. Only the rise of windswept drifts gives away any imperfections of the ground below. The deep red and grey of the Crimson Mountains stand in the distance, a dark contrast to the glistening plain.

Svarik's horse—Eriskatur, he'd called him—arches his neck and picks up his hooves in a pretty manner. It is the tamest rendition of impatience I've ever seen in a mount.

"I take it we've reached the open," Svarik chuckles and pats Eriskatur's neck. "Not yet, my boy."

We leave the road now, heading towards the mountains. Leaving the forest also means leaving the protection of the trees and I see Rhioa shiver with the bitter cold. But even as she gathers her coat more tightly around herself, I see her gaze follow the wind across the plain. I am drawn to it, too, as it tugs at our caps and plays with the snow. It pulls up stray snowflakes, swirling them and tracing patterns in the sky before sweeping them back down.

I glance over to Tirzah, riding beside Rhioa, and find her expression nearly as wistful as her sister's. I wonder if it has to do with their other forms. In Litash, most shape-shifters had a preferred form outside of the humanoid. They often took on characteristics of this 'alter ego,' such as tastes, preferences, ways of moving, and even personality. Perhaps Rhioa and Tirzah, having Dragon-like counterparts, feel the draw of the wind and sky.

With no help besides occasionally asking me about our position in regards to the mountains, Svarik leads us across the field and towards a slight rise. Then I begin to catch the muffled, gurgling sound. Something like running water but muted and more subdued. Then we reach the top of the rise and I realize we are at the edge of a steep riverbank.

"This is the River Noya," Svarik announces as Eriskatur halts. "It feeds into Lake Ondeveris a few miles from here. The residents of Tulstead take sledges there throughout the winter to cut ice for their cellars."

What an ingenious way to store food for a long period. I gaze over the edge of the bank and down at the thick swath of ice that cuts through the plain. The river has clearly melted and refrozen several times for the ice has piled up in heaps, looking like shattered glass. Somewhere deep below is the source of the gurgling. I can make out a few spots where the dark water lurks beneath.

I dismount and, heeding the warning that my mount tends to bite, keep my reins close in hand as I walk closer to the edge.

"Do be careful. The banks are quite slick," Svarik warns.

I kneel down beside what I presume is a small boulder and clear the snow away with a gloved hand. The dark stone is interrupted by a vein of deep pink that runs through it. "What a fascinating color. Salt, I presume?" It must be responsible for the color of the mountains.

I catch Rhioa leaning forward to see.

"If you are referring to a pink color, then yes," I look back to see Svarik nod. "It is what Tulstead is known for. Unfortunately, very little will grow here because of it. The villagers rely on mining and fishing to make their living."

I straighten, dusting my hand off on my long coat. "It must be difficult to mine in such cold," I remark.

Svarik's response is distracted. "I suppose."

I study him a moment, perched on the back of his magnificent horse. His posture is immaculate, his seat steady, his shoulders level; he seems as much a part of the landscape as the distant mountains. The biting wind, though strong enough to lift the fur collar of his coat, does not seem to affect him in the least.

And yet, here he is, trapped at the edge of the river that marks his county— the winding bars to his prison cell.

I set a foot in the stirrup and mount back up. We remain in still silence for a few minutes more before Svarik turns us all back towards the woods.

"Do you enjoy the countryside?" I ask Svarik as my little mount tries to catch up with his.

I can't see his expression now that he's back at the front, but Svarik sounds nearly tired as he replies, "I suppose it is rather charming."

"That sounds like something someone else has told you." I comment and glance towards Rhioa, Tirzah still riding beside her.

"To be fair, there does not seem to be much else to say of the place." Svarik's tone is uncharacteristically dry. "Nothing like the countryside to show one how much they miss the city."

I nudge my mare forward, catching up with Svarik before asking, "Do you?"

His head turns towards me, a quizzical look marking his brow. "Come again?"

I nearly wonder if my Arvenish has slipped and I've misspoken. "Do you miss the city?" I reiterate.

Svarik turns forward again, lips pinched together. "It is certainly far more private out here. And far quieter, too." He is a silent a moment. "But I suppose one could appreciate the energy and action of city life. It all depends on the person."

Before I can reply, Svarik gathers himself and twists around to call over his shoulder, "How are you faring, ladies? Can you bear the chill long enough to see more of the woods, or would you prefer to return to the manor?"

Rhioa's face is red with cold, yet her manner does not seem false when she calls back, "Let's go on to the woods."

Svarik addresses me next. "If you look towards the forest, you'll see a patch of spruce taller than the rest. Are we facing it head on?"

"Turn about twenty degrees to your right," I tell him.

"Here?" He adjusts Eriskatur to the new course.

"Yes."

With his bearings straightened, Svarik gathers his reins and pushes his stallion into a canter.

I double check that Rhioa and Tirzah are both set before I follow.

We wander the trails of the ever-green woods for about half an hour before we all agree that it is too cold to remain out any longer. Still, we take our time back to Tulstead Manor, letting our reins go slack and allowing the horses to stretch out at a walk. Svarik does the same, apparently trusting Eriskatur to lead us home.

"I have not met such creatures myself, but Arvenir has all sorts of tales," he goes on to Rhioa. He seems more relaxed than when we first left. "Children grow up hearing of river serpents and kitdste—the giant mountain wolves. Adults are more concerned with the snow gryphons, which come down from the mountains in flocks during the winter."

"What is a gryphon?" I ask as the stone turrets of the manor appear through the trees. I'm not sure if the word is just something in Arvenish that I have not come across before, or if the creature is one I've never heard of.

"Hm," Svarik frowns in thought. "I suppose it is rather like a small Dragon, but with the beak and feathers of a bird." He shakes his head. "And the brains. They are not bright, much less cognizant."

"Are they large?" Rhioa's question is nearly drowned out by the creaking of the gates ahead.

"They can get up to the size of a large horse, although those that make it this far north are no bigger than a dog," Svarik answers.

Seeing the size of the Arvenish hunting dog the stable master keeps around, that is still quite sizable.

I am distracted by the sight of three horses standing in the courtyard, all tied at the hitching bar. Each bears the mark of the great white Tskecz cat just behind the saddle.

Before I can warn Svarik, the gateman does it for me.

"Your Excellency!" The man is rubbing his hands to warm them as he steps out of the gatehouse. "Three men with the seal of the Grand Va' Kied arrived not ten minutes ago. The servants have shown them inside."

Svarik straightens his shoulders. "Thank you, Olsd. You may return to your post."

The man dips his head in a hurried bow, glances my way and then towards the ladies, then shuffles back to his warm gatehouse.

Jaw taut, Svarik leads the way into the courtyard. He dismounts and trades Eriskatur's reins for his cane. Rhioa, Tirzah, and I all hand our mounts off to the stable hands and climb the manor steps behind Svarik. Servants appear to help us all out of the heavy winter layers.

"Anva, please have lunch brought up to the western sitting room," Svarik instructs as he hands a woolen scarf off to another maid. "And something warm to drink, of course."

"Yes, Your Excellency," she curtsies. "Your guests are waiting in the parlor. We brought them tea, but they said they would not be here long enough to take it."

Svarik gives a curt nod of acknowledgment.

Thanking the servant who takes my coat and gloves, I trot down the hall to catch up with Svarik.

"Svarik, would you allow me to come with you?"

He keeps walking, cane sliding back and forth in measured movement. "There is no need to bore yourself with the matters of a lowly county," he replies. "Go take lunch with Lady Arhys; I'm sure that I won't be far behind."

"The men's horses had the Tskecz cat on their saddles—they've come all the way from Ilske, haven't they?"

Svarik stops. He lets out a quiet breath. "If that is so, then yes, they must be from the capital." His head turns and his pale eyes wander past me. "If you are certain that such business will not be tedious to you, then perhaps company would not be such a bad thing."

"I don't mind in the least," I assure him.

He tarries a moment more as if unsure what to say. Then he simply turns and leads on.

When we enter the parlor, the three men all snap to attention and give an Arvenish-style salute, clasping one open hand to the opposite shoulder in unison. Svarik gives no acknowledgment. He crosses to an armchair and sits down while I close the door behind us.

"Your Excellency, Count Ihail," one of the men steps forward. "I come with a message from the Grand Va' Kied."

I note that none of them had been sitting. Nor do any of them move to do so.

I take the chair nearby Svarik as he asks, "Then I presume you bear his seal?" He holds out a hand.

The courier gives Svarik a nearly blank look before going rummaging in his satchel. He pulls out a large, round token and places it in the count's outstretched palm. It looks like some sort of giant coin. Svarik runs his other hand over the metal token, letting the tips of his fingers brush across the top. He holds it back out and the uniformed man takes it back.

"So what is your message?" Svarik asks coolly. He sounds very different without his usual polite cordiality.

The man falters again, this time glancing towards me. "With all due respect, Your Excellency, I do not know who your guest is. My message was given to—"

"Are you here to give a message or to meddle in my affairs?" Svarik snaps, cutting him off. "What matter is it to Talsk who my guests are?"

The courier and his companions seem to bristle at the reprimand. The courier, especially, narrows his eyes and lifts his chin. His voice is taut when he recites, "By order of the Grand Va' Kied, the salt mines surrounding Tulstead are to be expropriated and their management brought directly under the Grand Va' Kied. This includes the mines in the Gvos Hills, the Crimson Mountains, and the Crystal Lakes. An allotment of salt shall be made for Tulstead Manor and its residents, as well as for the residents of the nearby village. All else shall be exported directly to Ilske. You have three days to withdraw any of your men or agents, as well as to hand over a full roster of the workers."

I look to Svarik. He barely reacts. The only giveaway is the set of his jaw. "Well, in one respect at least, I can spare you some trouble: There is no roster. The men of Tulstead, who know much more about mining than I do, run everything and simply report to my agents."

I do not miss the way the courier glances towards me again, as if looking for any giveaway that Svarik is lying. I return his scrutiny in even measure.

"Do you have any documentation? Or at least an attestation that you have none?" The man looks back towards Svarik.

"Since I cannot read, documents do me very little good. And since my handwriting is considered too poor for the Grand Va' Kied, I will abstain from sending him a sample." Svarik gets to his feet. "Do send him my regards, instead."

The courier narrows his eyes even further. But he snaps another salute and motions to the two other soldiers. "Your Excellency," he mutters, sweeping past him and out of the door.

With the men gone, I get to my feet and look at the sealed scroll they left on the tea table. Likely a transcription of the message.

"What are you going to do?" I ask.

Svarik's lips are pressed into a thin line. "Nothing."

"Nothing?" I echo.

He leans over, one hand feeling for the cane he left resting against the chair. "This is all for show. I don't do anything with the mines anyway—him taking them over is nothing but a show of power. It doesn't merit my attention."

I am unsure of how far to press this. "What of the residents of Tulstead?"

"I doubt they'll even notice the difference," he shakes his head, cane now firmly in hand. "Talsk has no interest in actually managing anything. He's had his little spiteful jab at me for the year, so I expect he'll forget about me until next cycle. Until then, the village will have their work and their salt and I will have my peace."

Svarik walks towards the door, but I don't move. "Perhaps peace is not always the best way."

He pauses at the threshold.

"Perhaps you should not let him forget about you," I venture a little further.

"And perhaps you should not tell a man what to do in his own house," Svarik says in tart reply.

"I would never presume to do so," I say earnestly, now stepping forward. "But I would be no friend if I kept silent in the face of your struggle. I apologize if it came off any differently."

Svarik sighs as he turns to face me. "Do not apologize. My reply was more unseemly than yours." He swallows, apparently conscious of how tightly he's gritting his teeth. "I admit that I am not used to having company. Especially ones with any real interest in my affairs. And you are," his mouth tips slightly. "Unusually open concerning such matters. I must confess that I am not entirely sure how to take it."

I shrug, despite the fact that he can't see it. I reply with humor when I say, "If it's any consolation, you are not the first person who hasn't known how to deal with me. It is quite safe to say that I am the common denominator in this matter."

The tension in his hands and shoulders seems to lessen. "I suppose that is marginally comforting," he says wryly. Then he turns back and steps into the hall. "Come, I'm hungry; let us go see if Lady Arhys has saved us some lunch."

The mention of Rhioa reminds me of our deal. I have two weeks. Hopefully, I have made more progress than Svarik is letting on.

"A splendid plan." I follow him out, lingering at the door when I spot the scroll still on the tea table. With a last glance, I shut the door.

CHAPTER 8

Rhioa

If I have to pretend to read one more book, I'm going to throw it at someone. Probably Tyron. He's a week and a half into the two weeks I gave him and what is he doing? Playing a board game. And not even with the count! Count Ihail had excused himself after luncheon and went up to his sculpting studio. Since then, Tyron and Tirzah have sat across from each other with a game of tin knights between them, going back and forth in the trade language.

"I think you've gotten the hang of this one," Tirzah remarks with a shake of her head.

I don't have to look up to know that Tyron has beaten her for a third time in a row.

"Well, as they always say, the success of the student is to the credit of the teacher," Tyron says as he helps her clear the board.

As usual, Tirzah's reply is blunt. "I've never heard anyone say that."

And as always, Tyron is irritatingly unaffected. "Oh. It must be a Litashian saying, then." He starts putting the pieces in their wooden case. "How about a different game?"

From my peripheral vision, I catch Tirzah glancing my way. But I keep my eyes stubbornly on the page before me. Not that I've been paying any attention to the words on it. It's as boring and dry as the past eleven days have been. The only reason I can bear any of this at all is because Tirzah and I have slipped out each night to go flying.

Apparently giving up on getting my attention, Tirzah picks up the case of tin knights and crosses over to the cluttered cabinet full of dusty game cases. I hear her rummage around.

"Do you know chess?" she calls back to Tyron.

"Yes—" He pauses. "Maybe? I suppose Litash may use different rules than Arvenir."

The sound of wood against wood tells me Tirzah has picked the next game. "That's alright; our country has different rules than anyone does."

I shoot her a look, reminding her to watch her tongue. No one is to know we are Myrandi. And if Tirzah lets it slip over something as silly as chess....

"How so?" Tyron asks with interest.

Tirzah, ignoring my glare, returns to the table and sets the case down. "For starters, we use three boards instead of one."

"Three boards?"

"Mmhm."

"Now you have my attention; you must show me." Tyron is already on his feet, returning to the cabinet and digging through. "Look—here's two more boards."

Soon they have the three boards laid out next to each other. "This one is supposed to have an extra row on this side, and the other end is supposed to have a row less, but I guess it'll do," Tirzah says. "We usually like to play with them stacked on top of each other. It makes some of the strategy easier."

I shift slightly, just enough to see the boards from the corner of my eye.

"Then this arrangement is perfect." Tyron is grinning. "This way I can blame it on the boards if I lose."

Tirzah raises an eyebrow and says nothing, instead setting up her pieces and having Tyron mirror with his. But I am still struck by the change in her expression. It isn't much, but it's...different. And to see a statue change at all seems monumental.

"Now comes the hard part: the rules." Tirzah looks over their makeshift setup. "I'm not really the best at this game anyway—Rhy is the expert. But everyone says it's a lot like the strategy of a battle...."

And on she goes into the longest monologue I've ever heard her give to anyone but me. She explains for nearly five minutes, gesturing to pieces or giving demonstration. She fumbles here and there when she can't quite recall the rules. But Tyron just sits and listens, taking in all the new information, never interrupting except for the occasional question. He takes me off guard when he catches my gaze, smiling a little before returning his attention to the game before him.

I hastily look back at my book. I keep myself strictly at it, turning pages now and then for show. Meanwhile, I listen to them go back and forth with chess pieces and banter. Is he...is Tyron doing this on purpose? The smile, the self-deprecating humor, the games—he's purposefully drawing her out. I nearly snap my book and get up to interrupt the whole thing. I might have, except that I suddenly recall the carriage ride two weeks ago. Tirzah had spoken all of three times for the entire journey. She hadn't smiled even once. And here she is, lips tugged up at the corners, explaining entire games.

"Wait, which pieces do I lose when a middle tier piece is taken?" Tyron asks.

"Uh," Tirzah falters, fingers tapping against her palms as she tries to recall. "I think it's the one right underneath and the one right behind."

"And the one afore," I add.

I feel them both look at me.

I give up my pretense, setting the book next to me on the cushion and getting to my feet. I haven't even taken a step before Tyron is pulling up another chair for me. With one brow arched, I accept it wordlessly.

"So it takes out anything in the corresponding space, as well as the one in front and behind?" Tyron restates, gesturing to where his bishop has just taken Tirzah's rook.

With a nod, I take the liberty of demonstrating. "When a nobleman falls," I remove the rook, then turn to the lowest board. "His men have no orders. The front line is scattered and defeated," I gesture to the foremost space. "Those around him are thrown into disarray," I point to the corresponding space. "And those behind him flee in fear." I take the pawn that Tirzah had in the one space behind.

Tyron watches the board. He is quieter when he asks, "So TetraChess is the game of war?"

I dip my head. "I presume that, being a noble, you are at least partially familiar?"

"Only from books, I'm glad to say," he replies as Tirzah begins her turn. His lips tilt in a wry expression. "Litash is too isolated to make war on its neighbors. But with so many pythanids and ligreans about, there's still enough for everyone to fight without having to turn on each other."

I watch Tirzah move her queen then reach for her knight. "And yet you are familiar with combat," I comment aloud.

Tyron's eyes do not leave the boards. "I've been sent out a few times. Nothing noteworthy. Usually only to help track down a band of thieves or such. Those spring up from time to time, usually near the border where they can hide in the outskirts of the Forest of Riddles."

"Why would a country of shape-shifters send a Human into battle?" I ask, dubious.

"Because sometimes said shifters have more important things to do," he answers. I can't tell if the dryness of his tone is the result of my question or of admitting his lesser importance. "And there were times where my Gifting was useful to them. Besides, as a lower prince, losing me would not have cost them too greatly."

The only time I've ever known a royal to downplay their worth was in some show of false humility. But Tyron puts on no airs as he watches Tirzah finish her move by taking out one of his pawns.

I decide to press the point. "I've never heard of the title. What does it mean?"

Tyron begins his move on the first board and I notice absently that he does what I would have—push the queen forward two spaces. "It means I am of the royal family and am given the appropriate lodgings, trappings, and so on. As far as authority, I could give orders to any standing guards so long as it does not defy previous orders. But I am not able to inherit the throne under any circumstances, and I am considered an outsider in any gatherings of the Ethian Council. I have no legal authority." He recites all of this simply, only hesitating when he can't seem to decide whether to move the castle or the bishop. He selects the castle.

"So in other words, you had all the benefits without the responsibilities," I remark.

He looks at me, pondering a moment. "Something like that, I suppose."

I continue my challenge: "Then why leave?"

Tyron nearly smiles, and yet his expression is somber. "Because I have no wish to waste my life on comfort and ease. I want to make a difference." His words are wry when he turns back to the boards. "And some people feel threatened by that."

I'm not sure if he's referencing his countrymen or if he's making a jab at me. Before I can decide, the study door opens without warning and the chamberlain stumbles in.

"Oh, my apologies," Elgraf says in Arvenish as he glances around the room. "I thought His Excellency was in here."

He begins to close the door but Tyron switches to Arvenish and calls, "Is everything alright?"

Elgraf pauses in uncertainty. "A villager is downstairs, seeking an audience with the count. She comes with some rather unsettling claims."

Tyron is on his feet. "I believe Svarik is up in his studio. Please, allow me to get him for you so that you may attend to the villager."

The chamberlain, again, seems unsure. But then he nods his assent and says, "Thank you. Please inform the count that her name is Amma Elsona, from the western edge of Tulstead."

And then both men are off, leaving Tirzah and I behind in the study. She looks at me as if awaiting orders.

"Let's wait it out," I murmur. "Better to not insert ourselves and look meddlesome. We can get the details from Tyron later."

We dawdle over the boards for a while. I take up Tyron's pieces even as I strain to listen for footsteps through the now open door. Nothing. That could mean that everyone is too caught up in the news the villager brought, or it could mean that the news wasn't of enough import to react to.

According to the winding clock on one of the bookshelves, twenty minutes pass before I hear voices from the hallway. I get up and cross to the door, listening.

"Don't be rash, Svarik," I hear Tyron reasoning. "Sending men will only end in disaster."

"Well, what do you want of me? Only days ago, you were urging me to do something. Now I am ready to act and you tell me not to!" Count Ihail's voice is raised and sharp.

What has happened? I step quietly out to the balcony and watch as the count storms up the staircase, Tyron close behind him.

"I'm telling you that what you're doing won't make a difference for those men," Tyron tries to point out. "Talsk will just send more soldiers and have his excuse to get rid of you. How will that help Tulstead?"

I step back as the Count Ihail reaches the top of the stair and stalks across the balcony to the next flight up. He's not even using his cane, just using one hand to feel his way along the railing. Tyron glances towards me but doesn't stop to explain. I fall in behind him and hear Tirzah do the same.

"He has no right! None!" the count thunders, already halfway to the next floor. "He won't get away with this!"

By the time I reach the third floor, Count Ihail has pushed open the door to his studio and gone inside—ranting all the while. Tyron stops at the threshold and I do the same. I have never been in this room before. It is open, spacious, containing nothing but a table, a pottery wheel, and row upon row of shelves. These are filled with ceramic sculptures of every shape, size, and color. I spy horses with arched necks and birds with proud eyes, trees and flowers alongside busts and Human profiles.

In the middle of it all stands the Count Ihail. He is silent now, shoulders heaving with his panting breath. His hands are clenched into fists, one wrapped tightly around his cane.

I look to Tyron and find him wearing a look of unerring patience, though I notice the way he presses his lips together. "Svarik," he begins quietly.

With a sudden roar, the count lashes out with one arm and sweeps an entire row of sculptures from their shelves. I nearly jump as they fall to the floor with a great crash. Shards scatter across the tile in waves. Svarik moves on, sweeping yet another shelf clean as his last victims crunch beneath his boots. Then again. Then he raises his hand, only to let it fall. He stands there breathless.

Tyron steps into the room. "Svarik," he tries again.

"I am so *tired.*" The count's voice trembles as he speaks. "So tired of smiling and nodding and taking orders from the very man who *ruined* my life. Talsk is nothing but a braggart and a bully. He took those men from Tulstead and enslaved them in the mines simply because he wanted to remind me of how helpless I am. I refuse to be helpless anymore."

"So what are you going to do?" Tyron asks. His calm manner is jarring against the backdrop of the shattered sculptures that litter the room.

"Apparently not send any of my guard to their aid," the count snaps.

Tyron remains unaffected. I think of all the times that I have been harsh towards him only for him to show the same persistent composure.

"Of course not," Tyron replies. "Because if you did that, it wouldn't fix the real issue: Talsk would still be Va' Kied and would still trample whomever he pleases."

Svarik turns around, pale eyes seeming to search for Tyron. His voice is low when he asks, "What are you saying?"

Tyron sighs. "I'm saying that so long as Talsk is Va' Kied, this is how life will be. If you truly want to change how things are, you must be willing to change everything."

I watch as the count's rage cools and his shoulders sag in defeat. His hands relax and he finally lets his cane settle back on the floor.

"I can never be Va' Kied," he says in a hollow voice. "No one would support me. I have nothing to offer and they're far too scared of Talsk."

Tyron immediately counters, "If they're all so scared of Talsk, then that's exactly what you have to offer: a way out. After all, you are the rightful heir—it's completely legal. All you have to do is get enough of the nobility on your side to call for an Assembly."

Svarik scoffs. "None of them are on my side. None of them stood up for me when Talsk drove me out of Ilske."

"Then show them you're willing to stand up for yourself. I think you'll find they're as tired of being helpless as you are." Tyron's voice turns softer. "Surely there is someone who is at least willing to hear you out. You could start with them and then begin to work your way up."

The delayed reply and the way Svarik shifts his weight from one foot to the other tells me he's actually considering it. Tyron has somehow played this perfectly.

"I would have to go to Ilske; everyone spends the winter there," the count says slowly. "And me showing up would draw Talsk's attention. But..." he is visibly mulling over the idea. "...I do know of a manor where I could stay."

"That's a good start," Tyron encourages. "And I presume that whoever it belongs to will be open to your cause." He phrases it like a question.

Svarik lifts one hand in an airy gesture. "Who knows. She always claims that she'd support me in anything, but she's never anywhere to be found when I need her."

Tyron steals a glance towards me and I shrug; I have no idea whom the count speaks of.

"She?" Tyron echoes.

With a bitter smile, Svarik replies, "The Baroness Ihail—my mother." He shakes his head and takes a step forward, only to stop when the ceramic pieces crunch underfoot. "I have not seen her in many years and that is entirely on purpose. But I suppose she's the best place to start."

Again, Tyron looks to me. "Alright. Then when do we leave?"

Tyron

"Can you see the bridge yet?" Svarik asks for the third time in the past hour.

I oblige anyway, peering out the sleigh window before replying, "Not yet."

Svarik returns to nervously rolling his cane in between his fingers.

If he is this nervous about visiting his mother's manor, I wonder how it will go when we leave for the capital.

"We should be close," Rhioa offers. Still under the guise of Lady Arhys, she had offered her support to Svarik. He had been anxious enough about speaking to his mother that he had accepted upfront. Then he had immediately sought me out to ask whether or not she was trustworthy. I'd guessed that Svarik was more suspicious of her than he'd let on, but I had not wanted to lie to him. So I'd reassured him of her motives and left out all of her methods.

"I can't say that I will mind being out of this sleigh for a bit," I mention in an attempt to lift the mood. After two days in the close quarters, I think even Svarik will be glad to stretch his legs.

"Let us hope it's not for too long," he mumbles in reply.

Tirzah, who had been resting an elbow on the window, suddenly straightens. "I think I see the bridge."

"What does it look like?" Svarik, too, straightens.

For a moment, I can't see it. But then the sleigh turns and I have a full view of the Dolsni Bridge. It spans the river with a graceful curve, with stone arches rising from the parted waters to support the snow-topped road.

"Exactly as you described," I report. I go on to illustrate the view as best as I can.

This seems to let Svarik relax, even if only a little bit. So I continue my narration as we cross the river and the distant Dolsni Manor grows larger. Only as we pass through its gates do I fall quiet.

This manor makes Tulstead look like a cottage. Not only is it at least three times the size, but its towering spires put it at nearly twice the height. The main body is of four different wings which unite under a single dome. While the masonry is just as flourished and detailed as on Svarik's home, it has been carved from two distinct types of stone: one a brilliant white, one a clay red. The striking contrast in color extends to the brightly tiled roof. I wonder what material they use to achieve such an intense, gleaming color.

The sleigh comes to a stop and so do my wonderings. As the footmen help Tirzah and Rhioa out, I pull on my gloves and double check that Svarik is ready. He has his coat buckled back up and his cane ready. But the hand that holds his hat taps in nervous rhythm.

"You are ready for this," I reassure quietly.

He takes a deep breath, grips his cane, then lets the footman help him down the step.

I am right behind him.

We are ushered across an immaculate courtyard, lined with carefully trimmed ever-green trees. I notice how many people there are: grooms already tending the horses, servants clearing snow or carrying wood, a huntsman with a dog at his heels and a hare slung over his shoulder. White birds with long, trailing plumage strut around the yard, squawking with offense when anyone passes too nearby. The many outbuildings beyond speak of the busyness just as much as the people do. I see barns, fenced fields, and an assortment of strange glass buildings.

A rush of neatly uniformed servants greet us as soon as we enter the broad front doors. I'm so busy gawking that I barely notice the man who offers to take my coat. I thank him and hand it over, along with my gloves and cap. But even as I straighten my tunic and vest, I'm back to peering around the vestibule. Like Tulstead Manor, the floor is a dark, polished wood. The walls, on the other hand, only use the material as a striking accent amid colorful patterns. These stretch up to an arched cupola above our heads and switch to panels of embossed tin.

"Right this way, Your Excellency." A servant addresses Svarik with a bow, drawing my attention back down.

From the corner of my eye, I catch Rhioa shaking her head. It seems my open fascination amuses her. I give a little shrug and gesture for her to go first as Svarik starts off down the hallway.

I follow at the very back, almost wishing we had more time to stop and look at the many paintings. I note how there are few portraits compared to the vast number of landscapes. Snowy mountains, thick forests, glens and valleys and waters, all captured in glossy oil and bordered by gilded frames. I get no more than a passing glance before we are brought into an expansive parlor and bid to take our seats.

This room is as richly decorated as the rest of the manor. The deep green walls provide a backdrop to the wood-framed furniture. The many narrow windows, edged with gold-tasseled curtains, look out over a wide courtyard with many snow-laden shapes. It takes me a moment to realize that these are plants, carefully covered with some sort of fabric.

Under different circumstances, I might have asked Svarik about this oddity. But seeing as he is gripping the arm of his chair until I fear he'll rip the upholstery, I don't think that light conversation will be much comfort.

Instead, I take a seat near his and assure him again, "You are ready."

"I suppose I have no other choice than to find out," he grumbles beneath his breath and tugs subtly at his collar.

The door opens and a footman steps through, holding it open for the woman behind him. Her fair hair, though touched by grey, is much like Svarik's in color. But it is her taut and perfect posture that makes mother and son look so similar.

"Welcome back to Dolsni Manor, Your Excellency," she says as she steps in. "It has been many years."

Svarik is on his feet almost instantly, turning around and accidentally knocking his cane across the arm of his chair as he does so. "It has, My Lady," he replies as if out of breath. There is a pause before he adds, "I hope all has been well with you."

The Baroness Ihail crosses the room until she stands in front of her son. She is a tall woman, thin in face and form. This is only accentuated by the richness of her attire—she wears the typical full skirts and structured bodice of Arvenir. In fact, her attire is nearly too typical; she, like Svarik, dresses *precisely* as her station requires. The baroness looks her son over in detail before her inspection turns towards Rhioa, Tirzah, and me.

"Life has been peaceful as always," she finally says. "Though I see yours has yielded some change."

"Ah, yes, do allow me to introduce you to my companions," Svarik steps back slightly so that he turns half way towards us. "This is Lady Arhys of House Saen, daughter of the Lord Saen of Beclian. Her escort is the Honorable Tahra of House Elaris."

Rhioa gives a graceful curtsy, Tirzah copying her in the background. "Such a pleasure to meet you, My Lady," Rhioa says with just the right amount of warmth.

Svarik's mother curtsies in turn and offers a smile that does not match her eyes.

"And this is Prince Tyron of Litash," Svarik goes on. "Son of King Otrian and Queen Casidia of the Ethian Council."

The baroness's eyes dart to me and narrow ever so slightly.

"It is good to finally meet you, my Lady." I bow my head. "It has been a privilege to know your son, and I am glad to know his family better." I am suddenly glad for all of Rhioa's lectures on Arvenish etiquette.

I do not miss the traces of suspicion that pinch the baroness's lips together. But she manages a thin smile. "That is very gracious of you. As it is to visit my son, for he does not get many visitors all the way at Tulstead."

With that arbitrary comment, she calls to the footman, "Ring the bell for tea, please," before gesturing for us to all take our seats.

Svarik is so nervous that he accidentally catches his cane on the edge of the carpet and trips. He catches himself and fumbles for his seat, face a shade redder than before. His mother looks at him a moment before taking the chair to his left.

"So how is Tulstead Manor faring this winter?" the baroness asks, straightening one sleeve.

"Quite well, thank you." Svarik takes up the small talk with the same polite tone. They sound more like strangers than mother and son. "And how are things here at Dolsni?"

"They are well as ever. Though I hope that the maintenance on the bridge was of no inconvenience to you." Her eyes wander back towards myself and Rhioa.

"None at all," Svarik quickly replies. "We didn't even notice."

The parlor door opens and an array of servants sweep in. Soon, there are enough trays on the tea table to provide a feast for a small family. The baroness surveys it all, selects a single piece of shortbread, and motions for us to serve ourselves.

"Do you still keep Morsiv's son as your chamberlain?" she asks as she holds her teacup and saucer out for the maid pouring tea.

"Yes," Svarik answers, feeling for his cup on the table. "He has been very faithful in his duties. He recently oversaw the hire of two new grooms for the stable." Then he accidentally knocks his teacup from the table to the woven carpet below.

"Stop gawking and help him," the baroness snaps at the maid. "Can't you see that he's blind?"

The maid apologizes and rushes to set down her kettle. Svarik, face flushed, searches the floor with one hand.

"Just a little to your left," I tell him.

Svarik adjusts and quickly finds the porcelain cup, returning it to its saucer. He murmurs, "Thank you," and holds it steady for the maid who pours his tea.

His mother, jaw taut, sips at her tea and returns to the conversation as if nothing had happened. "You should have your chamberlain keep in better touch with the tailors at Ilske. Your suit colors are fine, but the cut of the collar is quite out of fashion."

The statement is thrown out so callously that I can't help but try to soften the blow. "Perhaps I've rubbed off on you, Your Excellency," I joke to Svarik. "My sense of fashion is notoriously bad—even for a Litashian."

Svarik sips from his gilded teacup, the set of his shoulders giving away his anxiety.

"Do all Litashians have such...interesting taste?" With just the right touch of humor, Rhioa picks up the conversation and carries it further away from Svarik.

"Well," I take in a deep breath and make a show of letting it out. "Yes—but, to be fair, we are a nation of Bandilarians. With so many forms, fashion tends to be, er, oh, what's the Arvenish word for it?"

"Diverse?" Rhioa suggests.

I nod, holding out my cup for the maid. "Yes, precisely—diverse."

I see the baroness's focus turn to me and her eyes narrow again. Yet there is something protective in her posture, as if she wants to put herself between me and her son. It makes me wonder if there are good intentions behind her suspicion.

"Arvenir is used to foreign visitors: I'm sure no one will be unkind regarding your manner of dress," she says, pausing for a dainty sip of her drink. She pinches her lips together before adding, "If anything, they will be more surprised that you have no consort. Is that also common amongst Litashians?"

I credit her subtlety. She is challenging my claim to royalty while remaining within the bounds of etiquette. But I dislike double questions as much as their answers, so I reply honestly. "It's simply a matter of preference. Our governing structure is twofold—the king and his Council, and then the Court of Nobles. Since the nobles are generally legislative, they keep many people with them to help in the work. The Council, however, is a more active and protective: We tend to prefer light travel to remain efficient." Perhaps the detailed answer will help prove my station.

I hear Rhioa shift as she chimes in with a laugh, "This was his excuse to leave both his guard and his manservant in Krysophera—'efficiency.' To be truthful, I think he couldn't put up with their bumblings any longer. Neither man was worth their pay."

If it wouldn't be too obvious in front of the baroness, I would have given Rhioa a look. I know she's trying to make me sound more trustworthy, but I also know that lying is a terrible way of accomplishing such. I am frustrated that I have to play along with a smile and a shrug. "But see? I was correct. I haven't missed their help in the slightest."

The baroness seems to accept this, even if somewhat begrudgingly. She looks back to her son and the untouched scone on his plate. "And how has your health been, Your Excellency? You look rather pale. Have your servants kept the manor well aired?"

"I assure you that I am quite well." Svarik straightens. "And that my staff is quite attentive. Even if they weren't, I get plenty of fresh air thanks to Eriskatur."

His mother stiffens. "I hope, at least, that you do not ride unattended. I always told your father that he should have been more cautious in giving you that horse. Riding is dangerous enough, even for the sighted."

Svarik sets his cup and saucer down with a clatter that makes everyone jump. "Speaking of fresh air," He grabs his cane and stands up abruptly. "I do believe that I am in need of some. Perhaps we could take a turn around your lovely courtyard?"

Once more, the baroness pinches her lips. "Of course. But perhaps the greenhouses would be a better choice on such a chilly day."

"Whatever you think best." Svarik's voice is colored with his exasperation.

We abandon the half-full tea cups and have soon resumed our coats and gloves. Then the baroness, attended by a young maidservant, leads the way out the back of the manor. We cross a wide, snow-covered patio and descend into an open garden. It is full of the cloth-wrapped plants I had spied earlier from the window. But the baroness carries on towards the glittering buildings ahead. Only as we grow closer do I realize that it is a single, large building, with many wings connected to a central hub.

We enter one of the wings through a wooden door—the only wooden thing in this hall of glass panes and metal framing. I enter last, allowing the ladies and Svarik to pass through ahead of me. Even before I've stepped in, I feel the rush of warm, wet air. The baroness has already passed her coat off to her maidservant while Rhioa and Tirzah carry theirs. I drape mine over one arm and notice how Svarik simply keeps his on.

In slow parade, the baroness begins down the center aisle with Svarik beside her. I walk next to Rhioa, marveling at the array of exotic flora. How strange to be in the middle of such lush foliage while the white pall of winter lays only a few feet beyond. How do they keep it so warm? Is it a property of the glass?

Ahead of us, Baroness Ihail talks in detail about the many plants, the seasons, the loss of a batch of seedlings, the order she put in all the way from Fuerix, and so on until we have toured two whole wings of the greenhouse. As interested as I might have been on any other day, my focus is drawn more towards Svarik. He wears his silence with the same impatience that he wears his too-warm coat. I have a feeling that he will not bear either for long.

It comes when the baroness moves to discussing how Svarik could easily set up a greenhouse of his own.

"As useful as it may be, I'm afraid I lack your interest in agriculture," he cuts in.

"I suppose you do," his mother replies, stiffer than before. "I can understand how it might seem plain to you, since you cannot see the beauty of each plant or the harmony of a full garden."

Svarik stops in the middle of the walkway. "Why must everything be about my blindness? I simply don't like things that I find boring and dull—including botany. Why can't you just leave it at that?"

The baroness's face goes blank in a moment of shock. Then she blinks it away and glances towards Rhioa and me. Then she clears her throat and says, "Your Excellency, perhaps this is not the time to—"

"You're right," Svarik interrupts. "This is not the time. I'm here for other reasons: I came to inform you that I plan on going to Ilske, calling for an Assembly, and claiming my right to the crown of Arvenir."

I watch as the baroness stares at him blankly. Then she looks at me as if trying to see if I'm in on some joke. She is pale when she looks back at her son.

"You can't be serious," she gasps.

"Completely and totally," he replies without delay.

The baroness begins to shake her head. "No, no, you *can't*. Don't you understand? Who talked you into this?" Her eyes widen in apparent realization, then narrow as they hone in on me.

Svarik is back to gripping his cane. "I am not here to ask your permission, nor do I need anyone else's. Everyone knows that Talsk has no right to the throne and I'm tired of him making a mockery of my father's crown." He pauses, letting out a terse sigh. "I have let him get away with too much for too long, and now he has enslaved forty-two men from Tulstead to work in the salt mines. He has gone too far. And it's time I did something about it."

"This is ridiculous," his mother nearly hisses. "If you go making a spectacle of yourself by challenging Talsk, you're going to get yourself killed—and right on the anniversary of...." She falters, eyes darting to the side. "You should know no one will dare support you."

"No one?" Svarik repeats, the words pointed and sharp. "Not even my own mother?"

The baroness stops short. She looks at Svarik for a long moment. Then she sucks in a breath and says, "No. I will not condone this foolishness. I will not be part of you going off to get yourself killed, nor will I approve of these 'friends' who help you do it." She gestures towards Rhioa, Tirzah, and me.

Svarik straightens his shoulders, face red. "Very well. Then I will do it without you."

He spins on his heel and walks towards us. His mouth is twisted, his shoulders set. We part to let him pass and then follow hesitantly. The tapping of his cane on the stone walkway is the only sound in the entire greenhouse.

When he reaches the outer door, Svarik stops and turns back. "I will be leaving for Ilske in two weeks' time. I trust that I can expect the hospitality of your staff at your father's old house there?"

I glance back at the baroness and find that she has not moved.

"Surely you wouldn't leave me stranded in the streets again." Svarik's tone carries an edge. "Not after it caused so much gossip last time."

His mother's face is drawn, as white as the snow outside the greenhouse walls. "I will write to the servants and inform them of your coming," she finally says.

"Thank you." Svarik remembers enough of his manners to give a bow of the head. "And don't worry about seeing us off: I remember the way. Good day to you, Baroness." He opens the door and strides out.

With one last look towards the baroness, I, too, bow my head and leave. I can feel her gaze boring into me all the way out.

CHAPTER 9

Rhioa

In the sleigh back to Tulstead, the silence is uncomfortable and close quartered. Svarik sits very still, knuckles white around his cane. His pale eyes stare forward into nothing and I'm glad that I'm not the one sitting across from him. Tirzah is not one to be bothered, having already taken up her position with one elbow on the window sill. Tyron, sitting across from me, is in a similar position. Though I have the feeling that he has not forgotten about my lie to the baroness on his behalf. I'm sure he has some moral speech saved up for later.

"She wasn't always like this." The words are so sudden that even Svarik seems surprised to have said them.

"Like what?" Tyron prods quietly.

How does he always know what to say?

"She wasn't always, you know," The count makes a flustered gesture with one hand. "So afraid," he finishes.

Tyron glances at me and Tirzah before asking, "What changed?"

Svarik lets out a deep breath and his agitation seems to lessen. "I suppose my father was the only thing keeping her afloat, too. Her life was never easy, even when he was around. So when he was gone, I suppose that...." His voice trails off and he sighs again.

Normally, this sort of vulnerability is a perfect opportunity for me. A person is very malleable when they have opened themselves up so much. I've spent months getting people to such a place just so I can manipulate them properly. So why does it suddenly make me so uncomfortable?

"And yet, for all her flaws, you do not blame her?" Tyron phrases it more like a statement.

"I.... No. Not completely. I understand her." Svarik's grip relaxes from around his cane. "My father used to call her a 'dreamer.' She loved her books and her art and her botany. She was never very good at fitting in, no matter how much etiquette she practiced. My father never cared about propriety. He was..." His voice turns wistful. "...generous. Open. He filled the room just by walking into it. He could make anyone feel confident—even my mother."

And, apparently, even Svarik. I think of my own father and I look away.

"When I was born blind, things grew harder for my mother. Children are important in Arvenir, and so a mother is judged by her offspring." I hear Svarik shake his head. "My little brother, born two years after me, did not live past three months of age. She miscarried two others. After that, my mother would not appear in public without my father there with her."

The quiet that settles is heavy, seeming to mute even the sounds of the sleigh over snow.

"Such loss is a terrible thing for anyone to have to bear." Tyron speaks solemnly. "And, I think, it is that loss that has made her so afraid of losing you. These efforts to control you may simply be, to her mind, a way of keeping you safe. I doubt she sees the way that it causes you harm."

Svarik's brow knits together, his expression nearly troubled. "Perhaps," he says. "But whatever love she may have had for me seems to have turned into a love for herself. She will only ever accept me if I become the person that she imagines I am." He taps his thumb on the end of his cane. "I do not hate her, even if she did nothing when Talsk usurped me. But I cannot let myself turn into her."

As if suddenly self-conscious, the count clears his throat and tugs at his collar. "I do apologize—this whole visit has been more than you signed up for. And here I am, rambling on about it as if that will help."

I wonder if Svarik has ever spoken of this to anyone at all. How old was he when his father died? Seventeen, wasn't it? To be cast out at such a young age, alone and grieving and.... I stop the thought before it can go further. *Empathy is your weakness. Your emotions will get you and your sister killed.* The voice rises unbidden from the back of my mind and I suppress a shudder. I feel Tirzah look at me.

"You have nothing to apologize for," Tyron assures Svarik. "And besides, we all have families; we know how complicated things can be."

I nearly narrow my eyes, only to realize that Tyron isn't speaking of me or Tirzah. No, he isn't even looking at us. His gaze is unfocused as if seeing some memory instead of the walls of the sleigh. Curious. He has never mentioned family outside of his deceased parents. But then, if he is a lower prince, he must have at least one sibling in line for the throne....

"Complicated," the count echoes in a murmur. "That is a good word for it."

This time, when the silence falls, it is no longer awkward. The four of us sit in mutual agreement and the unspoken understanding that we'd rather not talk about it.

Why must it be so hot out? My breath comes in gasps and I scramble sideways. But my footwork fails and I feel my heel catch on something. I barely recover, using both hands to bring my sword up. The blow that follows leaves my ears ringing.

"You're slowing down," she taunts.

She doesn't have to tell me—the burning in my arms and lungs told me long minutes ago. I force my aching limbs to swing my sword again, this time to swipe away the stab towards my torso. It's so close that I feel it catch and tear the material of my loose tunic.

"What do you think?" Her voice drips sweetness and makes my stomach curl. "Three more blows, or only two?"

The bright glare of the sun and the sting of sweat in my eyes nearly makes me miss the shift in her weight. I try to adjust, but I'm too late; she's dropped under and around my guard. Pain explodes in my shoulder and I almost drop my sword as my whole right arm goes numb. Luckily, I'm too breathless to scream.

"Not even one," she makes a tut-tutting sound. "If these blades were sharps, that would have cleaved you right in half."

I nearly wish it had. I keep circling, making my left hand hold on to my sword. It feels like lead. Maybe...maybe it would be easier to just give up. I know how this ends. And I know that nothing I can do to change it. But then I catch a glimpse of the other figure, sitting in rigid silence at the edge of the ring. She is watching. I refuse to let her see me give in.

So, daft as it is, I charge.

For all of one second, I see something like surprise on Mother's face. Then she smiles and I feel my heart stop. She bats my sword aside and catches my wrist in her other hand. Then she twists. This time I can't bite it back and a yelp escapes my lips as she forces me to my knees. She lets go and I try to duck, but I'm not fast enough. The pommel of her practice sword hits me between the shoulder blades and sends me face down into the sand.

"Still so sloppy," she sighs in abject disappointment.

There is a sick sort of thud as she kicks me in the ribs, driving the breath from my lungs.

"Get up," she growls.

Gasping, I crawl towards my sword.

"I said," Another kick, this one accompanied by a stabbing sensation. "Get up!"

I can't, I can't. It's too late. I wrap my arms around my head and curl up as tightly as I can. It's not enough to protect me from the barrage that follows.

"Wait, no, Mother—please!" Tirzah's voice is pleading.

The rain of blows doesn't even lull.

"Stop!" I hear Tirzah's running footsteps and the beating stops.

I open my eyes just in time to watch Mother strike her across the face with such force that she stumbles backward.

"What? You want your turn already?" Mother spits.

I try to use the chance to reach my sword. But Mother spots the movement and brings her boot down on my hand. I scream as she grinds it into the sand.

Mother leans down and scoops up my fallen blade. "One day, maybe you'll actually learn."

All I care about is when she finally takes the crushing weight off of my hand. I immediately withdraw it, curling back up. I feel Tirzah reach my side and we both brace for the next blow.

But it doesn't come.

When I dare open my eyes again, Mother is looking down at us in disgust. "Weakness such as yours has no place among the Myrandi. If you won't let pain be your teacher, it will become your executioner." She smiles, tilting her head in the way that makes a shudder run down my spine. "And believe me, I'm all too happy to carry out its orders."

Then she turns away, walking to the edge of the ring and tossing both blades on the rack. "I expect better next week," she calls over her shoulder.

For a few minutes, neither Tirzah nor I move. We can't. We both lie there in the heat and dust and try just catch our breaths. My throat is swollen, my mouth dry and filled with a familiar metallic taste. My shoulders and torso throb with a pain that drives out any other sensation.

"Come on," I hear Tirzah croak. I look up to see blood dripping from the cut on her cheek. "Let's get you up."

I bolt upright with a gasp, one hand pulling my talon dagger from its hiding place. I remain frozen in place as I scan my surroundings. My eyes catch on movement—someone laying down. Someone asleep. The even measure of their breath is barely audible above the pulse still roaring in my ears. Then I notice the pale blonde hair and recognition clicks into place.

Calm down, it's just Tirzah. I return the dagger to its sheath but do not yet put it back under my pillow. I sit there for a moment, forcing myself through breathing exercises until I've regained control of my senses. Then I lie back down try to focus on the features of the room: the warm glow of the nearby hearth, the painted trim that edges the ceiling, the little chandelier in need of polishing, the frigid night air whistling along the stone outside the window.

The next step is closing my eyes. But I can't do it. Not when I see my mother every time I try. She's been gone for a century, so how does she still chase me? Why do I keep seeing the things she made us do? Or worse, the things she did to us if we did not cooperate....

Irritated, I get up and pull on a blouse and skirt. Normally I would wake Tirzah to see if she wants to go for a flight, but I'm not in the mood for my Dragon form. I blame this on that stupid visit to Svarik's mother. I shouldn't have volunteered to go. Tyron could have handled it by himself—it's not as though I even contributed anything. With a pause to make sure that Tirzah is still soundly asleep, I pull my shawl around my shoulders and exit the room.

I make sure to release the door latch slowly so as not to make any noise. Then I make my way down the corridor, my muted footsteps the only sound in the whole manor. What a change from the last few days. The moment we had returned from Dolsni, Svarik had given the order that everything was to be packed and moved. Sleepy Tulstead had roused itself into a flurry of activity within the hour.

My steps slow when I near the count's study. Svarik and his chamberlain, Elgraf, have practically sequestered themselves in there to deal with all of the provisions and documentation that Tulstead might possibly need in the count's absence. I check for light beneath the door before I dare pass, not wanting to run into either of them if they are working late. Especially not after the chamberlain had pulled me aside to tell me that they had found no trace of the herald I'd lied about sending. I had not missed the way he watched my reaction closely, as if judging my sincerity. He had seemed to buy my affected sorrow, agreeing to send a letter to the man's family once I had it written, but I know that it will only take one slip up to turn his misgivings into full suspicion. Thankfully, the study is dark and I pass safely by.

I pause again at the balcony rail. Up or down? Among all the packing and storage of household items, the upstairs is somewhat crowded. But the only room downstairs with real privacy is the eastern sunroom. It would be much too cold in there at such an hour. Upstairs it is.

My mind begins to wander again without my permission. For some reason, I keep thinking of what Svarik said of his mother: *I cannot let myself turn into her.* I had thought that the count was little different from the baroness. After all, both had holed up in their respective manors and hid themselves away from Talsk. Yet now, after ten years, Svarik has suddenly picked himself up and changed. I think of my mother, of how I am like her. Is it too late for me to change?

I shiver and pull my shawl more closely around my shoulders. I tell myself it's simply because the third floor is chillier than the second. Still, it's hard to push aside all my useless thoughts and focus instead on my wanderings. I've been upstairs several times since I volunteered to help with the packing and stowing of household goods. But I'd been too busy to explore.

I recall the mention of the stargazing tower from that first day we had arrived. Perhaps I can find that. The only place it could possibly be where I wouldn't have spotted it from outside is the end of the western wing. I turn and walk that way. I'd been annoyed when Tyron had brought up stargazing and, if only to keep from proving him right, hadn't sought it out.

The thought of Tyron brings up another issue. I don't want to leave for Ilske without first making some sort of plan that he agrees upon, but he has proved difficult to track down. He is helping with something entirely different every time I spot him. The only time I see him regularly is at dinner, where the count and his staff prevent me from speaking openly.

The hallway turns and comes to a sudden end at a thick, wooden door. This must be it. I tug on the cold wooden handle and it swings open with surprisingly little sound. All I hear is the slight hum of the wind scraping at the walls outside. I step into the drafty, stone stairwell and realize that it isn't lit at all. I consider borrowing one of the candles from the nearby candelabra but decide that the light would be of little help for stargazing. I shut the door, put one hand on the cold stone wall, and climb.

By the time I've reached the top, the thin light of the stars overhead feels bright. By it, I can make out the dim shapes of several chairs—all steeply reclined to allow for looking up at the glass ceiling. I spot what must be astronomer's charts hanging on one wall.

"Rhy?"

I nearly jump clean out of my skin.

"Oh, my apologies, it's just me."

I see him now, sitting on the floor with hands raised as if to show he means no harm.

"What in the *worlds* are you doing here? And why are you on the floor?" I demand, tone harsh if only to hide my breathlessness. I must be completely out of sorts to have mistaken the hum of his Gifting for a mere breeze.

"Just looking at the stars," Tyron replies, not moving. "I truly am sorry—I did not mean to startle you."

I ignore his apology, instead growling, "Looking at the stars? So late at night?"

"That is when they tend to come out. And actually, it is now technically morning by Arvenish standards," he says with some humor, lowering his hands. There's barely enough light to see the concern on his face when he adds, "But I suppose I could ask you the same thing. Are you alright? You don't look well."

I've regained my wits enough not to just turn around and leave. This is exactly the moment I've been needing to arrange a plan with Tyron. So I step inside the room and sit on the edge of one of the chairs.

"Quite well," I reply primly as I try to relax my grip on my shawl. "All of the packing and planning of the last few days has simply gotten to my head and is keeping me up."

The long pause that Tyron takes to evaluate me tells me that he doesn't quite buy my answer. But he doesn't challenge it. Instead, he shifts so that he can sit back against the wall when he asks, "I presume that includes planning ahead to Ilske?"

I hadn't expected him to bring it up for me. "Yes. There will be specific people that we need on our side if an Assembly would dare pick Svarik over Talsk."

Tyron smiles.

What did I say? Is he mocking me? The edge returns to my voice when I ask, "What?"

"You called him Svarik—not Count Ihail," Tyron replies.

"So?" I wave a hand in dismissal, irritated. *Never let yourself get attached to a mark.* The lesson echoes in my head and I move on quickly. "It doesn't change my point: We still need to have a plan on how to approach all these people."

Tyron gives a half shrug. "Seeing as Svarik will be the one doing it, I don't see why a plan is necessary. He'll know best who might listen to him, anyway. All we can do is offer encouragement and be ready to help if he needs it." Then he shakes his head slightly. "Though I should mention that lying on my behalf is not quite the help he needs."

I feel my cheeks color and am glad that he can't see it. "The baroness doubted your backstory, I remedied that, and everyone was happy. I don't see any issue."

"Except that we are trying to build trust," Tyron counters. "And being duplicitous is not a good way of doing that. The more lies that a person stacks together, the more likely they are to fall apart."

"And yet you had no problem with playing along with my role as 'Arhys,'" I point out.

"That was your choice. I cannot force you to change that." His voice is steady, even. "I am merely asking you not to make that choice for me."

I bite my tongue then nod. "Fine. But only so long as it does not jeopardize my work. Should that happen, I will act as I think necessary."

Tyron bows his head like one accepting the terms of a deal. Then I hear him draw breath as if to speak.

I'm not sure what he's going to ask, but I'm certain I don't want to answer. So I interject with, "How did you get here anyway?"

Even in the thin light, I can see his brow furrow. "Up here? One of the servants had mentioned—"

"Not the tower," I shake my head. "Arvenir. How did you make it from Krysophera to Arvenir? And then still afford a new suit and a transport to Tulstead? And how on Eatris did you manage to pick up Arvenish in just three months' time?"

"Oh." Understanding colors his voice. "I stayed in Krysophera a few days just to make sure that you weren't coming back then went back to the docks. I'd picked up enough skills on our crossing from Pershizar to trade work for passage to Arvenir."

I blink at him. Certainly he's joking. All of those days that he'd spent being absurdly helpful to the sailors...had he *planned* that? Or was he just that good of a person and it had actually worked in his favor? I don't feel like asking.

Tyron continues his explanation. "As for the language, I simply got lucky there. It turns out that, not only does Arvenish have the same root language as the trade language, but I'd studied the written form of it back in Litash. The books were very old and thus much of my knowledge was archaic, so I was fortunate that one of the sailors in the crew I sailed with was an Arvener. I traded a portion of my rations for language lessons." He pauses, head tipping slightly. "Admittedly, his use of language was a little, ah, different from what one might consider 'good etiquette,' but I had some time on land to smooth that over before I sought out Svarik."

He is absolutely ridiculous. If any other person had told me this, I would have laughed in their face and called them a liar. But this is Tyron—I believe every word. I move on to the next question: "Then what? How did you know we were coming here?"

"I didn't," he confesses. "The lists you had never mentioned Svarik. Still, I guessed that all of those other names on the list had something in common. It didn't take much digging to figure out that 'something' was him. Then after hearing his plight and visiting him...." He trails off and looks down at something he's fiddling with. His signet ring, I think. He is quieter when he adds, "I assure you that I did not mean to run into you again. I knew you wanted me gone, and I respected that. But I supposed that if I could figure out what your mission was, I could figure out who it was that had ordered it. Then perhaps I could have helped by appealing to them."

I go rigid. *Of all the stupid, senseless, idiotic....* My mind races over the different scenarios, each worse than the last. What if he had found Elescar? What if he had managed to find *Ovok*?

"You should be glad your plan went awry, then," I snap. "Because you have no idea how much harm you would have caused me and Tirzah, both." I stand up from the chair. "You may think that you are helping or making a difference or other such foolishness, but all you've done since I've met you is insert yourself where you don't belong. Someday, all that trouble that you get yourself into is going to come down on someone else's head and believe me: There are far worse things than staying in a ship closet for a few days."

Flushed, I turn to march back down the stairs. My imagination conjures up images of him enduring Elescar's brutal interrogations. Or worse, mine. If Ovok ordered me....

Tyron's voice stops me. "Rhioa."

If he had been angry, I wouldn't have cared. But the soft way he speaks somehow makes it harder to ignore. I stop in the doorway and look back.

"Stay. You came here to stargaze, and I've already been here awhile." He gets up and dusts off his breeches. "The second moon should be over the tree line within the hour and the rings are stunning from here."

Why is he so calm? I just yelled at him! If it weren't for his troubled expression, I would almost wonder if I'd imagined my harsh words. I almost leave anyway, then decide that the easiest way to get away from him is to just accept his offer. I return to my chair even as Tyron crosses to a cabinet on the side of the room. He opens it and pulls something out.

"Take this. It's cold up here," he says.

Baffled, I take the blanket that he hands out to me.

"Goodnight, Rhy."

And then he's gone, the faint diminuendo of his footsteps echoing in the stairwell. The hum of his Gifting lingers a moment more before it, too, fades to nothing.

I think I spend more time looking at the blanket in my hands than I do the starlit skies over my head.

Tyron

I spend a lot of time thinking on Rhioa's words over the next few days. Despite their sting, I know she didn't mean them—not fully anyway. They were the product of fear. So what has her so scared? Who could have so much control over her that she would react so drastically? Is she frightened of what would happen to me, or to her and Tirzah? And then there was her reaction when I didn't get angry in return: bewilderment. As if she couldn't even comprehend that I would still be kind. It speaks volumes as to how she has been treated by others.

Besides, how could I retaliate where there is some truth to her words? Even if I have not managed to cause harm thus far, I know I must be careful never to overstep my bounds. The reminder is a fair one. As for her accusation that I insert myself where I do not belong, I suppose she is correct. But if I do not belong anywhere, what else can I do?

Such are the thoughts that occupy my spare moments. Thankfully, Tulstead is too busy for me to have much idle time. There is plenty of packing, organizing, arranging, and more that goes along with moving a nobleman. For Svarik, I act as scribe and secretary when Elgraf is busy. For Elgraf, I act as messenger and overseer when he is helping Svarik. Then there are the servants, who have realized that I'm a good way to get a message through to both the count and his chamberlain. I see very little of Rhioa and Tirzah.

But finally, the five days are up. I stand on the snow-dusted veranda as I pull on my gloves and wait for the others. I take in the brisk air, the scent of pine, the sweeping snowflakes that drift lazily on the wind. Below, the courtyard teems with movement. Stable hands, cheeks red with cold, hold the reins of impatient carriage horses. Others are still double-checking all of the straps that secure the luggage to the sledge. The handful of servants who are coming along are busy stowing their trunks atop the old carriage that Elgraf had had brought out.

Fascinating how the Arveners build their carriages to be able to swap between wheels and runners.

The creaking of cold iron hinges has me look back over my shoulder. Rhioa and Tirzah, both in long, heavy cloaks, step out of the manor. I nod to each in turn and am glad when they return the gesture. Rhioa has barely even looked at me since that night in the stargazing tower. Even now she seems reluctant, as if worried I will try to bring something up again.

So to put her at ease, I glance up towards the blue skies and say, "A good day for travel, is it not, my lady?"

She and Tirzah join me at the top of the steps.

"It is," I hear Rhioa murmur in reply.

The door sounds again and this time I don't even have to look to know who steps out.

"And you wrote to instruct the tailor to be there the same day we are set to arrive?" Svarik's voice, a note higher than usual, rings across the stone landing.

"Yes, Your Excellency," comes Elgraf's patient reply. "I told him to expect a rush order."

"And what about the exchange station in Molos? They know we're coming?"

"Yes, Your Excellency."

I know that no amount of assurance will quiet Svarik's anxiety. Because it's not about the tailor, manor, or the trip—it's about Talsk. It's about going back home for the first time in ten years. It's about much larger things than even Svarik can control. And when people cannot control the big things, they tend to find solace in controlling the little ones.

I step to the side to make room for Svarik as he goes on. "If you need me for anything, or if any of Talsk's men come to try and cause trouble—"

"Then I will contact you immediately," Elgraf interrupts smoothly, stopping at the top step just as Svarik does. "Rest assured, Your Excellency, there is no reason for you to worry about things here at Tulstead. You have left instructions and means for every imaginable situation. And you have much bigger things to focus on going forward."

Svarik swallows and dips his head. His voice is nearly thick when he says, "Thank you. You have been of great help these past few days. And these past few years."

I note the pause and the surprise in Elgraf's demeanor. And then the hint of a smile. "It has been a pleasure, Your Excellency."

Svarik gathers himself and turns halfway to me. I shift again so that he can hear where I am.

"Is everyone here?" he asks.

"Here and ready," I confirm. "Your attendants are already in their sleigh and the luggage sledge has been thoroughly checked. Eriskatur is tied to the back of your sleigh."

"Then I suppose there is no reason to delay." Svarik takes a deep breath, adjusts his cane, and starts off down the stairs.

Rhioa and Tirzah climb in first. Then, with Elgraf's aid in finding the carriage door, Svarik goes next.

Before I can take my turn, the chamberlain puts a hand on my arm. I jump, startled, and jerk my arm away. I glance at him and then at the sleigh before stepping back and letting the door close.

Elgraf's voice drops to an undertone. "Forgive my forwardness: I presume that you are the one who put this idea in his head?" He doesn't wait for an answer. "It doesn't matter; you were not wrong to do so. But those at Ilske will come after him for it. Please just tell me that you will watch his back."

This rare show of earnestness is unexpected. And while I am fully aware of the gravity each word holds, I require no time to think on my answer. "You have my word."

Elgraf bows his head. "Thank you." Then he steps back, holding the door open for me.

I climb in.

"Is everything alright?" Svarik asks before I've even sat down.

"Quite," I reply steadily. "Elgraf was just double checking that all my things made it onto the sledge."

I see Rhioa raise an eyebrow and know she's thinking of our last conversation on the topic of lying. But I see no reason to go adding to Svarik's already taut nerves.

"Ah, I see." Svarik settles back against the seat.

Outside, Elgraf signals the driver and the whole sleigh lurches forward around us. The muted snap of driving whips mixes with the metallic jingle of the horses' harnessing. Beneath us, the scraping of cobblestones suddenly drops away and is replaced by the soft whisk of snow beneath the runners.

I just catch Svarik saying under his breath; "I suppose there's no going back now."

Five days in a carriage is a long time. Even as rapturous as the snow-drifted landscape is, I'd much rather be out riding through it than sitting in a little box as I slide through it. And besides, somehow, I always finish the day just as sore as if I'd spent the hours on horseback. I remind myself that at least it is warmer in here. And at least I have the benefit of sightseeing. Poor Svarik must be bored beyond words.

With his permission, I'd borrowed a few volumes from his study and brought them along. I read aloud from these whenever he seems interested and try to provide conversation whenever he's not. It's good practice for my occasionally flawed Arvenish. Sometimes Rhioa even chimes into help, volunteering to read a chapter or relaying some tale of her own. The only way I can tell how much of these stories is actually true is by how much Tirzah is rolling her eyes from the other side of the sleigh.

Rhioa.... It is hard to sit so near to her, to see her, to think of our last conversation, and not be able to say a word. Judging by her closed off and cautious expression, I wouldn't get far anyway. If only that knowledge would quiet the longing that constantly tugs at me. Maybe then I would be able to act out a role as easily as she does.

Today, at least, has everyone in a better mood. We have pulled into the change station at Molos and gotten the chance to stretch our legs in the warm, spacious inn. I stand at the window, sipping a cup of spiced tea and watching the station hands pull a wide, metal contraption beneath the sleigh. Then they crank a handle and the top of the device begins to rise. When it has reached the undercarriage of the sleigh, they give a few more tugs before turning their attention to the runners. Two men begin to unbolt these even as Svarik's coachmen pull spoked wheels from a compartment in the back.

"Is something wrong?" I hear Svarik call.

"Oh, not at all," I reply, turning towards the corner table. The inn is not terribly busy at this time of day, but Svarik had wanted to be out of the way all the same. "Just stretching my legs and watching them change out the runners. I'd been curious how they did it."

I sit down in the chair across from him as he replies, "Yes, from here to Ilske, the roads will be cleared and we'll need the rims." He shifts again, careful not to spill his half-finished tea, and pauses. "But are you certain nothing is the matter? You've seemed out of spirits these past few days."

His perceptiveness catches me off guard. I stop myself just in time to keep from looking up at Rhioa, but I can tell from the corner of my eye that she looks at me.

"I'm afraid I'm not quite accustomed to carriage travel," I say. The humor is to convince Svarik, the smile to convince Rhioa. "Rhy can bear witness to my wakingness—she had to put up with me for days on a boat."

Rhioa, warming herself by the hearth just next to us, pulls a face. Tirzah looks amused from beside her.

"Wakingness?" The former echoes. "Do you mean, 'restlessness'?"

I pause, trying to match up the Arvenish word to the Litashian meaning in my head. "Probably. Why? What does the first word mean?"

"Nothing at all," Rhioa replies, shaking her head. "It's not a word in Arvenish."

I set my cup down on the table, shaking my head. "I crossed two words together, then, didn't I?"

"That you did," Svarik affirms. "Although, this somewhat reminds me of a question, if you would abide my curiosity a moment." Svarik sips from his cup and returns it to his saucer. "How did you come by your nickname, Lady Arhys? I have yet to figure out how it comes from your name. Is it derived from something else?"

Rhioa turns towards us but does not leave the hearth. "That would be my sister's doing. I'm not sure why she felt that my name was too long, but she claimed that neither the shortened 'Arhy' or 'Rhys' was suitable. So she started using the middle three letters of my name instead." I watch her steal a glance towards Tirzah and smirk.

"I hadn't realized that you had a sister," Svarik comments. "What is she like?"

Her mischief fades and Rhioa's gaze returns to the fire. "She is quiet, and kind, and the best person I know."

I notice how Tirzah neither reacts nor moves.

"She is also very busy," Rhioa adds as she straightens her shoulders. "Hence why she was not able to come with me on the tour."

Svarik picks up his teacup again. "That is a shame," he says, voice more genuine than his usual polite affectation. "It would have been good to meet her, too."

Rhioa gives a thin smile before apparently remembering that Svarik cannot see it. "Well, I shall have to bring her back some souvenirs to make it up to her."

"A sound plan," Svarik affirms. "What about you, Tyron? Do you have any secret siblings hidden away that you have yet to tell me of?"

"Um," The unexpected shift in conversation leaves me at a loss. I clear my throat and reply, "Well, seeing as both are royals, they're hardly any secret. I have two brothers, both quite a bit older than me."

"Oh? What are they like?" Svarik presses on.

I catch Rhioa's attention drifting my way and sigh inwardly. Of all the times for Svarik to suddenly be curious.... While I have no wish to lie about this, I don't think an inn is the best place to elaborate—even with so few people around.

So I keep it simple. "Judican is the eldest and crowned king quite recently. Our father's health was not strong enough to bear the weight of ruling any longer. Euracia, the second eldest, is now crown prince until Judican's heir comes of age."

Svarik's brow furrows and I know he's caught on to my sparse description. "You are not close to them?" he queries.

I know Rhioa will notice, but I can't help but scan the room for eavesdroppers. "Not particularly," comes my slow reply. "Judican was always quite busy. Our parents kept him such to prepare him for his role as king and he was always more concerned with winning their favor than getting to know his brothers." I quash my discomfort as much as I can to keep it from my features. "As for Euracia, I'm afraid I can say little to his credit. He is little more than a brute and has been that way as long as I've known him."

The surprise on Svarik's face is mirrored on Rhioa's. I'm not sure if it is from the content of my blunt assessment, or my willingness to say it aloud.

Either way, I decide to move the topic along. "Fortunately, both of them have children who far surpass them. And fourteen nieces and nephews is enough to keep anyone too busy to deal with their siblings."

"*Fourteen?*" Svarik echoes, shock only growing.

So many explanations in one day. "They're not all related to me, technically. They are the fourteen chosen to be the next Ethians—the ruling class of Litash. Judican's two children and Euracia's son are among them. Somewhere along the way, I suppose I just took to treating all of them the same way."

The crackling of the nearby hearth seems conspicuously loud as Rhioa, Tirzah, and Svarik all seem to soak in this revelation.

"Do you miss them?" Rhioa is the one who asks, looking right at me.

Of course she would ask. She's likely the only one who knows that I have no intention of returning to Litash.

I open my mouth to answer but, oddly, the words don't come out. I close my mouth again and a foreign expression flits across Rhioa's face. Concern, perhaps?

Then the door of the inn slams and makes us all jump. There is the tromping of heavy boots as one of the station hands knocks the snow off of them. I stand up as the man approaches and bows towards Svarik.

"The sleigh is ready, Your Excellency," he announces, cap in hand.

"Ah, thank you," Svarik replies as he sets his cup down.

I move to help him with his coat and pretend not to notice how Rhioa's gaze follows me.

For once, this has been perfect timing.

CHAPTER 10

Rhioa

Unfortunately, riding in a carriage is far less comfortable than a sleigh. We spend the next day being jostled every which way by the cobbled roads. Svarik grumbles about "Talsk's neglect of infrastructure," and "No wonder the baroness had to repair the Dolsni bridge herself," but otherwise no one is in the mood for conversation. Not even Tyron.

We reach the capital of Arvenir by late afternoon. The sun hangs low in the sky and turns the snowy white world to glowing gold with its last, rich rays. But Ilske stands out like a bouquet of color, its shining domed rooftops and painted towers making it visible even at a distance. Tyron, of course, is glued to the window from the moment he spots it. Apparently, his time spent in reconnaissance didn't bring him this far inland. Then again, I have been to several Arvenish cities and even I cannot deny the draw of the gilded view before us.

The warm cast of the sun has paled by the time our carriage rattles through the city's blue gates, but the colors of Ilske have only begun. City dwellers, wrapped in long coats of brightly dyed wool, weave their way down snow-drifted street sides. Horses draw carts and carriages of varying size and expense, laden with everything from baked goods to live fowl. I note the general flow and busyness of traffic should we need to make a quick escape. The harder part would be the armed guards that occasionally mark a street corner, the white Tskecz cat emblazoned on one sleeve to set them apart from the crowd. Behind them, stone and brick buildings form a patterned backdrop edged with winter-white eaves. Beautiful, yes, but unforgiving if we should need to hide.

"Are they staring yet?" Svarik's voice is quiet and I turn to see him facing straight forward, gripping his cane.

"They seem to be more curious about your sledge than your carriage," Tyron replies.

He's not wrong. I see many stares towards the luggage cart that trails at the end of our little procession.

Svarik's posture seems slightly less rigid when he says, "I suppose a nobleman arriving at Ilske is odd for this time of year. Most who winter here settle in before the snows come."

The carriage rolls on and the crowds thin even as the roads widen. Lights begin to blossom at intervals as the lamplighters wake the city's famous street lanterns. Houses grow larger and further apart from each other, some with gates and drives and even small yards. I feel the carriage start to slow and we turn into one such yard, bordered by a low fence and immaculately trimmed ever-green trees.

The house is small compared to many of the estates we've passed. The three stories of pale stone act as a canvas for painted trim and elaborately carved cresting. Where the two wings unite, a paneled cupola of deep green tin rises from the snow-draped roof. According to Svarik, this house had been the winter home of his grandfather—the late Baron of Dolsni. It was left to Svarik's mother who, apparently, rarely uses it for fear of drawing Talsk's attention.

Nevertheless, as I let the coachman help me from the carriage, I can't help but notice how the baroness has kept up strict appearances. All the paint looks fresh, the stonework clean, and the gardens well covered. It would feel perfect to the point of unwelcoming if not for the warm glow that emanates from the many tall windows. The lure of light feels promising against the deepening dusk.

Servants emerge from the house and join with Svarik's hired hands to unload the luggage. Tirzah and I head inside to escape the cold, Tyron and Svarik close behind us. We are greeted immediately by the staff and helped out of our coats. They are all dressed in aproned uniforms, all courteous, with some of them better at hiding their curiosity than others. The young ones especially are not so guarded about their glances towards Svarik.

It is the house matron who brings everything into order. A stout, stern-faced woman, she manages to greet us, manage the storing of our outerwear, direct our luggage to the appropriate rooms, and usher us into the dining room all in one breath. No sooner that we are seated but another line of servants appears with platters of food.

It is good to have a hot meal again, especially outside of the jostling confines of the sleigh. Tirzah clearly mirrors my sentiment, leaning against the back of the chair as she eats. Even Svarik, who had been so nervous out in the streets, seems more at ease after the warm welcome from the household staff. Strangely, it is Tyron who seems the least himself. He is less talkative, less irritatingly interested in the minutia of his surroundings. He has been this way since he spoke of his brothers at the station inn yesterday.

As we finish and the servants begin to carry out our plates, the house matron reappears and addresses Svarik. "I hope the meal was to your satisfaction, Your Excellency."

"It was splendid, thank you," Svarik says as he sets his folded napkin on the table.

The matron receives the compliment with a bow of her head and moves on. "Now that you have eaten, I have some post for you. It arrived just this morning. Would you like to take it yourself or shall I pass it on to your manservant?"

Post? I see Tyron glance my way and know what he's thinking: Who knew that we were coming ahead of time? And even so, who would write Svarik a letter?

Svarik must be equally surprised as his answer comes after a long pause. "Oh, I will take it—thank you."

The house matron pulls a piece of parchment from her apron and lays it in Svarik's outstretched hand.

"Will you be needing anything else this evening?"

Svarik takes the letter. "No, thank you. I think we are all quite ready to retire."

"Of course. I will go ensure that your rooms are set." The matron turns slightly so that when she curtsies, it's to all of us. "If you need anything, please ask any of the staff." And then she is gone.

The table is clear, the room quiet, but all of us remain in our seats. Svarik uses one hand to feel out the wax seal and the creases on his forehead deepen. He extends the parchment to Tyron.

"Would you read it aloud, please?" he asks.

Tyron accepts the letter silently and pops the envelope seal. He pulls out several small cards which, after a quick look over, he sets aside. Then he picks up the letter and clears his throat. "To the Count Ihail, I hear tell that you are back in Ilske and planning on staying the winter. I hope you didn't plan on playing the stranger. After all, it's been so long since you've visited, and I've rather missed my favorite cousin. As a show of goodwill, I've included a formal invitation with my letter, requesting your presence at the celebration of my tenth year of rule. Your new friends, the Litashian Prince and the Lady Saen, are, of course, invited as well. You will have to let me know; do any of them enjoy hunting?" Tyron looks towards Svarik. "Signed, Udeneran Talsk, Grand Va' Kied of Arvenir, Lord of the Southern Snows, and...." He trails off, folding the letter and adding a droll, "So on and so forth."

Svarik is pale, visibly grinding his teeth. I can't see his hands beneath the edge of the table but I'm sure he's gripping his cane. "I suppose this is no surprise," he finally spits out. "Just a bit sooner than expected."

Tyron catches my eye and then Tirzah's. The three of us know that only person could have told Talsk far enough in advance for him to write the letter and have it waiting. And that person is Svarik's mother.

"Well, I think this will work in your favor," Tyron says as he inspects the cards that had come with the letter. Likely the formal invitations. "After all, everyone of import will be there. What better place and what clearer way to show that you are not afraid of Talsk?"

Svarik's expression does not change. His voice has a bite to it when he replies, "Yes, and what better timing than on the anniversary of my father's death?"

In the quiet that follows, Svarik's words seem to ring in the corners of the dining room. I remember, now, that moment when Svarik's mother had mentioned an anniversary only to trail off. This must have been what she was referring to. I look to Tyron. He wears an expression I've seen many times now: understanding, colored with sympathy and a touch of sorrow. But he does not speak.

I'm not quite sure why that prompts me to. "If I may," I straighten in my seat. "I think I might understand some of how you feel. My, um, my mother was taken from us many years ago. I, too, remember it each year when that season comes again." The sentiment is real enough, even if it is in a far different vein than Svarik's beloved father.

I note how some of the tension eases from Svarik's jaw. And I ignore that Tyron is looking my way.

"But with it, I remember her legacy and how I wish to be. Otherwise that memory would go to waste." Not that I would mind wasting the memory of such a vicious woman.... But if this is what gets through to Svarik, then: "So yes, maybe it is the best time. What better day to reclaim your father's legacy than on the day when you think of him most?"

Svarik lets out a long breath, a motion that seems to deflate him entirely. He looks tired as he replies, "My apologies, you are right, Lady Arhys. I suppose I just...." He swallows hard and clears his throat. "Talsk always dredges it back up. Always. His mention of the hunt...." His tone turns gravelly and he shakes his head as if to clear it. "My father died on a hunt. It is said that he was killed by a Tskecz cat, the animal Talsk uses for his coat of arms."

My disgust is mirrored on Tyron's face.

"But I was not there that day." Svarik's words are dull, hollow. "For all I know, Talsk could have done it himself."

"Do you think that is an actual possibility?" Tyron is watching the count intently.

"I-I don't know. Not that it would matter—there would be no evidence after ten years." Now Svarik sighs, rubbing the side of his face in an unusual show of fatigue. "I simply wouldn't put it past him. He is the sort of person that could kill without a second thought."

Never have I felt like so much of a fraud. To sit here and listen in confidence, to speak as if I understand, and all the while knowing that I am no better than Talsk. Perhaps I am worse. I glance towards Tirzah and find the same discomfort showing in her stiff features.

With a deep breath, Tyron says, "We are all tired. Perhaps it is best to sleep on this and reconvene tomorrow. We'll have three days to prepare for the celebration—which is plenty of time to talk this out."

Svarik is leaning on the arm of his chair, chin resting on one hand. "Perhaps you are right," he murmurs. He straightens and pushes his chair back. Yet he does not get up. "Thank you for your support. And, for listening. It has been a long time since anyone has been willing to do either."

The moment of sincerity only rubs salt onto my already stinging conscience. *And here you thought you'd smothered that pesky thing years ago.*

Of course, Tyron is fully earnest when he replies, "You are very welcome. And I think you'll find that there are more willing people than you realize—they only need a chance to know you in the same way that we have."

I have to grit my teeth to add, "And if it did not take me long to see, I doubt it will take much for your fellow countrymen."

"I hope, for all our sakes, that you are right." With that last statement, Svarik gets to his feet. "But I will leave the worrying to tomorrow and bid you all goodnight. Hopefully morning will hold better news."

We echo our partings and Svarik exits, the tapping of his cane fading down the hallway. Tirzah stretches and gets to her feet to show that she is also ready to retire. Slowly, I follow suit. But when we reach the door, I pause and turn around. Tyron is still at the table with brow furrowed in thought over the invitations in his hand. He notices my hesitation and looks up.

"Is everything alright?" he asks, concern lacing his tone.

I blink at him. How can he be so sincere, so open, when he just sat and listened to me tell such shameless lies?

"Yes," I recover as smoothly as I can. "Just be sure not to lose those."

Tyron dips his head in acknowledgment and looks back down at the cards. "Goodnight," he calls back. "And to you as well, Tahra."

Tirzah gives no reply.

Neither do I.

We go up to our room, full of every comfort and lavish thing, and spend the night tossing and turning.

We spend the next day talking through the upcoming celebration and everything it will entail. Despite having purposefully avoided coming this far south, Tirzah and I carefully researched which of the nobility are wintering at Ilske. We help lay out a list of them for Svarik and claim that we learned our information from the social circles of the port cities we visited; Svarik takes it from there. He is able to name each one that would take part in an official Assembly and then arrange them in order of who is the most likely to take his side.

"Duke Sohlv was a good friend of my father," he explains from his spot on the overstuffed chair. "A very rational fellow. They enjoyed debating politics and philosophy together. But I have heard that he is not so involved in politics since my father's death. Even if he sides with us, he may not have much sway."

Tyron scribbles this down next to the Duke Sohlv's name. The various parchments, covered in his neat, flowing script, have taken over the sitting room table. I can just see enough from my chair near the hearth to double check his work.

"And what of Lord Runim?" Tyron asks as he goes.

Svarik taps a finger on his cane. "He won't budge unless we can convince Lord Veldost, and Veldost tends to follow Count Tskei. He often disagreed with my father about the agricultural taxes. Perhaps if I could promise him a reduction...." He shakes his head. "Of course, if Archduke Grimvold goes against us, then all of them will fall in line with him—and Grimvold never did like my father." His tapping stills. "Let me think on how to handle that one. What's the next name we have down?"

I have to admit, this whole process has left me with far greater confidence in Svarik's political ability. He had seemed so rusty at it all back in Tulstead that I had worried he might not be able to navigate the complexities of Ilske. And while it took him the better part of an hour to get warmed up, he seems to be remembering more and more.

"Next is Duchess Os, Osk—uh—Oskoristiv?" Tyron pauses long enough to look up.

"Oh, her," Svarik waves a hand. "The duchess is obsessed with anything she deems 'exotic.' You and the Lady Arhys will be able to talk her into practically anything so long as you claim it's in fashion." Suddenly, he frowns. "Although, I suppose that brings up another issue. We have the rare visit from Beclian, but no one has even *heard* of a visit from a Litashian. Not everyone will be as quick to believe your heritage as I was."

Tyron's expression turns thoughtful and he twirls the quill in between his fingers. "Hmm. Well, what was it that convinced you?"

A marvelous question. I look to Svarik as he chuckles.

"You forget, I was raised in a similar position to you. I knew the signs well enough to know you weren't lying about your status." The count gestures vaguely with one hand, still smiling. "My chamberlain was able to tell me that you didn't look Arvenish, but it was a few more days before I was sure you were from Litash. The accent, the many names you listed off, your account of the Forest of Riddles, your fascination with mundane Arvenish things—especially my huntsman's snowshoes—all drove the point home."

His observations surprise me. I hadn't thought the count so perceptive. It makes me a little more worried about what he's noticed about me and I make a mental note to be more cautious.

Tyron looks nearly sheepish. "Ah. I don't suppose that being enamored with footwear will help me establish my credibility among other nobles." His attention shifts towards me and Tirzah as he asks, "Does anyone have any better ideas?"

I exchange a glance with Tirzah. She does not seem thrilled with what I am going to suggest, but neither does she offer any alternative.

"A small show of Gifting may do the trick," I say. "Gifting is rare here in Arvenir, is it not, Svarik?"

Tyron looks at me, his question clear: Will it harm me or Tirzah? I wave a hand to tell him we'll discuss it later. In truth, being around him for so long seems to have left me more accustomed to the constant hum. I rarely notice it anymore. I'm sure him using a little of his Gift will not be too much of a problem.

"It is," Svarik's voice is colored with surprise and he raises both eyebrows. "But you are Gifted, Tyron? You never mentioned it."

Tyron shrugs, a slight motion. "My apologies. Gifting is so commonplace in Litash that it's not something one would even bother to mention unless there is need. I'm sure I could find some smaller use for it at Talsk's celebration so long as it won't cause too big of a sensation."

Svarik's chin dips in apparent thought. "As long as you keep it small. And of course, if you can find a way to use it in some sort of natural context and not make it seem like you're trying to prove a point. That would only make them suspicious."

"Understood." Tyron dips his quill in ink and jots this down with everything else.

Hopefully his experience on the boat to Krysophera was enough to keep Tyron from going too far with his Gifting. *If I have to pull him out of prison again....*

"Now, one of our biggest obstacles is going to be the Speaker of the Assembly, Mikaud Lenstativ." Svarik leans back in his chair. "He is quite firmly in Talsk's pocket. Even if there was a way to get him on our side, I have a feeling it would require more time than we have to work with. We will have to find a way around him."

"What is his role, exactly?" Tyron asks as he writes.

Svarik crosses one leg over the other as he explains, "As Speaker of the Assembly, Lenstativ oversees the Assembly of Lords—any of us who own land. Normally, that doesn't mean very much. Assemblies are generally held once a year and are little more than a quaint social visit where noblemen compile their list of complaints for the Va' Kied to ignore." Svarik shifts in his seat. "But...there are very rare occasions when an Assembly is *called*. When this happens, the nobles are usually riled up enough to threaten their one actual power: challenging the Va' Kied's right to rule. The Speaker is then the one that handles negotiations with the Va' Kied to see if everyone can come to terms." Here, Svarik tilts his head back and forth. "In Talsk's time, this has changed. Lenstativ is more like Talsk's representation among the nobles than the other way around. My hope is that enough members of the Assembly are tired of this arrangement that they will opt to sidestep the role of Speaker entirely"

Tyron's thoughtful frown tells me that he is thinking all of this through. I had known of the role of the Assembly and its Speaker, as well as how Lenstativ had not quite lived up to his duties. But whether or not the Assembly-members are dissatisfied enough with him to cast him out is another matter.

Before the conversation can continue, a soft tapping on the sitting room door draws all of our notice.

"You may enter," Svarik calls, head turned.

A maid in a neatly ironed apron steps in and curtsies. "Sorry for the interruption, Your Excellency, but the tailor and his apprentice are here."

Svarik is on his feet with cane in hand. "Perfect. Please show them into the parlor." Then he motions in Tyron's general direction. "Come, Tyron, they should have your suits for adjustments, too."

Oh, good, someone is sorting out his attire. I'd not been sure that he had proper formal wear for anything as formal as an Arvenish ball.

Sprinkling pounce across the last parchment before stacking it with the others, Tyron comments dryly, "Ah, yes, my favorite activity: standing in front of a mirror whilst getting repeatedly stabbed by the tailor as punishment for my outdated wardrobe."

"Or perhaps as punishment for your poor taste," Svarik returns and I see humor playing out on his lips. "It seems that your sense of fashion is poorer than even a blind man's."

Tyron makes a face in my direction as he narrates, "Since you can't see me, I'd like to inform you that I'm rolling my eyes."

As he joins the now chuckling Svarik, I smirk and add my own opinion. "Don't worry, Svarik, my taste is much better than Tyron's; I can confirm that he's only put out because you're right."

"And now they're ganging up on me." Tyron throws his hands up. "Tahra, please tell me that you're on my side."

I open my mouth to answer for her, thinking she has no wish to participate with Svarik around.

But Tirzah surprises me by replying in monotone: "Seeing as I am only allowed to be here if agree with whatever Lady Arhys says, I'm afraid you're on your own."

Tyron's sigh is overly dramatic. "So much for reinforcements. I suppose I shall have to surrender this round. Lead the way, Svarik."

Tyron

I adjust the collar of my new suit and wish again that Svarik had not insisted on paying for it. When he had found out that the cost was the reason I wouldn't put an order in to his tailor, he would not be dissuaded.

"I do hope that Lady Arhys and her attendant had no issues with their hired coach," Svarik says as the carriage rattles through the lamp lit streets.

Rhioa and Tirzah had opted for a separate carriage simply for appearances' sake.

"I'm sure they're right behind us." I reassure. His anxiousness is in full swing and I cannot blame him. "Though I doubt it is Arhys's timeliness that is causing you to wear a hole in your carriage floor."

As if only suddenly aware of the habit, Svarik stops spinning his cane in between his gloved fingers. "I have not been in a crowd for many years," he murmurs. "I rather wish I'd gotten a chance to acclimate first."

I know this evening will be a hard test for him: the anniversary of his father's death and of Talsk's takeover, the open return to the public eye, and all in the very place he used to call home.

"Either Arhys or I will be with you at all times. If you think you need to step out for some fresh air, all you have to do is say so. We'd be glad to accompany you." The clamor of a crowd can be difficult even with one's vision to help decipher it all—I can't imagine how much more disorienting it must be for Svarik.

"Thank you. I will bear that in mind." He lets out a long breath and his shoulders relax ever so slightly.

Beyond the frosty pane of the carriage window, I see the palace gates pass by like ghostly stone sentinels. Svarik must hear the change in the cobblestones for he asks, "Are we here?"

The carriage turns and slows as it waits its turn to approach the great steps. But I can see the palace now, glowing as it is in the many torches that line its walls. It is a giant of spires and columns, with rich swathes of color and gleaming tin ornamenting its many faces. Cupolas, balconies, buttresses, all of it trimmed with snow as if it were part of the architect's original design. Light from the hundreds of windows chases away the dark until it seems a veritable fortress against the night.

"I'll take that as a yes." Svarik tries to chuckle, but the sound falls flat.

"Yes, sorry," I reply quickly. "And it is every bit as stunning as you said." The carriage lurches again and we are one measure closer to our turn at the steps. So I take the chance to say, "If you can make it through tonight, Svarik, then you can make it through anything."

He's back to rolling his cane back and forth. "I am not so certain that I can," he admits. "I've never done anything like this. And I'm not my father—he commanded the room simply by entering it. He was never afraid of anything."

I keep my voice firm and even as I say, "Then you are braver than he was, for you are afraid and yet are doing it anyway."

Svarik opens his mouth as if to refute me then pauses. His brow furrows and his chin dips in thought.

The carriage moves again and this time all the way to the grand staircase.

"Our turn," I say.

Svarik straightens his shoulders and collects his cane. "After you, then."

We step out into the frigid evening, giving our thanks to the coachmen as we turn towards the wide staircase. I watch Svarik as we climb to make sure that he does not lose his footing on any patches of ice. But even that focus cannot distract me from wondering how the builders moved such large slabs of stone as the pieces used for the stair.

We reach the top and pass between two massive pillars to reach the arched double doors. Two attendants, well dressed in fur coats and caps, pull them open and bow as we walk through. Another set of attendants relieves us of our outerwear; I wonder how many times the poor doormen will have to do that tonight.

"Is my suit laying correctly?" Svarik asks quietly as soon as we are beyond the vestibule.

I take one moment to inspect before replying, "Impeccably so." I note again how carefully he is dressed. Usually he takes such pains to exactly match his station. Tonight, he has dressed just the slightest bit finer.

With so many servants practically forming a trail, I don't even need Svarik's instructions to find the main hall. Besides, I can already hear the distant notes of music echoing through the gilded corridors. The unfamiliar instruments have a tone both sweet and full that is utterly enthralling. It is jarring to have such wondrous sound layered over the macabre sight of the hallway we turn into.

Though it is decorated with the same lavish taste as the rest of the palace, there is one alteration: animals of every kind hang from placards on the wall, motionless and glassy-eyed. Winged creatures, various deer with broad antlers, wolves and great cats, all frozen in place. Some only feature the heads or pelts or horns. But they're far too real to be sculptures. My best guess is that they are the skins of Talsk's kills, stuffed and shaped to look as they did before death. Such a thing would never be done in Litash. Too many Bandilarians take the shapes of animals to go about desecrating them for trophies. I don't know if this is common practice in Arvenir but, after remembering what Svarik said about his father dying on a hunt, I decide not to mention anything.

We stop at a wide-framed doorway and wait for the nobles ahead of us to finish being announced. The system is a curious one; in Litash, only the hosts or guests of honor are generally announced. I double check that Svarik has his card in hand before I hand mine to the herald and wait.

When he begins to speak, I begin down the staircase and towards the ballroom floor below.

"Announcing Lower Prince Tyron of Litash, son of King Otrian and Queen Casidia of the Ethian Council."

If my name is enough to make a room fall silent, I wonder what effect Svarik will have. I keep my smile pleasant despite the open stares and wish that this staircase was not quite so long. The crowd is a shimmering array of colors. Silk bodices, satin skirts, woven dress coats, military jackets with cording and wide collars. The glint of jewels is not limited to necklaces: Precious stones are embroidered on bodices, pinned up in elaborate hairstyles, and stitched onto caps and sleeve cuffs.

As soon as one foot touches the ballroom floor, the herald calls out again. "Announcing the Count Svarik Ihail, Count of Tulstead Manor and the Far East County of Arvenir, son of the late Grand Va' Kied Ordrin Ihail."

I step to the side of the balustrade and wait. All by himself, Svarik steps forward to the very center of the staircase. I wonder if he even knows. He must, for he doesn't reach for the railing, His cane dips over the first stair and he stops, adjusting it so that it hovers at an angle. Then he walks slowly down.

It's a terrible thought, but it's all I can think: *Please don't trip. Please don't trip.*

To my immeasurable relief, he doesn't. His steps remain measured and sure all the way down.

"I'm right here," I say as the herald begins with the next person.

Svarik stops and waits for me to come up next to him. Just as we'd discussed, he puts one hand on my arm just above the elbow. I walk just a little bit ahead of him as we move away from the stairwell.

"How about something to drink?" I suggest lightly. I am still conscious of the shocked, open stares that are directed our way. Those who aren't gawking seem to be looking elsewhere a touch too purposefully.

"A marvelous suggestion," Svarik replies.

We don't have to go far. An entire wall of the room is lined with ornate tables which bear trays of, well, everything: sweet breads, tarts, cheeses, fruits, cakes, jellies, and many things I don't recognize at all. They come in more shapes and colors than I can number and are arranged in patterns that seem too pretty to disturb by taking from them.

The beverages are thankfully a more limited selection. Nevertheless, I'm forced to tell Svarik, "I'm not actually sure what most of this is."

"Pick whichever one is warm." Svarik instructs. "Should be safe enough,"

I pick a still-steaming cup that gives off a rich scent. Out of habit, I check the inner lip before handing it to Svarik. Then I take one for myself. No need to get poisoned on the very first night out.

"There. Now that we look like properly occupied gentleman," I turn us away from the tables. "All we need is Lady Arhys to tell us who is who."

The stares have lessened, now. I try to keep an eye out for those Rhioa had described to me, but it's difficult with so many unfamiliar faces. It doesn't help that all she had been able to give me was second-hand details. Whatever identities she and Tirzah had assumed while gathering information, it would seem they were separate from 'Arhys' and 'Tahra,' and therefore, they had not personally met anyone they would have to interact with later on.

Svarik and I end up near one of the room's many columns where we can remain out of the way but still see the stairs. Having the physical landmark is also helpful for Svarik, who had not wanted to be hanging on anyone's arm all evening.

"I think someone's headed our way," I murmur as I sip my strange drink. I hope I'm loud enough for Svarik to hear me over the music. "Somewhere in his late fifties. A baron?—no, a duke." I'd spent the past few days going over the various aspects of Arvenish insignia.

"Married?" Svarik asks, confirming he heard me.

"Unsure." There is no woman with him, but that doesn't put it out of question.

There is no time for any further inquiry before the man reaches us, glancing very quickly from side to side even as he bows. "Count Ihail, I am not sure whether you quite remember me but allow me to reintroduce myself." His voice is nearly hushed, as if he is afraid of being heard. "I am Duke Sohlv of the Northern Moors."

Svarik bows his head. "I remember you well, Duke Sohlv, and I am glad to be reacquainted." Something in his voice changes when he asks, "Tell me, how is your family?"

Duke Sohlv's lips press together until he nearly frowns. I see his eyes flick towards me as he answers shortly: "They are well." Then his voice drops and he says, "Please forgive my forwardness, but *what* are you doing here? Do you have any idea what a risk you're taking?"

I immediately note the man as a potential ally. He is frightened, unsure about even being seen with Svarik, and yet still hazarding this little speech.

"Yes, I do," Svarik replies, voice soft and brow furrowed. "But it is past time I take it."

The shake of his head and the sharp sigh he gives shows Duke Sohlv's exasperation. But then his attention turns elsewhere and he gives a hasty bow. "Watch for my courier. And be careful."

With that, he fades back into the crowd. And only just in time.

"Announcing your esteemed host, the Grand Va' Kied Udeneran Talsk, Lord of the Southern Snows and the Crimson Mountains, Ruler of the Iron Door, and High Huntsman of Arvenir."

As if the herald's words summon the man himself, a figure steps forward while the music around us fades. He is tall, broad-shouldered, holding himself so that his chest is nearly puffed out. He wears a dress coat such as those worn by the Arvenish military officers, but with far too much decoration to be of practical use. The abundance of gold cording, the lavish embroidery, the wide lapels and cuffs—all of it exaggerated beyond good taste. His crown seems almost out of place in its simplicity, consisting of a filigreed gold band and a single, iridescent stone.

"Welcome!" Talsk opens both hands in a broad gesture, stopping halfway down the staircase as he addresses the crowd. His smile is predatory as his gaze sweeps the room. "I'm delighted that all of you could be here tonight to celebrate with me. But seeing as there is plenty of food and drink and dancing to be had, I won't bog you down with long speeches." His dark eyes stop on Svarik then on me. "In fact, all I wanted to give was a single toast."

It has been less than thirty seconds and I already cannot stand him. But perhaps it is his familiar manner; he reminds me far too much of my brother. The resemblance is not flattering.

At his beckoning, a servant approaches with a single goblet on a tray. Talsk takes this and holds it up. I mimic the crowd around me as they do the same.

"To the late Grand Va' Kied Ihail, my dear uncle. May I continue to hold up his fine legacy for the next decade as I have done for the last." Talsk is grinning directly at me.

"To the late Grand Va' Kied," I hear echo around the room.

Talsk downs the contents of his goblet and places it back on the tray. "Oh," he holds up one hand as if highlighting his afterthought. "Be sure not to crowd my good cousin, the Count Ihail. For those who may have forgotten, he is quite blind. We wouldn't want him to take a fall on his first time out in years, would we?"

To his credit, Svarik gives no reaction to the open affront. Unfortunately, the way he keeps his calm makes it that much harder to keep mine. I take another sip of my drink and turn away as the music resumes.

"I take it he is coming our way?" Svarik murmurs.

"You are correct." Talsk is talking to someone else, but I see the way he is angled towards us. "He's just taking his time."

Svarik shifts his weight from one foot to the other and straightens his taut shoulders. "Lady Arhys may yet get out of talking to him."

I peek up to the stairs that busy again with arriving nobles now that Talsk has finished his little speech. But no Rhioa.

"As unfair as the prospect is, I suppose it's only proper for such allowances to go to the ladies," I say, trying for some humor.

I get only a grunted response, but I see Svarik's grip loosen around his cup.

"Ah, there you are, Cousin!"

"Here we go," Svarik mutters, even as he turns towards the source of the sound.

Udeneran Talsk strides towards us, that patronizing smile pasted across his entire face. My dislike of him doubles.

Svarik dips his head and I give the half-bow as is befitting my rank. Talsk acknowledges neither, clasping Svarik roughly by the shoulder, making him jump.

"So good to see you again," Talsk says in a voice that is one notch too loud. "To be honest, I wasn't sure that you'd come. I know that dances aren't quite your scene."

The curve of Svarik's lips is closer to a grimace than anything else. "On the contrary, I find that any event is enjoyable if one has the right company."

With an open laugh, Talsk begins to nod. "True enough. But speaking of," his focus shifts to me. "Why don't you introduce me to your new friend?"

I note the way he says 'new.' And then the way he is so blatantly sizing me up. Ah, he thinks that I am the one leading Svarik along. I wonder if Svarik's mother told him such, or if he came to the conclusion himself.

"Cousin," Svarik half spits. "Meet Prince Tyron of Litash, son of King Otrian and Queen Casidia of the Ethian Council."

I am accustomed to the feeling of fake smiles. I give no more than the minimal amount of warmth to sell the act as I say, "A pleasure to meet you, Your Highness. I must say, your reputation precedes you."

Talsk cocks his head, eyes narrowing ever so slightly as if trying to ascertain what I'm implying. "I'm afraid I cannot quite say the same, for I have never met any of your countrymen. What brings you all the way to Arvenir?"

"Simply my own enjoyment," I reply. "I've not had the chance to travel before, but I've been touring at leisure for some months now. The Count Ihail was kind enough to host me at Tulstead for a few weeks and offered me the chance to see Ilske with him."

"I see. Then we will have to make sure you come by for a full tour of the palace." Talsk finally lets go of Svarik's shoulder, but only to wave up an attendant. He inspects the tray of drinks even as he says, "I would certainly like the chance to get to know more about you and your homeland. I'm sure you have many fascinating tales and," he plucks a glass and takes a sip before finishing, "I admit, you have me quite curious."

I chuckle politely. "Oh, you can ask the Count Ihail—I am all too willing to talk. I'm told that getting me to stop is the real trick. Isn't that correct, Your Excellency?"

I look to Svarik as he gives an emphatic nod. "Indeed it is. But I'm sure my patient cousin can put up with your inquisitive mind."

Talsk gives little reaction as he follows the exchange from me to Svarik. But the hesitation makes me think that he didn't expect me to bring Svarik into the conversation.

Suddenly, from the droning of the herald's announcements in the background, a name sticks out. "Announcing Lady Arhys of the Beclian house of Saen, daughter of the Lord Saen."

I look up and my heart sinks. *Oh my....*

Rhioa nods her thanks to the herald, one graceful, gloved hand on the balustrade as she descends the stairs. Her golden hair is braided and pinned up in the fashion of Beclian but her deep crimson gown is nearly Arvenish in style. The gathered waist, the full skirts, the rippling silk that trails behind her on the steps.... She looks more like a queen than the daughter of a lord.

Idiot. You blithering, vacuous—

"*That* is your other companion?" Talsk asks Svarik, nearly incredulous. He doesn't wait for an answer. "No one mentioned she was such a beauty. Although, I suppose you wouldn't know the difference."

The statement irks me in too many different ways to number.

"Well, please excuse me, Cousin, but I think I'll go introduce myself." Talsk turns to leave without waiting for any parting gestures.

In the span of seconds, I watch Talsk's eyes turn down towards the cup in Svarik's hand. Then I see the way he steps just a touch too far to the right. As he makes contact with Svarik's arm and the cup tips towards my friend, I am already pulling at my Gifting.

"Oh—watch out, Your Highness!" I call.

Talsk jumps back, eyes wide.

CHAPTER 11

Rhioa

After making sure that Tirzah has caught up with me, I scan the crowd again for Tyron and Svarik. I was sure I had spotted them by one of the nearby columns. I catch a glimpse of black hair, just a few inches taller than everyone else in the room. That would be Tyron.

We weave through the crowd, giving a few polite smiles and nods, without stopping for introductions yet.

"Oh—watch out, Your Highness!" I hear Tyron call. Then I hear that familiar hum.

I come into view just as the Grand Va' Kied of Arvenir jumps back, looking in shock at the liquid that is suspended in midair. Judging from the tipped cup that Svarik is holding, someone bumped into his drink.

"One moment, Your Excellency," Tyron addresses Svarik. "Don't move just yet."

In full view of the now *very* attentive crowd, Tyron sweeps one hand out and the liquid follows until it pours itself back into Svarik's cup. Then Tyron reaches to straighten the errant goblet.

So dramatic. He doesn't need to use his hands to use Gifting.

"There you are," he announces cheerily. "Didn't want that getting all over your jacket."

Svarik does his part wonderfully, dipping his head and speaking in a completely casual tone. "Why thank you. Seeing as it is brand new, it would have been quite the shame to douse it in chocolate."

I decide that this is a good time to make my own entry. "There you two are. Already up to trouble, I see." I step up alongside Svarik.

"Ah, Lady Arhys," the count greets me. "We were just wondering when you would arrive. Please, allow me to introduce you to my cousin, the Grand Va' Kied Talsk."

"Your Highness," I drop into a deep curtsy and hear Tirzah do the same from behind me.

Talsk is still blinking away his startlement. He recovers enough to give a scattered smile and a gesture of acknowledgment. I watch him survey me with a glance and swallow my loathing. As much as I hate this part, allowing that spark of greed is the most effective way. After all, people are so good at justifying the things they want. If a pretty face means they justify me, then it makes my job that much easier.

"What a delight to meet you, my lady." He inclines his head. "And all the way from Beclian! What affords my country this rare pleasure?"

I pretend to be flattered. "My father has recently taken up the role of Head of House Saen. He wanted to increase knowledge of our country beyond the Macridean Sea, as well as to learn more of others, so he has sent me abroad on tour."

"He was very wise to have picked you for such an endeavor," Talsk says. "After all, if the ladies of Beclian are half as beautiful as you are, I'm of half a mind to make a trip there myself."

I ignore Tyron spitting his drink back into his cup as I manage a blush. "You are too kind," I say.

I'm sure that Talsk thinks his grin is dashing, but it has about the same amount of polish as his flirting. "Oh, no, don't presume my compliments come for free—you now owe me a dance before the end of the night."

With a fluttering laugh, I let my chin drop ever so slightly as if feeling shy. "Then I shall have to be sure to settle my debt."

"Marvelous," Talsk claps his hands together, making Svarik flinch. "I have a few others to greet, but I will come to collect soon." He makes his exit with no more than a brief nod to Tyron and the count.

I turn to address them both, but stop at the comical expressions they both wear.

"That was..." Svarik trails off, brow furrowed.

"Nauseating?" Tyron suggests.

Tirzah bites back a laugh from next to me.

I shoot Tyron a look while Svarik mutters, "I was thinking 'unexpected.'"

I open my mouth to scold them both, only to notice all of the tension in Tyron's posture. Wait. Did I miss something with Talsk? Or something with Svarik? Such questions will have to wait for more private quarters.

So I move on, saying, "I hope I didn't keep you two waiting for too long."

"Not at all," Tyron replies. "It was just enough time for us to have a lovely chat with Duke Sohlv."

Duke Sohlv? Interesting. Seeing as Svarik and Tyron were waiting for Tirzah and I, the duke must have approached them.

"Perhaps now that we've gotten through the introduction of my cousin, we'll get a little further with everyone else," Svarik says in an undertone.

Perhaps. We have, at least, caused a good stir. But there will still be work involved to turn that attention into anything useful. It will be best to follow the plan we'd made to split up. "Well, I think Tahra and I will go see about something to warm ourselves up with after that chilly carriage ride."

Svarik nods, getting the hint.

But Tyron looks uncharacteristically displeased. "It might be prudent to avoid certain company," he says quietly.

Does he really think I'm trying to sidle up to Talsk just for the fun of it? "And it might be even better to remember your manners and not insult our host," I reply, keeping my tone even solely to keep from drawing notice.

He holds my gaze for several seconds, jaw taut. Then he tips his head and resumes a pleasant expression that is impressively convincing. "Of course."

With Tirzah close behind, I take my leave. We stop to pick up a drink—and some of the gossip from the married ladies who tend to gather around the table there. Their shawls, varying in length and material, give away their marital and social status. But their tittering over Svarik and Tyron gives away little else.

So, taking our time, Tirzah and I wander towards the center of the room where the dancers are. I spot a group of unmarried women towards one edge and hazard that they are all waiting for partners. A few are seated, others with drinks or nearby attendants holding drinks for them. The majority are clustered together, giggling and glancing out towards the dancers. I see a few outliers and decide to start there.

I wander closer as I pretend to take in my surroundings. After all, I am playing the tourist. While Arvenish taste has always struck me as somewhat overdone, there is something about the symmetry of the intricate, inlaid patterns that is strikingly beautiful. The marble floors, polished to a near sheen, reflect the ornate ceilings and walls until the entirety of the hall feels like a kaleidoscope. The swirling of silks and suits brings the effect to life.

"Oh, hello, I hope you don't mind me introducing myself." One of the ladies who had been on the fringe of the group addresses me. She is bedecked in a fur-edged shawl despite the warmth of the room. "I am Viscountess Lina Postorik, wife of Viscount Postorik," she says with a curtsy. "You are the lady from Beclian, are you not?"

"I am. Lady Arhys Saen, daughter of the Lord Saen, at your service." I return the curtsy and then gesture to Tirzah, even while I mentally add this woman's name to the long list I'm already juggling. "This is my companion, the Honorable Tahra of House Elaris."

Viscountess Postorik nods to us each then discreetly elbows her friend. "Oh come, Elsze, don't be shy."

The friend, I notice, wears no marriage shawl despite her age. She must be mid-twenties—almost too old to be marriageable by Arvenish standards. But then she turns and I see why. Despite the attempt to cover it with decorative ribbons and deeply parted hair, there is no missing the red, knotted scar. It starts nearly at her temple and runs down her face, jaw, and neck until her high dress collar hides it. It is clearly from a severe burn, though I estimate it to be well over five years old.

"Lady Elszebet Sohlv, daughter of the Duke Sohlv, at your service," she murmurs. She makes no attempt to smile, yet neither does she avoid my gaze.

"A pleasure to meet you both," I say, allowing my shoulders to relax slightly and so give the impression of warmth.

"How long have you been in Arvenir, Lady Saen?" The viscountess picks up the questioning.

I shake my head. "Please, call me Lady Arhys. And I've been here a few weeks now, simply touring the landscapes of your beautiful country."

"Touring? In the middle of winter? You are braver than most Arveners." The viscountess laughs.

"I'll admit, in southern Beclian we don't have to worry about anything other than rain. I didn't even think anything of it when I was delayed in Cadbir." I give a sort of rueful sigh. "But I like to think of it as a well-fated accident. As challenging as the weather has been, the snows have been absolutely breath-taking."

Abruptly, Lady Sohlv cuts in with, "You've been staying with the Count Ihail at Tulstead, have you not?"

The viscountess's smile turns brittle and her gaze darts towards her friend.

"Yes, I have. He has been quite a generous host. In fact, he was the one who offered to take me as far as Ilske. I don't know that I would have made it this far south otherwise," I reply, pretending not to notice the tension.

Lady Sohlv narrows her eyes, but the viscountess quickly changes the subject.

"What about your other companion? I've never met a Litashian." She hides the nervous twitch of her lips with a sort of smirk. "Did he escort you this evening?"

I can *feel* Tirzah holding back a snort.

"Oh, no," I assure. "We are genial acquaintances, but nothing more."

The viscountess seems amused by my nearly hasty reply. Her voice drops to a conspiratorial whisper as she winks at her friend. "Hear that, Elsze? Best not to tell the other girls yet. Not until we've gotten you a proper introduction."

'Elsze' Sohlv rolls her eyes.

I give a slight smile and shrug to try and establish some sympathetic rapport. It could come in handy when trying to get on her father's good side.

But Lady Sohlv's expression drops to a near glower that takes me aback. Then I realize it's pointed at someone behind me.

I turn just as Talsk calls, "Ah, there you are, Lady Arhys. I've come to collect my dance."

I curtsy as he reaches us, the viscountess and her friend doing the same. And yet, all the while, Lady Sohlv does not temper her stare.

Talsk meets it with smug derision. He straightens his shoulders and gives a haughty tilt of the head as he greets them. "Good evening, ladies. I hope you are enjoying yourselves."

He holds out his arm to me and, after passing my drink to Tirzah and quashing my distaste, I accept. But he doesn't turn towards the dance floor.

"Tell me, Lady Sohlv, how is your father doing?" he asks, tone clearly gloating.

Elsze's gloved hands are curled into fists, a fact she apparently tries to hide by pressing them into the folds of her full skirt. "Very well," she says, every word cold and crystalline. "Thank you for inquiring, Your Highness."

Talsk adds an over-gracious smile as he says, "But of course. Pass on my regards to him, would you?" He doesn't wait for her reply, placing his free hand over mine and pulling me with him as he turns away.

I feel Lady Sohlv's steely eyes follow us into the crowd of dancers.

"So, Lady Arhys," Talsk says as we take up position across from each other in the long line of couples. "How have you enjoyed your time in Arvenir?"

I notice the way he uses my given name without permission. Normally, this would be a good sign—he's already getting comfortable. So why does it bother me so much now?

"It has been lovely. Cold, but lovely," I reply as the music begins.

His laugh is unpleasant. "I'd hazard you have far less snow in Beclian." He holds out his hand in time to the music and I take it, glad that Arveners always wear gloves at formal dances.

As we begin to circle in slow, measured steps, I give a nod. "Yes, snow is almost unheard of in my region. But I can't say it's all so bad—sleighs are certainly more comfortable than carriages."

"And seeing how long you've likely spent in both, you would be quite the expert." Talsk turns the subject as we turn in the dance. "Which makes me wonder: What took you all the way to little Tulstead? I can't think of anything there worth the notice of such an intrepid traveler."

"Everyone in Krysophera told me that I must see the ever-green forests and the red mountains. And everyone here told me that the Far East County had the best of both," I explain.

We both swivel to face each other again. In time to the music, the men all fall into line alongside their partners and we step forward in unison.

"Well I am glad you've made full circle to Ilske," Talsk says from beside me. "A dancer as fine as yourself shouldn't be hiding in the countryside."

His hand brushes my waist and my skin crawls. *What is wrong with you? You've done this a hundred times before—tonight is no different from any other.* But why does it feel so different? Why does it feel so *wrong*?

"You are too kind," I say, wrangling my thoughts back into line. I need to make better use of this conversation. "Just as you were too kind to extend Count Ihail's invitation to me and Prince Tyron."

His smile thins as we stop and circle again. "In Arvenir, we hold that one must be charitable to the weak and infirm. If I don't watch out for my dear cousin, who will?"

I recall Svarik sweeping shelves of porcelain sculptures to the floor with a horrible crash. *Weak. Infirm.* And yet, would I not have used the same descriptors mere weeks ago?

"Indeed," I hear myself murmur.

Again, the men and women line up shoulder to shoulder as we parade back towards the end of the room. I can see Tyron and Svarik across the way, engaged in conversation with a lady in a bright green dress. She is speaking rather animatedly about something, while Tyron stands quietly and wears an expression I've seen many times—the one that shows he is listening carefully. Then he looks up and his eyes meet mine. I almost halt in the middle of the dance floor.

"And it's as I always say. But tell me, what do you think of Ilske so far?" Talsk asks and I suddenly realized that I've missed whatever he said before that.

I hope it's not important. "It is truly a wonder. I've never seen anything like it. And this palace of yours..." The dance turns me to face Talsk again and I feign awe as I scramble for something more to say. I try to think of how Tyron would describe the room. "...I've never seen such details and patterns, and all in such perfect balance. Your people must be masterful craftsmen."

Talsk takes the flattery in the manner of someone long accustomed to it. "So they are. But if you think that this room is a sight, I'll have to show you the rest of the palace." He stands in place, allowing me to take a turn around him before we swap places. "What would you say if I invited you to stay here? As a royal guest, of course."

"I would be deeply honored," I reply even as I feel nearly sick to my stomach. "But I couldn't. Not just yet. I promised the Count Ihail that I would remain with him for another two weeks at least to tour the city proper." We join hands and circle again.

"Oh, surely he wouldn't mind you taking up such an opportunity," Talsk coaxes.

We change directions to circle back. "Perhaps not, but I'm afraid my father would." I sigh as if disappointed. "It is hard to explain, but the idea of one's word is paramount in Beclian. And as I am acting as an emissary of my father, he would be livid if he heard that I had backed out of even this small promise."

Talsk seems skeptical of this foreign custom but finally accepts it with a smile. "We couldn't have you getting in trouble. Perhaps after you've fulfilled your obligation, then."

"I would be delighted," I lie.

The dance ends soon enough, but Talsk doesn't let me escape just yet. I am dragged to meet several of his officers and officials. I try to make the best of all these introductions, but I can't seem to focus. And those who don't seem scared stiff of him seem to be just like him. I end up just smiling, nodding, laughing, and trying not to flinch when Talsk puts his hand on my shoulder. I finally extricate myself when Talsk gets caught up in a card game with his friends. I give the excuse of needing to check in with my own friends and, after making me promise him another dance, Talsk lets me go.

Tirzah says nothing as she walks beside me, but she hands me the drink she's been holding for the last hour. I down it in the hopes that it will do something for my churning stomach. No such luck.

We find Tyron and Svarik only a few yards from where they had started the evening. They are talking with an elderly couple that I don't recognize. I step up discreetly without interrupting the conversation.

As soon I approach, Tyron takes one look at me and asks, "Are you alright?"

His hushed voice is so genuine. He angles towards me, brow furrowed in concern, but he makes no move to touch me.

"Just a little warm, is all," I say despite my tightening throat. I make a show of fanning myself for good measure. "Too much dancing."

His green eyes linger a moment more then drift to Tirzah. His attention returns to the elderly couple still talking to Svarik.

I feel a sudden, strong urge to turn and walk away. I don't belong here next to Tyron. I am far more like Talsk: belittling those I see as weak, shamelessly using others to my gain, full of fake smiles and bravado and half-truths. Did I not plan to use Svarik in the same way? Did I not spend an evening putting up with Talsk so that I could use him, too? *No, you're not like Talsk, you're even worse: You're like your mother.*

And just like Mother taught me, I put all of this aside to keep smiling and nodding. Anything to keep the mission intact.

Tyron

The carriage ride back to Svarik's borrowed house is a silent affair. The evening has left us too drained for any more words. On top of it being past midnight, we have both been standing for hours and making small talk with anyone who was brave enough to look our way. The only person who had really stopped for any length of time was the Duchess Oskoristiv. And she, true to Svarik's warning, had simply been after tales of the exotic. When she'd had her fill of those, her curiosity turned to a near interrogation of Svarik concerning his blindness. I'd closed the conversation off rather quickly.

We reach the house and Svarik immediately bids me goodnight. I return the parting and wander up towards my own room, noting the light beneath Rhioa and Tirzah's door. They had left a little before us. I pause in the hallway, recalling how pale Rhioa had appeared. Not that I suppose I can be of any help at such an hour. Nonetheless, my steps feel heavy as I pass by.

I pull off my dress coat and close my door behind me. The nearby hearth is full of glowing coals that, while filling the room with a steady warmth, do little against the dark. With Gifting and a thought, I light a set of nearby candles and the room becomes a little more bearable. If only it was so easy to banish memories as it is to banish the dark.

I hang the coat in the heavy, oaken wardrobe and sit to take off my boots. The new leather is stiff and uncooperative and it takes work to wrestle the things off my feet. They, too, go into the wardrobe. Next comes a night shirt, then washing my face, and all the other motions of preparing for bed. But when I go to lie down, I don't even bother with pulling back the coverlet. I lie on top of it and watch the candlelight flicker on the canopy above me.

And so, both thoroughly exhausted and wide awake, I think of the evening. Svarik's arrival, then Duke Sohlv's furtive approach. Then came Talsk, his open insults and direct reference to Svarik's father. I think of Rhioa and let out a long breath. *Here you go again.* She had been utterly breathtaking, and that was all anyone had cared about. Did no one see she was so much more? Did *she?* Talsk certainly hadn't cared. With irritating clarity, I recall flashes of them dancing, laughing, Talsk parading her around on his arm as if she was some trophy.

I close my eyes. But it's too late—my mind wanders on. I think of other balls, not all quite so tedious as Talsk's. I'd passed many evenings in pleasant, knowledgeable conversation and many more just dancing until the musicians could not be coaxed into another song. I nearly smile to think of those rare nights when Ameri and Destrin Verzaer would attend—*that* was always memorable. Then there were the occasions where I'd catch all fourteen of my nieces and nephews spying on us from one of the balconies, all up well beyond their curfews. After letting them plead and beg, I'd always give in and teach them a few of the dances. We'd have our own little party in the corridors above the ballroom.

And yet for every bright spot, there is always a shadow. I remember how tiring it was to spend a whole night surrounded by fake smiles and thinly veiled condescension. I think of my adopted parents, never looking my way unless they had some use for me. And then there was Judican and his practiced expression of disapproval whenever he thought I had crossed some line. I could always expect a private lecture the next day. Still, I preferred that over Euracia and the way he would watch the whole evening from the sidelines. He always had the lazy manner of a wolfcat watching fish swim circles in a barrel, not bothering to strike until he decided he was hungry.

With a sigh, I sit up. Instinct drives me to glance towards the windows— despite knowing that the curtains are already drawn for the night. I know better than to try to sleep with such thoughts for my only company. And I know from experience that I won't bother anyone by holing up in the little house library.

So it's back up and back to the wardrobe, trading my nightshirt for a tunic and breeches. I extinguish the candles one by one until I reach the last little flame. On a whim I pluck it—holder and all—from its place on the stand.

Perhaps it is a pitiful defense against the dark hallway I step out into, but anything feels better than facing it alone.

The next morning, I am the only person who comes down in time for breakfast. I try to persuade the matron of the house that there is no need to set a full table when I am the only diner, but she will hear none of it. I suppose it works out for the best as Svarik joins me halfway through.

"Good morning," I say as he takes his seat. I notice that while his attire is as neat as ever, not even that can hide the weary droop of his shoulders.

"Good morning," Svarik returns, adding his usual polite, "I hope the accommodations were sufficient and that you rested well."

I watch as a maid reaches around to pour his drink. "As well as ever," I reply with as much cheer as I can muster.

With the pleasantries out of the way, conversation lulls. I finish my breakfast and wait until he's had a good measure of his before attempting to revive it.

"I'd say that last night went well," I venture.

Svarik takes another forkful of some kind of hash before giving a half-hearted reply. "It could have gone worse, anyway."

"At least we know we have a starting place with Sohlv," I persist. "He said to watch for his courier. I presume he'll send a letter, if not an invitation to his home."

"Mm." Svarik feels for his cup, takes a draught, then suddenly comments, "You never mentioned that Lady Arhys was particularly pretty."

The jarring subject change takes me a moment to wrap my head around. I'm not sure how he expects me to respond. "I did not think it mattered," I say with a shrug.

Svarik sets his cup down and gives a slight shake of his head. That's all I get before he switches the subject again. "Are you still up for a trip out into the city today?"

"Quite," I nod. Svarik had planned this in advance, saying that it would reinforce his public presence and show that he was yet undaunted by Talsk. "But I haven't seen anything of Arhys or Tahra yet. Arhys did not look quite herself yesterday evening."

"After putting up with my cousin the whole night, I can hardly blame her." Svarik's tone is even enough, but it holds a sour tang.

"Please don't misunderstand her. She was trying to keep from making us even more conspicuous targets by offending him," I explain quietly. "And she still has duties to her own country. But I can assure you that she has your best interests in mind."

Svarik's pinched expression relaxes. "My apologies. I meant no slight." His empty fork hovers midair. "I have not known her as long as you have."

Unspoken questions echo in the recesses of the room and I know that Svarik has noticed more about Rhioa than he has let on. But I cannot reassure him of her identity, only of her motives. Even those are better left unexplained.

A set of muted footsteps catches my attention and I look to the doorway. "Good morning, Madam Tahra," I say as Tirzah walks in. Rhioa is not with her.

"Good morning," she returns, glancing at Svarik. "Lady Arhys sent me down to ask if you two might excuse her from this afternoon's outing. She is not quite feeling herself."

Worry blossoms even as Svarik asks, "Is she alright? Should I send for a physician?"

Tirzah shakes her head. "Oh, no, I think it is simply fatigue from last night. A little rest and she should be back to rights."

This seems to satisfy Svarik.

But I catch the disquiet in Tirzah's eyes and decide to investigate further. "Have you two eaten?"

"Not yet. I was going to fetch some trays to bring back up with me," Tirzah replies.

"Allow me to help you." I get to my feet. "Svarik, I can meet you in the vestibule after you've finished with your breakfast."

Svarik acknowledges this with a nod and, "Alright."

I follow Tirzah back into the kitchen and wait for the two breakfast trays to be loaded. Then, kindly refusing the servants who offer their help, we each take a tray and head for the stairs. I wait until we are closer to the rooms and further from possible eavesdroppers to voice my question.

"Is she alright?"

Tirzah's lips are pressed together when she glances back at me and murmurs, "She is not ill. She is...." She faces forward and her taut posture becomes more evident. "Her work is difficult for her to bear."

We reach their shared room and halt, but Tirzah makes no move to enter. Her eyes dart from the door, to the ground, then suddenly fix on me. "She hasn't been so deeply affected by it since we were young."

My brow furrows. I'm not exactly certain if that is positive or negative.

"I think you remind her of how things once were," Tirzah says slowly. Her lips press together again. "But hope can be a cruel thing. It has tricked us before."

There is a quiet pain to the words—a fleeting glimpse of a much greater anguish. It occurs to me that showing any of it at all must take an enormous amount of trust for Tirzah. I wish to come up with some sort of comfort or reassurance that would ease her fears, but I know that words cannot undo whatever it is that life has wrought on her and Rhioa. I can only show them that I am willing to help.

"I am sorry," is all I say.

Tirzah tilts her head slightly, lips parted. Whatever it was she was going to say, she seems to think better of it and instead shifts her tray to one hand. "Here: I can take them both in."

I hand her my tray and make sure she has both securely before letting go. I hold the door open for her and she nods in thanks as she steps through. Making sure to do so silently in case Rhioa is still asleep, I close the door and head back downstairs.

"I've actually never wandered the streets without an escort," Svarik admits as we navigate the crowded city square. He is half a pace behind me, hand looped around my arm just above the elbow. It's a little more difficult for him between my heavy coat sleeve and his thick gloves. At least we had the sense to leave his purchased gifts back with the carriage.

"Really? Never?" I question. "You were a much better-behaved child than I was."

"I don't doubt it." A glance over my shoulder confirms that Svarik is grinning. "But I had my moments."

I survey the row of shops as I reply, "Oh, really—do tell."

"Well, there was this one occasion...." Svarik clears his throat. "I was maybe nine or ten and we had just had two blizzards within a week of each other. The snow was at least ten feet deep—far more if you found a good drift." Someone brushes against him and his story pauses. "I had this friend who convinced me it would be fun to jump off the second story balconies and into the snow."

I'm already smiling, picturing a smaller version of perfectly postured Svarik leaping into a snowdrift. I only smile more to think that Svarik considers this a rebellious act. Maybe I ought to keep some of my tales to myself....

He goes on, saying, "Well, like any gentleman, I let her go first. The drift was, um, a little deeper than we had estimated, and she got rather stuck. So naturally I jumped in after her to help her out."

I can't help but laugh aloud.

"Not my brightest idea." Svarik comments sheepishly. "Especially paired with the other part of our plan: You see, we had jumped off of the ballroom terrace since we knew no one used it except for parties. And while that meant we wouldn't get caught, it then meant no one was able to pull us out."

"Seeing as you are here and not an icicle on display in the palace," I shake my head, still laughing. "I presume you figured something out."

"Sort of. We were fortunate enough that my father happened to be walking the palace with a visiting duke. They heard us hollering and found us still flailing around in the powder." There is a lightness in Svarik's face and shoulders that I've never seen before as he recounts the story.

Speaking of snowdrifts.... I have to sidestep to bring us around a pile of cleared snow and to the row of shopfronts. Various lords and ladies, all bundled in furs and thick wools, glance at us as we walk by.

"My father was really quite kind about it all, given the circumstances." Svarik muses. "I think he forgave me simply because the duke's reaction was so comical. Imagine: You are touring the royal palace with the Grand Va' Kied himself, and he pauses a moment to go pluck the crown prince from a snow drift." He chuckles as we skirt a patch of ice. "Of course, I quickly caught pneumonia and wasn't allowed out of bed for two weeks. He deemed that sufficient punishment."

As the humorous story plays out in my head, I can't help but wonder who this friend of Svarik's was. He so rarely mentions anyone from his past. "Was your friend so unlucky?"

Svarik gives something like a scoff. "Oh, no, she was of much sturdier constitution, apparently. Didn't catch so much as a sniffle. Her parents made her come sit and read to me every day for her bit of penance." His smile is softer, more wistful than before. Then he suddenly straightens. "Come, we have work to do. Read off some of these shop names for me."

With that, we are back to our errand: purchasing gifts for any potential hosts. Apparently, it is customary to bring a 'token of appreciation' when visiting the home of another nobleman. Svarik knows exactly what items will and will not do, making me describe them in detail even though he feels everything out himself. Meanwhile, I try to take stock of any familiar faces from last night's ball.

Finally, we have enough goods ordered to satisfy Svarik. But as we are making our way back to the far end of the square and the waiting coachman, I spot a small store decked with several ever-green wreathes. A wooden sign with a painted flower hangs above the door. I wonder if the city has greenhouses like Svarik's mother does. An idea springs to life.

"Svarik, are you up for one more stop?"

CHAPTER 12

Rhioa

I pull my cloak more tightly around my shoulders, watching my breath make soft shapes in the air. The glass panes of the little sunroom, covered as they are in lacy frost, keep out the biting wind but offer no other protection from the cold. Today, somehow, the chill is refreshing. Or perhaps, numbing. I am thankful either way.

Muted voices pull my attention towards the door behind me. Svarik and Tyron must have returned. I consider getting up and going to see how it went, then decide they'll come find me if there was anything of import. Tirzah knows where I am if I am needed.

The voices fade and the mournful drone of the wind takes their place. It whistles over the windows, scraping through frozen tree branches and lifting miniature flurries out of the snow drifted garden beyond. I close my eyes and let the desolate, winter chorus drown out my own deadened thoughts.

At the sound of footsteps, I open my eyes. I turn just as there is a soft tapping on the door. It opens a crack and a voice asks, "May I come in?"

Tyron.

I turn back to the view of the yard. "If you wish."

He enters with quiet footsteps and lets the door close behind him. He sets something down on the side table next to me before taking his seat in a nearby chair.

I look down to find a steaming cup of tea. "What is this for?"

He shrugs, adjusting his coat as he replies, "Tirzah said you had been out here since we left. I thought you might be cold."

I look back down, hesitate, then slip one hand out from the protection of my cloak to pick it up. I don't even need to drink it. I cup the porcelain in both hands, taking in the rich aroma and letting the warmth seep down my arms.

"Thank you," I murmur.

When Tyron says nothing, I glance over and find him wearing the strangest expression. What did I say? It clicks all at once: I've never thanked him for anything before. I feel even worse as I force my gaze back out to the garden.

"You are always welcome," comes his delayed reply.

For a while, we just sit there without a single word between us. But the longer the silence draws, the more my stomach twists and tightens. I expect it any moment—that lecture that I'm sure he's been thinking of all night. I know he was not pleased by me playing along with Talsk's advances. Does he have any idea how many times I've done this? Does he realize that, of all the things that are required of me, this part is the easiest? I have done far worse than even Talsk has. And judging by his reaction to Talsk, Tyron wouldn't even be able to stand the sight of me if he knew it all.

My thoughts run for cover as Tyron draws a deep breath. But instead of a lecture, all I get is a gentle, "Are you alright?"

I shouldn't have looked at him. The piercing green eyes, the brow furrowed in concern—both make it harder to keep my voice even when I reply, "Of course. Just a little tired after last night's festivities." I'd hoped mentioning last night would be enough to deter him, but his expression doesn't change. So I try a different approach, "Being around so many people is rather taxing. Some time to myself is all I need." *Please just leave me be.*

Tyron makes no move to leave. "Tirzah is worried for you."

My throat tightens. "She always spends too much time fussing over me," I try to say dismissively. "Very bossy for being a younger sister."

"And yet, she knows you better than anyone," Tyron counters.

I know better than to look at him this time. "She does," I admit very softly.

There is a pause before Tyron ventures, "Did something happen last night?"

"Is *that* why you're in here?" He's back on Talsk, isn't he? I knew it. I straighten my shoulders and muster as much voice as I can. "I have no need for a lecture. I did my work and I did it well and," I know I should bite my tongue, but the last sentence comes out anyway. "As much as it might surprise you, I would rather not have had to do it at all."

Tyron takes all of this very quietly. I can't tell if it is in reaction to my words, or I only just notice it, but he suddenly looks quite tired. "I know you don't want to do this," is his simple response.

Somehow, it takes all the wind out of me. I sit back again and just cradle my teacup in my hands.

"No one as empathetic as you are could enjoy a life so completely detached from others," he goes on.

I try to scoff as I echo, "Empathetic?" Why would he, of all people, call me that? How many times now has he tried to be kind to me only for me to turn and berate him? I think of the night in the stargazing tower and the way he'd made sure I had a warm enough blanket before leaving.

"Yes," I catch Tyron's nod from the corner of my eye. "I imagine that it is what makes you so good at reading people." He pauses and I see him run a hand through his hair. "You know, in Litash, it is held that all Gifts have two sides. Take healing as an example: The same knowledge and ability that allows me to close a wound could also be turned around and used to open one. I think that all 'Gifts' are the same way, even ones of character. A person who is brave can use that courage to rob others or to help them. A strong leader could lead others forward or astray." His hand returns to the arm of his chair. "Someone who is empathetic—who truly feels and understands that which others feel—can use that knowledge to bring joy or pain. The choice is up to them."

A shudder runs down my spine as Mother's voice taunts me: *If you won't let pain be your teacher, it will become your executioner.* I can't stop myself from the weak defense: "I was not always this way." I was not always like my mother.

"What changed?" Tyron asks.

I shake my head, finally reining in my loose tongue. I have said too much.

"Then how did you used to be?"

"I...." My attempted answer trails off. I realize with near fright that I can't even remember how life used to be. When I was younger, I had cherished daydreams of returning to that happier life. But then I had grown up and such dreams had become a painful reminder of how stark my reality was; I had locked those childish thoughts away. "I suppose it doesn't matter. That was a long time ago."

Tyron watches me very carefully, thought marking his brow. Then he straightens in his seat and says, "Perhaps it is not so distant as you think. When you first found me, I was dehydrated, practically starving, and too weak to defend myself. Bringing me with you posed many risks: I would slow you down, take up supplies, leave you vulnerable to attack, and possibly reveal aspects of your mission and identities to others. I was, in every aspect, a threat to your work." He lets out a breath and shakes his head. "To top it off, I wasn't even conscious when you found me; it would have been so *easy* to simply walk away." His eyes meet mine. "But you didn't. You woke me up. You gave me food that you didn't have to spare and protected me when I couldn't hold up against those raiders. And when my acts in Ajhal jeopardized my safety again, you took me to Krysophera—likely another huge risk for you."

I don't even know what to say. I try to recall all the rationalizations I had given Tirzah at the time but can't manage to do so.

"You are much more than your orders, Rhy," Tyron goes on in an undertone. "And you are worth far more than your usefulness to whoever it is you are bound to. You should never be forced to cheapen yourself for another."

Wordless, I stare at him openly. My mind turns his bold statements over and over, unable to fathom any of them. I look back out the wide windows and try to remember how to breathe.

A knock from behind us makes us both jump. But the pattern of two slow, then two fast, tells me exactly who it is. I look over my shoulder as Tirzah enters.

I see her glance from me to Tyron before she says, "The courier has just come. Svarik wanted you to read the letters."

"Ah." Tyron looks to me, reluctance in his pursed lips.

I set down my now lukewarm tea and get to my feet. Tyron follows suit. Tirzah turns back into the hallway but Tyron stops at the door to hold it open for me. I keep my head down, not daring to look at him as I pass by.

Tirzah leads the way into the sitting room where Svarik is already comfortable in one of the chairs by the heart. As cold as I am from being in the sun room for so long, I opt for the settee across the room instead. I keep my cloak on.

"There you are," Svarik holds up three envelopes as I sit down. "These just came—all within minutes of each other."

Tyron is the one who walks forward to take them, quickly looking them through. He pulls off his coat and drapes it over the back of a chair before sitting down. "Should I read them in any particular order?"

Svarik shakes his head.

As Tirzah takes her seat next to me, Tyron breaks the seal of the first envelope and three title cards fall out.

"This one is an invitation to a solstice dance hosted by the Duchess Oskoristiv," he says, scanning it. He looks down at the cards. "All of us are invited. That would be six days from now."

Svarik sighs reluctantly. "Well, I suppose it is a good opportunity."

Tyron nods and opens the next letter. "This one is from Duke Sohlv." His gaze flicks across the parchment in quick intervals. "He has asked that we join him for luncheon in two days' time, but he asks that we do so discreetly. He says not to send any written confirmation."

I realize that I have not yet had the chance to catch up on everything that happened with Tyron and Svarik during last night's ball. They had briefly mentioned Sohlv but no specifics.

Svarik seems more stiff when he replies, "Alright. Did he say anything else?"

"No." Tyron checks the back as if making sure. "It was quite brief."

"Hm." Svarik appears to be lost in thought for several seconds before he snaps out of it. "What is the last one?"

Tyron picks up the last envelope and I see him look to me. He angles the parchment so that I can see the wax seal, pressed with the sign of the Tskecz cat.

Talsk.

He opens it and begins to read. The further he goes, the more intent his expression grows.

"Well?" Svarik prods.

Slowly, Tyron says, "This one is addressed to me. It is an invitation to join Talsk on a hunt in four days' time."

There is a delay as everyone soaks in the news.

"Absolutely not." Svarik speaks with sudden vehemence, knuckles white around his cane.

Tyron does not reply. He has one elbow on the arm of his chair and one hand to his temple as he scans the letter again. He's not actually considering this, is he? I exchange a glance with Tirzah.

"This is absurd," Svarik's voice rises with his apparent temper. "This is nothing more than another one of his little threats—one of his childish attempts to frighten me. I refuse to play along."

"Perhaps this is more than that," Tyron says, still unerringly calm.

Svarik freezes. "Don't tell me you're *actually* considering this. This is ridiculous."

"I think I rather agree with Svarik," I say, clearing my throat.

The look Tyron casts my way is an odd one, as if he expected me to be on his side. "I think this could be a good opportunity," he explains as he holds up the letter again. "We need people to see that I am not running some power scheme and using you as a puppet. Now, I presume that there will be plenty of other noblemen there, correct?"

Flustered, Svarik stammers, "I mean, traditionally yes, but—"

"—Then I will have a good audience. No doubt this is Talsk's way of getting me into a corner and trying to figure out all of my motivations. I'll gladly tell him the truth: I am simply a friend of yours, not some master." Tyron leans back in his chair.

I'm sitting right on the edge of mine. "But what then? What if he decides to take his threat further? You will be without any sort of backup."

"Exactly." Svarik gestures wildly in my direction. "Talsk is not above physical threat. There's already plenty of rumors around about things he has 'arranged'— including my father's death. Proving a point is not worth risking your life."

Tyron is still irritatingly unruffled. "I don't think it would be any more risk than what we took on by coming to Ilske. Especially since, if getting rid of me was his goal, turning down the invitation won't do anything except make him find a more creative way."

I almost don't care if he's right. The nearly casual way he speaks of his own safety makes me want to throttle him.

He doesn't give Svarik or myself any room to interrupt, quickly adding, "And should I feel like I'm in any danger, it would take less than a second to transport myself to safety. Gifting will allow me to get well out of reach without even having to put up a fight."

Here, Svarik goes silent. His jaw is clenched and his fingers are tapping in uneven rhythms atop the arm of his chair.

I try to use the moment to make eye contact with Tyron, but he's not looking at me.

"So there is not that much risk, it is a good, public opportunity to reinforce your status and show we aren't afraid, and it is a better alternative to turning the invitation down," he summarizes. Then he softens. "I understand your fears,

Svarik, and I know that they are not without reason. But please, trust me in this. Have I not proven myself to you this far?"

I look to Svarik, hoping he will bar Tyron from going. He is still sitting there in rigid silence. He swallows and lets out a sharp breath before replying in a low voice, "I will think about it." He stands abruptly and collects his cane. "I will reach a decision by supper. Until then, I would like to remain undisturbed in my quarters."

"Understood," Tyron says in quiet acknowledgment.

Svarik bows his head in the general direction where Tirzah and I are sitting. Then he exits without another word, letting the door close behind him.

"This is a bad idea," I say under my breath.

Tyron folds the invitation and tucks it in the pocket of his woolen over shirt. "But it is the best alternative."

"At least let me come with you." The impulsive words leave my mouth before I have a chance to think them through. I try to make them sound more rational by adding, "You ought to have someone watching your back."

"But then who will be watching Svarik's?" Tyron returns. "Besides, should I need to use Gifting, it will be much easier for me to be by myself."

I don't like this—any of it. And yet somehow, I can't quite find the means to say exactly why. I sit there with several different arguments in my head that never get as far as my lips.

Tyron gives me a slight smile, the expression somewhere between sympathetic and reassuring. "It will all work out. For now," he gets to his feet and plucks his coat from the back of his chair. "I think Svarik had the right idea. A little rest before supper sounds good to me."

I say nothing. I give a terse nod to acknowledge his departure and nothing more.

Once he's gone, Tirzah turns to me. "Maybe you should do the same," she suggests. "Or at least go up and get out of your cloak and boots."

I'd forgotten I was wearing them. My mind, still running in frustrated circles around the issue of Talsk's hunt, is at least able to decide I want to take the warm things off.

"Alright," I murmur as I get up.

Then I pause. Tyron left the other two letters out on the tea table. With a frown, I scoop them up and fold them. They should not be left out for the prying eyes of servants. I slip them in a cloak pocket as Tirzah and I exit the sitting room and head for the stairs.

Between my earlier conversation with Tyron and then the three letters, my thoughts keep me busy all the way up to my quarters. But the moment I enter the room, I freeze. Something is different; someone has been in here. A quick scan doesn't reveal anything out of place except....

I cross to the stand by the frost-edged window, puzzled. A vase of cut crystal holds a single flower. Its slender stem reaches up to wide, layered petals, the same shade of blue as the pale morning sky. I can't help the childish urge to pick it up to take in its delicate scent.

Then I hear Tirzah come in and I hold the flower up to ask, "Where did you find this?" She must have sent one of the servants to get it. And seeing as it's still the dead of winter, the greenhouse must have charged her a pretty penny for it.

"Oh, that wasn't me," Tirzah shakes her head. "Tyron said that he saw it while they were out in the city and thought you'd like it."

I turn back towards the window, blossom still in hand. I breathe in the lovely scent for a second more before returning the flower to its vase. I don't want to think about Tyron right now.

Tyron

The ride to Duke Sohlv's city manor is a quiet one. But then, everything has been quiet since Svarik acquiesced to me going on the hunt. I can't tell if that is why Rhioa won't speak to me, or if it is because of the conversation we'd had before the letters. I suppose that, either way, it isn't too different from how much we spoke before. Perhaps the only reason it weighs on me more now is that I had thought that there had been some kind of rapport between us. Apparently, I was wrong. Whatever the explanation, I decide it's better than telling them why I'd been so insistent in taking Talsk up on his invitation.

The carriage jolts sharply as it turns into a wide, stone gate. In the smaller space of the servants' carriage, the motion sends us bumping into one another. It was decided that using this one would better suit Sohlv's request to remain low profile. However, while it might make the duke feel safer, I am fairly sure that Talsk has set a watch on Svarik's house and thus it will make no difference in the end.

The horses come to a stop and the carriage with it, and I wait only until I make sure everyone has coats and gloves ready. Our attempt to remain discreet has also meant no footmen—just a driver. So I step out, straightening my coat and then turn to hold the door open. Svarik comes next, carrying his cane, thanking me as he steps into the snow-dusted square.

Then comes Rhioa. On a sudden impulse, I offer my hand.

She pauses and eyes it with one brow arched.

...what are you doing?

Just when I am about to withdraw in embarrassment, she places her gloved hand in mine and descends the carriage step. The graceful flourish of her skirts stirs up a scattering of snowflakes that dust her cloak like frost-bitten lace. Her eyes, turned up to the winter sky, reflect the pale blue expanse and all its wonder. In this one, single step, she is still nothing short of enchanting.

Then her gaze brushes past mine and she releases my hand without a word.

When I turn to help her sister down, I realize Tirzah is smirking.

I can feel my face redden as I murmur, "Oh, hush."

The smirk widens to a grin that I promptly ignore.

I shut the carriage door and catch up to Svarik, letting him take my arm so that I can lead him up the shallow front steps and to the modest doorway. No one comes out to greet us so I step up and use the wrought iron knocker. The maid that answers casts a look between and beyond us before ushering us in.

There's the usual delay of everyone taking off coats and gloves and caps, aided by another maid that appears in the vestibule. Then we are led through the paneled corridors with Svarik at the front. The tapping of his cane traces a path all the way into a long, rectangular room. The space is lit by the typical tall, narrow windows, and holding only a dining table with its high-backed chairs. A richly embroidered runner, dotted by several sets of candles, spans the length of the table.

"Please, have a seat," the maid tells us. "The duke and his family will be right in."

Family? No one had mentioned that Duke Sohlv had children. A glance to Rhioa shows that she is not surprised—has she met them? A look to Svarik only tells me how nervous he is.

We have just taken our seats when there are footsteps from the corridor on the other side of the room. Svarik immediately stands as the Duke Sohlv enters. The duke's attire is far less formal than two nights ago, but he wears the same solemn expression beneath his close-cropped beard. Behind him, I presume it's his wife in plain colors and pinned up hair who enters. Then comes what must be their daughter: a younger copy of her mother, somewhere between my age and Svarik's, and with a burn scar that reaches from temple to jawline and down to her collar.

"Welcome to our home, Count Ihail," the duke says, bowing his head as we all do the same. "And thank you for being understanding of the...circumstances."

"Of course," Svarik replies nearly too quickly. "I know that the situation is delicate for many here at Ilske."

Duke Sohlv sucks in his cheeks. "Perhaps more so than you realize." Then he takes a deep breath. "But duty before conversation: I have invited you here for lunch, have I not?" He signals to a maid who curtsies and exits. "Allow me to reacquaint you with my family. Do you remember the Duchess Zylua Sohlv?"

Svarik bows his head in the direction of the duke's voice while Rhioa, Tirzah, and I all copy him. "How could I forget? It is wonderful to meet you again, my lady."

The duchess is gracious in her half-curtsy, but her bearing is uptight and her brow knotted in worry.

"And I'm sure you recall my daughter, Lady Elszebet Sohlv," the duke gestures to his daughter.

She is staring right at Svarik, eyes darting towards Rhioa and myself only briefly. She gives no curtsy.

When Svarik doesn't reply, I turn and see the shock in his slack expression. Wait. What did I miss?

"Oh, Lady Sohlv, I did not know that you were still..."

Oh no. Please don't say 'unmarried.'

"...at home," Svarik stammers.

I nearly groan as everything clicks into place: the nervousness, the way he asked after the Duke Sohlv's family at the party, the fond tale of jumping into snowdrifts with a young friend....

Elszebet is visibly grinding her teeth when she replies, "Yes, I'm afraid I've turned into quite the old maid since last we met."

"Oh, no, I-I didn't mean...I just, when your father was alone at the ball...." Poor Svarik stutters on and I try to think of a way to intervene.

"I was there," Elszebet says primly. "In fact, I even spoke to your friend, Lady Arhys."

I don't dare look at Rhioa.

"Ah. I, um, didn't see you." Svarik winces as soon as the words leave his mouth, as if realizing their obvious nature.

I take the ensuing awkward silence as my cue. "My apologies; I realize that I have not yet introduced myself. My name is Tyron, the Lower Prince of Litash and son of King Otrian and Queen Casidia."

"And I am Lady Arhys of the Beclian House Saen," Rhioa says from beside me, picking up the conversation before it can slack. "This is my companion, the Honorable Tahra of House Elaris."

"A pleasure to meet you all," Duke Sohlv says as his family takes their turn to bow. He then gestures to the chairs before us as his wife takes up the questioning.

"Out of curiosity, how did nobles from such far countries end up in Arvenir at this time of year?" The duchess's question is carefully worded.

We all take our seats as Rhioa replies, "I have been touring at the behest of my father for well over a year now. Madam Tahra came along to assist me and to garner some experience for herself. But we had some delays that, unfortunately, set us here the same time as your snows. I'll admit that few in Beclian are used to planning for winter weather."

I notice that Elszebet is no longer staring at Svarik, having taken up a thorough inspection of her plate to keep from looking at anyone.

"Ah, I see," Duchess Sohlv eyes move on to me.

"I am also touring, though only for my own pleasure and not for diplomatic purposes," I begin, pausing as servants enter with trays of food and set one in front of each of us. "When I met Lady Arhys, she spoke of going to Arvenir and I found myself intrigued. I decided I had no reason not to come see it for myself."

A look passes between the duke and his wife as they both pick up their dining utensils. Doubt flickers through the silent interaction.

"So, how did you come to meet the Count Ihail?" Duke Sohlv clears his throat before broaching the subject.

There is always this check—this subtle screening to see how we are controlling Svarik. Even Elszebet is observing now from the corner of her eye.

"Duke Sohlv, if I may," Svarik cuts in unexpectedly. "I have known you since I was a boy and respect your input immensely. These three have proven themselves to me several times over. There is no need to test them on my behalf. However far you trust me, you may trust them to the same extent."

It takes effort to keep the surprise from my features. The unexpected speech leaves me with a nearly warm feeling, both at the measure of Svarik's trust and his initiative in speaking up on our behalf. When Duke Sohlv looks at me in open evaluation, I meet his gaze without wavering.

"Well, then I suppose I shall get right to the point." Duke Sohlv sets down his silverware. "What are you doing here? And why so suddenly? We've heard nothing from you in ten years—we weren't even sure you were still *alive*. And now you waltz in at the height of Talsk's paranoia?"

Well, there is a lot to unpack in those several questions.

"I stopped writing after two years of receiving no replies. And after eight more years without a single inquiry, I did not think it would be of much use to send word ahead of my arrival." Svarik's voice borders on taut.

Elszebet head snaps up from across the table. "We never received any letters."

Both of her parents look at her, but there is agreement in their silence.

"None at all?" Svarik repeats, quieter than before.

"None," Elszebet confirms.

Leaning out of the way of a maid who is refilling my glass, I suggest, "Perhaps Talsk decided the distance was not quite enough to keep you isolated."

By the looks on everyone's faces, my suspicion is all too plausible.

Picking up his silverware, the duke says, "Whether you wrote or not, it does not answer why you have suddenly decided to come back now."

The meal resumes slowly as Svarik replies. "For years, I let Talsk do as he pleased. But he finally went too far. A few weeks ago, he took forty-two men from the village of Tulstead and enslaved them in the salt mines. And there was nothing I could do to stop him." He takes a deep breath. "So I decided that I had had enough. I am done watching Talsk harm the people that he is meant to protect. He has squandered my father's legacy, and it is long past time that I take it back."

"You're making a bid for the throne?" Duchess Sohlv wears her shock openly.

"As is my right," Svarik answers.

The duke shakes his head and sighs, but I see how his daughter looks nearly approving.

"You may not realize this, but you could not have come in at a worse time," Duke Sohlv tells him. "Rumor says that Talsk is preparing for war."

War? Now I look to Rhioa, but whatever emotion it is that shadows her expression is hard to read.

Duke Sohlv continues as he cuts a piece of meat on his plate. "There is nothing official—and he does not seem to be targeting any of our neighbors—but he has been appropriating supplies, repairing old barracks, and even introducing legislation that widens the draft ages for troops."

"And he's been more controlling than ever," his wife adds. "Usually he is content with leaving management to his underlings, but now everyone is talking about how particular he's become over even the smallest details."

I wonder what it is that has Talsk scared. Is it the same reason that Rhioa and Tirzah were sent here to oust him? Or...is it of whoever sent them?

"Then perhaps this is perfect timing." Svarik takes a sip from his glass and sets it back on the table. I see Elszebet glance his way. "If he has become even more unbearable, then I could have a better chance at convincing an Assembly to take my side."

The duke sighs again. "Your optimism is admirable, but I'm not so sure it's realistic. I think you underestimate the hold that Talsk has on Arvenir. Fear is a powerful thing."

"And now Talsk has begun to succumb to it," Svarik points out. "Is that not grounds enough for hope?"

"Svarik," The duke using his first name does not seem like a good sign. "Things are run very differently than in your father's day. Talsk may not openly punish those who speak up against him, but there are...happenings." Duke Sohlv swallows, now looking at his daughter. "We and a few others protested your expulsion. Baron Varix and his son disappeared in a blizzard. Lord Ulsthur took suddenly ill a week later and never fully recovered. Count Lirskinov was found with incriminating letters hidden in the floor of his carriage and thrown in prison for over five years. When we were the only ones left, we became very cautious." His shoulders sag. "It wasn't enough. One night, while we were all still asleep, our home went up in flames. Zylua and I were very lucky—we were having some masonry redone in our quarters and had been sleeping in another wing. Elszebet was not so fortunate. She was caught in the blaze and barely made it out with her life."

I watch Svarik's hands turn to fists around his fork and knife. This must be why Elszebet is yet unmarried. I know Arvenir puts great stock in strength and image so, between her scar and the reminder of her family's standing with Talsk, she must have faced a similar isolation to Svarik's mother.

"I did not know." There is a rasp to Svarik's tone. "I am truly sorry. Elsze, I...." He stops himself, head bowed. "I cannot let this continue. My father always had the saying, 'those who desire power most are those who least ought to have it.' Talsk has proven that over and over, and he cannot be allowed to keep abusing the people he is meant to protect. I know that you may not be able to risk supporting me when it has already cost you so much, but that does not temper my resolve. I promise you that I will make this right."

As tense as the silence around the table is, I imagine it must be even worse for Svarik who cannot see the Sohlvs' reactions. Hope and fear wrestle back and forth to paint a vivid indecision. The exception is Elszebet, whose steely eyes match the determined lift of her chin.

"I, for one, am quite tired of living under Talsk's thumb and would rather take him down with me than sit around waiting for him to pick me off when he feels like it." She sets her napkin down beside her untouched food. "But you've been gone ten years—how much do you even know of current events? Do you even have a plan once you have the crown? If not, I frankly see no point in trading a ruler who is ruining his country purposefully for a ruler who will do it out of ignorance."

Her challenge, laid out so bluntly, gives me hope: She is taking this seriously. Judging by how her parents are also watching Svarik for his response, they are doing the same.

But he doesn't reply right away. Nearly a minute ticks away in silence and I catch the sound of Rhioa shifting in her seat beside me. *Be patient. He can do this.*

"I would start with the confiscated lots of grain." He takes a deep breath. "Those must be returned to the farms, both so that they can have food through the winter and seed for the spring. Next, I would get rid of laws protecting hunting grounds. Too much land that could otherwise be used for farming or lumber has been parceled off for the idle pastimes of nobles. And too many citizens have been punished for hunting these lands out of need. Why should we punish those who would work to feed their families?"

Elszebet's expression remains impassive. "That would certainly put you in poor graces with half the nobility of Arvenir."

"Of course," Svarik tips his head. "Which is why the move would have to be paired with both a reduction in agricultural taxes—which is long overdue—and a repeal of tariffs on goods from Fuerix. The repeal would benefit both citizen and noble, as it would make imports far more affordable during the winter months when the citizenry need it most and also open up accessibility for many of the luxury goods that the nobility favor."

"What will you do when the merchants begin to complain of competition from those imports?" Elszebet gives no ground.

Yet Svarik builds momentum and confidence with each reply. "Remind them that Fuerix will likely follow our example, making it easier and cheaper for them to conduct their trade. Besides, it would be the start of repairing our relationship with Fuerix overall. Our trade lines through their waters are currently hanging by a thread, and that's not a thread any of our merchants can afford to have cut."

I notice that Duke Sohlv's features are not quite so taut as before. Beside him, the duchess has even resumed sipping at her drink.

"But then there will be traditionalists in both the Assembly and the army who will accuse you of being set on the throne by Fuerix," Elszebet argues on. "Then what?"

"Then I reiterate my stance that being diplomatic never requires a lapse in sovereignty. Opening trade does not mean I will bow and give up the disputed western isles—which is what they always bring up. Those were legally purchased under my great-grandfather's rule, and while I am open to negotiations about their ports, I will affirm that the land will remain under Arvenish rule." Svarik is more sarcastic than I've ever heard him when he adds, "And if my countrymen still say I am a puppet run by Fuerix, maybe they should thank Fuerix for sending them a Va' Kied who doesn't murder them in their beds."

Elszebet purses her lips. Her voice is lower when she asks, "And what will keep you from that? You'll have the same power as Talsk once you're in his place. What assurance will your people have that you won't turn into him?"

I watch Svarik process the question and all of its gravity. "I would form a cabinet among the Assembly and set them over the army. Any military action I wish to take would require majority approval before I could proceed."

Now Elszebet raises her eyebrows. Has he managed to take her aback? "That is a lot of power to give up. They will call you weak."

Svarik shakes his head. "Accountability makes one stronger—not weaker. Anyone who is afraid of it is not strong enough to rule."

Perhaps I am letting hope get the better of me, but I think I catch some kind of approval in Elszebet's gaze. Finally, she says, "His Excellency is right. He might be too late, but he is right." She looks to me, then to Rhioa and Tirzah, then settles back on Svarik. "As long as Count Ihail has a solid plan on how to get to the throne, I think we should offer him whatever support we can to get him there."

This time, the duke and duchess don't even have to look at each other to sigh in unison.

"Well then, Count Ihail," Duke Sohlv turns to Svarik. "What exactly is your plan?"

CHAPTER 13

Rhioa

I adjust my cloak and shiver, watching Tyron double check his girth.

"Are you sure about this?" Svarik asks for the hundredth time.

"Utterly certain," Tyron replies again. He gathers his reins and mounts up in one fluid motion. I spot both swords buckled beneath his coat. "There's no need to spend the day fretting. You and Arhys focus on your visit with Count Tskei and don't bother waiting up for me."

Count Tskei was one of two that had sent letters after our meeting with Sohlv. Apparently, we had convinced the duke and duchess enough that they had written to others on our behalf.

"Alright." Svarik is still visibly uneasy.

I don't blame him. I step up alongside Tyron's mount as he adjusts his stirrups. "Be careful," I say quietly.

His green eyes snap up to meet mine. "I always am," he replies with a smile. But the effort is tenuous and the bad feeling in the pit of my stomach only grows.

Then Tyron straightens and I step back as he spurs his borrowed horse forward. I watch him canter out of the yard, leaving a trail in the snow behind him. I stand listening to the hoof beats recede before turning back to Tirzah and Svarik.

"I suppose there's no going back now," Svarik says with a deep breath, gathering his cane.

"I suppose not." I shiver again as I reach them. "How long until we have to leave for the Tskei house?"

Svarik turns back to the house, feeling out the stone as he walks. "We have a few hours yet." He pauses when he reaches the door and, at first, I assume it's to find the handle. But then he asks, "Do you think he'll be alright?"

I wish he wouldn't act so worried. "Oh, quite. As kind and innocent as he may appear, he's really quite capable," I reassure, now opening the door for him.

"He is..." Svarik shakes his head and walks though. "...unusual for a nobleman. Or for any man, for that matter. So full of contradictions."

Tirzah and I follow.

"What do you mean?" I ask as I unbuckle my cloak and hand it to Tirzah. I am wary of any conversation without Tyron here, as I know that Svarik is not so certain of my character as he told the Sohlv family.

Svarik comes to a stop in the middle of the foyer to take off his own coat. One of the servants steps forward to take it. "Take what you said, for example. You called him 'kind' and 'innocent.' I think another word would be 'sincere.' In fact, he's so sincere that you feel obliged to be the same—you've poured out your life story before you even know it. But," he pauses, head tilting slightly. "While he means everything he says, you eventually realize that he says very little about himself." His smile is wry. "He's managed to get me to willingly tell everything about myself while I barely know anything of him."

Somehow, this has never occurred to me. Tyron always seems so open that I've never really stopped to question more of his past. I've spent so much time trying to escape his inquiries that I've never made my own. The only time that I recall hearing of his past was that time we'd stopped at the inn and Svarik had asked about Tyron's siblings. But despite the sudden realization, I am too aware of how quickly this topic could turn down a prickly path.

"I suppose you're right." I speak slowly, eyeing Tirzah as she rejoins me. She has something in her hand. "I admit, it's a hard tactic to fight. You feel bad for even trying."

"Exactly," Svarik agrees. "Like the titles—he never asked to use my given name, only insisted on me using his until I felt bad for any title at all."

That sounds like Tyron. I allow myself a chuckle and a small quip. "He's nearly shameless about it, isn't he? He helps whether you want him to or not."

"Ah yes, his favorite word." Svarik's chuckle matches mine. "'Help.' But have you ever tried to help him? He barely even allowed me to pay the tailor for his suit. And he wouldn't have even needed the thing if it weren't for the fact that he was helping me."

"Leave it to Tyron to make helping others a flaw," I say. Though, come to think of it, I suppose I've never really tried to aid him either. Not since Pershizar where it was simply a matter of staying alive.

Svarik's chuckle fades and his more serious air resumes. "Yes. Let us just hope that it does not cost him too much in the end."

"Mm," is all the agreement I can give. Then I regather myself. "If you don't mind, I will excuse myself. I have a few letters I wish to write to those back in Beclian and I would like to send them off before we leave for the Tskeis." The excuse will keep me from having to spend unnecessary time with him. The more I have to talk with him, the more I will have to catch Tyron up on. I don't need this falling apart over small talk and swapping stories.

"Of course," Svarik raises a hand in a gesture of dismissal. "I can ask a servant to give you a half hour's notice before we depart."

I start to bow my head, remember he can't see it, and carry through anyway. "That would be very helpful. Thank you."

With Svarik's nod, he heads for the corridor and I for the stairs. Only when I reach the top does Tirzah hold something out to me.

"These were in your cloak pocket," she says.

I look down to find the two letters I had picked up from the sitting room table several days ago. I take them, then stop right outside the door to our quarters as I remember the third letter: Talsk's invitation.

"Do you know what Tyron did with the third one?" I ask, remembering with new suspicion how he had pocketed it before anyone else had a chance to read.

Tirzah shakes his head. "I presume it's in his quarters somewhere."

Hmm. I glance up and down the hallway before giving the letters back to Tirzah. "Stay in here. If you hear a servant coming, stop them and ask for tea or something."

Tirzah gives a shrug that I decide to take as assent.

I continue down the hallway, taking my time and listening carefully for any servants. I reach Tyron's door and do one last check before I slip inside. Slowly, I lower the doorlatch so that it makes no sound as it settles back into place. I turn and survey the space, scanning for possible hiding places. I start with the most obvious option: the large wardrobe in the bedroom.

The room is very tidy, a fact that spares me much of the work in putting it back together. A folded tunic is much easier to replicate than the particular position of one sprawled haphazardly over a chair. Replacing a closed book on a shelf is far quicker than recalling what page it was open to or what angle it was left at on a desk or table. So I go through Tyron's room in short order, starting at the most obvious places and ending with the least. I find nothing.

I recall how Tyron searched my pack on the boat to Krysophera and realize that he might be somewhat familiar with these tactics. After all, I didn't even know that he had done so until Tirzah guessed it months later. I stop in the middle of the two rooms, turning a slow circle. If I was Tyron, and I was trying to keep the letter from me, where would I hide it? But then again, judging by the conversation I only just had with Svarik, perhaps I wouldn't bother hiding it at all.

My gaze catches now on a chair near the hearth. By the imprints left in the carpet, it's supposed to be facing the divan. Instead, it's pulled up to the little side table and angled towards the fireplace. A favorite reading place, I'd imagine. I cross to the side table and note the position of the book—or, rather, books. There are four left in a pile. I pick up the top volume and leaf through.

I shake my head as I pluck the folded piece of parchment from the pages. Was he *really* using it as a bookmark? Leaving the book open, I scan the letter.

To the Lower Prince Tyron of Litash,

I am writing to you personally to invite you on a royal hunt, to take place on the third day of the next cycle. This is an esteemed and longstanding tradition in Arvenir and few grounds are kept as well as the royal Woods of Rhasur—reserved solely for the Grand Va' Kied and his officers. I trust that you understand the rarity of such an invitation and will be able to attend. Should you find yourself otherwise engaged, I, of course, understand—I will simply avail myself of other, more pleasurable company.

Provided that you do accept, you may report on horseback to my hunting lodge just beyond the eastern gate of the city. Arrive by the tenth hour. All hunting implements will be provided. But dress warmly— Arvenir is unforgivably cold this time of year.

Grand Va' Kied Udeneran Talsk
Lord of the Southern Snows and the Crimson Mountains
Ruler of the Iron Door
High Huntsman of Arvenir

I fold the letter, but I do not return it to its book. I leave that wide open on the stand—I no longer care if he knows I went snooping. *More pleasurable company...*Talsk meant me. If Tyron did not go, Talsk would have invited me. I head for the corridor, pause at the door to listen for any servants, then exit.

"I take it you found the invitation?" Tirzah asks as soon I step into our quarters. She's sitting in a chair that she'd dragged up against the wall.

I reply in the trade language, knowing few would speak it this far south. "Yes. And Tyron lied."

Now Tirzah gets up, confusion in her scrunched-up expression. I hand her the letter before she can ask. I watch understanding dawn as her features relax.

"I don't see what the matter is," she says as she hands it back.

"Don't see?" I point out the veiled threat on the page. "Talsk meant me."

"And?" Tirzah shrugs.

Her lack of reaction only incites mine further. "Tyron didn't have to go. That whole speech he made up about it being a good opportunity was pure rubbish—he only went because he thought I would go otherwise." I can't *believe* he managed to lie so easily. And with only seconds to scrape the act together, too.

"Was he right?" Tirzah asks, sitting back.

"What?" I blink at her.

"Was he right?" she repeats. "Would you have gone?"

"Why does that matter?" I sputter.

Tirzah rolls her eyes. "Because, if he was right, what other choice did he have?"

Her question, topped with her attitude, does little for my mood. My voice turns dry as I say, "He had the choice to sit back and let me do my work. Or at least to let me go with him."

"And here I thought you were the perceptive one," Tirzah mutters. "Look. You would have gone because you had to, correct?"

Arms now folded, I nod.

"And you would not have wanted to, correct?"

I hesitate, a reaction which Tirzah takes as confirmation.

"And clearly, Tyron knew this," she points out. "So the only way for him to actually give you what you wanted was to lie to you. Is that really so baffling?"

I fight to remain irritated. "It wasn't his choice to make. And what baffles me is that it was so easy for him to lie to us all."

"Why?" Tirzah shrugs again. "You lie to him all the time."

Her words take mine away. I stand there for a moment, stunned. And yet I don't even know why. She's right, after all. Finally, I manage a thin, "He is supposed to be different."

Tirzah sighs, shaking her head and walking towards her bedroom.

Whatever it is she's thinking, I decide that I don't want to hear it. I shove the letter back in my pocket and head for the door. Only outside do I recall the rest of Talsk's letter and the other veiled threat:

Dress warmly—Arvenir is unforgivably cold this time of year.

Tyron

The sound of the courtyard reaches me before I can even see it: horse hooves against cobblestone, the baying and barking of hounds, all mixed with loud laughter and conversation. I've walked into traps before—most far more likely to spring on me than this one—and yet cannot help the sense of dread that builds in my chest. I rather wish I could turn around now and ride back to Svarik's house. Instead, I press my mount forward and around the corner.

The sight of it all is just as busy as the sound of it had been. Between the long row of stables and the stone walls of Talsk's hunting lodge is a crowd of movement and color. The majority are younger men, many attired in the long jackets that indicate military status. But I do pick out several noblemen in their furs and bright colors. The ladies seem to be in the minority, gathered in clusters or hanging off the arm of some officer. None wear breeches—apparently a scandalous act here in Arvenir—but favor thick riding skirts instead.

"Ah, there you are!" Talsk's voice somehow cuts through all the noise to reach me. He's standing between two of his officers, waving for me to join them.

I dismount and, with quiet thanks, hand my reins to the stable boy who is managing the line of horses. I make a mental note to double check my tack and saddlebags for any tampering before mounting up again. Then I turn away, walking towards the right corner of the square where I'd spotted Talsk. I exchange a few nods and greetings on my way and note that, even if I don't know them, the officers and nobles all seem to know who I am.

"I was beginning to worry you'd gotten lost," Talsk comments as I reach him. He's traded his crown for a tailed fur cap. Yet, just like at the palace ball, his heavy coat is cut in a fashion more similar to his officers than to his noblemen.

I give a half-bow before meeting his gaze and replying, "Oh, no need to worry on my account, Your Highness."

He surveys me openly, sizing me up before turning to the man on his left. "This is my Grand Officer, Iveros Kstoren. He is head over the armies of Arvenir."

The officer is of typical Arvenish stature: broad-shouldered, fair-haired and bright-eyed, and several inches shorter than myself. He stands with the same straight posture and puffed chest that Talsk bears, but his expression is that of near skepticism. We exchange a nod as Talsk goes on.

"And this is the Speaker of the Assembly, Mikaud Lenstativ," Talsk gestures to the man on his right. "He is a good friend of mine."

Lenstativ. I remember what Svarik had said of him being soundly on Talsk's side. The nobleman is quite the opposite of Officer Kstoren, as lean as the former is broad. His hair is long enough that he wears it tied up. Despite Talsk calling him a friend, his body language is strained around the Grand Va' Kied.

"A pleasure to meet you," Lenstativ murmurs, meeting my gaze only briefly.

"And this is the huntsman who scouted out our quarry today," Talsk goes on before I can return Lenstativ's greeting. "He has found us a whole herd of treiset."

The fourth man in the group, dressed in similar fashion to Svarik's huntsman back at Tulstead, nods and holds up the map in his hands. "The herd was between thirty and thirty-five animals, at least five with their yearling spots. They were right on the edge of the tree line and will likely move out to find food as the day warms up." The huntsman has his mittens pulled off so that he can trace all of this out for us.

Either I have never seen a treiset, or I have not yet learned the word.

"Then let the dogs be brought up through the woods so that nothing escapes back into the trees," Talsk says. "The rest of us can ride around the edge and begin the chase."

Svarik had explained some of this, saying that hunting was nearly ritualistic in Arvenir. The animals were scouted, a plan made by the master of the hunt, then agreed upon by members of the party. The usual method was to run the quarry until they were either cornered or too exhausted to put up much of a fight.

- 239 -

"We can run them right up to the riverbank and take our pick from there. What say you, Officer Kstoren?" Talsk turns to his friend.

The Grand Officer surveys the map with a nod of approval. "A solid plan. Who gets first kill?"

Talsk cocks his head and looks at me with a dare in his grin. "How about our esteemed guest?"

"As honored as I would be," I put little effort into sounding flattered. "I may not be the best choice. My country has no such sport as this and I'm afraid I have little idea of how it operates. I wouldn't want to ruin your catch."

I notice the way Lenstativ's gaze flits from me to Talsk as if gauging reaction.

The Va' Kied accedes to my point with smile still intact. "Then this is the perfect opportunity for you to learn. Ride up in the leading party with us so that you can observe. I will take the first kill."

Kstoren and Lenstativ both dip their heads in agreement and I do the same.

"Excellent," Talsk claps his gloved hands together. "Huntsman, sound the call. To arms and to mounts!"

A horn blares and the scurry begins. Talsk goes off to check with the houndsmen, sending me with Kstoren to procure a weapon.

"Javelin or crossbow?" The Grand Officer asks, gesturing to the wide rack even as his sharp eyes watch my every movement.

I scan the rack for a recurve and see none. If I should find myself in trouble, I won't have time to reload. "Javelin," I reply.

He plucks one from its place and gives a cursory check of the shaft and head. He handles it with the ease of an experienced fighter. "I'll give it to the retainers. They'll bring all the weapons in the sledges so that we don't have to carry them all day. When we reach the herd, you can get it from them." He holds out a leather keeper. "Have you used a keeper before?"

I nod, accepting the item.

"Then I'll leave you to it. Everyone lines up by party, so ride to the front when you're ready." Kstoren is off before I can reply.

I head for the picket line where my mount is one of the only ones left. Thanking the stable boy who is holding my mount's reins, I attach the keeper to the outside of my stirrup. This gives me a quick chance to check over my girth and reins without seeming too blatantly suspicious. Then I mount and ride to the front of the courtyard.

The line of lords and ladies and officers wraps nearly around the whole yard. Some are on horseback, others in light sleighs. Heavier sleighs are lined up behind, manned by only a single retainer and laden with all sorts of goods. I spot wooden chests, blankets, furs, quivers of crossbow bolts, and more. How much does one need for a single day of hunting?

"The hounds are set," Talsk announces, mounting his own animal. The large, dapple grey destrier tosses its head and chomps at its heavy bit, jigging in place. "Let's be off!"

As soon as the dogs and their handlers have cleared the courtyard gate, Talsk lets his restless mount break into a trot and leads us through the archway. The single set of ringing hooves gathers to a resounding thunder as the whole line follows. Between the eagerness of my mount and my own taut nerves, I have to make a conscious effort not to be hard on the reins.

We leave the shelter of the courtyard behind and venture forth onto the wide plain beyond. Our colorful procession stirs up the snow, cutting a bright swathe through the pale drifts. The combination of snow and icy wind only adds to the horses' impatience. A few of the groups behind us give in and allow the animals to break into a canter but, while they spread out on both sides, I notice that none pass the Va' Kied.

The general air of conversation and laughter continues as we ride on. Talsk and Kstoren exchange some banter and small talk, but nothing more than a few sentences. Lenstativ rides a few paces behind without a word. Besides those three and myself, there are two more officers to round out our party. A few retainers ride behind us with their masters' crossbows and spare javelins.

We top a slight rise and the dark expanse of a forest appears. The wind, stronger here, pulls up so much snow that it nearly obscures the woods in sections. Talsk turns his mount to ride parallel with the forest edge, slowing now to a walk. I recall the huntsman's map and mentally trace our route around the narrow arm of the forest.

"Come, Prince Tyron," Talsk waves me up. "No need to hang behind. Not unless you prefer the back of Lenstativ's head over the view of the woods."

And here I was just thinking that Talsk is easier to bear from the back than the front. I take a breath, brace myself, then prod my mount forward. "No discredit to the Speaker, but the forest is a difficult view to surpass."

Talsk chuckles, Kstoren smirks, and Lenstativ gives no reaction at all.

"Speaking of beautiful views, it's a shame that you could not bring your lady with you," Talsk says. I don't have to look at him to hear the smirk in his tone. How I wish I could wipe it off his face.

The one benefit of my flaring temper is that it takes the edge off of my nervousness. I simply have to be careful to not let it go so far as to take down my guard. "Unfortunately, Lady Arhys was otherwise occupied today. And while I consider her a good friend, she is by no means mine." Perhaps I would have done better to leave off the last part, but I cannot abide the thought of Rhioa 'belonging' to anyone.

Talsk chuckles. "Ah, she turned you down, did she?" He turns to Kstoren, commenting, "You remember the Lady Saen, don't you?"

The officer nods as he fights the wind for his cap. "A true beauty."

"Any man would be a fool not to pursue that one," Talsk adds, turning again to me. "No one could blame you for trying. But I suppose her father has higher aims than a lower prince for her." The way he watches me for a reaction is so strongly reminiscent of Euracia that my mouth turns sour.

"I wouldn't know." I keep my voice and features steady. "But I hope that, whomever she picks, they are worthy of her. She is too strong of mind and character to be bound to anyone but an equal."

Talsk only laughs. "So long as she doesn't require an equal in face, I'm sure it won't be too hard to find."

Of all the slimy, self-important....

"Which does make me wonder how she ended up as the guest of my dear cousin...." Talsk still wears the too-purposeful smile even as his posture settles and stiffens. His horse tosses its head in protest when he regathers his reins. "As fun as these little guessing games are, there's no need for them out here," he nearly cajoles. "Come now—man to man—what is your use for the Count Ihail? We've all tried to puzzle it out. You may be a bit young for politics, but surely, you're too smart to think he could get you the throne." He lets the last statement trail off into a question.

Man to man? No one who threatens a woman to get what he wants can call himself a man—no matter how big a crown he might wear. I don't even bother to look at him as I reply, "I'm afraid the answer is not so interesting as to be worth your puzzling. I am merely a friend of Svarik's—I have nothing to gain from him."

"Really, you don't have to play at this humility," Talsk's humor holds an edge. "I'm frankly impressed that you've dragged him out this far. He's a skittish little shut-in—always has been. To make use of his type requires a hefty bit of strategy, and I'm simply curious as to how you've done it."

He lays it all out so shamelessly. I can't help but shake my head as I regard him evenly. "You might find that your cousin is not the same man he was when he left. He is not a puppet to be dragged about on strings, but a man with a will and purpose of his own."

I notice how both Kstoren and Lenstativ are watching me closely.

Talsk turns us to follow the ridge down towards the forest's edge. "Oh? And what are those?"

"I'm sure Count Ihail would gladly explain if asked." I doubt Talsk will test that statement, but perhaps others will.

"Alright, alright, I see how it is." Talsk laughs again. "Stick to your little charade if you so please. Just remember," he holds up a finger in emphasis. "The player is always guessed in the end. I'm sure we'll get it out of you one way or another. Isn't that right, Grand Officer?"

Kstoren doesn't bother with Talsk's feigned humor. He inclines his head and meets my eyes when he affirms, "Quite right, Your Highness."

My first thought is for Rhioa. I know she is very capable, but if anyone was to even touch her or Tirzah.... "I suppose we'll see, won't we?" The rash taunt leaves my lips before it has a chance to go through my thoughts. But, if drawing attention to myself means it keeps it away from the others, I can't say I regret it.

Talsk raises both eyebrows, amusement still intact. He drops the subject and twists around to address his retainer. "Sound the call for a canter. I want to get clear of this ridge."

In response, the young man lifts a horn and blasts a long, clear note, followed by three in shorter succession. The chill of the wind must have the riders as eager as the horses to get moving, for the pace of the whole group picks up within seconds. I glance over my shoulder to see the array of mounts and sleighs churning up the powdery snow.

For the next hour, we continue on around the forest. We often return to a walk to spare the horses. Once Talsk and Kstoren take up some subject on a hunting technique, I let my horse drop back a few strides from Talsk. I stay in this position and try to remain aware of those around me lest any 'accidents' have been arranged. The closest rider is Lenstativ who, despite his title of Speaker, does not seem to have any interest in conversation. He rides with his gaze so fixed ahead that it is nearly disconcerting. My worry is only quieted by his current lack of weapon.

Now and then, one of the parties further back will sound a call and the whole group stops. I look back two or three times to see one of the nobles set their hunting bird loose, or for the bird to return with some small prey. This is always followed by a series of whoops and horns until I can't help but wonder how they're catching anything when they're making so much noise. I'd have thought we'd scared off anything within several square miles by now.

Around mid-morning, there is a break and everyone regroups around the sleighs. Tea, somehow still steaming hot, is passed out in tin cups. Many dismount and stretch their legs. Others show off their prizes: hares, small foxes, forest sprowls, and even young mearin. Conversation flies as fast as the banter and I force myself to participate. I try to remember every new name that I'm introduced to, as well as how likely they might be to sympathize with Svarik's case. It's difficult when I'm acutely aware of either Talsk or Kstoren watching me at all times.

Refreshments are stowed away and those who had left their weapons with retainers now take them up as we remount, so I follow suit. Between that and how much quieter things are when the ride resumes, I take it that we are growing close. But it's another half hour before we ride around the curved arm of the forest and I notice how the sleighs drop back. I tighten my grip on my javelin.

The blast of a horn nearly makes me jump right out of my saddle. Ahead, figures I hadn't even noticed pick up their heads. The animals' coats, a mottled mix of white and grey, blend in to the snow around them. Their massive antlers are so dark and angular that I initially mistake them for fallen branches. I estimate more than thirty animals all together.

One horn call is joined by another, then by shouts and the baying of the hounds that emerge from the forest's edge. The herd of treiset bolts almost in unison. They make no sound at all, their slim legs carrying them as fast as any horse.

Svarik had called this next section of the hunt 'the chase.' And thus it is. The hounds are freed of their leashes and set after the treiset. Us hunters, now divided again into groups, follow. The groups from the back are the first to take up the gallop. About half of them press forward at an angle, looping from around the back of the herd up one side. The dogs remain on the other side to keep the herd from swerving out. The rest of us follow at a comfortable canter.

After a little more than a mile, the hunters ahead of us begin to lag. Talsk gives the signal and the horn blares once more to signal our turn. We press our horses into a gallop and overtake the front parties, who then allow their horses to fall back.

I can't even see the riverbanks but already the weak of the herd are beginning to falter. Some are the very young, their antlers are not yet formed and their coats speckled with dark spots. Others are the old and infirm, with noticeable limps or patchy coats. None of the hunters so much as glance at them. Even the dogs ignore them after a signal from their handlers.

The treiset slow when we reach the river. The banks have clearly frozen and refrozen many times, piling enormous sheets of ice until the river is practically walled off. Some of the treiset try to climb or jump this. A few manage; most slip and fall. With another horn blast, the ring of hunters reforms and tightens until the exhausted herd is trapped. They pace anxiously, bumping into each other, throwing back their heads as they balk. I notice the way any hunters with javelins keep their weapons level and forward. I do the same. If anything is going to happen, it is going to happen now.

"All yours, Your Highness," Kstoren calls from somewhere to my right.

Talsk waves up his retainer. The assistant hands the Va' Kied a crossbow, then steps back as Talsk pushes his mount forward.

"Watch how it's done, Prince Tyron!" he calls with a grin. Then he hefts the weapon up, using it to point towards the milling herd as he shouts to the dog handlers, "I want the tall one there."

There's a shrill whistle and the dogs charge forward. Barking, growling, snapping, they drive one section of the herd further in, successfully pushing another section forward. I spot the massive animal Talsk had pointed out among them. As he brings up his crossbow and takes aim, I can't help but watch with disgust. What about this requires any skill? The scout found the herd, the dogs and retainers managed the chase, the ring of hunters keeps the animals trapped. Talsk has no more prowess than a man who catches a fish from a barrel.

The bolt flies from the crossbow and strikes the treiset behind the foreleg. Talsk drops the crossbow, grabbing another loaded one from his retainer. He shoots again before the animal can even try to move back with its panicked herd. I don't see if it falls or not, for at that moment, the trumpets ring out again. The hunters around me cheer and raise their weapons.

The once orderly ring of riders breaks into fragmented parties, splitting off and picking their targets. One by one, in order of rank, the hunters take their marks. The mounted retainers and the houndsmen continue to manage the fearful herd by forming a loose wall. Any animal that does not fall by crossbow, or tries to run at the riders, is quickly felled by javelin. I keep my mount back, along with a few others who seem to only be here to watch the whole spectacle. My ears ring with the sounds of horns and cheers and the screams of animals.

"What do you make of the hunt?"

I turn my head to realize it's Speaker Lenstativ. He sits on his horse, watching with the irritated air of someone who has better things to do.

"This...tactic is unfamiliar to me," I reply.

Lenstativ shrugs. "It is typical of Arveners: use numbers and brute strength to round them up and then pick them off."

My mind goes to how Talsk handles any opposition among the nobles. I wonder if the Speaker is referring to the same matter.

My suspicions are confirmed when Lenstativ muses aloud: "It would be interesting to see what would happen if someone with a little more skill came along."

I wonder where he's going with this. Is he discontent? Is he trying to evaluate any possible threats to Talsk? Or is he simply seeking to preserve his own position? I look out at the hunters, watching as Kstoren lands the killing blow on a large treiset.

"I'm not sure many would recognize such skill if they saw it," I comment in turn.

There is a pause before Lenstativ replies in a dry tone, "True. I frankly think this whole affair is a trivial waste of time. The dogs deserve more credit than any of the hunters."

A shrill sound erupts to our left, distracting me entirely. I watch as one of the younger treiset runs out of the fringe of the herd with several hounds hanging on to it. It tries to escape the ring but the mounted retainers brandish their spears, pushing it back. It stumbles, bucking and kicking at the dogs that tear at it—all to no avail. It falls, thrashing in the snow.

I have hunted many times in order to sustain myself and others. I have killed many more animals in self-defense without thinking twice. But this is not the same. Watching the dogs maul the frantic, dying treiset, listening to the laughter of the hunters and houndsmen, I feel suddenly like a boy again. The memory is so vivid: me trying so desperately to heal the little bird that Euracia had torn to pieces. One of the groundskeepers had found me crying and had ended the tiny thing's suffering. The man had explained why, and I had forgiven him, but I had never forgotten how much Euracia had *laughed* over the matter.

"Come, Prince Tyron!" Talsk's call interrupts it all. He rides towards me at a trot, grinning and holding a reddened javelin. "Pick your animal! Kstoren and I can back you."

In a moment, I make my decision. I grip my javelin and spur my horse forward. The hounds scatter even as I raise the shaft and hurl it forward. The point strikes right where the neck meets the jaw and the animal falls still.

I slow my mount and turn it back, noticing how the laughter has ceased. Talsk surveys me in a way that is somewhere between wary and annoyed. But then he resumes that overdone smile as he nods to the retainers.

"Bag it up for him. But maybe don't bother with the pelt," he laughs. "I'm afraid our foreign guest may not quite understand how to pick the best animal. We'll teach him how to do that for next time. Isn't that right, Mikaud?"

Mikaud Lenstativ is looking at the dead treiset. "Quite right."

I decide it's best I say nothing at all.

CHAPTER 14

Rhioa

I tap my fingers idly on the upholstered arm of the chair, watching the slowly dying fire. I see why Tyron favors this chair for reading; it's quite comfortable. Perhaps a little too comfortable. I've already caught myself nodding off twice and resorted to skimming the book Tyron left on the stand just to stay awake. I hadn't dared to get up and walk around in case a servant should hear me. It would be quite difficult to explain what I'm doing in Tyron's quarters at such an hour. For the same reason, I forego any candles and stick to the light of the hearth.

For possibly the twentieth time in the past ten minutes, I glance at the little winding clock on the mantel. It is now past midnight. Svarik had told me that the hunt is followed up by a feast that can often last late into the night, but I hadn't thought it would be quite this late when I'd decided to stay up. I'd wanted to confront Tyron about Talsk's letter and, well, be ready to act if he didn't return. But without any way of knowing when the feast has ended, this whole idea is seeming more and more futile.

Just when I am contemplating giving up and going to bed, I hear muted footsteps from the hall. I remain in the high-backed chair just in case I'm wrong. I'm less likely to be seen from here than if I stand up. The slow steps halt outside the door, replaced by the quiet click of the latch. I glance cautiously around the edge of the chair and see a dark-haired figure close the door behind himself.

I get to my feet, saying, "You're rather late."

Just as suddenly as the figure vanishes, it appears mere inches in front of me. I don't even have time to raise a hand to defend myself before I'm slammed back against the wall. The force drives the breath from my lungs, sending the room spinning. The disorientation is furthered by a nearly unbearable hum that fills my ears. But my instincts are still sharp and I have pulled my dagger before I've even pulled together a thought. Just as I have the tip of it up against his ribs, I meet his eyes and the conscious side of me takes back over.

"Tyron," I gasp, fighting the forearm he has pressed against my throat. "It's just me, it's just me."

Green eyes widen and the pressure releases all at once. The hum of Gifting lessens with it. "Rhy? What in Eatris—what are you...." As quickly as he had stepped back, he now steps forward. "Are you alright? Did I hurt you?"

One hand to my throat, one still clutching my dagger, I shake my head as I try to catch my breath. "I'm unharmed," I wheeze. "Just...just lost my breath. Give me...one second."

"I am so sorry. I-I didn't know you were in here." Tyron sputters, one hand running through his hair. "Here, come sit down."

I accept the seat, if only to calm him some. Then I close my eyes and focus on taking deeper breaths. The tight feeling around my ribs eases slowly. When I trust that I can speak again, I open my eyes and find Tyron on the very edge of the nearby settee.

"I didn't prick you, did I?" I ask, now aware again of the dagger still in my hand. I quietly sheathe it.

"No, no," Tyron shakes his head quickly. "Not at all. How is your throat? Do you feel any bruising?" He stands up as if to come check for himself.

I wave him away. "I'm alright, really. No need for all this fretting." I keep my tone dry to hide my embarrassment.

He doesn't reply to this, instead turning to the mantel and taking one of the wooden spills from a holder there. He lights this from the hearth and begins to go around the room lighting candles.

"I didn't mean to startle you," I say, now cognizant enough to be concerned by his reaction. I turn to watch him and notice that he's having a hard time lighting anything with how badly his hands are shaking. What happened on the hunt?

"I didn't mean to react so...." Tyron's sentence trails off as he returns to the hearth.

"Did something happen out there?" I ask.

He shakes his head as he tosses the leftover stub of the spill onto the glowing coals and sits back down on the settee. "No, it all went smoothly. Talsk had his questions, but that was that; no tricks." The new candlelight gives a better view of his haggard expression. "Why are you in here, again? Did something happen while I was gone?" He's back to running a hand through his hair.

"I'd wanted to make sure that nothing went wrong and..." I falter, glancing at the letter on the stand and realize how bad my timing has been.

"And?" Tyron follows my gaze to the letter and his whole posture slumps. "Please, not right now," he murmurs. "You can scold me all you want in the morning, just please not now."

I shouldn't have waited in here. I can't tell if the lump in my throat is from guilt or Tyron striking it earlier. Either way, I silently take and fold the letter and get up to leave. I make it as far as the door, one hand on the cool metal of the latch, before I make the mistake of looking back over my shoulder. Tyron is sitting with his head in his hands, shoulders drooped. He hasn't even taken his heavy overcoat off. If I had stumbled across Svarik in such a state, I would have immediately told Tyron so that he could help him. But if Tyron is the one who needs help, who can I fetch? I recall this morning's conversation with Svarik: *Have you ever tried to help him?*

I take a deep breath and let go of the door latch. "Are you sure nothing happened?" I ask as I turn around.

Tyron picks his head up. "Hm?"

"You seem..." I search for a fitting term. "...out of sorts."

"Ah." Tyron straightens, gathering himself and offering a bleak sort of smile. "Just tired, I suppose."

He's obviously lying, but I have the feeling that I shouldn't say as much. What do I say instead?

Apparently, my silence is enough to do the trick. Tyron's smile fades and he lets out a long breath. "Really, nothing happened. Talsk simply," he swallows. "Well, reminds me of someone."

Someone? I draw the sudden connection. That day at the inn when Svarik had asked Tyron about his siblings, he had had a similar—albeit lesser—reaction. I hazard my guess aloud. "Your brother?"

Tyron seems reluctant to admit it. He looks away towards the hearth as he quietly says, "Yes."

With measured steps, I return to the chair and set the letter aside. "What about him bothers you so?"

Now Tyron's eyes are fixed on mine, searching, evaluating, nearly pleading though I know not why. Is it a matter of trust? Does he fear I will use this against him?

"I have told you of my birth parents," Tyron finally says, now leaning back in his seat and rubbing one temple. His gaze returns to the glowing coals in the hearth. "I did not mention my adoptive parents because there was not much to say; I saw them perhaps once or twice a month and usually at a distance. But I knew I was not theirs and I did not resent them for it." He sighs. "But their second son, Euracia, was not so forgiving. From what I hear, he was a fairly normal child. But our parents did not spare much time for anyone other than their eldest and heir. As Euracia grew older and his good works failed to catch our parents' attention, he turned to other means: cruel pranks, bullying the other young Ethians, and even torturing small animals. Anything bad enough meant he would be brought in for reprimand—a bit of the attention he craved." Tyron lets his hand fall to the arm of the settee. "Euracia is more than ten years my senior so, by the time I knew him, he did such things simply because he enjoyed them."

He relishes the pain and fear of others and gladly uses both to manipulate people. I'm not sure he is capable of feeling either himself."

I think of Mother, that horrible smile she used to wear when she hurt us. Tyron's description fits her eerily well. While the Va' Kied does not seem quite as brutish as Tyron's brother, and certainly not as sadistic as my mother, I can understand Tyron's reaction completely.

Which brings up another question. I roll it around in my mind, trying to find a better way of putting it and finding none. I finally just spit out, "Did he harm you?"

Tyron shrugs and leans forward enough to pull off his overcoat. "He could never go too far—that would have gotten him in too much trouble." He lays the coat over the back of the settee.

A sick feeling churns in my stomach.

"I suppose I can at least thank him for my proficient Gifting." Tyron tries a lighter tone as if sensing my unease. "It was my best means of defending myself and as such, I became rather good at it. Sometimes it even led to me discovering things by accident." He shakes his head, lips tugging upwards. "There was this one day where he'd tied me to this tree in one of the little gardens. After three hours, I realized that no one might come through for another day or two. That's how I learned to transport myself."

All I can do is stare at him. "That is..." *awful.* "Is he the reason you left?"

Weariness settles over his expression once more, somehow accentuated by the warm cast of the candlelight. "He was the final straw, anyway. In truth, I was rather sick of all of them." He glances up and catches my confusion, adding, "The Ethians—the ruling Council of Litash. They're mostly reasonable people, but they're rather self-centered leaders. They act as if the good of the country and the good of the people are somehow two separate interests and only ever serve the former." He seems to realize the tirade he's begun and brings the subject back around. "It didn't help that all of them are too scared of Euracia to do anything about him. He has a way to *everyone* inside that palace."

"What about your other brother?" I ask. I can't remember his name. "He's king, isn't he?" Wouldn't he do something?

Tyron nods. "Judican, yes. He was crowned shortly before I left. But he's more interested in pleasing people than ruling them well. In the end, he does more harm than good." Now his jaw goes taut and he's back to running his hand through his hair. "After his coronation, there was an incident with a band of thieves attacking a village near the Forest of Riddles. This happens from time to time, but Judican wanted his first public act as king to be successful. He sent me, Euracia, and one of the other Ethians out with a handful of soldiers to deal with it." As his story goes on, his voice grows quieter and quieter. "We set an ambush, but things went awry and we only caught one man. No matter how high a bribe or how severe a threat we tried, he wouldn't talk. So, Euracia requested permission to 'interrogate' him privately."

The sick feeling spreads and I have to keep myself from looking away.

"Judican, anxious as he was to catch everyone responsible, wrote back and granted his permission." Tyron's voice is low, barely above a whisper. "They sent me off to gather firewood or some stupid task just to keep me out of the camp. But I could hear the screaming all the way from the woods." His fingertips dig into the fabric of the armrest. "I couldn't take it. I intervened and made Euracia stop. The Ethian in charge took my side—though likely only because we'd already gotten the information by then." Tyron swallows, mouth twisted into a near grimace. "I healed the man as best as I could and presumed that would be the end of it. But the next morning, he was missing."

My heart sinks. I find myself bracing against the back of my chair.

"The men found him off in the trees—mauled beyond recognition." Tyron lets out a sharp breath. "They blamed it on animals, but everyone knew Euracia had done it. So when we returned to the capital, I went straight to Judican and demanded something be done. You know what he told me?" Tyron looks up and quotes, "*Nobody cares about a thief.*" The curve of his lips is bitter. "And apparently, no one cares about a man in power with a taste for blood. When I told Judican that I would take the truth straight to the citizenry, he sent me on 'border patrol'—that's the Litashian way of getting rid of someone for eight months and hoping they're better behaved by the time they get back." One hand returns to his temple. "So I said my goodbyes, went the border with my assigned men, and told them I was crossing the Forest. They agreed not to stop me and off I went."

"And that's when Tirzah and I found you," I finish.

He gives a nod. "At first, I simply wanted out of Litash. Then I suppose I wanted to see a part of the world that wasn't dominated by Euracia." He gives a defeated shrug. "Perhaps I was naive—perhaps even willfully so—for hoping such a place existed. For all I have found is more Euracias. Not always so bad, and not so powerful, but still him packaged up in different forms: debt collectors, usurpers, rulers, officers." One hand ticks off his list in the air. "That same greed for power drives them all. It seems the nature of all beings to either be like him or to be afraid of him."

I can't help but feel like the lowest form of hypocrite, knowing that I am flawed in both respects. On one side, I am like Euracia in the things I have done and the means I have used to harm others. On the other side, I have been controlled by such people since I was a child.

Then it strikes me all at once that this is why Tyron is so carefully withdrawn: He expects people to either be like his brother or controlled by the people like him. And thus he can trust neither. I can't help but wonder how, with such an outlook, he manages to be so persistently kind. Why does he keep trying to fix a world that he sees as so irreversibly broken?

"But what of people like you?" I find myself leaning forward slightly. "You fit in neither category but seek to amend both."

Tyron's demeanor does not change. "Yes and no. I already gave up on my home country, didn't I?" I draw breath to argue, but he doesn't give me time before going on. "But if I am an anomaly, then it is still to no avail. The only reason that Euracia has never been able to use me is because he has nothing to use against me. And if the only way to be free of both greed and fear is to have nothing you hold dear, then it is not worth it."

For nearly a full minute, the only sound in the room is the faint popping of the coals in the hearth. In the pause, all I can think of is Tirzah. She has always been my one friend, my comforter, my support when I had no other. I could never have survived without her. And yet to Tyron's point, she has also been what has kept me bound. For I cannot leave without it coming down on her head and she cannot leave without it coming down on mine. We are both each other's refuge and prison all at once. And we would never let the other go. Life without her is unfathomable, which makes me wonder how Tyron has borne a life so utterly alone.

"I don't think that that is true, and I don't think you believe it either," I say, surprising myself and, judging by his raised eyebrows, Tyron as well. "If it was, then you would not be in that irritating habit of helping every soul you set eyes on. Don't you, by the very act of putting yourself on the line, give those 'Euracias' something to use against you?"

This time, it is Tyron who starts to argue and I who cut him off. "Take what you did in Ajhal: By intervening for that mother and her child, you became invested in them. That debt collector knew that they mattered to you and thus it gave him something to use against you. But you stood your ground and that child was saved because of it."

He looks at me, lips parted and head tilted slightly to the side. Then he catches himself and straightens. "Well, yes, I suppose—"

"—Can't one be afraid and yet act bravely?" I persist, not even sure why this matters so much to me. "Isn't that exactly what Svarik is doing right now as he stands up to Talsk?"

Tyron goes back to staring at me. When he does move, he dips his head in concession. "You are right—forgive my foolish words. I have let myself dwell too long on such matters."

I'm not really sure what to do with his apology. I'm really not sure what to do with any of this. Did I make him feel as though he had done something wrong and that's why he is saying sorry?

"There's no need to apologize. It was not my intention to make you feel bad," I murmur, frustrated. Why can't I always know what to say the way he does? "I'm not like you—I'm not good at this."

Now Tyron's brow furrows. "What do you mean?"

My exasperation gets the better of me and I make a loose gesture around the room. "I mean, *this:* talking, listening, helping. That is your expertise, not mine. It seems that, unless it is false or fake, I am no good at it."

Tyron looks openly surprised. He shifts in his seat, saying, "On the contrary, you have always seem worn out by fakery. You might be forced to use it, but it is not who you are." His voice drops and yet his earnestness is only heightened as he goes on. "Rhy, I've never told anyone what I just told you about my brother."

"Never?" How can that be? Surely there has been someone in his twenty years that knew.

"There was no one I could tell," he replies simply. "I was rather the outsider in Litash. To the commoners, I was a noble. To the nobles, I was a commoner with a tacked-on title. To the Bandilarians, I was Human. To the Humans, I was adopted by Bandilarians. No matter which angle you approached me from, I did not fit in. Not that it was all bad; I grew up with a much wider perspective than most are granted. But it was, admittedly..." He hesitates. "...well, lonely."

It has never occurred to me that someone so good at being a friend should never have had one himself. And yet, I have witnessed it in the way he is with Svarik. He's always giving and giving and never allowing anyone to give in return. Up until now, it has been the same way with me.

"So thank you. It was strangely nice to have someone listen to all that." Tyron's smile is still tired, but there is a warmth to it now.

I don't actually know how to respond to such heartfelt thanks. A 'you're welcome' would feel out of place after such sincerity. Still feeling as though I don't quite have it right, I say, "If you ever find yourself needing someone to listen again, you need only ask."

Tyron's expression is hard to read. He is back to searching my face, green eyes lit by the gold of the fireplace, as if trying to verify that I meant it. When he replies, he is nearly hoarse. "Thank you."

This time, I nod.

Then Tyron gathers himself and glances at the mantel clock. He clears his throat. "For now, I think I have kept you up late enough for one night. We ought to both get some rest."

He gets up and I follow in silent agreement. He crosses to the door first, holding it open for me as I pass through.

"Goodnight, Rhy."

"Goodnight, Tyron."

Tyron

I wake up slowly, registering light on the canopy overhead. How is there light in my room? I sit up and realize that it's peeking around the edges of the curtains. I must have overslept. Rousing myself, I make the bed and cross to the wardrobe. I pull out the usual heavy tunic, vest, and woolen breeches. Then comes the boots and jacket.

I cross into the other room of my quarters and find that the household staff have already left me fresh water on the wash stand. I must have been very soundly asleep not to have heard them. I feel a little disoriented as I wash my face and comb my hair. But then, in the mirror of polished tin, I spy the letter from Talsk laying on top of my pile of books.

It triggers the memory of Rhioa, sitting across from me in the chair. I'd been so sure that she was going to be angry with me over the way I'd concealed the letter and its contents. I think that, at first, she was. What made her change her mind? Whatever it was, the conversation that had followed had been wholly unexpected. I had thought up until then that she considered me, at best, a tool in her mission. But now I replay her words and cherish the sense of warmth they bring. And the hope—the hope that I have earned more of her trust than she lets on.

I take the quick precaution of tucking the letter beneath a book and then head downstairs. I find everyone still at the dining table, just finishing their breakfasts.

"Good morning," I greet them all as I take my seat.

Across from me, Rhioa offers a nod and the semblance of a smile in return.

"There you are," Svarik says, straightening in his seat. "I was beginning to worry that you were unwell."

"Not at all," I assure, leaning out of the way of the maid who sets down a tray of breakfast for me. I thank her before adding, "I was just a bit tired from getting back so late. It was past midnight by the time I returned."

"I see. How did it go?" Svarik asks almost hesitantly. Another maid clears his breakfast and refills his tea.

My empty stomach tugs at my attention nearly as much as Svarik does. I take a quick bite of toasted bread, waiting until both maids exit the room before replying, "Fairly smoothly. Talsk is still convinced that I am somehow controlling you, but I think others are not so certain."

I notice both Rhioa and Tirzah listening closely. I also notice that they hold their teacups in the same exact fashion, cupped in both hands as if trying to warm them.

"Hm. Who did you ride with?" Svariks taps one finger on the table in thought.

"Talsk, Grand Officer Kstoren, and Speaker Lenstativ," I list off after another bite. "There were two other officers in our party, but they were lower ranking and were not formally introduced. I presume they were more guards than anything."

Svarik's tapping stops. "Did you say Lenstativ? How interesting. He never enjoyed the hunt."

I take this as a cue for more information. "He did not seem pleased to be there. He spent most of his time in the back of the group and did not participate in conversation unless addressed." I pause, remembering the one exception. "Though there was one moment when Talsk wasn't with us. Lenstativ commented on the hunt and how it embodied Arvenish tactics—'round them up and pick them off,' he said. Then he commented that it would be interesting to see what happened if someone with a more skilled approach came along."

"Hm." Svarik leans back in his chair.

"Could it be that he is not so devoted to Talsk as you first thought?" Rhioa takes up the question.

It gives me a chance to actually eat some breakfast as Svarik replies, "I'm not sure. Mikaud Lenstativ is...an unusual case. Back when he came into his position, he was not technically a member of the Assembly: He had a title, but no land. Talsk was the one who helped him to gain the position through various loopholes. Lenstativ has returned the favor by advocating for Talsk ever since."

"Perhaps, then, he is tired of paying back his debt to Talsk," Rhioa comments. "If you are that someone with a 'more skilled approach,' perhaps he would consider switching sides."

Svarik considers this quietly. Then he says, "Perhaps. But it would be too dangerous to approach him and be wrong. I think it would be safest to continue speaking with the other Assembly-members and see what they say about him." Svarik takes a sip of his tea and continues to a new subject. "But this also brings up the visit with Count Tskei. He admitted to Arhys and me that he has been very upset with Talsk's unexplained seizure of crops. Apparently, enough has been taken that he is concerned about having enough for next spring's planting."

"Which matches Duke Sohlv's information on rumors of coming war," I muse. "Did Count Tskei say anything on that?" I look to Rhioa, but she is suddenly busy stirring her tea.

"Not outright," Svarik shakes his head as he sets down his cup. "But there were many mentions of 'unrest' and 'hysteria.' He seemed too nervous to say more."

One of the words is unfamiliar. I look at Rhioa and repeat, "Hysteria?"

She translates it into the trade language and I nod in understanding.

"Tskei did agree to put in a good word to Lord Veldost for us, though," she goes on. "He even mentioned that he could introduce us at Duchess Oskoristiv's solstice dance."

Oh, right. "That is being held tomorrow evening, correct?"

"Correct," Svarik confirms.

"Do we know who will be there besides Tskei and Veldost?" I take the last bite of sliced fruit and push back my empty plate. I try to tally who we already have on our side. The Sohlvs, the Tskeis, possibly Veldost and from there, the Runims. Then there had been mention of one of the southern lords showing interest, along with one of his cousins from further west.

"Fortunately, it does not sound like Talsk attends such things—especially not so soon after a hunt." Svarik's tone is dry. "Solstice dances are a traditional affair, held on our winter solstice to celebrate the coming lengthening of days. Such parties will be held in various houses by those who enjoy the tradition. Since Duchess Oskoristiv is well-established among the socialites of Ilske, her guests will likely be those most involved in the social season."

Which, in Arvenir, means those who are yet unmarried. Hmm.... "Will the Sohlv family be in attendance?"

Svarik reddens. "I, um, am not certain."

Across the table, Rhioa looks at me oddly.

I grin.

"But come, let's go over some of the party traditions so that you know what to expect." Svarik changes the subject quickly.

I follow along, letting him change the subject—for now, anyway. He won't have such luck tomorrow night.

Svarik and I reach the top of the steps and I can't help but look back across the courtyard. I must admit, the duchess knows how to put on a good show. Lanterns are everywhere: bordering walkways, lining the broad entrance, and sitting on both sides of each stair. The flickering of the candles is refracted by snow and ice until everything shimmers.

Inside is much the same. Besides the already elaborate décor of the manor, every available surface bears some sort of arrangement. I spot cut branches of ever-green, live flowers, ornaments of glass and metal—all nestled around white candles of every shape and size. Above these, garlands hang from the walls, often entwined with rich swathes of satin and clusters of bright berries.

In a now practiced manner, Svarik and I hand our coats and caps off to the servants and follow another group of party-goers to the hall. We wait through the usual introductions, handing our cards to the herald in turn and waiting for his announcement. But without Talsk in the audience, and without having an entire stairway to descend by oneself, I barely even mind.

The hall is already quite full, a busy pattern of bustling white against black. Svarik had explained the solstice tradition of men wearing all black to symbolize the long nights up until now, and the women wearing all white to symbolize the coming lengthening days. At midnight, the host of the party would pass out some sort of colorful token as a pronouncement that spring was on its way. Svarik had also added that the tokens were a way for the host to show off their wealth—the more lavish the token, the better the boast.

We haven't been in the room for a whole minute before the duchess spots us.

"Count Ihail, Prince Tyron, how wonderful of you to join us this evening." She gives a deep curtsy, making the strange high collar of her dress wobble slightly.

"And how gracious of you to invite us," Svarik replies with a bow.

I smile and follow suit from behind him.

Duchess Oskoristiv beams. "But of course! I do hope you find everything to your liking. Be sure to help yourselves to refreshments; I've had delicacies brought in from as far as Cadbir just for tonight."

I can't help but think that, if it made the journey all the way from Cadbir, one probably shouldn't be eating it.

"And as for the drinks...." The duchess goes on through various aspects of the menu, the decor, the music, and a few of the dances. She even launches into a full explanation of the new chandelier. "Isn't it just dazzling? It has sections of glass imported all the way from Pershizar. You can spot them even from here—they have the reddish tint, see?" She stops suddenly, her blush showing even beneath her cosmetics. "I beg your pardon, I did not mean to be rude," she says in a rush.

It takes me a moment to even figure out what offense the duchess thinks she has caused.

"No apology is necessary," Svarik says graciously, dipping his head. "I'm sure the chandelier is quite enchanting; I appreciate your description of it."

Duchess Oskoristiv is a little less flustered when she says, "Oh, in that case, I am glad to oblige." Just as I fear she has taken it upon herself to describe the entire room, she apparently spots another guest that merits her attention. She quickly tells us, "Should you need anything, simply avail yourselves of the household staff."

Svarik squeezes in a "Thank you," before she is off to the next person, the white ruffles of her dress flouncing all the way.

"At least she spares one the trouble of figuring out what to say," Svarik says under his breath.

I smile, glad that Svarik is relaxed enough this time around for jests. "Indeed. But, for all her, um, effervescence, she seems sincere." Nosy, yes. But in the harmless manner of a curious child.

Svarik and I meander towards the drink table as I scope out the room. I see several faces from Talsk's celebration, particularly among the dancers, but not so much from the hunt. There's Lord Uteir, of the western reaches, and Marquess Dromrv, a sympathetic but not particularly influential figure. And of course, the young Lord Toldorist is among the dancers, still trying to find a bride so that he can fulfill his father's stipulations and inherit his estate. Then I notice the Duke Sohlv, his wife on his arm as they converse with a couple I don't recognize. Now to find their daughter....

"Tyron?" Svarik is tugging on my arm.

"Hm? My apologies, I was distracted."

"They just announced Lady Arhys and Madam Tahra," he tells me.

Ah, perfect timing. "Then let's fetch our drinks and go meet them."

We are on our way back to the room, drinks in hand, when I spy Elszebet Sohlv standing on the sidelines of the many dancers. A plan begins to form.

"There you are," Rhioa's voice reaches us before she does, and a good thing too. It gives me enough time to brace myself before she comes into view. She is as stunning in white as she has been in every color I've seen her wear. My breath catches at the flow of her skirt, the woven silver necklace at her throat, the strands of white woven into her golden hair, the warm brown eyes...that are regarding me quite strangely.

I clear my throat. "Arhys, you're just in time," I say, skipping the formalities. "They're dancing duets and I'm inclined to try one."

Rhioa's expression matches her baffled question: "What?"

I'm already handing my drink off to Tirzah, who seems far less confused than her sister. "Would you mind staying here with Svarik a moment? We'll just take one turn."

I extend my arm to Rhioa and she takes it more instinctively than anything. I lead her towards the swirl of dancers.

We reach the floor and she turns to face me, skepticism very thinly veiled.

"Just trust me." I keep my voice low as I hold out a hand.

Rhioa looks dubious. But she accepts it, stepping forward and placing her other hand on my shoulder. "Only if you explain."

With one hand just barely brushing her waist and one hand holding hers, I suddenly wish that I could forget Elsze and just have this one dance. Instead, I force myself to listen to the singing of stringed instruments and then step into the beat.

"That's hardly trust, now, is it?" I comment wryly. But then I explain, "I need to speak with Elszebet, and I need help getting close enough without it looking too obvious."

Rhioa blinks at me. "Are you...are you playing a matchmaker?" Disbelief is evident in her raised eyebrows. "And making me help you? This is ridiculous."

I can't help but notice what a graceful dancer Rhioa is. Every step is light, every movement in perfect response to my cues. "'Matchmaker' might be a bit much. I like to think of it more as giving them a nudge in the right direction."

Now Rhioa's face settles into something unimpressed.

"Oh, don't tell me you didn't notice the way they were," I say, guiding our steps a little closer towards the side of the floor where those without partners wait.

"Yes, emphasis on *were*," Rhioa replies. "That was years ago. Besides, don't they have better things to focus on?"

I ignore her hint. "Believe it or not, I do have some experience in this realm of expertise."

The skepticism returns. "Experience?" Rhioa repeats dryly.

I nod, allowing myself a little mischief in my smile. "It was a survival tactic, really. My parents had realized that, thanks to the title they had given me, I made a nice little bargaining chip. So when they were having trouble with a nobleman from one of the border cities, they promised me off to his daughter in return for his cooperation."

"I don't see what matchmaking has to do with this," Rhioa intones.

"Ah, but it's how I got out of the engagement." I wait for her twirl before going on. "See, in Litash, even arranged marriages are expected to have a certain length of courtship and engagement. So when the daughter came to the capital, I got to know her and," I feign a thoughtful expression. "And I couldn't help but think of this one young noble that she would get along with brilliantly."

Understanding dawns and Rhioa shakes her head. "You didn't."

I grin. "I did. In fact, I did it so well, that neither her nor the young nobleman had any idea I knew. They eloped within the month and she left a very apologetic note behind for me."

Rhioa is still shaking her head, but I see the way she fights to keep her lips from curving. "What did her father do? What of your parents?"

We weave past another set of couples in black suits and white dresses. "The father was upset, but only with his daughter. He let the matter slide when he heard that she at least married a noble. As for my parents," I shrug. "They suspected I had done something, but could hardly prove as much. I got off with nothing but a scolding."

"You are unbelievable," Rhioa's humor leaks into her voice and makes me smile all the more.

"Which is why I'm here to help Svarik," I say.

Rhioa just rolls her eyes.

As if taking that as its final cue, the song comes to an end and our dance with it. I'm right where I wanted to be, with Elsze only a few yards away, and yet.... I am suddenly reluctant to let go of Rhioa's hand.

I shake myself and step back to give the closing bow. "You look a little flushed, my lady," I say, now a bit louder than before. "Could I fetch you some refreshment?"

Rhioa plays along, giving her curtsy and replying, "Thank you, but don't let me get in the way of your dancing. I'll fetch something myself."

With that, we part ways and I turn around to let myself bump into Elszebet.

"Oh, pardon me," I immediately spout. Only when I've stopped and stepped back do I add, "Oh, Lady Sohlv."

Recognition flashes across her face and she gives a small curtsy. "Prince Tyron," she greets me without warmth.

"My apologies for my clumsiness," I say, giving a sheepish smile. "But I am glad to see you; Count Ihail was wondering if you would be here this evening."

"He was?" Elsze's features remain impassive.

I nod and let my voice become more serious. "Indeed. He speaks quite highly of you."

"Does he now?" She murmurs the question, something in her expression flickering.

"He also has more, um, interesting tales." I'm taking a bit of leap here, but I'm fairly certain that she was the one Svarik was talking about. "Something about jumping into snowdrifts from second-story balconies?"

Elszebet blushes.

I am quieter when I go on. "But I understand that things are...complicated. If you wish, I will not mention to him that you are here."

Elsze does not reply for a moment, looking out across the sea of dancers. Then she straightens her shoulders and meets my gaze. "No, actually, I think I would like to speak with him. Is he currently occupied?"

I keep my victory off of my face and reply, "Not when I last left him. If you would like, I can show you to him."

Sucking in a breath, Elszebet nods.

So we walk together back towards the front of the room, saying nothing more but a few trivialities about the decorations or dances. Well, I say such and Elszebet nods the bare minimum number of times required to remain polite.

We find Svarik, still standing with Tirzah, chatting with an elderly lady and what I take to be her daughter. Both curtsy and take their leave as Elsze and I approach.

"Svarik, you won't believe who I've stumbled across," I say. "Or rather, stumbled into."

"Oh?" Svarik angles himself towards me without moving from his spot.

Elszebet announces herself with, "Hello again, Count Ihail."

Svarik's jaw drops and he quickly snaps it shut. Perhaps I should have warned him. Then again, perhaps the reaction is good for Elsze to see.

"How wonderful to see you again, Lady Sohlv," he stammers as he bows.

I turn to Tirzah. "Tahra, have you seen Lady Arhys anywhere? She went off to get something to drink and I've quite lost track of her."

"No, I haven't," Tirzah shakes her head. "I think I will go find her."

Perfect. Now we can leave these two alone. "Allow me to assist you."

"Um," Svarik's expression is that of panic. But I merely pat him on the arm in reassurance.

"No, no, don't worry about coming with. You two catch up and we'll be right back." I nod to Tirzah and we take our leave before Svarik can even argue.

We head for the drink table, taking our time. I notice the side eye and smirk Tirzah gives me and have to fight off my smile.

"What?" I ask innocently.

Tirzah glances over her shoulder and back towards Svarik and Elsze.

"I was just, helping them along," I insist.

Tirzah rolls her eyes—an identical reaction to the one her sister gave on the matter.

I've just spotted Rhioa standing near a table of drinks when I see a servant among the crowd of dress jackets and flourished skirts. And he's heading towards us.

"Prince Tyron," the man bows as he reaches us. "Forgive the interruption, but you are a companion of the Count Ihail, are you not?"

"Yes," I nod.

"His footman asked us to fetch him, saying something about damage to His Excellency's carriage," the servant explains. Then he hesitates. "Under the, uh, circumstances, I thought that it would be better to inform you."

Normally, I would be irritated by such a presumption. But seeing as Svarik is otherwise engaged I am, for once, glad they didn't go to him. "I see. Madam Tahra, would you let Lady Arhys know that I'll be right back?"

Tirzah glances between me and the servant before giving a nod.

I follow the servant from the gilded ballroom, through the corridor, and back to the vestibule. The young footman is still waiting there. The boy has his cap in his hands and his gaze flits about the grand room as if quite nervous. He must be worried about getting in trouble for this.

"Just my coat, please," I say to the maid who stands by the coat closet. Then I turn to the lad. "Are you alright?" I try to recall his name.

He seems surprised by the question. "Oh, um, yes, sir. It-it's just some nasty damage to His Excellency's carriage."

I accept my coat from the maid with thanks and pull it on. At my gesture, the young footman leads the way out into the cold.

"What happened?" I ask, noting that it has begun to snow.

"Me and...me and Foriv—that's the driver, sir—we were putting the carriage in the line with all the others and," he glances up at me and then back at his feet as he shuffles on. "One of the horses slipped, sir. Backed the carriage right up over this little rock wall and damaged the axle."

We enter the barn and I realize that there is no back exit. I'd thought we were simply going through the building. After all, if it was a carriage line, and there was a rock wall, that would all be outdoors.

"What's your name, lad?" I ask, stopping in the middle of the barn aisle. Horses shift in the stalls around us.

The young footman stops, too, dropping his head. He's still holding his cap. "Miko, sir."

"Miko," I repeat. "If the carriage is damaged, why are we in the barn?"

"Um, I...." The boy looks up, fear in his eyes.

I gather my Gifting and turn, but I'm too late. Whatever it is that strikes the side of my head leaves my ears ringing and my knees weak. I draw a knife, only for my attacker to grab my wrist and wrap something around it. The drain on my energy is instantaneous. I barely register the familiar coppery color of red-bronze.

I pull back with all my weight and the man staggers forward. I make use of his imbalance, grabbing him by the shoulder, kicking the inside of his knee, and sending him to the ground. My still colorful vision makes it hard to take stock of my situation. There are four men—no, five, six.... Well, never mind how many. They're between me and the door anyway.

I shift my knife to the other hand and grip the chain that's still bound to my wrist with the other. The second shackle that hangs from the end of it feels weighty enough. When the first man charges, I slash towards his midsection to keep him distracted. Then I swing the shackle towards his head and it connects with a solid thud. The man stumbles back.

The horses are getting riled up now, stomping and banging in their alarm. The thugs ignore it and four of them encircle me cautiously. I note swords strapped to their belts and realize with grim reassurance that they're at least here to take me alive. Then one stops to pluck a shovel from a nearby barrow. Alive, but not necessarily unharmed, it would seem.

"There's no use in putting up such a fuss," the man reasons in an accent I don't recognize, emptying the shovel of manure as he does so. I note that he is the only one wearing a full set of armor.

"Ah, but there's no fun in surrendering," I reply, dagger and chain held out in open invitation.

Shovel raised over his head, he charges first. The only way I can avoid him is by ramming into one of his companions. We both tumble to the ground and I roll away, back on my feet as quick as I can manage. I'm still surrounded, but now I'm behind one of the thugs. I leap forward and lock one arm around his neck as my other hand holds the dagger to his back.

But I've miscalculated. The thug seizes the chain still locked around my wrist and drops to his knees, twisting forward. The momentum yanks me off my unsteady feet and throws me to the stone floor. I have just enough wherewithal to scrabble up and back to free the chain from his grip. The same does not go for my dagger hand. The shovel that I'd lost track of slams into my forearm and sends pain screaming up into my shoulder. My dagger clatters to the floor.

There's no time to act before I'm seized by both arms and the other shackle locked around my throbbing hand.

"Get him on his feet," the armored man orders, setting his shovel against a stall door. Then he turns around. "Run along now. This doesn't concern you anymore."

It's the young footman, cowering in the corner beside the barn door. The boy is shaking, eyes wide, and yet he doesn't leave. Instead, he looks to me.

It's best that he not see this. I give a nod and the boy scrambles out the door.

"Now," the man turns back to me as I'm hauled to me feet. I realize that what I first took to be chainmail seems to be...feathers? Their metallic tint reminds me of Rhioa and Tirzah's Dragon forms. "How about we have a nice, civil conversation?"

"I'm afraid that such a conversation would require you having both manners and intellect," comes my breathless retort. "So I don't see that going well."

"It will go as well as you behave," the man corrects me. Then he smiles. "Which, yes, probably doesn't mean too well."

They drag me towards the far end of the barn and I can't help but think that, if these men don't do it for her, Rhioa is going to kill me.

CHAPTER 15

Rhioa

"What was that all about?" I ask Tirzah as she joins me.

She glances back towards where Tyron just exited, following one of the servants. "Something about damage to the count's carriage," she shrugs. "He didn't want them to interrupt Svarik."

Ah, yes. Not when Tyron had just spent all that time to get them talking. I roll my eyes and comment, "He is ridiculous."

"But it worked," Tirzah points out, one eyebrow raised.

"Not yet, it hasn't." I shake my head and take a sip of my drink. "Talking may yet make them decide they don't like each other at all."

Now Tirzah looks at me. "You would be a terrible matchmaker," she drolls.

"Perhaps," I concede. "But that still doesn't mean that Tyron is a good one."

Tirzah gives her usual expression that tells me that I am impossible and she is giving up. Which, of course, only makes me smirk all the more.

We wander for a bit, always staying within sight of Svarik and Elszebet. A few people strike up passing conversation, a few others ask for a dance. The latter are put off with a variety of polite excuses.

"I wonder what's taking him so long," Tirzah says as we head for a row of benches along one wall.

Hopefully the carriage is not too damaged for use. "Knowing Tyron, he's stopped to help someone along the way and won't be back for another hour yet." My reply is only half-joking.

But right as we reach the benches, I pause. There is a man in one of the side entrances that the staff have been using. He is arguing with a young boy in livery dress.

I nudge Tirzah. "Isn't that boy one of Svarik's footmen?"

She follows my gaze to the side door and her brow furrows. "Yes."

We wander closer.

"I don't care what the matter is—you can *not* go in there dressed like that. The duchess would have your head!" The man insists.

"B-b-but, please, you don't understand, I need to speak to the Count Ihail," the boy pleads.

I decide to step in. Adopting an expression of concern isn't too hard when I ask, "Is everything alright?"

"Oh." The servant jumps slightly, startled. He gives a rushed bow before saying, "Of course, my lady. It is one of these visiting livery boys; they're always such trouble. I'll have him sent right back to the stables."

Now that I'm closer, I can see what a state the young footman is in. His eyes are wide, his cheeks tear-stained, panic in his nearly hunched posture. "Lady Arhys!" He recognizes me with evident relief. "Please, I-I need help. The prince is in trouble."

Oh no. What has he done now?

"He keeps saying this, but I have no idea what nonsense he's talking about," the servant huffs.

"It's alright. I'll take care of this," I assure the man. I immediately turn back to the boy, taking him by the coat sleeve and half dragging him down the corridor. Tirzah follows.

"Where is he?" I keep my question low.

"The barn," he whimpers. "Th-there were a bunch of men. They threatened to hurt me and Foriv if I didn't-didn't fetch the prince."

I wait until we reach a section without any possible eavesdroppers to stop. Then I lean down, place both of my hands on the boy's shoulders, and force him to look at me. "Listen very carefully. I need you to go get the driver, get the horses ready, and have the count's carriage in the courtyard as soon as you possibly can. Do not say a word to anyone. If anyone asks you what you're doing, tell them the count is unwell and is leaving early. Do you understand?"

Tears are still dripping down his cheeks as he nods.

I let go and he hurries off.

"What do you know of the barn layout?" I ask Tirzah under my breath. We keep to a careful walk.

"I didn't notice much," she replies. "Double front entrance. My guess is a single aisle lined by stalls on both sides."

"I'll take the front; you find a way in the back. Signal when you're ready."

We resume polite smiles as we reach the vestibule and the maid offers us our cloaks. We accept, claiming the need for a little fresh air.

Only once we're outside does Tirzah ask, "What about Svarik?"

"He's with Elsze and far too public for them to do anything now." I descend the manor steps, barely able to see as far as the barn through the heavy snowfall. The ground reveals two sets of faded footprints: one smaller one that has made the trip and back twice, and another larger set that has only gone once without returning. "Besides, they specified that the boy bring back Tyron."

Tirzah grunts her acknowledgment.

Then we grow close enough for me to see the lone figure that stands in front of the two barn doors. Whoever it is has posted a sentry, meaning Tyron must still be in there.

"I've got him," I murmur. "You go around."

Tirzah veers off to the side. For once, these dresses have worked in our favor; the white should camouflage her perfectly.

I pull my hood up and gather my cloak about me as if cold. I wait for the sentry to address me.

"Can I help you, my lady?" he asks.

"Oh," I bring my head up, feigning surprise. "I didn't see you there." I peer past him at the closed doors. I can hear muffled voices through the thick wood. "I need to check on my horse. He's stabled in there."

The sentry shakes his head. "I'm afraid there's a big mess in there and no one's allowed in until they've cleaned it up. Perhaps if you check back in an hour, it'll be all set."

"But I really need to check on him." I let my lower lip droop in a pout, letting the sentry think I'm going to be difficult about this. But then I ask, "Could you check for me? If I gave you his stall number?"

"Uh," the man turns to glance over his shoulder.

I take the opportunity. With one motion, I side-step and pivot so that I am directly behind him. One arm wraps around his neck while the other hand braces against his head. He gasps, trying to kick at my legs and use his height against me. But I keep myself angled and his feet slide on the fresh snow. He goes limp after ten seconds, I wait ten more, then drag him around the side of the barn.

I return to the doors and press one ear to the wood.

"Let's try this again," a male voice says. The accent is familiar. "How do you know the Myrandi? Who is your contact? Did they send anyone else with you?"

I feel suddenly cold.

"I'm afraid to tell you that your technique could use a little brush up." I instantly recognize Tyron's voice, but he sounds badly out of breath. "When interrogating someone, you should never ask more than one question. That way, when you get them to the breaking point, they actually remember what to tell you."

I try to peer through the crack in the doors. I can only see a single figure— either they are in one of the stalls, or my view is too limited.

"I'll keep that in mind," the first voice replies in monotone. "Put him back under and let him think about it."

There is a sound like something heavy hitting water and my stomach twists. *Where is Tirzah?* I take off my cloak and hike up my skirts, belting them so that they fall just past my knees.

"Why isn't he fighting?" Another voice asks.

"He's holding his breath, you clod. Kick him in the ribs."

There's a thud and then a nearly frantic splashing.

"See, there you go," someone laughs.

How long could it *possibly* take to find a back entrance?!

"Give him a little longer," the first speaker instructs. "This one is stubborn."

The cold feeling is turning into something like rage. Signal or not, I'm not waiting. I draw my knife and pull open the door.

"Hey, what are you doing in here?" The one thug in the aisle takes one step towards me only to stop and gape at my knife, protruding from his chest.

I reach him in seconds, pull the blade out, and drive one elbow into his diaphragm. He is too weak from shock to keep his balance. Before he even hits the ground, I've identified which stall the rest are in. Another thug is opening the door to see what's going. I seize the heavy door and slam it into him, sending him careening backward. I hear the subtle scrape of someone drawing a sword and I pause.

My eye catches on a shovel, leaning against a nearby stall. In quick succession, I've sheathed my dagger, grabbed the shovel, and circled to the other side of the occupied stall. The moment the stall door opens and the gleaming blade appears, I bring the shovel down on it. I step forward and follow through by ramming the handle upwards to catch the thug under the jaw. There is a sickening crack and his eyes roll back as he collapses.

I've grabbed his sword before he's even hit the ground. Then I evaluate the space: five left, spread throughout the stall—a roughly fifteen-foot square with walls that are taller than I am. Tyron is on his knees in front of the water trough to my left, both hands shackled behind his back. Everything from his head to his torso is sopping wet and the side of his face is bloodied. He's bent forward, coughing, with a sword point held inches from his neck. The man holding it is no hired thug like the others. He wears armor of hardened leather with Myrandi feathers woven into it, his blade has a slight curve and hooked end, and I catch sight of looped chain buckled to his belt. The hum of his Gifting confirms it: This man is a Drogan Hunter.

"Well, this is a bit of a surprise," the Hunter says, surveying my hiked-up, blood spattered dress. "I take it you're here for your friend?"

This could be a good way to buy more time for Tirzah—*wherever she is*. "You presume correctly. Why don't you let him go so that I don't have to kill any more of you?"

The Hunter raises an eyebrow in near amusement. "I'm afraid I can't do that yet. Not until he answers some questions, anyway." He adjusts his grip on the sword. "But perhaps you could do that for him."

From the corner of my eye, I catch Tyron looking at me. My gaze locks on his and his eyes dart to the man next to him and back. I open one hand slowly in the slight signal: *Wait*.

"What exactly do you want to know?" I ask, shifting my weight slightly to give the impression of weighing my options.

"I want to know about the Myrandi. I presume you're working with them, too." He looks me up and down once more.

Then I hear something. It's just barely there, nearly imperceptible beneath the nervous pacing of horses in their stalls. A flash of silver beyond the bars of the stall window behind him confirms my suspicions.

"Wrong," I reply, tilting my head and allowing myself a smile. I want him to know before he dies. "I'm one of them."

The hand that told Tyron to wait now balls into a fist and he throws himself against the Hunter's legs. At the same time, the wooden bars of the stall window shatter and send splinters everywhere. The narrow snout and neck of Tirzah's dragon form reaches through and snatches the thug nearest the outer wall.

As the barn fills with the worried neighing of horses, I charge forward. The thug by the door is so distracted by Tirzah that he doesn't even raise his weapon. I dispatch him with my borrowed sword and then drop to my knees. A blade whistles over my head and buries itself in the wooden wall. Before the man to my right can recover it, I stab upwards into his thigh and grab behind his ankle. In the same motion I stand, pull his feet out from under him, and send him crashing into the thug behind him. Tirzah grabs the second man and breaks his neck with a single twist.

Then I turn on the Hunter. He's back on his feet and scooping up his fallen weapon, the hum of his Gifting starting to swell. I pull one of my red-bronze knives as I raise my sword. He raises his own blade to block my downwards stroke, giving me a window. My other hand slashes towards his exposed wrist with the red-bronze. He deflects it with a bracer, ripping the small knife from my grasp. I don't have time to pull out my spare. So I kick him square in the gut and send him reeling backward.

Instead of distracting him from using his Gift, this gives him the space to do so. The Hunter releases a blast of energy that nearly makes my legs give out. I stagger, trying to maintain my grip on my blade, shaking my head in an attempt to clear my senses. Then I realize my biggest mistake: The Hunter now stands between me and Tyron.

The Hunter has realized this, too. One hand keeps his sword raised and the other hand points a threatening mass of flames towards Tyron. Tyron, who has gotten his shackled hands in front of himself, but who is on his hands and knees coughing.

"If you don't want your friend burned alive," The Hunter's voice comes in between heaving breaths. "Then drop your weapon."

I hesitate, glancing towards Tirzah. She can't reach him—not without acid, which might hit Tyron. He's still coughing so much that I'm not sure he's aware of his surroundings. Maybe I could reach my spare red-bronze knife.... Slowly, I lean over to place my sword on the ground, letting my other hand drift back towards the knife.

The Hunter keeps his Gifting and blade up. "Good, now—"

Tyron moves so fast that even I'm caught off guard. He reaches out, using the chain that connects his manacles to wrap around the Hunter's hand. It's not until the flames dissipate and the hum of Gifting with it that I realize the chain is red-bronze.

The Hunter steps back, trying to twist away. I see him raise his weapon. Without even thinking, I scoop up my sword and lunge forward in the same motion. I catch the Hunter's blade on mine and sweep it out to the side—away from Tyron. This puts me inside his guard, allowing me to hook one foot behind his ankle and thrust my dagger into his throat. His eyes go wide and his hand goes to his throat as he stumbles backward into Tirzah's waiting maw. With one vicious shake, he goes limp.

I check the stall over once to make sure no one's moving before I nod to Tirzah. My attention immediately goes to Tyron, back on his knees and breathing hard.

"Hold out your wrists," I instruct, pulling two pins from my hair.

He does as he's told and I set to work on the locks.

"Thank you. And sorry—" He's interrupted by his own coughing. "—about all this."

He's apologizing. Why is he apologizing? I'm still seething over what they've done to him, and he's sitting here apologizing. One shackle clicks open and I start on the next.

There's a set of footsteps, but I recognize them and don't pause in my work. "What took you so long?" I grumble as Tirzah enters the stall.

"They'd bolted all the back and side doors," she replies, making her rounds to check each man.

"I thought the window entry was rather effective," Tyron offers, still breathless.

I ignore him and ask, "Did you check the two in the aisle? And the sentry outside?" None who have seen us shift may live. Especially not now that there are Hunters involved.

"All quiet," Tirzah confirms.

The second lock clicks and I pull the chains free.

Tyron's shoulders sag in relief and he murmurs his thanks, rubbing one wrist.

I dare not even look at him.

I get up and turn to Tirzah. "Let's pile them all in here and get out of this place."

She nods and exits the stall.

But Tyron is still on his knees.

"Need a hand?" I reach to take his left arm and his breath catches in a sharp hiss.

"Not that one," he says, wincing.

He holds out his right hand and I haul him to his feet. When I'm sure he won't fall over, I let go.

Tirzah and I drag the two other thugs into the stall and close the door. As Tirzah completes the horrible work of hiding any bite marks on the bodies, I use the flat of the shovel to even out the trails their boots left in the sandy aisle. Our protocol dictates that if we can't hide all the evidence, we get rid of any that would link back to us—or better yet, plant false evidence to pin blame on someone else. Since Talsk will already know, there's no point in doing that. All we can do is keep from giving him proof to use against us.

"Here. You're going to need this." Tirzah holds out the cloak I'd taken off earlier.

I look down at my once white dress, now covered in blood, dirt, and bits of straw. I accept my cloak and undo the belt that is holding my skirts up. "You'll have to be the one to go fetch Svarik," I say, pulling my cloak on.

"Don't," Tyron shakes his head. His wet hair is plastered against his face and he leans against a stall door as he speaks. "Eight men are going to be found dead in the morning and they're going to check the list of visitors—including those who left early. We don't need anyone being able to connect this back to Svarik."

He's right. But clearly neither of us can go back inside in this state. Tirzah, at least, is still well ordered. "Tell the count that Tyron wasn't feeling well and went home. That's all he needs to know for the time being. If anyone asks about me, let them presume Tyron and I sneaked off somewhere."

Tirzah nods.

Tyron looks utterly mortified.

But there's no time for arguments. "Come on. The carriage should be waiting."

Tirzah goes out first to do a quick scan, then she ushers us out. We wait several long minutes before being rewarded with the clatter of carriage wheels. Only once we confirm it's Svarik's vehicle does Tirzah return to the manor. I help Tyron in and he collapses onto one of the seats, propping himself up in the corner.

The carriage ride feels much longer on the way back than it did on the way here. It doesn't help that Tyron is now shivering quite badly, despite me forcing him to take my cloak. He still gives the occasional cough.

"How bad is it?" I ask, trying to keep my concern from my voice.

He doesn't even open his eyes as he answers, "Mostly just bruises, maybe a cracked rib or two. Didn't swallow too much water. A night's rest and I'll be fine."

I know he's an experienced healer, but somehow, I don't trust his reply. "You look far worse than anything a few hours of sleep can fix."

Tyron opens his eyes and gives a pathetic excuse for a smile. "I suppose I left out the bit where I will also need to dry off."

I say nothing. But if he's telling the truth, perhaps he is right. I've been through enough beatings to know there's not much one can do for a bruise. And I suppose it would be difficult to find a physician at this hour anyway. Frustrated as I am to not be able to do anything, I keep my mouth shut.

We finally return to Svarik's borrowed manor and I step out without waiting for the footman. That boy has caused enough harm for one evening as it is. As I help Tyron down, the boy comes scrambling from the front of the carriage.

"I-I'm so sorry," the young footman sputters. "I didn't know they were—"

I move to shoo the boy away but Tyron reaches out a hand to stop me. "It's alright," he says softly. "It's alright, Miko. You did what you had to and it all worked out. Go finish your work and get some rest."

With a pause and a trembling nod, the boy returns to his post.

Tyron and I enter the manor and I'm glad to find it completely silent. The servants have already gone to bed.

We head for the stairs and I offer to help Tyron again.

"No, no, I've got it, thank you," he tells me, one hand on the rail.

I stay directly behind him—just in case.

He is slow and stiff and clearly sore but he makes it all the way to his room by himself. He has one hand on the door latch when I stop him.

"Tyron...."

He stops and looks at me.

I bite my lip. I still don't like the idea of him simply going to bed like this. This isn't good. Maybe a hot bath or drink or *something* to get him warmed up. Surely, we could wake one of the servants or—

Tyron sighs. "Don't worry, Rhy. I didn't tell them anything."

The words are like a slap to the face. I stand there, numb with the shock of them.

"Thank you again for helping me." He opens the door. "Goodnight."

And just like that, he's in his room with the door closed behind him.

For a moment, I don't even move. He thought that I was concerned over him giving away information. How could he....

Just as quickly as that defensive thought rises, it dies away. Of course, he would think that—that's exactly how you've lived for over a hundred years, isn't it? 'Anything to keep the mission intact.'

Still numb, I turn back towards my own quarters, vaguely aware that I need to get out of my blood-spattered dress. If only it was so easy to get out of my mission.

Tyron

Soft as they are, I catch the sound: footsteps. I summon my Gifting as I bolt upright, only to immediately regret the decision.

Ow.

The fiery, pulsing sensation of pain works its way up and down my body in a nauseating rhythm. The pressure on my chest makes it hard to breathe, an issue that's only exacerbated by the sudden feeling of being far too warm. Why can't I open my right eye?

Movement reminds me of why I sat up in the first place. My Gifting dissipates as I recognize the figure that stands across the room, rummaging through a chest that's up against the wall.

I try my voice and find it hoarse. "...Rhy?" My head throbs in response to even that soft sound and I put one hand to it.

Rhioa turns around with a blanket on her hands. "Lie back down," she instructs. "You need to be resting."

I realize that I'm on the settee, still in my half-soaked finery from the ball. My boots are in a pile on the floor. I remember sitting down and taking them off and then.... I must have fallen asleep. But then how did I end up under this blanket? And for that matter, how long have I been out?

"No, no, I—" The cough that racks my lungs is so violent and painful that I completely forget whatever it was I wanted to argue about.

Rhioa is by my side within moments, holding out a glass water.

I have to drink deeply before I am able to murmur a "Thank you."

"I think it's time to send for a physician," she says, studying me closely.

I don't have time to be sick. Not right now. But I know that I can't be entirely foolish about this—that will only create more delay in the end. So I set the glass on the nearby stand and try to test each limb with gentle stretching. My left arm screams with the effort, sending pain up my arm and across my chest. I have to catch my breath before using my right hand to feel around my ribs. More needles of pain confirm that at least four are definitely cracked. Then I close my eyes and breathe as deeply as I can. Which, regrettably, is not very much.

"There's more fluid in my lungs than I realized," I admit. "I should probably draw it out."

"With Gifting?" Rhioa asks, brow furrowed. "Is that safe?"

Well, technically, it is never safe to heal oneself. But I think that part is better left out. "It won't take much," I say instead.

Rhioa frowns slightly as if not quite convinced. "Fine," she eventually relents. "But you should get out of those damp clothes first. I doubt those are helping."

She has a point.

Rhioa helps me pry off the wet coat—an arduous process, thanks to my left arm being so swollen—and goes to wait in the hallway. I make it through the challenge of changing my tunic and breeches, though not without my drumming headache reminding me that I'd rather be back on the settee.

Then I try to think of the best way to do this. Drawing fluid out of my own lungs is definitely the most ambitious thing I've ever attempted on myself, but I don't have many options. I don't want to be the thing slowing Svarik down. I end up at the wash stand with the basin in front of me, ready to catch whatever might come out.

It's just the usual process: deep breaths. As my breathing deepens and slows, I pull at my Gifting. Then I twist it back and send it through my veins. I have to ignore the sharp twinge it causes, sending it even deeper and into my lungs. *Deep breaths.* It is difficult. I can feel the buildup of fluid, the way my lungs struggle to take in air. So I begin to pull at the water in the fashion of one pulling a thread from a spool. I ignore the growing, burning feeling as I weave this strand upwards.

The first setback comes when I start to gag. The reflex makes me drop all of the water and sends me into a coughing fit. *Ow.* I have to start all over. This time, I decide, I will just have to bring it all up at once and let my reflexes take over to cough it all out. I resume my deep breathing and try again. I reach the fluid, search it out entirely, then try not to brace myself as I yank on it as hard as I can.

The flare of pain is so bad that I have to hold on to the wash stand just to keep from falling. The coughing takes over almost instantly and I can't stop it. But I have a bigger problem: I'm coughing up blood. Lots of it. Panic fills me with adrenaline and makes it even harder to breathe. *Deep and slow, you fool!* I try to focus, searching out the patch that I must have torn from my lungs. But it's hard when I can't stop coughing.

I can't breathe; I can't breathe. I force myself to ignore how weak my knees are. But no amount of ignoring will fix the black that has begun to edge my vision. I've just found the wound, I've just stopped it up, but I can't stop the coughing.... My hands try in vain to hold on to the wash stand. I feel myself falling....

Someone is calling my name. Have I overslept? I should get up. But wait— I'm already sitting up against something. I open my eyes and find a panicked face only feet from mine.

"Rhy?" I croak. "What's wrong?"

"What's *wrong*?!" I've never heard Rhioa's voice reach such a pitch. "You're covered in blood!"

"What?" I look down, shocked by the crimson stains that cover my tunic. Oh. *Oh.* "It's alright, it's alright—calm down," I try to reassure.

"Tirzah—quick, send for a physician!"

"No, Tirzah, wait." I grab one of Rhioa's hands, which is difficult since she's gripping both of my shoulders. "Rhy, please, *listen.* Give me ten seconds to explain." *And please let go of my shoulder—that hurts.*

Her eyes are riveted on mine. "You'd better hurry."

"I'm alright," I say first, wishing I wasn't so breathless so that I might be more convincing. "It was just a stupid mistake: When I was drawing the fluid out, I clenched up and took a chunk out of my lung. That's what the blood is from. I healed it, but I must've used too much energy and blacked out for a moment. But I'm alright now—really."

Rhioa's brown eyes are unrelenting. "That's what you said before."

I sigh. She has a point. "I know. I was just...tired."

"And you aren't now?" she challenges.

I stammer a moment, trying to get my groggy brain to muster a coherent reply. "Rhy," I try to reason as I sit up straighter. I immediately wish I hadn't. "Even if I did need a physician, it wouldn't be worth the risk. If I'm found all roughed up, they could connect me to all the bodies they surely found in that barn this morning. Things could get complicated—it could jeopardize the mission."

"I don't care about the mission," Rhioa hisses. "I am far more worried about coming in and finding you dead on the floor."

...what?

"Now swear to me that you truly are alright." Her grip tightens on my shoulders then lessens when she catches my wince.

I can't help but stare at her, her features still fixed in such intensity. It's a moment before I can even tell her, "I swear it."

Rhioa's scrutiny does not lessen. "So help me, if you are wrong or lying and you die for this, I will...." She trails off, swallowing. She finally lets go and gets to her feet. "Tahra, help me get him to the bed."

I realize we both used Tirzah's real name a few moments ago. Rhioa must have really been scared to have forgotten such a detail.

With one of them supporting me from each side, they help me into the next room and to the edge of the bed. I am so stiff and sore that even the short journey taxes me. The pain makes my head swim until I'm nauseous. I must have done more damage than I realized.

"Tahra brought you some tea and breakfast," Rhioa says, voice now a forced sort of calm. "You should eat some before you rest."

The thought of food makes me suddenly aware of that unpleasantly familiar taste in my mouth. I wipe it with one sleeve and the white fabric comes away red. *You dullard; you have blood all over your face—no wonder she panicked!*

Rhioa is already fetching a new tunic from the wardrobe as Tirzah reenters with the tray from the other room.

The latter glances from my face to my shirt sleeve and says, "I'll go get you something to clean up with."

Tirzah leaves while Rhioa sets the fresh tunic on the bed. "Wait until you've cleaned up so that you don't get blood on this one, too."

I nod mutely, too busy watching her to reply. Her otherwise collected demeanor has a single flaw: Her hands are shaking. I open my mouth to ask her if she's alright but she quickly cuts in.

"Elszebet Sohlv has agreed to meet Svarik at one of the concerts in Estarvos Hall in two days' time," she says, sitting down in one of the small chairs up against the wall. She gives a pointed look at the tray of food and I pick up the still warm tea just to satisfy her. "It seems your matchmaking has come to something after all."

I sip slowly, letting the tea wash away the metallic taste of blood. I try not to cough. "That's good," my response is slow. Speaking takes such effort. "How is Svarik?"

"Upset," comes her blunt reply. "Talking up and down about how Talsk won't get away with this. He wants to tell people what happened. I told him that we should wait and weigh out our options first. We technically have no proof to link this back to Talsk, but he could link the death of those thugs back to us."

I nod, stopping when my throbbing headache increases its tempo. "Your point is a good one."

My gaze falls to her hands. They lie quietly on her lap, but her knuckles are paler than parchment. Not even my exhaustion can temper the impact of her earlier statement: *I don't care about the mission.*

"Rhy, I am very sorry," I nearly whisper. "I did not mean to frighten you like that."

Rhioa swallows, looking away. "It was a mistake. It was not your fault."

Oh dear. Now I have to tell her. "Not entirely," I confess. "There, um, there is an unspoken rule among healers..." I run out of air and have to pause. "...that one should not heal themselves except as a last resort. Because of the pain healing causes, it can interrupt the healer's focus and they can do more harm than good." I take as deep of a breath as my cracked ribs allow and brace myself. "Which is what happened just now."

Her gaze returns to me and I wince, waiting for her anger.

Rhioa sits there, utterly rigid. She is so still that she seems nearly a part of the room. Then she takes a tremulous breath and looks down at her clenched hands.

"In all our lives, there has only been one other person besides you who ever dared to help me and my sister." Each word is clear despite the hush with which she speaks. "One. And he died because of it." When she looks up, her eyes are welling with tears that she does not allow to spill. "Few people are granted second chances; I do not think we will be granted a third. If you die, our hope dies with you."

The statement holds a weight that makes reply seem impossible. I open my mouth to try, but nothing comes out. I hadn't ever imagined that I mattered so much to her. And I don't know what to say now that she has told me. My stupid, muddled brain can't hold on to a single thought.

The door latch announces Tirzah's return from the other room and Rhioa gets to her feet.

No, wait, I have to set this right. I reach out a hand and Rhioa shakes her head.

"Now is not the time for conversation," she says. "You need to clean up, eat what you can, and rest. We will speak of this another day."

I suppose I have no choice but to accept this. Besides, the sheer exhaustion that pulls at me tells me that she's right. "Thank you," I manage one last time.

And for the first time ever, Rhioa replies, "You are welcome."

"...his left collarbone, and five ribs. I suspect he may also have a slight fracture in his left forearm, based on the extent of the bruising."

Even in this half-conscious state, I register the droning voice as one I do not know.

"From what you told me, I do suspect that he damaged his lungs. But they sounded clear enough that he should make a clear recovery there. He is really very lucky to have escaped with such minimal damage to his organs."

"So what else can we do—besides keeping that arm in a sling?" The question, asked in the same low tone as the stranger's, belongs to Svarik.

I force my eyes open, slowly making sense of the bedroom around me. It's full of soft light that emanates from the adjacent room along with the murmuring voices.

"Keep him in bed with plenty of food and water," the stranger replies. "He should remain there for a few days at least, and nothing strenuous for a few weeks more."

I recognize the scoff immediately: Rhioa. "That will be difficult."

I begin to recall waking up on the settee, seeing Rhioa...then scaring her half to death.... Wait. The stranger. Did they summon a physician? The fog of sleep is dispelled by pain as I slowly push myself upright. *Ow.* I try to swing my legs off the bed, but the wave of nausea that hits leaves me reeling.

"I'm afraid there's not much I can do there. I will come back in a few days to—"

Svarik interrupts. "I think I hear him."

Rhioa appears as a silhouette in the doorway. "What do you think you're doing?"

"Rhy," I feel as exasperated as she sounds. "I told you not to send for anyone."

She's already at the bedside. "You also told me you were alright," she replies. "Which, judging by the amount of broken bones you have, was rather an exaggeration." She makes as if to push me back on to the bed.

I fight the burning feeling that wraps around my torso and squeezes the air from my lungs. "But if he tells someone—"

"—Relax." Rhioa doesn't let me finish. "Svarik is no dunce. He went to the Sohlvs and they lent him their personal physician. The man's been with them longer than Svarik's been alive." Her mouth tips in a wry expression. "And, just in case, Svarik has compensated him generously. Now will you please get back in the bed?"

That creeping sense of paranoia does not ease. The dizziness, the throbbing and burning and aching, it all leaves me disoriented. I still can't take a deep breath, or open my right eye, or use my left arm, or....

Rhioa sighs. In a softer voice, she tells me, "Stay here. I will be right back."

She returns to the other room, leaving me still stranded on the edge of the bed.

"He's awake, but he's a little distressed. Why don't you three continue this conversation downstairs and I'll get him calmed down?"

There are quiet murmurs and padded footsteps, followed by the closing of a door. Rhioa reappears, now carrying something under one arm, and crosses to the closed curtains. She pulls at one just enough to let a thin shaft of light into the room. The visual is accompanied by a stabbing sensation that makes me wince and put a hand to my head.

"Do you need help to get back into bed or can you do it yourself?" Rhioa asks.

I don't have any rational arguments left. Only a plea. "At least let me sit in one of the chairs."

Rhioa studies me closely, making me wonder if she's considering it. Then she shakes her head. "The more you rest, the faster you'll recover."

"But Svarik doesn't have time to—"

"—Tyron." She cuts me off. "You have done so much to help Svarik; why can't you allow him to return the favor by letting you recover? Let us take care of you for once."

I blink at her, at a loss. "It's not that," I try to argue.

"Then what is it?"

"I..." I suppose I don't know. Is she right? Perhaps. But the thought of being useless, vulnerable, stuck here in a bed—it makes my mouth go dry.

Rhioa does not speak. She steps forward to help me and I shake my head.

"I can do it," I mumble.

I get myself sitting back against the bed frame and pillows, closing my eyes when the dizziness hits again. Not even sitting still lets me escape the sharp, persistent pain. *Just breathe, you dolt.* I expect to hear Rhioa leave. Instead, the scraping of wood against wood sounds and I open my eyes to see her pulling a chair over. She sits down, crosses her legs, and pulls out the book she had tucked under one arm.

"There's tea for you on the side table, there. Some kind of Arvenish draught. The physician says you should have three cups of it a day." She holds up the faded leather volume. "Now, where were you?"

The tea, I understand. But the book... "...what?"

"This was the book you were reading, correct?" she asks. "It was on your usual table."

Still lost, I nod slowly.

"So where did you leave off?"

"Um...." What is this for? "I think I left something to mark the spot."

Rhioa flips through until she finds that old invitation from Talsk wedged in between the pages. She raises an eyebrow, sets the parchment aside, then clears her throat and begins to read. "According to the accounts set down by the ancient historian, Denevor Rulst, it was foreigners from the Iron Door who were hired to build the palace at Ilske—not Arveners."

...what is she doing? Despite me staring at her, Rhioa goes on.

"Rulst describes a variety of great machines, saying they used these to lay the foundations and the massive front steps. But he refers to many diagrams that have since been lost. There is no way to guess at how these machines were built, operated, or even what their exact uses were. Modern architects say that a variety of Gifting must have been used, as was common for travelers from the Iron Door. They also surmise that—"

"—I'm sorry. What are you doing?" I can't help but ask.

Rhioa looks up. "I thought this would be a good way to keep you in bed. Isn't this what you do when you are too uneasy to rest? Find something to do or study until you are calmer?"

I'm taken aback by the observation. I always knew that she kept a sharp eye on all the goings-on of those around her. But for her to know *why* I stay up so late, and without me ever saying a word about it, seems like another matter entirely.

I finally stammer, "Well, I mean, yes..." but no one has ever noticed before. No one has ever understood. Oh, great, all of the pain is making you even more of a sentimental fool than usual.

"So, short of tying you up, this seemed like my best option," Rhioa says with dry humor.

With that, she goes right back to reading.

I don't interrupt this time, still just trying to process all of this. First, there was our conversation the night she'd waited up for me. Next, she rescued me. Then she said that she didn't care about the mission. And now finally this.

That stupid, stubborn hope begins to unfurl and I do my best to stuff it back down. Why torture myself with it? I know it can never be fulfilled. Yet I can't help but close my eyes and allow myself to listen as Rhioa reads. Her voice rises and falls in such a gentle rhythm, each syllable in its perfect place so that the words make a music of their own. The lovely sound slowly edges out every anxious thought that had filled my head and lets me forget the discomfort of my battered body.

It's only been a few minutes before Rhioa asks, "Is this boring you? Should I skip to the next section?"

"No, no, this section is fine."

To be quite honest, I haven't a clue what she's reading about anymore. All I know is that I could listen to her read all day.

CHAPTER 16

Rhioa

I read for about half an hour before I am sure that Tyron is sound asleep. Then I read a little longer, just to be sure. But even after that, even once I've set the book aside, I don't move from my chair. I sit watching the gentle rise and fall of Tyron's chest as he sleeps.

I remember the day Tirzah and I found him, alone and half-starved in the woods. I suppose he was not much better off then than he is now. And yet, the mottled trail of black and purple that runs from his jaw to his temple is so horribly, intrinsically familiar that it makes my stomach churn in a way that his gaunt frame never did. I have seen the same garish mark on my sister. For that matter, I have seen the same mark in the mirror; I know exactly how it feels.

I close my eyes, wishing I could get rid of that image of Tyron on his knees and held at sword point. He'd been soaked, bleeding, laboring to breathe. Even worse was yesterday, hearing the thud of him hitting the floor and running in to find him covered in blood. I'd thought he was dead. And I'd thought it was because of me. All I could think of at that moment was what he'd said in the hallway: *Don't worry, Rhy. I didn't tell them anything.*

Rousing myself, I debate whether or not to go downstairs. I don't want to leave Tyron alone for too long in case he wakes up. He might need something or be disoriented and try to get up again. Still, I want to know if the physician had told Svarik anything else before he'd left. So after making sure that both food and drink are within his reach should he need them, I exit the room as quietly as I can.

I have only just stepped out into the hallway when I'm greeted by Tirzah and Svarik. Apparently, they've been waiting.

"How is he?" Svarik asks.

"Calmed down and sound asleep," I assure. "What else did the physician say?"

Svarik is rolling his cane around in one hand, jaw taut as he replies, "Not much. He said he will return in three days' time to make sure he is healing well and to check the set of any broken bones. Should Tyron develop any new symptoms, we are to send for him immediately."

Now to hope that, for once in his life, Tyron doesn't get himself into the worst trouble possible.

I let out a long breath, unable to let out my tension with it. It's the same stress I see in Tirzah's closed fists and Svarik's clenched teeth. And the one who is always so good at putting them at ease is the very one who they are so worried for.

"He'll be alright." I try to offer some encouragement. "As the physician said, he managed to avoid anything that would cause long-term damage."

This does not seem to do have any effect on Svarik. He swallows whatever he clearly wants to say, instead giving a stiff nod. "I suppose I will get out of the way, then. Should anyone need me, I will be downstairs." He swivels around and stalks off down the corridor.

For a moment, I simply watch him go. What should I do? I know Tyron would go after him, tell him it's not his fault, somehow convince him to believe it. But I'm not Tyron. I don't know what to say when I actually mean something.

"You go," Tirzah interrupts my dilemma. "I'll stay with Tyron."

I look at her in confusion.

She rolls her eyes. "Oh, please. Don't pretend you weren't already trying to think of what to tell him."

I give her a narrowed look but have to concede to her point. "I don't know what to say, though. I hardly know him."

Tirzah shrugs. "You'll still do better than me."

"True."

Now she's the one giving me a look. I try to smirk, but the effort falls flat. We part ways on that dull note.

I find Svarik in the parlor, seemingly having just taken a seat near the window. He's holding one of the stringed instruments he'd brought from Tulstead.

Before I can announce myself, he calls out, "Arhys?"

"Yes, just me." I clear my throat as I close the door, now feeling doubly awkward.

"Is something wrong?" He angles towards me as I cross the room.

I take a nearby seat. *Now what?* "No. I just wanted to make sure that you knew that this is not your fault."

Svarik's shoulders go rigid and he sets the instrument down. "You're right, it's Talsk's—I'm simply the one who handed him the throne."

"You were seventeen," I argue back. "What could you have possibly done?" Well, I suppose Tyron is yet twenty...but Tyron has always been different.

"What my father raised me to do. What Elsze and Baron Varix and Lord Ulsthur and all of Talsk's other victims *needed* me to do." Svarik is back to grinding his teeth.

Why is it so much harder to convince people when I actually have their interests in mind? "But aren't you doing that now?"

"Yes," Svarik spits. "A good ten years too late. Possibly too late to even make a difference."

"So? What does it matter? You can't change the past. Your only options are to do exactly what you've been doing or to just give up." *That is definitely not what Tyron would have said....*

Svarik's mouth is pressed into a thin line. "Except it does matter. Just look at Tyron: a broken collarbone, five ribs, a fractured arm, a lacerated wrist—how long do you think it will be before he'll be up and about again?"

I'm glad Svarik can't see my wince.

"He's alive by sheer luck. If he had died—if those men had *beaten* him to death—would you still tell me that this is worth it?" Svarik's hands are balled up on the arms of his chair. "Talsk has proved over and over that he is willing to use whatever force is necessary in order to get his way. How many more lives will I jeopardize by continuing?" He scoffs, shaking his head. "Even if I do win the Assembly over, I'm not sure it matters. Talsk still has the army. What's stopping him from seizing the country that way? Then all I will have done is turn Arvenir from the rule of many over to the rule of a dictator. *And* given that dictator the motivation to execute the half of the Assembly that tried to get rid of him."

The thought has crossed my mind before. But I can't exactly tell him that Tirzah and I have backup plans if it comes to it. What do I say instead?

When I don't reply right away, Svarik lets out a long breath. "Then again, if Talsk is already willing to rough up foreign dignitaries and kill his own nobles, I suppose the situation wouldn't have changed that much." He drums his fingers a moment before murmuring, "I guess all I can do is allow the Assembly their own choice. If I give up, all I do is rob them of that." The drumming stops as if he is suddenly aware of it. "Do forgive me—I did not mean to put all of this on you. I was just," his shoulders droop slightly. "Well, taken off guard by what happened to Tyron. I'd been so worried when he went on that stupid hunt that when it went well, I thought that perhaps he was safe—that Talsk wouldn't risk harming a visiting foreigner. And then it happened in such a public place and I didn't even know until afterwards and...." He trails off into nothing.

So I finish for him. "And all of this reminded you of your father." Just as it reminded me of Kassander.

"Yes." The single word is heavy, tired. "I am not sure that I could live with that happening again."

More than ever, I understand him. I recall what I told Tyron yesterday: *If you die, our hope dies with you.* I meant every word.

"I'm not sure any of us could," I finally murmur.

Svarik's expression phases through surprise into something like relief. "I'm glad to hear that."

The reaction is so opposite of what I'd expected that I don't know what to make of it.

But before I can ask, he clears his throat and regathers himself. "While you're here, could I enlist your help in writing to Elsze? I wanted to thank her for sending the physician and to let her know I won't be able to meet with her tomorrow."

I hesitate before deciding I'd rather not ask what Svarik had been inferring earlier. "Of course. But why can't you meet her?" I cross to the small desk in the corner and rummage for parchment in the drawer.

"It would hardly be right to leave while Tyron is still so ill," he says, twisting in his seat so that he nearly faces me.

"But he would want you to go," I counter as I sit down and take up the quill. "There is still much work to do."

Svarik sighs as if this confirms some thought of his.

"I can go with you. I'm sure that Tahra would be glad to stay with Tyron while we're gone." I am at least certain that Tyron would not want all of his matchmaking to go to waste. And as much as I don't want to leave him, I also don't want Talsk to have the victory of thinking he's scared us into staying behind locked doors.

Svarik still purses his lips in reluctance as he gives in with a nod. "Alright. So long as you don't mind acting as chaperone for an afternoon."

"Not at all." I uncap the inkwell and dip the quill. "Ready when you are."

I step down from the carriage and scan the bustling new surroundings. Estarvos Hall is several stories of pale stone, glowing with rosy color from the setting sun. I note the rows of windows along the second and third balconies that are made of showy, leaded glass. I'm willing to bet that the whole building makes use of such a feature—meaning plenty of escape routes. Although, judging by the hum of chatter and the stir of people around us, exits will still be difficult to reach through the crowd.

"Elsze said she would meet us inside," Svarik says as he climbs out behind me. "She said she'll be sitting on the far-left edge, about halfway in."

I turn around. "Sounds easy enough to find."

Svarik nods, gathering his cane. "I suspect that it is already quite packed in there and my cane can be a bit unwieldy in such close quarters. Would you mind leading the way?"

I feel a flush of self-consciousness. I've seen Tyron do it often enough, but I'm not sure if there's any specific knack to it that I might mess up. "You might just have to tell me what to do."

Svarik doesn't seem the least bit put off as he holds out a gloved hand. I step up next to him and put his hand right above my elbow like I've seen Tyron do.

"Perfect. Now all you have to do is walk," Svarik tells me. "I'll be half a step behind you so that I can follow. I'll also be a bit to your side, so no scraping up against walls or doorways, please."

I take a tentative step, still feeling as though I'm doing this wrong. But I keep my voice dry when I say, "It sounds like you have some experience being run into things."

Svarik chuckles. "Let's just say that Elsze could not manage to walk anywhere when we were children—she was always running from one place to another. I got dragged, quite literally, into all sorts of obstacles."

The mental image of Elszebet Sohlv running poor Svarik into various furniture is oddly amusing. I find myself smiling as we start up the stairs. "I didn't realize you had known each other for so long."

"Oh, yes," Svarik clears his throat. "Our fathers were good friends, so we practically grew up together."

It makes sense, then, why Duke Sohlv had been brave enough to approach Svarik at that first ball. And then why Elsze had been so quick to take up his cause. I suppose I have to give Tyron some credit for reviving the relationship.

"She must be glad to have you back home, then," I comment, nodding to the doorman as we enter the hall.

"I'm not so sure," Svarik admits. "It is a bit more complicated than that. A lot has happened in my absence and I'm not certain that she can forgive me for not being there. Even if she could, a lot of time has been lost." There is a pause before he adds, "I do not blame her. But even if I cannot have her friendship, I am grateful for her aid. She has risked much to help us."

I don't reply, too busy handing my cloak and gloves off to the waiting staff. Yet the way Svarik is willing to put aside his own hopes and desires out of respect for Elsze strikes me in its rarity. I have seen very few who would ever do the same. It makes me want to encourage him, but I haven't seen enough of Elsze and Svarik together to judge what she thinks of him; I would hate to give him confidence only for it to be misplaced.

We join the flow of people out of the vestibule and into the main hall. The room is enormous, taking up almost the whole of the building. The sound of a thousand conversations rises all the way to the ceiling three stories above our heads. Rows of curved, stone arches run all the way back down. Between these are little balconies, most with a chatting couple or two sitting in chairs that are angled towards the front wall.

Making sure that I'm not running Svarik into anyone, I steer towards the left wall. Only when we've broken free of the crowd do I see the row upon row of long, low-backed benches that fills the vast space. The far wall, with its low platform, is the only cleared area. I can't help but wonder what Tyron would think of all this.

The thought reminds me of why I'm here and why he can't be. I refocus on scanning the seats for Elszebet, all while keeping an eye out for any of Talsk's men.

We find Elsze exactly where she said she would be. She gets to her feet as soon as she sees us, smoothing the dark green fabric of her dress. She gives a quick dip of her head in greeting, glancing around before skipping the usual pleasantries to ask, "How is he?"

She means Tyron. I check over my shoulder for any eavesdroppers, though knowing the clamor of conversation around us should be plenty of cover.

"He was awake for a few hours this morning," Svarik replies, matching her low tone. "Lady Arhys said that he is still in a good deal of pain, but no more than expected. He'll be confined to bed rest for a few days more."

At the mention of my name, Elze's eyes flick towards me. There is a certain caution in the way she studies me before looking back to Svarik. "I'm glad to hear he'll be alright. He's luckier than most."

Svarik's shoulders sag as he nods. Then he picks himself back up to say, "Thank you again for all you did. I don't know who else we could have trusted."

"It was the least I could do," Elsze states simply. Then she steps out of the rows of benches. "But here, I should let you both sit."

I see my opportunity. I guide Svarik to the bench and let him feel his way to his seat. Then I turn to Elsze and say, "Would you mind terribly if I sat on the outside? I always prefer being close to the aisle."

Elsze gives a stiff shrug. "I don't mind."

But despite the apathetic assent, I catch a slight satisfaction in her face as she sits down next to Svarik on the padded bench. I wonder if her earlier suspicion had more to do with jealousy than distrust. Maybe Svarik's chances are not so poor as he thinks. Either way, I plan on informing Tyron of my contribution to his work.

"So what is your next step?" Elsze asks quietly, still glancing around. "Surely if he is already making such open moves, then you don't have much time before he takes more drastic measures." She doesn't have to say Talsk's name for us to understand who she means.

"Agreed. I need to find a way to convince several nobles at once. Visiting one house at a time has proved effective but slow." Svarik adjusts his collar with his free hand.

"What if you held a dance or some other formal function?" Elsze suggests.

Svarik shakes his head. "Our borrowed house doesn't have a hall large enough."

"Hmm." Elsze pauses as a well-dressed couple passes us from the aisle. Then she asks, "What of the Grand Inn in the city square? They don't have a dance hall, but it's become quite fashionable to host a luncheon or tea there."

"That's a good idea," Svarik muses. "But I would still have to figure out how to convince such a crowd."

"What's there to figure out? Just do what you have done thus far." Elsze's blunt attitude reminds me of Tirzah, even down to the way she squares her shoulders.

"You mean appeal to old alliances with my father?" Svarik remarks under his breath.

Elsze casts him a look. "You really think that all of these nobles would risk their lives over the memory of someone who's been gone for ten years?" She seems to realize the harshness of her own words and softens when she goes on. "Your father was well loved, but he can't save anyone from Talsk. Those who take up your cause are doing so because you are the one leading."

Svarik is quiet when he says, "Then let us hope I do not let them down."

"I don't have to hope," Elsze replies firmly. "No matter how this goes, I know that you will do right by your countrymen."

The declaration leaves me feeling like an intruder on a personal moment. And yet I can't help but admire Elszebet's confidence. From her vantage, Svarik did nothing for ten years—and still she puts such faith in him.

"What?" Elsze asks, now studying Svarik.

He must have made some face that I missed.

"Nothing," he answers a touch too quickly.

"Oh, come on, what is it?" Elsze prods his arm.

I barely catch what Svarik says. "Have I ever told you that you have the most beautiful voice?"

Elsze's entire face goes crimson. She glances over her shoulder and I scramble to pretend that I've been looking elsewhere the whole time.

"No, you haven't," she mumbles shortly before promptly turning the subject.

She doesn't have to keep up the small talk for long before the faint sound of instruments echoes through the hall and silences all conversation.

"Good evening, Noblemen and Noblewomen of Ilske," a herald calls from somewhere in the front as the crowd takes their seats. "The famous singers of Estarvos Hall are eager and ready to entertain. But before they begin, they and their benefactors wish to give special thanks to one particularly esteemed guest: our Grand Va' Kied himself, Udeneran Talsk."

From a balcony on the other side of the hall, a caped figure gets to his feet and raises a gloved hand in acknowledgment. Recognition clicks and disgust rises with it.

"Perhaps this concert is not worth staying for," I murmur, standing with the crowd as they rise to give salute. I'd always supposed that Talsk had someone watching Svarik's house, and yet I hadn't thought Talsk would take it upon himself to come personally.

"I'm staying." Svarik's reply is firm. "I refuse to be chased off by him ever again." He is quieter as we all take our seats. "But Elsze, it wouldn't be good for him to see you with me."

Elsze huffs. "As if he doesn't know already. I'm staying too."

Svarik says nothing more, but I feel again to make sure my talon dagger is reachable beneath the folds of my dress.

The herald finishes his announcements and the singers take their place at the front of the hall. For a moment, there is only the hush of expectation. Then a strummed instrument casts notes across the silence in handfuls that float over the audience. One voice joins, then another, until the woven layers of harmony fill every chink and crevice of the stone chamber.

On some other day, I might have been swept away by the glorious sound. But today I am thinking of Tyron and how much he would have loved this. I remember days on the ship when I could always find him by the sound of him humming a tune while he worked. Does Litash have halls like this one? The thought of him missing out on such a thing—and all because of someone as low and base as Talsk—only adds to my growing ire.

I seethe through the entirety of the performance. The only distraction I allow is to check our surroundings for Talsk's men. I wait through the songs, the applause, an encore, and more applause. I'm all too ready when Svarik collects his cane and stands.

He clears his throat and says, "Let's meet him head on then, shall we?"

When the hall is a little clearer, I step out of the row and let him and Elsze lead the way.

We take our time as we make our way back to the vestibule. We exchange a few greetings, a few snippets of conversation, but little more. We have just reached the stairwell when I hear the heavy, armored steps descending. The crowd makes room as two bodyguards step down. Then comes Talsk, straightening his short cape as he searches the crowd. I see his gaze lock onto Svarik.

"Why, hello there, Cousin!" Talsk calls as we approach. There is a certain brittleness to his usual bravado. "Fancy meeting you here."

The conversation around us lowers a notch.

"I suppose you know where to find me any time you fancy," Svarik returns flatly.

My attention is drawn the man who stands behind Talsk. He wears an Arvenish overcoat, but his attire beneath is reminiscent of countries further north. His stance is more relaxed and observant than that of the bodyguards at strict attention. It is the slight hum of his Gifting that confirms my suspicions: He is one of the Hunters.

Talsk chooses that moment to recognize me. "Why, Lady Arhys, how nice to see you again."

I curtsy, grinding my teeth as I fake a smile. Best to play dumb for now. "And you as well, Your Highness."

"I'm glad you were able to come see an Arvenish performance," Talsk says, gaze now flicking back towards Svarik and Elsze. "Many of the foreigners who make it as far as Ilske do so just to hear our singers."

"Oh, I quite understand why. The experience is unmatched." I give just the right show of awe.

Elsze jumps in then, speaking in her usual blunt fashion. "I didn't realize that you also enjoy music, Your Highness."

Talsk's smile is thin. "Who could possibly do without? Although, that does make me realize," he lets the sentence drag out. "Aren't you missing a companion? Where is the Litashian prince on this fine evening?"

I am struck by the sudden temptation to send him face first into the nearest wall—not even the thought of the Drogan Hunter bothers me.

"Prince Tyron was feeling unwell after supper and opted to stay home," Svarik replies evenly.

Talsk shakes his head and declares, "What a shame." Then he holds out one hand to me. "Well, let's not block off the whole vestibule, shall we? Allow me to walk out with you."

Svarik accepts with a nod, meaning I have to take Talsk's arm.

I'd rather break it. It would be so *easy*. Just a firm grip around the wrist, one hard twist to get him on his knees, and then....

We reclaim our coats and gloves from the waiting staff and head out into the frigid night air. Rows of glass lamps line both sides of the stairway, illuminating the steps and the waiting carriage below. The white Tskecz cat marks the coach door.

"I suppose this is where we part ways," Talsk says.

He starts to reach for my hand as if to kiss it, so I quickly drop into a curtsy. He makes an awkward recovery by bowing his head.

Then he turns towards Svarik and Elsze. His voice is a poor imitation of friendliness as he speaks. "Do watch your step, Cousin. I would hate for any of your other companions to end up...unwell."

Svarik looks calmer than I feel. "Not everyone is afraid of a fall or two, Cousin. There is no need to worry about me."

Talsk's eyes narrow and his voice drops. "I'll keep that in mind."

He swivels on the stair and descends to his waiting coach, followed by his guards. The Hunter, still watching the crowd filter out of the hall, takes longer. I try to ignore the way his gaze lingers in our direction.

"Well, Elsze, would you like a ride home?" Svarik asks suddenly. "Perhaps being unaccompanied is not a good idea this evening."

"Perhaps not," Elsze replies slowly.

Speaking of unaccompanied, I hope that Talsk was content with simply interrupting our evening and left Tyron and Tirzah alone.

I clear my throat. "I think I see our coach. Why don't we walk to meet it?"

Tyron

"Are you cheating?"

"How could I possibly cheat at checkers?"

Tirzah grumbles as she clears the board of her sixth defeat in a row. "If anyone could find a way, I'm sure it would be you."

"I'm not sure whether or not that's a compliment." I reach to help her, but Tirzah swats away my hand.

"And I'm not sure whether or not you should really be talking this much," she retorts. "I have a feeling Rhy wouldn't be pleased."

I sit back against my pillows. She and Svarik have been gone for almost two hours. "I'm beginning to think that Rhy believes Humans are made of glass."

These past few days, she hasn't even let me speak beyond a few sentences to describe symptoms. It's frustrating when all I keep thinking of is that afternoon when I'd scared her. I can recall the way she'd sat there with folded hands and rigid shoulders as she spoke of someone else who had tried to help them. But when I try to bring it up, she only tells me the same thing: wait.

"I think that has more to do with being you than with being Human," Tirzah says as she begins to set the chips back in their rows.

I study her, trying to figure out what she means. Is she just referencing my penchant of getting myself in trouble? Or perhaps my apparent inability to be of much use when Rhioa is around? Or...could she mean that Rhioa really is somewhat attached? Before I can ask, a knock comes from the door to the other room of my borrowed chambers.

Tirzah frowns as she gets to her feet. "I told the staff not to bother us unless necessary," she mumbles. She pulls back one of the curtains briefly and I see her scan the exterior yard before exiting the room.

There is a brief exchange of muted voices that, despite my straining, I don't catch. Then Tirzah returns, expression even more serious than usual. "They say there's a visitor downstairs that refuses to leave. Single traveler on horseback—wouldn't give his name." She's checking outside the window again when she adds, "Apparently he is specifically asking for you."

I try to process the unexpected information. If Talsk had sent someone, there would be more than one person and I doubt they'd bother knocking. But who would visit at this hour? Only someone who couldn't risk coming in daylight. Perhaps that is also the reason they came on horseback, not in a coach. For someone to take such precautions means that they must be under scrutiny from Talsk.

"Can you help me into the other room?" I ask.

Tirzah narrows her eyes and opens her mouth to argue.

I run through my logic quickly. "Clearly, they are afraid, or they would have come openly. And clearly, they must have something important, or they wouldn't have come when they're afraid." I glance towards the other room. "Besides, should we need to escape, we have much easier options from the other room."

The last point seems to win her over. "Fine. But if Rhy gets angry at me, I'm telling her that this was all your doing."

"Fair enough."

It takes an embarrassing amount of effort to get out of bed and all the way to the settee in the adjoining room—even with Tirzah's help. My embarrassment is only furthered by my attire. I suppose it could be worse; the tunic and the loose nightwear trousers that are common in Arvenir are better than the simple nightshirt most Litashians opt for. Still, I'm glad when Tirzah fetches a jacket from the wardrobe for me before calling to the maid, "You may send him up."

Tirzah sets a blanket beside me then takes the chair next to mine as I pull the jacket over my shoulders. My arm and ribs hurt enough from walking that I know better than to try and loosen my sling to pull on the sleeves. Instead I take the spare minutes to try and steady my breathing, hoping to ease the sharp ache.

Tirzah, on the other hand, seems to become more rigid. I note her one hand that rests close to her hidden dagger.

Footsteps echo in the hall and the maid knocks twice before entering. "Here he is, my lady."

"Thank you," Tirzah replies; I watch as a cloaked figure enters behind the maid. "You may be dismissed."

Only when the maid is gone does the figure step forward towards me and push back his deep hood so that the firelight reaches his face.

...Mikaud Lenstativ?

"Ah, so you survived, then." He looks me up and down.

"I did," I reply slowly. "But you'll have to excuse me not standing to greet you." I turn my head. "Madam Tahra, allow me to introduce you to the Speaker of the Assembly, Mikaud Lenstativ."

Tirzah's gaze darts from me to Lenstativ. She does not offer a greeting.

"To what do I owe this unexpected visit?" I ask, gesturing to the settee across from me.

Lenstativ steps forward to take a seat, but I see him watching Tirzah. "A few matters of business," he replies. Looking back towards me, he adds, "Perhaps not matters for delicate company."

I wonder how hard Tirzah is trying to keep from rolling her eyes

"Madam Tahra is of a strong enough constitution for conversation, I assure you." I keep my tone dry.

Lenstativ takes one last, long look at Tirzah before finally sitting down. He pulls off his gloves and sets them on the side table but doesn't bother to remove his cloak.

He doesn't get a single word out before there are voices in the hallway. "And you let him in? How long has he been in there? What do you mean, you don't even know who it is?!"

I hope that Rhioa has the sense to not come in waving a sword. But hearing the rising pitch of her voice, my hopes are not very high.

"It would seem my friends have returned from their outing," I murmur, glancing towards Tirzah.

Lenstativ appears unperturbed. "Perfect timing, then."

The door bursts open and Rhioa storms in, cloak and skirts whirling with the motion. Her face is fixed in the same dangerous intensity I'd seen the night she'd rescued me. She'd looked like some specter then, her white dress splattered with crimson as her dagger dripped the same color onto the barn floor. This probably isn't the best time to repeat that dramatic entrance.

"Lady Arhys, you're just in time." I give a polite smile, trying to get my silent point across. "We have a rather esteemed guest who dropped in while you were gone. Allow me to introduce you to the Speaker of the Assembly, Mikaud Lenstativ."

Lenstativ gets to his feet, giving the customary bow. "You are the lady from Beclian, are you not?"

Rhioa looks him up and down with narrowed eyes before replying sharply, "I am." She gives no curtsy.

"Did you say 'Lenstativ'?" Svarik's question comes through the doorway just as he does.

"That he did," Lenstativ replies as he sits back down. "With Talsk off to the concert hall for the evening, I thought this might be a good time for us to conduct some business."

Wait. Talsk was at the concert hall? At the same time that Svarik and Rhioa were there? I look to the latter, but she's still glaring at Lenstativ.

"What business could be so urgent that you had to drag a sick man from his bed instead of waiting downstairs?" Svarik asks as he reaches us. His tone is almost *too* even, as if it takes him effort to control.

Lenstativ takes no affront. "He is part of it; I came to see if he was still alive."

There is a pause as Svarik feels his way to a seat. Rhioa is slow to follow his example and, even after she has taken the last chair, sits on the very edge as if ready to spring up at any moment. She looks away from Lenstativ only long enough to examine me. I have a feeling that I will be getting an earful for this.

Svarik clears his throat. "You knew of what happened?"

"More than that, I knew it was going to happen." Lenstativ speaks bluntly, putting on no airs. I notice how he still carries all of the tension that he'd worn during the hunt. "I have my sources. And now that I've seen that you at least have some means to stand up to Talsk, I'm willing to offer you a deal on all of that information."

This is...sudden. By the total lack of reaction around the room, I am not the only one who finds it such.

"You have an interesting sense of timing, Speaker Lenstativ." Rhioa's tone is hard and thin, a brittle overlay to her anger. "You come at night without any announcement like some sneak thief, claiming to have known of a threat to our friend—a friend who was nearly killed in the incident you apparently could have warned us of. And then you want to strike a deal on information you supposedly have?" She tilts her head, a motion that reminds me of the moment right before she'd killed those thugs. Maybe I should cut in.... "I'm not sure that you've given us any reason to trust you or your sources. For all we know, this could be your way of getting information to bring straight back to Talsk."

Lenstativ raises one brow as if mildly surprised, yet he does seem the least bit concerned by Rhioa's accusations. "If you want to understand my timing, I'm afraid you'll have to go a bit further back. See, when you lot arrived in Ilske, I was under the same impression as the Va' Kied—that the Prince Tyron must be using the count for his connections to the throne." He nods to me. "Then I met you on the hunt. I'd heard a few things, but nothing quite clicked until I saw the way you interacted with Talsk. You clearly loathed him, and not in the manner of a man who views another as competition. You refused to play any of his games and wouldn't even claim to speak on Svarik's behalf. So, I decided to do some digging."

I note that while Rhioa's jaw is still clenched, she seems to buy Lenstativ's story thus far. Svarik is harder to read. He remains perfectly still as he listens.

"Information is my responsibility. Talsk expects me to be knowledgeable regarding every nobleman and their situation, as well as how best to correct any behavior which Talsk does not approve of." Lenstativ's explanation continues as my dislike of him grows. "It didn't take much investigation for me to realize how many nobles you had already spoken with. Certainly not enough for an Assembly majority, but enough for me to realize you were serious."

"I still don't see what that has to do with Prince Tyron being abducted and beaten half to death," Rhioa says flatly.

Lenstativ looks directly at her. "Talsk ordered it because he thought the prince had information on some of Talsk's newest enemies. I was the one tasked with finding out how and where it should be done."

I try to make eye contact with Rhioa, if only to will the thought into her head: *Please don't kill him. We might need him.*

"I supposed that it would be a good test. If you all didn't have what it took to get through one of Talsk's 'arranged accidents,' then I would know you could never get as far as toppling him." Lenstativ's attention shifts to Svarik. "There have been others who have tried and met quicker ends."

Rhioa is gripping the rim of her chair, presumably—or perhaps, hopefully—in an effort to remain on it.

I clear my throat. "Perhaps we have passed your little test and survived Talsk. But you still seem too afraid of him to be able to say the same. After all, you've taken such precautions: waiting until he was occupied, coming after dark, taking a single horse, and not even giving your name to the staff."

"And as convenient as it is that we have proven ourselves to you," Svarik now breaks in. "Lady Arhys is right: You have yet to prove yourself to us. I have no reason, nor inclination, to trust you. Wasn't it Talsk who gave you your coveted position to begin with?"

Lenstativ sucks in his cheeks. "Talsk and I had what was supposed to be a simple deal," he says tautly. "If I backed his claim to the throne and helped with a few...other matters, he would ensure that I received the position of Speaker." The hand on the armrest of his chair is gripping his gloves with a vengeance. "Yes, I realize that such a deal puts me in a bad light. But you don't understand: I had so many ideas, so many changes that could bring about so much good. And nobody cared—I wasn't even allowed in the building simply because I had no land to my name." His jaw sets. "I thought that as Speaker, that would change. But then Talsk began asking favors." He scoffs. "Favors that I soon tired of, so he threatened to reveal the things I'd done to get my position."

If nothing else, Lenstativ has a special talent to be able to get an entire room angry. It is hard to feel any sympathy for someone who has brought around his own situation and yet refuses to take fault for it. Especially when he has so little consideration for what he has wrought on others.

"Before you say that I do not understand, remember who you are talking to." Svarik's voice is low, each word enunciated to a sharp point. "In case you have forgotten, I was tossed out of my home and stripped of my title because I was deemed 'unfit to serve'—despite the fact that I had spent my entire life preparing for the role."

By the look on his face, even Lenstativ has to acknowledge this misstep.

Svarik goes on. "And to make sure that we are clear, I am not here to make good on any of my cousin's deals. I have come to put an end to his methods—not use them."

"I am not asking for my position," Lenstativ replies tersely. "But I would like to make it through this with my life and without getting thrown in some rank little cell for the rest of it. And seeing as the only thing I have to offer in return is information, that is what I came to barter."

I suppose that, being so involved in Talsk's underhanded dealings, Lenstativ has a healthy enough fear of being on the wrong side. If he is genuine in this, then he has likely calculated all of the risks and found Svarik the safer bet. Perhaps this could be in our favor.

Svarik remains quite still, the firelight casting shadows over his pensive expression. He is quiet when he says, "Should you hold up your end of the deal, I am willing to grant you full pardon when this is over. But before I make such a promise, I think it only fair that I have my chance to put you to the test. After all, we passed yours."

Lenstativ glances to Rhioa then me before refocusing on Svarik. "Fine. What do you want me to do?"

"Tell me why Talsk is preparing for war," Svarik replies calmly.

From the corner of my eye, I watch Rhioa. She gives no reaction.

"Shortly after he came into power, Talsk was approached by a representative from a foreign nation known as the Myrandi," Lenstativ begins, leaning back in his chair. "A very quiet deal was made that gave this nation access to a region in the far south known as the Iron Door."

Myrandi.... That's what Talsk's thugs had kept asking about. Then Rhioa had showed up and, right before killing them all, announced she was one.

"As in, the ancient ruins?" Svarik interjects.

"Yes," Lenstativ nods. "I guess they had an interest in the site and its lore. I don't know anything more because Talsk didn't care what they did—so long as they paid well for the privilege."

Rhioa hasn't moved, but I catch Tirzah's subtle shift.

"As best as I know, the Myrandi wanted to bring in some kind of equipment," Lenstativ makes a loose gesture with one hand. "Talsk got greedy and asked too high a price. When the Myrandi refused, he decided to send a message by killing their courier."

It's always hard to read Rhioa in front of others, and it's even harder now with her being so fixated on Lenstativ.

He doesn't seem to notice. "Only, the courier apparently turned into some kind of Dragon and killed twelve of Talsk's soldiers before flying off. Now Talsk is convinced that an army of Dragon-folk could appear on the horizon any day now."

Svarik collects himself, as if trying to process the unusual tale. "How long ago was this?"

"About four months. Talsk believes they are simply waiting out the winter," Lenstativ answers. "Hence why he has been so busy preparing. He hired these people from the north who call themselves 'Drogan Hunters' and has done everything to their recommendations. Our engineers are designing their weapons, our strategists defer to their experience, and even some of our troops and scouts have been made answerable to them."

Hunters.... Was the head thug from the barn one of those? He had been the one leading the questioning.

One finger tapping the arm of his chair, Svarik addresses me. "Is this what those thugs were asking you about, Tyron?"

I hesitate, catching Rhioa's gaze. She gives that slight up-and-down signal with one finger, so I reply, "I believe so. They kept asking about the Myrandi and who my contact was. At the time, I had no idea what they meant, but it all lines up with Speaker Lenstativ's story."

Lenstativ nods to me as if in thanks, but I do not acknowledge him. I said what I did purely to help Svarik.

"Hm." Svarik's tapping stills and he takes a breath. "Well then, Speaker, it seems you've passed the only test we have. What do you have to offer that will help us?"

"The Archduke Grimvold," Lenstativ replies.

The name vaguely rings a bell. Rhioa looks almost confused while Svarik sounds skeptical.

"...Grimvold? But he hated my father. He wasn't even polite enough to keep the fact to himself. How could he possibly help us?"

"He may have disliked your father, but Talsk has tromped on his toes one too many times. I have...information there which you might find useful." Lenstativ moves on, explaining, "And his purpose is twofold. First, if you can convince him, you'd win yourself a good percentage of the Assembly just from that."

Svarik mutters, "Or fail to convince and have him turn me right over to Talsk."

Lenstativ charges on. "Second, if you win him over, you have a path to Kstoren."

Wait, Kstoren? As in, the Grand Officer?

"What does Grimvold have on Kstoren?" Svarik asks, visibly bewildered.

For the first time since I've met him, Mikaud Lenstativ smiles. "Everything: Kstoren married his beloved daughter."

"...Ah. I must have missed that." Svarik clears his throat.

"Kstoren and Grimvold share that same old-fashioned sense of patriotism and duty." Lenstativ doesn't bother to hide his derision. "And since Kstoren has such respect for his father-in-law, it makes Grimvold about the only person who can get anything through Kstoren's thick skull."

I gather that Lenstativ and Kstoren do not quite get along. "And if we can convince Kstoren, we take Talsk's army away from him."

"Exactly." Lenstativ gestures my way.

"Simple as that," Svarik says dryly.

Lenstativ's reply is blunt. "Much simpler than taking on the whole army of Arvenir by yourself."

Svarik lets out a long breath. "Perhaps. Perhaps not. I suppose we'll see."

CHAPTER 17

Rhioa

Lenstativ does not stay long, but he still manages to outstay his welcome. It doesn't help that, as he is getting to his feet and gathering his gloves, he says, "Just make sure to watch your backs. Talsk is more spooked than a skittish horse since you managed to kill that Hunter." He addresses Tyron. "He's tasked me with finding out whether or not you had help that night, but I think he's still operating under the suspicion that you are Myrandi—or at least working for them."

Tyron's wry expression is somewhat marred by the bruise that covers half his face. "I'm afraid he'd be quite disappointed to learn that I'm nothing more than what I say I am."

"Well, if I can convince him of that, then perhaps I can convince him that killing you has too many repercussions." Lenstativ seems to think on this. "After all, if he's scared of the Myrandi, a fear of Litashians shouldn't be too hard to foster."

I swear it, if Talsk so much as *looks* at Tyron again....

Svarik gets up, clearing his throat and gathering his cane as he says, "Allow me to walk you back to the door."

Lenstativ takes the hint, bowing his head to Tyron and then to me and Tirzah before heading for the hallway. Svarik is close behind.

I make brief eye contact with Tirzah and she gets up to follow them out. Whether he's telling the truth or not, I don't trust Lenstativ even as far as the front door. It's the same reason I wait for their footsteps to recede before addressing Tyron.

But Tyron has no such inhibitions. "Talsk was there?" he asks in the trade language as soon as the door has shut.

I frown, my temper ebbing. He already sounds winded; I suspect he's been sitting up for too long. But he looks concerned enough that I also switch to the trade language and answer, "Yes. We stayed through the whole performance anyway and ran into him only briefly afterwards. He made his veiled little threats, Svarik stood his ground, and that was that."

Tyron dwells on this a moment. "Talsk must be getting desperate," he muses. He starts to shake his head, then stops when the action seems to pain him. "How else would his Speaker find the guts to come to Svarik?"

"Then we can take that desperation as a good sign." I get to my feet, presuming that the conversation is done and Tyron will need help getting back to his bed.

"And as a warning," Tyron adds quietly. Then he lets out a breath. "I think it's time we had that conversation, Rhy. The stakes are higher now. If nothing else, I need to at least know what Talsk knows."

I swallow. Instinct makes me glance towards the closed door—whether out of fear of being overheard or for hope of escape, I'm not sure. I'd known this moment would come soon, yet I can't help but hesitate a few seconds more before replying. "Alright. But I'm going to do the evening check so that you can go right back to bed afterwards."

As usual, he looks somewhere between reluctant and embarrassed. "Alright," he acquiesces.

I head for the bedroom, scooping up the vials and jars and bandaging that litter Tyron's nightstand. I deposit these back on the tray they'd once been organized on and carry it back into the other room. With the tray balanced on one hand, I pull the little book table closer to the settee. I set the tray there before sitting down across from Tyron.

"Let's start with your hand," I instruct.

With a slight sigh, he holds out the one hand that isn't bound in a sling. I steel myself as I undo the bandaging around his wrist and begin. "As you know by now, my sister and I are Myrandi. You may know of us by another name: Drogans."

A glance upwards shows no more than a vague recognition in his expression.

"Many think we are Dragon-shifters, but that is not so. We are both fully Human and fully Dragon and can move at will between either." I tip his wrist and inspect the cut that wraps around it. Then I reach for the jar of ointment on the tray. "We were created to be Guards—protectors of the world. But that was a long time ago. There were wars among us, all sorts of infighting, and others who walked away from the responsibility altogether. Some even stifled their Dragon side until all they had left was the Human. And like Humans, they began to age and were lost to time." I apply the ointment as gently as I can to the laceration.

"So if your people are no longer guards, what are they?" Tyron asks, watching me work.

"Mostly, we are outcasts. Whether out of fear of our power or resentment of what they blame us for, few races would have anything to do with ours. So we withdrew to our own borders to let them forget about us. But it seems that hiding only made us something worth hunting. The less they understood us, the more scared of us they became." I finish with the ointment and wipe my hands clean.

Tyron's countenance is both somber and sympathetic. He does not interrupt me as I continue.

I put the cap back over the ointment and make sure it's sealed tight as I explain, "The man who led those thugs—the one with the armor—was a Drogan Hunter. There are many different kinds from many different countries, but they all have the same goal: to kill my people. Thankfully, they are little more than prize seekers and bounty hunters. With too few of them and too much rivalry between them, they could never unify in enough numbers to instigate a war. They settle for picking off any of us that they find outside our borders."

Now Tyron's brow furrows in a mixture of horror and revulsion. "That is *disgusting.*"

It is somehow a relief to hear him say that. "It is what we live with," I reply. "Which is why our ruler, Ovok, though he carries out the ancient role of protectorate of Eatris, does so quietly." I turn back to the tray and pick out a fresh length of bandaging. "He has a select number of us that he uses to carry out his orders. He keeps countries in check, dictators in line, and replaces both if need be. But all without drawing notice so that none can accuse us—nothing is ever connected back to the Myrandi." I tuck the end of the bandage under his wrist and begin to wrap it.

"And you were given no choice but to be one of these 'select number,'" Tyron guesses.

I do not look up. "As Ovok's daughter, there was no escaping it."

Tyron pulls his arm out of my grasp and I look up to see his shock. "You're telling me that your own *father* is the one doing this to you?"

I take his hand again, stubbornly finishing my bandaging instead of meeting his gaze. "Perhaps 'doing' is too active a term," I murmur. My throat feels thick and I have to force the words out. "He more of 'lets' it happen. My mother was the one who started it all." I don't need to look up to know his horror has only doubled. "For the first years of our lives, Tirzah and I were quite normal. We barely saw anything of our mother, and our father was often busy, so we spent most of our time with others in the community. But among the Myrandi, this is not unusual. Our childhood is so long and children so rare that all adults are expected to help raise them." I tug carefully on the bandage to make sure it's at the proper tension before tucking in the end. "We were in our forties—around eleven or twelve years by your race's comparison—when my mother decided it was time Tirzah and I should start our training."

My tightening throat makes it hard to even swallow and I falter. I have never told anyone this. Tirzah was the only person I ever could, and we had lived it together; it was better left unspoken.

Tyron's hand turns and wraps around mine, squeezing it in quiet assurance.

The gesture makes my eyes well and I look back at my tray, fumbling for the salve. I suck in enough air to continue, "Our mother was very particular about how she wanted things done. And she was very creative with punishments if we did not meet her standards. She claimed she wanted us to be able to withstand anything that we were able to do to others. And she found out very quickly that she could get one of us to cooperate by threatening the other." I turn his wrist back over and push his sleeve up to uncover some of the bruising there.

"I have told you before that, among my people, twins are considered two halves of a single whole. This is because one tends to take on more Dragon-like characteristics, and the other more Human ones. Tirzah takes after the Dragon; she is quicker, stronger, more instinctive. And she was honed into a weapon. She can kill with practically anything—or nothing at all." I start to apply the salve to the bruise. "I take after the Human and thus can more easily establish rapport with them. I was drilled on different forms of deception, of how to assume identities, how to identify and exploit weaknesses." I keep my eyes fixed on his arm as I say, "We went along with it until Mother started bringing in real people for us to practice on. But she quickly stamped that little rebellion out of us."

"And your father did nothing? All those people who helped raise you did nothing?" Tyron asks, still audibly aghast.

I have to press my lips together to keep them from trembling. I take up the salve again and this time motion for him to hold still. I put one hand to his stubbled jaw to keep him steady, using the other to apply the salve to the side of his face. "We used to go through each day hoping that someone would notice— that someone would help us. At first..." My voice cracks and I swallow hard before resuming. "...at first, I think they were simply too afraid. But then I began to notice the sideways glances. The looks of disgust." The one green eye that isn't swollen shut is focused on me. "Parents would cross the street so that their children would not have to walk near us. They knew, we knew, and it was easier for everyone to pretend we were doing it by choice."

"Oh, Rhy...." His tone is so soft.

"And my father just...never said a word. He was the only one who could have put a stop to it all, and he just let it all happen." I have to turn away again with the pretense of putting away the salve and wiping the excess off my hands. They're shaking too badly for me to attempt any more bandaging right now, so I fold them and let them sit in my lap. I keep my gaze fastened on them, toying with my puzzle ring as I recount the last bit of my tale.

"We had only done two or three missions when Tirzah and I knew we couldn't bear it any longer. We decided to run away." It may have been a hundred years ago, but the memory still makes it hard to breathe. "We, um, we made it a good seven months. Long enough time for us to hope, anyway. But we were finally discovered and dragged back. My mother, she...." I swallow again and grip my hands as tightly as I can. "She was much like your brother, Euracia. We never saw her angry. Disappointed, perhaps, but usually she was enjoying her work. Until that day they brought us back." I close my eyes as if it would keep me from seeing it all over again. "She was in a rage. She blamed me, saying I was the one who must have planned it all. She chained us up and..." My breath catches and I feel Tyron's hand on my arm. The warmth of his presence is somehow enough comfort for me to spit it out: "...I thought she was going to kill me. She might have if no one had intervened."

I open my eyes, staring at my lap and seeing nothing. "His name was Kassander Knyte. He was once a friend of my father's. While he also kept up the old responsibilities of the Guards, he differed with my father when it came to his methods. Tirzah and I had regarded him as an uncle of sorts but hadn't seen him since we were children." I shiver. "He must have come to visit my father and then heard the screaming. There was a fight, him and my mother, and," I start to shake my head. "I couldn't even do anything. I couldn't even get myself free. By the time Father had arrived and reined Mother in, she'd already fatally injured Kassander." Tyron's hand remains on my arm, steadying me. "We never knew exactly what happened. Tirzah and I were carried off to the healers and kept there for days. By the time we returned home, we were told that our mother had been locked up. No one said a word about Kassander." I feel cold as I finish, "But you see, Myrandi are not taken out so easily. To kill us, you must kill both Dragon and Human. My best guess is that after his first form was killed, my father made sure that someone else finished the job."

For a while, there is no sound besides the crackling fire in the nearby hearth. Then Tyron says, "So this is why you are so afraid to leave. And this is why you tried to get me to stay in Krysophera."

Feeling numb, I nod.

He is even quieter when he asks, "What happened after your recoveries?"

"For a time, nothing," I reply, eyes now glued to the fabric of the settee— anywhere but Tyron. "We-we sort of held our breath and hoped it would stay that way. Then one day we received orders. It was an easy job, in and out—no casualties. And yet," I let out a shuddering breath. "We knew. The missions became steadier, longer, more...complicated. We have been doing them ever since."

Finally, I look up. Tyron's face, bruised and battered as it is, holds many things: anger, sorrow, empathy. His hand remains on my arm in a quiet sort of support as he speaks. "No one deserves to live this way, Rhy. I know you are afraid of endangering anyone else, but this cannot be allowed to continue."

"I'm not sure it can change." I wish I did not have to say this part. I wish I could keep his good opinion. "Not all of my missions are so ethical as this one. I...I have done things to people—*horrible* things, Tyron. If you thought your brother was so awful for—"

"—Rhioa. My brother is reprehensible because he *enjoys* the suffering of others. It is his very nature. Do you enjoy hurting others?" His gaze is locked on mine.

"What? No." I shudder again.

"Why do you do it, then?" Tyron persists.

"Because if I don't, or if I fail, they have Tirzah. They have hurt her before." Why must he make me say it?

Tyron tilts his head. "Don't you see it, then? You have spent your life trying to make the best of your circumstances. I do not know anyone except the most heartless who could abandon their own sister to torture simply to secure their own freedom. Why do you blame yourself for not being able to do so?"

I want to look away from him, his features brimming with that open kindness. He makes it all sound so simple—hopeful, even. "It does not change the harm I have done. I cannot undo the lives I've ruined," I remind myself as much as I do him.

"Perhaps not," he concedes. "But why must past wrongs keep you from doing good in the future?"

"I..." I guess I don't know. It just seems wrong, fraudulent even, as if goodness would be nothing more than another charade for me to act out. "I suppose it doesn't even matter so long as Tirzah and I are still under our father."

Tyron's whole demeanor shifts. That openness turns to something more intense, the hope to something more resolved. "Then that is what needs to change. When this is done and Svarik is crowned, we go to see your father."

"No," I shake my head, pulling away from him. "No, you don't understand. Ovok is the Lord of the Myrandi, with every resource at his disposal. Where I am susceptible to Gifting, he carries one of the old Drogan blades that renders him immune. He has many more trained vassals like me—some more powerful. And he's over *two thousand* years old; not even you could hope to outsmart him."

Tyron is unfazed. "We will find a way."

Why is he so stubborn?! "Tyron—"

"—Rhy, please. Trust me." His voice is soft again, a salve to my rising fears. "You can't just ship me off to Krysophera again. I understand why you are frightened—I really do. And I promise you this: I will do my utmost to make sure that you, your sister, and myself all make it out of this."

I swallow. I want to trust him. I really do. But how can anyone go up against my father and survive? "I can't watch you die," I say, voice now hoarse.

"And I can't watch you wither away in the cage that your father has left you in," Tyron replies. He reaches out again, this time taking my hand. "We will do it together—all three of us. We will find a way."

He doesn't even understand what he's taking on. How can I let him promise his help? But I know him well enough by now to know that he will not let this go, not even when he's barely well enough to stand. I decide that this battle will have to wait for another day. So I simply whisper, "Alright."

That incessant hope lights up his face and he squeezes my hand before releasing it.

I can't help but sit and watch him. I don't understand him. Here he is, all beaten up and yet still making it his mission to help *me*. Why is he so willing to risk his life for me and Tirzah when he won't gain a thing in return? How can he give and give when he has nothing?

"What is it?" Tyron asks, concern furrowing his brow.

Suddenly conscious of the fact that I've been staring, I try to find somewhere else to look. My gaze catches on the one arm that rests in his sling. "Nothing. How is your arm and shoulder?"

Tyron

I shift in my seat, making sure not to grimace with the effort. I'm certain Rhioa is still watching me out of the corner of her eye. It had taken so much coaxing for her and Svarik to let me come. The last thing I want is to get all the way there and be made to wait in the sleigh. After nearly a week in bed, I think I've done enough waiting for the next five years.

At least riding in a sleigh is not nearly so bad as the jolting of a carriage. We're nearly to the Archduke Grimvold's estate, but even these few hours from Ilske have left me sore. Svarik had explained that the close proximity of his land to the capital denotes the archduke's high status. And apparently his tendency to remain at this estate instead of his city home indicates his lackluster attitude towards social events. If we weren't armed with information from Lenstativ, I doubt Svarik would have ever attempted coming out here.

As we pull in, the first thing I notice about the large manor is how quiet it is. Nothing moves outside the austere, stone walls. It reminds me of the home of Svarik's mother in its stiff orderliness. The air of efficiency starts in the courtyard, which is clear despite the snow that has been falling all day. That efficiency carries on to the grooms, who are polite as they confer with our driver, and then the uniformed and courteous staff as they take our coats and usher us into an expansive parlor.

I don't miss all the widened eyes and sideways glances that are cast in my direction. One poor maid even trips over a carpet and nearly drops the coats she's carrying. I know from shaving this morning that my face is still a proper mess. The swelling has gone down enough for me to open both eyes, but the green-and-purple blotches look as sickly as the former black ones. I'd thought briefly of trying to cover it up with cosmetics, the way I used to as a child, then decided against it. Better to let Grimvold see the stakes.

For nearly half an hour, we sit sipping our tea and looking around the elegant room. We'd expected the wait since Svarik had foregone the usual letter in advance. What is harder to predict is whether or not the archduke will see us at all. Just when Svarik has begun his usual restless tapping, the door swings open. The archduke strides right in without any announcement.

He is exactly how I pictured him: tall, broad-shouldered, his hair and beard almost completely grey. The squared cut of his jacket is reminiscent of an officer's uniform. While there is no weapon at his side, he walks like someone accustomed to wearing a sword. His countenance is steely as he watches us all get to our feet. We haven't even finished bowing before he speaks.

"I didn't think you'd have the guts to come here, Count Ihail." His pale blue eyes are fixed on Svarik. His tone turns dry when he adds, "I also presumed you'd have enough manners to write first."

Svarik's squares his shoulders. "I supposed that if I did, you would not see fit to admit me. I figured that I'd have better luck catching your interest if I showed up at random."

The Archduke Grimvold's expression does not change. But then he grunts, "Well, seeing as the tactic has worked, I'll have to allow you that point." He gestures to the chairs around the parlor, signaling us to take our seats.

Rhioa, Tirzah, and myself all do so. Svarik hears us and does the same. The archduke takes his time, surveying us one by one before sitting down across from Svarik.

"So," Grimvold takes the kettle from its stand and fills the cup in front of him. "How did you come by that pretty face?" He glances towards me as he sets the kettle back.

"A little chat with some of Talsk's lackeys," I reply evenly.

Grimvold shakes his head, picking up his teacup and blowing on it. "You know, I rather miss the days when a man had to do such things himself. Then overstuffed sots like Talsk would never make it to such a rank."

An interesting response. I process it as Svarik replies, "I'd prefer an Arvenir where we hear out other opinions instead of beat or blackmail them."

"Ah, yes, the pacifist—I see that you take after your father," Grimvold shakes his head before sipping his tea.

Svarik gives a slight smile. "I'll take that as the highest form of compliment."

The archduke huffs. "Take it how you wish, but remember that Talsk is the one alive and in power—not your father."

"Yes, and how *is* that working out for you?" Rhioa's icy question catches me by surprise.

"Excuse me?" Grimvold raises grey eyebrows in her direction.

"Clearly, you found Va' Kied Ihail to be soft and weak. But how have you fared under his replacement?" Rhioa tilts her head and looks him up and down. "If I were to guess, he finds your opinions a little...old-fashioned."

Oh dear.

"Um." I clear my throat. "Lady Arhys, perhaps—"

The archduke waves a hand. "—No, no, let the lady continue. I'm curious as to what insight a foreigner could possibly offer into Arvenish affairs."

I try to make eye contact with Rhioa, but she's clearly avoiding it. I have a feeling that this is going to be like Lenstativ all over again.

"I may be a foreigner, but I still know that the archduke of the central regions is typically head of the Va' Kied's war council," Rhioa says. "I also know that, rather suddenly, you resigned that position. So either the Va' Kied decided your input was out of vogue, or you decided that he was not worth reasoning with."

"Or," Grimvold leans one elbow on the arm of his chair in the irritating manner of someone watching hired entertainment. "I retired because I have better things to do here at my estate than sipping tea with capital socialites."

Rhioa presses on. "Ah yes, your estate, famed far and wide for its fine horses. But I hear you have been less busy as of late—not more. Perhaps something to do with the recent acquisition of several horses for the Va' Kied's officers? Or maybe it's due to the commandeering of several fields and forests by the palace hunting parties." Still balancing her cup and saucer, she gives a slight shrug. "Either way, I hear your replacement on the council is half your age, with less than half of your experience."

I try not to sigh aloud. So much for being subtle about bringing up the information Lenstativ gave us.

The archduke's show of ease has grown thin. He takes another sip of his tea before saying, "If you came all this way to try and convince me to join you based on a few scraps of gossip, I'm afraid you've quite wasted your time." He shakes his head as he regards Rhioa. "Did you really think I'd revolt over a horse or two?"

"It's not about a horse—it's about a ruler who would trample even the most loyal among his ranks." Rhioa's tone turns blunt. "A ruler who would have a visiting dignitary beaten half to death."

I see Grimvold cast a quick glance towards me.

"A ruler who would have many of his own citizens killed or wrongfully imprisoned," Svarik breaks in now. "Come, Your Grace, let's be forthright: We both know what Talsk is. We both see what he's made of Arvenir. Our roads are so deteriorated that one can barely reach Ilske. Our taxes are so high that few can afford to travel anyway. And that's presuming anyone is left in the villages after his expansion of both the draft and labor crews. Even if you refuse to acknowledge his many violations of our law, there is no denying his neglect and mismanagement in every other area."

Grimvold holds up a finger. "And here is where you make your mistake. A country in disarray needs stability—loyalty—not someone going around and sowing dissension."

I see Svarik's grip tighten on the head of his cane. "How is there any loyalty in letting one's country fall into ruin? If it does not happen soon from within, it will come from without. Few of our allies will have anything to do with us anymore. Even Krysophera, which you worked so hard to establish an alliance with in my father's day, has grown tired of being continually snubbed. We are fortunate that they have not taken any action against us." The set of his shoulders softens. "But not everyone will be so forgiving as Krysophera. Talsk has made bigger enemies for himself and it will not be long before his people begin to pay for it."

The archduke swirls his tea in one hand. "You mean the 'Dragon-folk' he's always raving about?" Lenstativ had told us that this had been the exact matter that had forced Grimvold to resign. Still, the archduke manages to look decently calm as he places the cup back in his saucer. "I doubt they even exist. No one has ever seen a single shred of evidence. If you ask me, Talsk is either covering something up or is simply losing his mind."

"Does it matter?" Svarik asks. "If they are real, Talsk is about to try and go to war with *Dragons*. And if they aren't and he's using it as some excuse, then why he is still confiscating massive amounts of resources? What happens when half the country is starving before the snow has even melted?" He leans back in his seat. "And if he is a madman, well, then we are doomed all the same."

Grimvold does not respond right away. He sits there with one arm still propped up, one hand idly stroking his beard. I see his gaze flick from me, to Rhioa, then back to Svarik. He straightens and takes a breath. "Well, this has been quite the nice little presentation. I'm sure it's even gotten you a few, desperate followers who have made weak-kneed pledges to back you in an Assembly. But there are still some left in Arvenir that have a sense of duty; I will not be joining you."

Svarik straightens his shoulders. "Duty to what?"

The archduke blinks at him. "Come again?"

"You said you still have a sense of duty, but to what?" Svarik asks. "To Arvenir? To Talsk? To whoever happens to sit on the throne on any given day?"

I watch Grimvold pick up his chin, shifting from offense to defense. "To Arvenir—as she is represented by her leader. For now, that means Talsk."

"So what if Talsk continues to act in detriment to Arvenir? What if he continues to kill any who disagree with him, or enslave his own citizens, or confiscate the food and seed they need to survive? Then what? How can two conflicting interests be treated as a single entity?" Svarik shakes his head. "Perhaps 'duty' is nothing more than a way to get out of making your choice."

Although his beard hides his clenched his jaw, the vein that appears at Grimvold's temple gives his anger away. "A bold statement from one who has been running for ten years," he replies sharply.

Now he's making it personal. Perhaps Svarik has managed to reach his conscience.

"I had to face the same choice," Svarik admits, voice soft and sure. "But I have made mine. I came here to ask what you will do with yours."

Grimvold's hard eyes remain on Svarik for several seconds more before he sets down his cup and saucer. "I think it's time you leave."

Svarik hesitates. I catch the slight disappointment in his tightly pressed lips, but he does not express any of it as he gathers his cane. "Understood." He gets up. "Thank you for the tea."

Rhioa looks my way as if trying to see if I need help. Given the fact that she still looks mad enough to knock Grimvold out, I give a slight shake of my head as I slowly push myself up.

The archduke holds the parlor door for us as if ensuring our exit. What surprises me is that he then accompanies us back to the front foyer and waits with hands folded behind his back as we put on our coats. I notice the way he watches Rhioa help me with my sling, making me feel rather awkward and clumsy. But Grimvold doesn't say a word. Not until several minutes later when he announces, "Here is your sleigh."

Through the tall, narrow window panes, I can just see the horses come to a stop at the front steps.

"Then we will take our leave." Svarik removes his hat and bows his head. "Thank you for hearing our case."

Grimvold does not return the gesture. Instead he asks, "Why now? You've been in Ilske for weeks."

I watch Svarik let out a deep breath. "Because I doubt we have much time left. If Talsk is willing to attack foreign dignitaries almost openly, I doubt he will hold back much longer from quietly getting rid of his own cousin—or anyone else who dares disagree with him. Besides," he gives something like a shrug. "You and my father may have always been at odds, but he spoke well of you. Called you the 'stubbornest, most pig-headed, and most dutiful man in Arvenir.' I know the respect that others have for you, and I know that you seek to live up to that. So that's why I hoped that you might be willing to stand up to Talsk on their behalf." With one hand, he puts his hat back on before giving a sad sort of smile. "But it would seem not."

With one last farewell, Svarik turns towards the doors. The faint tapping of his cane across the foyer is suddenly conspicuous.

With a bow of my head, I follow behind. Even Rhioa manages a stone-faced curtsy, copied by Tirzah, before stepping out into the falling snow.

All the way down the steps and into the waiting sleigh, there is the vain hope that the archduke will change his mind. Even when the whole cabin lurches forward, I find myself listening for someone calling out behind us. I think the others share my sentiment for the sleigh remains quiet until the manor has faded into the bleak landscape behind us.

"That did not go as hoped," Svarik sighs.

Rhioa huffs. "Just because the archduke has no manners does not mean he should mistake yours for weakness."

I wonder again at what has so awoken her ire. Perhaps I should take it as a good sign. It seems so long ago when she wouldn't even use Svarik's given name— now she's willing to speak up in his defense.

"But he has his point," Svarik says quietly. "From what he knew of me ten years ago, he is not wrong to think me weak." He sighs again. "The bigger question now is whether he will take this to Talsk. If he agrees to testify against me, they could try me for treason and get rid of me without even breaking the law."

I turn away from the grey, windswept view beyond the sleigh window. "I don't think that that would quite fit Grimvold's rigid sense of duty. But we will still have to find some other way to get through to Kstoren."

"And quickly," Svarik murmurs.

I try to think of some encouragement, some comfort, but find nothing besides, "Well, we have made it this far. We can find our way from here."

The conversation turns to bandying about various lackluster ideas on how to proceed. It's generally agreed that Elsze's idea of hosting a tea at the Grand Inn is our best attempt to appeal to wide array of nobles at once. However, it is also agreed that such a public move will likely be the final straw for Talsk; Svarik will have to call for the Assembly there in front of the whole crowd. From there, we'll only have two days before the meeting and vote. And if that goes awry.... I look at Rhioa and Tirzah. I'm not sure what their back-up plan is, but I know better than to ask in front of Svarik.

It has been a few hours when I feel the sleigh pick up its pace. We must be close to Ilske. A check out the window reveals nothing except that the snow is coming down too heavily for me to see more than a few yards. I nearly make a comment about it, then decide against it. Tirzah has been on the verge of dozing off for the past mile and I don't want to wake her.

Then the whole sleigh jolts to the side, slamming my bad arm against the wall. I hiss in pain as Rhioa and Tirzah straighten in alert across from me.

"What was tha—"

Svarik's question is cut off by another jolt, this one tipping the sleigh precariously towards one side. A muted scream comes from outside as our pace doubles. Adrenaline spikes and I gather my Gifting, waiting for Rhioa's cue. She nods to Tirzah first and the latter opens the sleigh door before leaping clear.

Svarik recoils from the sound of the open door. I grab his shoulder with my free hand, calling, "I've got you; I've got you. Hang on—there's something out there."

I don't have tell him. From the blurred wall of white that speeds by the still open door, I hear the shriek of some animal. Wait, that's not Tirzah, is it? I don't have time to ask before a heavy thump sounds over our heads. I look up to see two large cracks in the ceiling of the sleigh, quickly followed by a set of talons that pierces the decorative woodwork. That shriek comes again at a now ear-piercing volume.

"Get Svarik out!" Rhioa yells, already half way out the door.

One hand still firmly on Svarik's shoulder, I imagine the last spot I remember seeing outside the sleigh window. Then I wrap my Gifting around Svarik and myself and tug us both away. The sleigh vanishes, replaced by the dizzying white expanse around us.

But I have made one miscalculation: our momentum. Svarik and I both go tumbling as soon as our feet hit solid ground. If I didn't have a mouthful of snow, I might have screamed as my own weight is thrown against my bad arm and sore ribs. It's only through adrenaline that I'm able to drag myself back to my feet and hurry to Svarik's side.

I wait until I'm close to announce myself in a low voice. "I'm right here." The shrieks of the animals are still too nearby for me to risk saying much more.

"Wh-what happened?" Svarik pants, trying to pick himself up.

His efforts are so weak that I fear he's injured. When I reach to help him, he recoils. "It's just me, it's just me," I assure as I try again. "I had to transport us out of there. Are you hurt?"

His head lolls slightly as if he's dizzy. "I-I don't think so...."

A dull thud draws my attention upwards and I see a large shape land yards away in the snow. Then it shrinks down to the size of a person, coming closer until I recognize Rhioa through the swirling white. Relief spreads across her expression as soon as she sees us. "Is he alright?"

"I'm not sure yet. We both took a fall. We—"

"Get him back to the city," Rhioa orders.

"What? No—what about you? What about the driver?" I try to ignore my own dizziness. The bite of cold wind against my skin is not pairing well with the burning sensation that still runs up and down my rib cage.

Rhioa gives a single shake of her head that tells me the driver is dead. Then she says, "There's no time to argue. And you can't Gift us all that far. Can you or can you not get Svarik to Ilske?"

I open my mouth, sputtering. Then I remember that night on the dunes of Pershizar. I'd stayed then, hadn't I? And look what had happened. So why does it kill me to say, "I can. We will meet you at the manor."

With a final nod, Rhioa turns and shifts. I barely catch a glimpse of her golden feathers as she vanishes into the falling snow.

"Hold on, Svarik, I've got to transport us again," I tell him as I kneel next to him.

Svarik is still visibly disoriented. "Wait, what about...Arhys? And Tahra?"

"They have another way back; they'll be alright."

So help me, if that turns out to be a lie....

I summon my Gifting once more, wrapping it around us, and then pulling us towards the warm hearth of the borrowed house in Ilske.

Rhioa, so help me....

.

CHAPTER 18

Rhioa

I squint against the disorienting blur of white around me as the wind and snow batter away at my feathers. Gravity can tell me up from down, but it gives no warning of potential obstacles. All I have is scent, my limited vision, and what little I can hear above the wind.

But sound is enough. I hear another shriek to my right—the same high, bird-like cry as before. I tilt my wings and veer towards the sound.

"Tirzah?" I roar, the gravelly tones of my Draconic voice cutting through the snowfall.

All I hear is more animal cries, still distant. I take the risk and speed up.

"Tirzah!" I call again.

I barely catch the moving shape amid the pummeling snow. It's the ear-piercing shriek that gives me just enough time to act. I open my wings, using the drag to pull my shoulders up and get my talons out in front of me, then collide with the other creature.

For a moment, we are falling, fighting, tearing at each other with claws and teeth. I don't know how long I have until we hit the ground and it has its talons wrapped around one of my legs. So I grab it with both front claws, avoiding its sharp beak, and then throw my whole weight into a spin. It takes three rotations to get the right momentum. Then I brace myself and push against it as hard as I can.

I flare my wings, letting the air fill them and launch me skywards. A muted thud comes from beneath me as the animal slams into a drift below. In a split second, I make my decision: I dive after it. The creature doesn't even have time to right itself before I've swooped down. With wings and claws, I pin it to the ground. A single swipe across the neck and it writhes before finally going still.

I make a quick check of my surroundings before examining the dead creature. It is feathered, four-legged, with the head and beak and talons of a bird. Wait—Svarik had described something of this ilk. Gryphons, he'd called them. But he'd said the ones that came this far north weren't any larger than a dog. Why is this one bigger than a horse?

More gryphon cries remind me that questions can wait. With two beats of my wings, I propel myself back up into the icy sky and let the sound guide me forward. I use the time to gain altitude. When the scuffle is directly beneath me, I gather my breath, let out a roar, and plunge downwards.

With the snow blurring by at such blinding speed, I'm barely able to catch sight of a target. It's more luck than skill that I seize one of the gryphons by a wing. I redirect my momentum and go into a spiral. I feel bones snap in my claws and the creature screams. Its downwards weight confirms it can no longer fly and I let go, propelling myself up at the next one. With no time to pull my talons up, I grab it by the neck with my bared teeth. I twist up and around to try and get away from its talons.

But this one is bigger than the rest and I feel it catch one of my wings. I'm forced to release the gryphon and pull back to get free of it. Now with no momentum, no element of surprise, and no altitude advantage, I've lost the offensive. I dive off to the side to get out from beneath the animal and I hear it shriek as it follows close behind.

Then the shriek gets cut off halfway. I crane my head around to watch a flash of silver ram into the already bleeding gryphon. I waste no time, tucking into a roll and doubling back. Before the gryphon can try righting itself to lash out at Tirzah, my claws are wrapped around its throat. It goes limp and we both let go.

"What took you so long?" Tirzah pants, wings beating in rhythm to keep herself up.

"Do you have any idea how hard you are to see in all this?" I growl as I match her rhythm.

Her silver head tips down as she looks at herself. Not even her Dragon form can hide her dour expression. "Point taken."

"Was that all of them?" I ask, still trying to listen despite the whistling wind.

"I think so," Tirzah says. "What of Tyron and Svarik?"

I start to explain that Tyron had Gifted them back, then stop. "Wait, do you feel that?"

Tirzah flares her wings, letting the wind hold her for a brief second. "Gifting," she nods.

"That idiot," I grumble, my Dragon form turning the last word into a snarl. "I told him to wait at the manor. Let's go get him before he freezes to death looking for us."

I swivel around and fall into a glide, following that low hum. Of all the rash, impulsive things he's done. Didn't he learn anything from that night in Pershizar? And he's not even recovered! He should have—

"Rhy!" Tirzah's roared warning comes too late.

By the time I've processed the metallic sound, the net has wrapped around my wings. The weight of iron and of gravity leaves me no chance; all I can do is tuck in my limbs and brace myself. I hit a deep snow drift, tumbling for several yards. The motion breaks much of my fall but only further entangles me in the net. I have no chance to regain my footing before I'm surrounded.

Futile or not, I fight back. I thrash and writhe and snap at those who try to take hold of the longer chains that trail out behind the net. My wild movements drag several soldiers off their feet, even running them into their compatriots. I pull free enough to let off a stream of acid. It falls short of the soldiers, but the sizzling of it in the snow is enough to scare some into dropping their lines.

I am nearly free when I *feel* it—the humming. It grows louder, harsher, heavier, until it is unbearable. I struggle vainly, aware of how my movements growing slower and slower. There is nothing I can do as the soldiers regain their grip on the chain leads and pull them taut, pinning me to the ground.

Heavy footsteps crunch in the snow, stopping inches from my head. Helpless, trapped beneath chain and the burning, crushing sensation of Gifting, I can't even turn my neck and look. But I don't need to look to know that it's the Hunter who speaks.

"You have two options, Drogan," he says in heavily accented Arvenish. "Shift and come peacefully, or keep up your useless struggle. Then I will have an excuse to give Talsk when I bring you back wounded."

I push through the pain, wrangling my thoughts into order. If Tirzah is following our procedures, then she is likely circling overhead and waiting for my signal. With the snow and wind, I doubt the Hunter even knows she's up there. Yet I know there are likely other nets still loaded and at the ready if she should appear. Full capture on a mission is considered a failure. My best bet is to go with them and wait for Tirzah to break me out of the palace.

So I shift, pulling myself back into Human form. Years of stifling my own instincts allows me to sit there calmly, taking deep, even breaths. I don't even allow myself a grimace at the bite of the freezing metal net nor at the caustic sensation of Gifting.

"The lady of Beclian." The Hunter wears a mask that covers the lower half of his face, but the way his eyes scrunch up tells me he's smiling in satisfaction. He motions to a pair of soldiers and they come forward with shackles and collar. "Talsk was still betting on the Litashian, but I'd suspected you from the beginning."

I don't say a thing. I sit and watch, fighting to keep my expression carefully bored.

"Get the collar on first—that will keep her from shifting back," the Hunter instructs. Then he pauses, looking up at the sky.

My pulse quickens. Don't do it, Tirzah—you know better.

The Hunter looks back down, inspecting me once before turning away. "Get her in the cart and let's get back to the palace before this storm gets any worse," he calls.

Relief comes and goes quickly as the bombardment of Gifting lessens but then the soldiers lock the icy manacles around my wrists. If Tirzah was able to keep her head and stick to procedure, then I know that she'll continue to do so. I can trust her not to make any rash decisions.

Tyron, on the other hand....

Tyron

"What?!"

Tirzah's glare is the visual equivalent of being shushed.

I restrain myself to a strangled sort of whisper. "What do you mean, caught? Who? Where did they take her?"

"It was one of the Hunters," Tirzah replies. "The animals must have just been a means to flush us out. They took her to the palace."

"Then we have to get in there." I knew they'd been gone too long. I should have gone back! "We have to—"

"—calm down," Tirzah cuts me off, brusque and nearly irritated as she glances up and down the corridor. "We've done this a hundred times at least. Rhy knows what to do. If we break in there and throw out the whole mission, she's more likely to kill us than thank us."

The only thing that keeps me from losing my temper is the worry I see in Tirzah's tightly pressed lips. But that worry adds to my own. "You know as well as I do that Talsk is in a panic over the Myrandi. How far do you think he'll go to get information out of her?"

Tirzah rolls her eyes in typical fashion, yet the gesture holds more empty bravado than usual. "He'll never get that far. Knowing Rhy, she'll be leading him in circles and getting far more information from him than she'll ever give in return."

I run my good hand through my hair and try to remain logical. I know Tirzah is right. I know Rhioa is very capable. And yet I can't help the urge to go right up to the palace and tear down the gates with my bare hands. "Fine. Then we find a way to finish the mission and rescue her in one go. And we do it quickly. If we can't figure it out in two days, we get her out and then clean up the mess from there."

"Three," Tirzah says. "That is our protocol."

I decide neither to agree nor disagree, instead turning the subject. "What do we tell Svarik?"

Footsteps sound from further down the hallway and interrupt Tirzah's answer.

I turn around just as the servant bows. "Pardon the interruption—there's a man here to see you. He's the same one who came a few nights ago."

Lenstativ. Several thoughts run through my head in a matter of seconds. First is the possibility that he could have tipped Talsk off to Rhioa. The second thought comes along, reminding me that Lenstativ still had no indicators that she was Myrandi. Third is his warning from last time about how Talsk suspected me. And lastly, I think of how we knew we'd been tailed before, and how Grimvold's was the only nearby manor to the southeast of Ilske.

This is more my fault than it is Lenstativ's.

So help me, if Talsk harms a single hair on her head, I'll....

"Have him shown to the sitting room," I instruct the servant. "Count Ihail is already there." Despite it being late into the evening, and despite him still being tired and sore from his earlier fall, Svarik had insisted on staying up until both ladies and his sleigh driver had returned. I'd simply not had the restraint to wait in the sitting room and had spent the past two hours pacing the foyer.

As the servant goes to fetch Lenstativ, Tirzah and I head for the sitting room.

"If he asks how it happened, just leave the explanation to me," Tirzah murmurs.

I give a sharp nod to show I've heard her, knock once on the sitting room door so that Svarik knows I'm coming in, then enter. It takes every ounce of willpower I possess not to immediately launch into the bad news. Instead I manage to ask, "How are you feeling?"

"Still fine," Svarik replies. "Like I said, I simply lost my wind when I fell. I'm perfectly fine now." He shifts in his seat to face more towards us as we walk in. "Is that Arhys I hear?"

I physically bite my tongue, taking a breath before replying, "No, it's Tahra. Arhys has been taken captive."

Svarik stiffens in visible shock. "What?"

"The attack was a set up," Tirzah speaks now. "They took Arhys, but I got away."

Before he can ask for details, I break in to add, "We're hoping Lenstativ has come to give answers."

"Lenstativ is here?" Svarik gets up from his seat. "But wait, is it possible that he's the one who sold us out? Is he just here to collect the rest of us?"

"If that were so, I would have brought soldiers," Lenstativ's voice comes from the sitting room door as he strides through.

This time, I don't wait. "Where is she?" I demand.

"The palace," Lenstativ replies, sitting down heavily in one of the chairs.

No one else sits.

"That Drogan Hunter is convinced she's one of the Dragon-shifters. Personally, I think he's just trying to get his money's worth out of Talsk." Lenstativ pinches the bridge of his nose. "And getting us into a war with Beclian in the process." He shakes his head. "They're holding her in one of the lower cells— unharmed. They plan to bring her forward as evidence in the Assembly."

Slowly, Svarik resumes his seat. "Talsk has called for an Assembly?"

I see Tirzah look at me from the corner of my eye.

"The announcement goes out at dawn. By law, he must give a minimum of one full day's notice," Lenstativ answers.

Svarik lets out a long breath. "So we have one day."

Lenstativ gives a tight-lipped nod. His voice drops and he looks between me and Svarik when he asks, "Do you think you can win the majority?"

The silence that falls is answer enough.

"We did not win over Grimvold," Svarik quietly admits. "Without him—without Kstoren on our side—winning the majority wouldn't even matter. Talsk will just keep power by force."

I run my good hand through my hair, trying to remind myself that Talsk needs Rhioa unharmed as far as the Assembly. Surely, he knows that torturing a woman and then dragging her onto a stage wouldn't win him any favor. But wait, if she hasn't given any information, how does he expect to use her as proof?

"Has Arhys said anything?" I ask suddenly. "How exactly does imprisoning her give him any proof?"

Lenstativ rubs one temple. "As far as I know, she's been completely silent. A wise move, diplomatically. But that Hunter tells Talsk he can force her to shift into a Dragon in front of everyone."

I wait until Lenstativ turns back to Svarik before I glance at Tirzah. By the expression she wears, the Hunter's claim is true.

"But, then again, when she doesn't turn into a Dragon, Talsk will have publicly confessed to abducting and illegally detaining a foreign dignitary," Lenstativ muses, straightening at the thought. Then he freezes. "She...won't, will she?"

I blink at him, trying to cover my reaction with a facade of confusion. "Lady Arhys? ...turn into a Dragon?"

"I know, I know—it sounds ridiculous." Lenstativ is back to rubbing his temple. "But after hearing Talsk and that Hunter go on for so long, it's starting to wear off on me."

I can't help but notice how very still Svarik is sitting. Is he piecing it all together? He gives no indication either way when he clears his throat. "Well, with that issue aside, Lenstativ is right: Lady Arhys may have given us an advantage. And seeing as our only hope of rescuing her is deposing Talsk, I think we should use it. We have one day to spread the word of what Talsk has done and to make our case. The day after, they will have to make their choice." He shifts in his seat, head turned towards me. "Do you agree to this, Tyron?"

In spare seconds, I run as many scenarios as I can conjure through my head. It feels wrong to agree to this—to letting Rhioa be leverage. But it's the best way. And, infuriatingly, it's what she would want. I lock eyes with Lenstativ. "Can you swear her safety until the day of the Assembly?"

Lenstativ meets my gaze. "It is not mine to swear. But Talsk knows he has little sympathy among the nobles and is at least smart enough not to harm her publicly. I will do what I can to remind him of that."

The assurance is thin, yet it's the best I'll get. I regather myself and look at Tirzah.

She gives a quiet nod. "As backup, I will have a letter drafted out to Beclian. If things go awry, it will be sent immediately to our liaison in Krysophera. He could be here within six weeks."

"Then it is settled," Svarik says. "Now we need to figure out how to spread the word." He shifts back in Lenstativ's direction. "I hope you have better tips for us this time, Mikaud. We can't afford another Grimvold."

Mikaud Lenstativ leans forward to take off his coat. "Thankfully, your friend from Beclian is rather charming. With all the heads she turned, her peril makes a very convincing bit of motivation. I would start with the Duchess Oskoristiv. From there..." he begins to tick off names and the best manner of approach.

Finally accepting that we will be here a while, I take a seat nearby. I see Tirzah do the same. Then we exchange that silent look and I know we're thinking the same thing: How are we going to keep Rhioa from being revealed in front of the entire Assembly of Arvenir?

Next time, Rhy, I don't care what you tell me or threaten me with. I'm never leaving you behind again.

CHAPTER 19

Rhioa

I can't quite make up my mind on what the most annoying thing is: the freezing cold, or the fact that the most comfortable position I can find makes my hands go numb after two minutes. No, maybe it's the neck collar after all. Besides the fact that it will decapitate me if I try to shift, the metal thing is rather heavy and won't let me lean my head back. I suppose it's for the best, considering that the wall behind me is probably as cold as the stone floor I'm sitting on.

Muffled footsteps filter through the heavy door of the stone chamber and the high-pitched protest of the key in the lock echoes off the walls. The first to enter is the guard, who does a quick walk around of the chamber and a visual check of my shackles—of course from the safety of a few feet away. Only when this cursory examination is complete does he return to the door and call, "It is safe to enter, Your Highness."

In marches Udeneran Talsk, followed closely by the Hunter.

If there is any benefit to having been seen in Dragon form by nearly thirty soldiers, it's that I don't have to grovel or cry or otherwise put on a show. Talsk has too much proof of who I am for me to sell him another act. So as he walks up to me, I simply sit in the same relaxed fashion I have for the past few hours.

"How?" he growls.

"I warned you before," the masked Hunter replies thinly, staying a pace behind Talsk. "These beasts can forge anything Human—letters of introduction, records, reputations, and even Human form."

"Where are the others?" Talsk demands, apparently addressing me.

I tilt my head to one side, looking him up and down a moment. Then I raise one brow and smirk.

Talsk raises a fist as if to strike me. "Answer me!"

"Don't waste your breath," the Hunter interjects. "You can shout at her and starve her all you please, but you won't get anywhere until you let me do my work."

Talsk finally tears his gaze from me and turns to face the Hunter. "Not until after the Assembly. If I bring her in there all torn to pieces, no one will care whether she's Drogan or not—there will be uproar. I can't fight them and the Drogans all at once."

The Hunter scoffs. "From what you've said of your cousin, she's probably the only reason that he's made it this far. Without her, this Assembly will be nothing more than a formality, will it not?"

Talsk gives an unflattering grunt. "That's what Lenstativ tells me. But the Litashian isn't dead—for all I know, he might be pulling Ihail's strings in her absence." He mutters something under his breath and runs a hand over his face. "The Assembly will be first thing tomorrow morning. After that, she's all yours." He turns back to look at me, gaze lingering a moment before he shakes his head. This time, I catch what he mutters: "What a waste." Then he stalks out the door.

The Hunter does not leave right away. He stands in the shadows of the cell, his silent attention now fixed on me. I meet his gaze, tilt my head again, then straighten and give a wide yawn. The Hunter's eyes narrow and I catch the subtle way his gloved hands turn to fists. He exits the cell in nearly the same huff that Talsk had.

My little bit of entertainment gone, I go back to trying to find a more comfortable way to sit. Then it's back to counting the stones in the wall just to pass the time. Part of me wonders what Tyron and Tirzah are doing. The other part of me decides it's best not to think about it. Whatever it is they're up to, I should probably come up with a backup plan.

Tyron

I drum my fingers on the edge of the carriage seat, mentally reviewing the plan for the millionth time. There are so many ways this could go askew. Part of me wonders if we should really be trusting Lenstativ's information after things went so badly with Grimvold. If Lenstativ is even the slightest bit off on today's timing, it could be catastrophic.

The carriage jolts forward again as we inch closer to the palace steps and Svarik's turn to exit. But then we pause, waiting once more for those in front of us. I take the chance to triple check Tirzah's disguise. I'm not quite sure how she has managed it so convincingly but, with her neat uniform and her hair secured under an Arvenish style cap, she looks like a young manservant.

"Are you sure that you will be up to this?" Svarik's question interrupts my busy thoughts. "The physician had said—"

"—it will be fine. I healed what was needed." I wave off his worry. My arm and ribs are still sore, but they're functional enough.

Svarik and Tirzah frown in unison. "Isn't that risky? I thought you weren't supposed to heal yourself," the former comments.

"It was less risky than me trying to do this with one arm," I reply. Rhioa can scold me all she wants once she's free. For now, the carriage rolls forward again and I announce, "This is it."

Svarik gathers his cane while Tirzah pulls on her gloves. As soon as the carriage settles to a stop, she steps out and steps back to hold the door.

But Svarik does not get out yet. Instead, he leans forward and says in a low voice, "About Arhys..."

My breath catches.

"...and what Lenstativ said about the Hunter—you'll take care of it, right?"

He's worried she'll transform into a Dragon in front of the Assembly. He knows that, in this one regard, Talsk is right.

I'd figured as much. "Yes, I will make sure of it."

With a bow of his head and a simple, "Alright," he feels for the door and steps down from the carriage.

"Good luck," I call after him.

The only thing I get before the door closes is a nod from Tirzah. It says what she does not: She will watch Svarik's back.

The carriage lurches forward and I watch the steps of the palace slide out of view. *Here goes nothing.* I force myself to remain seated until we've pulled all the way around to the stable yard and have joined the long line of vehicles there. Once there are carriages on either side of me, I let myself out.

The uniform of a palace servant that Lenstativ had smuggled to us keeps me from drawing any attention as I cross the open square. Just in case, I pull the folded parchments from my inner pocket and keep them in hand as I take the staff entrance on the left. Lenstativ had warned us that there would likely be guards at each door and I know that my hair and complexion don't help me blend in. I've used too much Gifting to heal myself over the past few days, and expect to use it too much today, to risk using it now to disguise my features.

Sure enough, the soldier leaning against the corridor wall straightens as I enter. I pretend not to notice as I close the door behind myself and stomp snow off my feet. When I do look at him, I give a slight wave—a greeting that simultaneously shows off my papers and their important-looking seals. The guard's eyes dart down to my hands and then back up. He returns my greeting in the form of a nod as I go on my way.

One left, down the stairs, another left—the papers and my purposeful stride continue to ward off suspicion. Nevertheless, I take the door on the right and enter what had appeared to be a storage closet on the palace map. I shut the door behind me and use Gifting to light the small room. The closet is lined on one side with shelves, the other with racks of tools. First, I take off my outdoor coat and stuff it beneath a shelf along with the papers I'd been holding. My gloves stay in my jacket pocket. Next, I pull on the armband that indicates I'm cleared to work in the prison levels. Then I grab a pail and mop, extinguish my little light, and stand by the door to wait.

Several minutes tick by in dim silence before I hear the coordinated beat of footsteps and the faint clatter of armor. Still I wait. The sound grows, climaxes just outside the door, then fades. I wait until it comes from the far end of the hall before quietly opening the latch and stepping out. I catch a glimpse of the masked Hunter and eight soldiers just as they disappear around the corner.

With my mop and pail in hand, I follow. I keep always one turn behind the Hunter and his group. Right, down two doors, right again, and then I wait at the top of the last staircase until I hear them clear with the front guard. That's the signal to make my descent.

"What are you doing here?" A soldier asks as soon as I've come into view. "We've already had the morning cleaning."

I make sure to match his Arvenish accent as I reply, "I was told someone vomited in the back corridor." I stop as I reach the bottom of the staircase and pull an irritable expression. "Actually, I was told that someone was 'sick of stepping in it,' but they sent me to clean it up either way."

The guard looks me up and down, eyes my mop and pail, then shrugs. "Just make sure you stay clear of the left passage. They're pulling a pretty dangerous prisoner out and you know the protocol for that." His head tips towards my armband.

I nod and step through the barred door as he opens it for me. "Alright, will do."

Knowing he is likely watching, I take the hallway to the right. But the main cell block is a simple square set up and all I have to do is loop around. The left passage extends further beyond the rest of the block to a higher security cell—the cell where they're keeping Rhioa. So I go until I reach where the back corridor meets the left passage, check both ways, then set my mop and pail against a wall. I don't want them getting in the way later.

I keep my footsteps quiet down the long passageway until I've reached the reinforced door. I press my ear against it, catching the muted clicking and jangling of chains. I continue listening as I take my gloves from my jacket pocket. Only once I've pulled them on do I reach for one of the little red-bronze daggers that Tirzah had lent me.

My timing is perfect. As soon as I have the knife ready, the sound settles within the cell. So I raise one hand and knock.

For a moment, silence.

Then, "You—see who it is."

I step back, veiling my face with Gifting and allowing the soldier room enough to peek out the door. His brow furrows in instant confusion.

I assume a polite tone as I say, "Would you kindly inform the Hunter that a friend of the prisoner would like to speak with him?"

The door slams shut and a chorus of alarm echoes from the other side of it.

I press myself in the small corner where the cell wall meets the passage wall and wrap myself from head to toe with Gifting. If I have bent the light correctly, I will be completely invisible.

The door now bursts open and soldiers charge through, the last half of their orders streaming out after them: "—in a separate cell. Do *not* bring him back here!"

I count seven of them rushing off. That means one is still with the Hunter and Rhioa. As soon as all seven have cleared the bend I drop my illusion, step into the cell, and close the door. Gifting locks it behind me.

The first thing I register is Rhioa, on her knees and bound in chains from head to toe, with the Hunter right behind her. Torchlight gleams off of the dagger that he has pressed right behind her jaw. But he is not holding her with the other hand; he must not want to get too close to her.

"Easy now," the Hunter says beneath his mask. I see him twist the blade tip against her skin until blood begins to dribble down her neck.

Rhioa doesn't even flinch.

I can't say the same.

The Hunter continues in a low voice, "I take it you don't want her dead, so why don't you do as I say? Drop the knife, kick it over to my friend, and put both arms straight out in front of you—wrists together."

I have seconds to work each factor out: the soldiers still in the hallway, the guard still in the cell, the Hunter's position to Rhioa, Rhioa.... I can't help but meet her gaze for a moment just to make sure she's alright. Her eyes dart side to side in an effort to tell me not to do it. But I have to ignore her. I bend over and place the red-bronze knife on the stone floor, kicking it away and holding my wrists out as instructed.

I see Rhioa's shoulders drop in a sigh. At the Hunter's signal, the guard takes a pair of cuffs from his belt and steps cautiously forward. I simply wait. But as soon as the soldier is close enough to grab my arm, I summon my Gifting and whisk us both away.

We appear in one of the walled cells I had passed earlier. The soldier's momentary disorientation lets me snatch the cuffs right out of his hand, close one around his wrist, and pull the other end around one of the iron rings on the wall. It clicks shut just as he has enough wherewithal to try and pull away. The chain goes taut, but it all holds.

"My apologies," I tell the baffled soldier even as I take out my second red-bronze dagger. With that I steady myself, envision Rhioa and the Hunter, and Gift myself back.

As intended, I appear directly behind the Hunter. What's less intentional is my knife catching on his pauldron as he twists around. I nearly lose my grip on the blade, a problem that is only doubled by the Hunter's elbow ramming into my ribs. *You probably should have healed those more.* I'm left gasping as I get one foot beside his, using my other arm and his own momentum to trip him. The Hunter hits the floor and rolls once before vanishing.

No, no, no.

I swivel around as fast as I can as I whisper, "Rhioa—down!"

She hits the ground just as the Hunter materializes in front of her, his blade leveled where her throat would have been. I see his eyes track her downwards and I react instinctively. My blast of energy hits him square in the chest and knocks him all the way back against the cell wall.

But while the distance lessens the danger of his dagger, it does nothing to stop his Gifting. I move forward with red-bronze in hand just as the Hunter looks at the torch sputtering next to him. He reaches out and the fire pours like water into some invisible vase, a burning mass that swirls in his hands. I step in front of Rhioa as he hurls the fireball at my head.

I see my chance. I grasp at the air in front of me, hardening it to a thin layer and hoping this works. The mass of flame bursts up against it and flares out into a blinding wall. I ready my knife, release my invisible shield, and charge though the dissipating fire. The Hunter has one sleeve held up in front of his eyes to protect his face from the heat. Only, his other arm is moving....

I duck as another wave of flames roars over my head, the searing heat nearly enough to throw me off balance. I come up with my forearm raised and deflect the dagger he swings at me. Carrying my weight through, I smash his arm against the wall and drive my red-bronze knife into the unarmored area just inside his elbow. He yowls and drops the dagger. He tries to grab me with his free hand but doesn't get the chance before I drive a closed fist into his stomach. He lurches forward and I let him, maintaining my grip on the arm I stabbed. I twist it and push down to drive him to his knees. Then I double it up behind him and he howls again. But this time I wrap one arm around his neck, maintaining the pressure despite his struggling, and wait until I feel him pass out.

It takes all of my self-control not to just drop him and rush to Rhioa's side. I have to secure him first and, before I can do that, I need his pauldrons, coat, and mask. I set to work even as I try look Rhioa over.

"That seemed like an unnecessarily complicated way of doing it," Rhioa pants as she picks herself up off the floor, still bound in chains. "I take it you have a larger plan?"

"Yes," I nod, using rope from my pockets to bind the unconscious Hunter's hands behinds his back. "We're taking away Talsk's only evidence of the Myrandi. All you have to do is keep playing along." I risk another glance up to ask, "Are you alright?"

Rhioa is back her knees now, visibly trying to take deeper breaths. "I would have preferred a little less Gifting," she grumbles.

"I apologize—I didn't have many options."

With a spare length of rope, I make sure the red-bronze knife is securely against his skin so that it won't come out if he moves. I grab the one I had dropped when pretending to surrender and strap it to his other arm—just in case. Then I drag the Hunter to the corner of the cell and start to put his coat on over my servant's uniform.

Rhioa begins to chuckle.

"What?" is my baffled question as I fumble to strap on the pauldrons.

She chuckles a little more before replying, "That is *far* too short for you."

She's right. The Hunter may have had broader shoulders than me, but he was half a head shorter. Yet somehow, despite the haste and tension of the whole situation, Rhioa's humor is reassuring. She really is alright. I take a deep breath for the first time in two days.

"Hopefully these soldiers are more concerned about the consequences of insulting their commander than about pointing out his poor fashion sense," I reply in kind.

As if on cue, there are footsteps in the hall. Then an unsuccessful tug on the door handle. I hurry to tie the Hunter's mask around the bottom half of my face and pull up his hood, all while the shouting escalates outside the door.

Here comes the hard part. I haven't done this since I was a youth and trying to mess with Euracia. Hopefully, I still have the knack for it.

"What are you waiting for? Someone go fetch the key!" I shout. "We need to get moving."

The mixture of my feigned accent and the use of Gifting to manipulate the air as my voice carries is a tricky balance. But it seems to be convincing enough through the cell door, for the banging fists quiet and there's a scurry as someone shuffles off.

I have less than a minute now, yet I can no longer help myself. I cross to Rhioa and kneel in front of her. "Are you sure that you're alright?" I whisper, looking her over again. My gaze catches on the blood on her neck where the Hunter had pricked her. I frown. "Let me check that."

Rhioa twists away from my outstretched hand. She replies in the same hush, "Now's not the time. It's just a scratch. Move my hair to hide it from the soldiers."

The order goes against my instincts to help, even though I know she's right. I gently adjust her loose hair so that it lays on the other side of her neck and hides the red stain.

"Wait a moment—" Rhioa manages to make a whisper sound sharp. "—Did you heal your arm?"

The movement I hear in the hall could not have been more opportune. "Like you said, now's not the time," I say as I stand.

Rhioa narrows her eyes at me but keeps her reply to herself.

The clicking and scraping of a key in the lock sounds through the room and I take a deep breath, envisioning the Hunter as I had entered the cell. I use Gifting to make up for the remaining disparities between his appearance and mine. Eyes are always the most difficult to fake. At least it's much easier to give the unconscious Hunter his disguise; so long as no one gets too close, all they'll see is the empty stone corner.

The door opens and the soldiers spill in.

"Did you find him?" I ask, my borrowed dagger level to Rhioa's throat as if I've been standing guard the whole time.

"No, not even a trace," their officer replies. Then his brow furrows. "Where's Dras?"

That must be the guard I left in the neighboring cell. "He went after the rest of you. But we don't have time to wait for him—the Va' Kied won't appreciate us being late."

The thought of an angry Talsk seems to be motivation enough for all of them to leave their fellow guard behind. They begin taking up positions around Rhioa, picking up the chain lines attached to her hands and neck collar to double check their security.

But I dare not let myself be relieved just yet. As we get Rhioa to her feet and begin to move, I know the biggest gamble is still ahead.

CHAPTER 20

Rhioa

The irritating sensation of Tyron's Gifting chafes more than my shackles as I'm led down the corridor. I don't know how the feeling manages to be somewhere between a prickling across my skin and a ringing in my ears, but it's more aggravating than both. All the same, I can't help but wonder how he's managing to control so many facets of it at once: his appearance, his voice, all of the transporting and fighting that he'd done earlier. With each step, I worry that a soldier will notice. Or that a guard will come running and telling of the Hunter they found in the cell.

But it never happens. No one gives Tyron so much as a second glance as he follows close behind me. Not until we our final door, that is.

"You," Tyron speaks. The hum of his Gifting increases as he bends his voice to match the Hunter's. "Go in and wait for the Va' Kied's signal."

Personally, I think he's made the voice a touch too low. The soldier doesn't seem to notice as he nods and slips through the door.

"You two, take post at both hallway entrances," Tyron continues. "No one gets through—not even sentries. This 'friend of the prisoner' may have disguised himself."

Two more soldiers nod and move to follow his orders, leaving only the four who hold my chain leads.

I'll admit, it's fairly clever of him. This way if someone *should* come running to warn them about Tyron, Tyron can simply accuse the intruder of being, well, him.

The corridor falls quiet and I catch sound on the other side of the closed door. Sometimes it's a single, loud voice, other times it's a hushed, collective murmur. All of it is too muffled to catch what's being said. I am left to hope that Svarik is able to hold up beneath the pressure of it all.

I refocus on my part. Tyron is clearly here to keep the Hunter from exposing me but he isn't here for a rescue, meaning that Lady Arhys is needed to help win some of the Assembly over. So I use the wait to prepare: I create space in the back of my throat as if about to yawn, I keep myself from blinking as much as possible, and I make my breath more rapid and shallow.

By the time the soldier returns to give us our cue to enter, I've drummed up a good bout of tears. It's the perfect pairing with my dungeon-stained dress. Add in a little trip over the threshold, some rapid blinking as if unused to the bright lighting, and I look properly pathetic as I let the soldiers drag me into the hall. The gasp that runs through the entire Assembly is instantaneous.

"Is that—"

"Why is she—"

"What is the meaning of this?!"

The overlapping chorus reverberates through the hall until it builds to a roar.

"Enough!" Talsk's shout climbs above it all, but it takes two heavy thuds of the Speaker's staff to rein the clamor in. Talsk's voice is still raised as he says, "This so-called 'Lady Arhys' is not who she says she is—she is one of them! The Myrandi!"

He must still be quite scared of me to have me brought in from the side door instead of through the main door behind him. I keep my eyes wide as I look towards the raised platform that sits centered against the wall, where Talsk is pacing and making his wild hand gestures. Across from him, right in the front row, sits Svarik. I instantly recognize the young attendant next to him as Tirzah.

"I-I don't know what he's talking about," I stammer breathlessly, addressing Talsk when I repeat, "*Please*, your Majesty, I don't know what you're talking about." I look out across the Assembly now, manacled hands raised as I plead. "Someone, p-please—help me."

"Silence." Tyron's harsh command is followed by a jerk on my chains.

Perhaps it's a *touch* overboard, but I stagger and drop to my knees.

"Lady Arhys?" Svarik has leapt to his feet. "Is that you? Are you alright? Have they—" Tirzah makes a good show of holding him back.

"Count Ihail! Yes, y-yes, it's me." I throw a fearful glance back at Tyron, which serves to move my hair to the other shoulder. The blood that the Hunter drew earlier is on full display when I turn back to the crowd. "Please, they hurt me, I don't know why. Please—help me!"

The baffled look on Talsk's face is rather enjoyable. Especially combined with the Assembly's growing tumult. Even Talsk seems to gather that the situation is slipping from his grasp.

"Everyone settle down!" he shouts again. "This is nothing more than a staged act—and a pitiful one, at that."

"Then show us your proof." The deep voice turns several heads. Especially as its owner gets to his feet: Archduke Grimvold. "Because if she's not one of these 'Dragon-shifters,' then you've arrested and harmed a foreign dignitary from Beclian—meaning we're facing war on two fronts."

Talsk turns, holding out a hand in signal to Tyron. "Hunter, show them what she really is."

The entire hall holds its breath.

"Spread out; keep the leads even," Tyron orders the guards around me.

The four spread out, each still holding the chain lead taut as they retreat to a safer distance. Then, slowly, Tyron raises his hands until his gloved palms face me. The illusion of the Hunter's face is fixed in absolute concentration.

He's so dramatic.

As the expectant pause strains and threatens to give out, so his brow begins to furrow as if in confusion. I keep up the act by glancing back and forth between him and the crowd in utter bewilderment.

"It's..." Tyron keeps his palms outstretched as he looks to Talsk. "...It's not working."

"*What?*" Talsk's gaze darts out across the Assembly. "What do you mean, not working? Try again!"

Tyron resumes his little pretense as the Assembly-members resume their murmuring. The sounds doubles when Tyron lowers his hands and begins to shake his head.

Talsk's eyes narrow, first at me and then at Tyron. He turns back to the Assembly to proclaim, "It doesn't matter. I have several witnesses of her transformation—Speaker Lenstativ, tell them what you saw."

Mikaud Lenstativ, sitting in his raised booth in the center of the platform, purses his lips. His hesitation is long enough to make me worry. When he clears his throat, he says, "I'm afraid, Your Highness, that I have nothing to tell them since I have not seen the lady in any Draconic form."

"Lenstativ," Talsk growls his name in warning.

"The only witness I have is that which you and your hired Hunter have given me," the Speaker continues as if he hadn't heard the Va' Kied at all. "I'm sure the Assembly would gladly listen to his account."

Wait. This isn't good. Tyron has gotten away with a sentence or two of speech, but an entire account—of something he wasn't there for, no less—could blow his cover.

"On the contrary: I raise an objection," Svarik cuts in. "Not only is this person employed by you and thereby biased, he is employed with the sole purpose of hunting these 'Dragon-shifters.' Of course he would try to cover up his failure!"

Talsk opens his mouth, but the thudding of Lenstativ's staff intervenes.

"The objection of a witness needs the backing of three other Assembly-members in order to be sustained," the Speaker announces in reminder. "Are there any who will back it?

I watch the crowd, keeping my eyes wild for the sake of those who watch back. Svarik's intervention, while timely, has its weak spots. Will people support it anyway?

I catch Duke Sohlv looking to his wife and her quiet nod in response. He gets to his feet and says, "I will back it."

We still need two more.

"I will back it." Duchess Oskoristiv stands next. I can only recognize her at the distance by the bizarre, feathered hat she wears. I vaguely recall saying something about feathers being in fashion at her last party....

I risk looking to Grimvold, but he doesn't notice. He's too busy studying Tyron.

It's those friends of Elsze, the Viscount and Viscountess Postorik, who stand and announce, "We will back it."

"Then the witness has been rejected and may not speak in this Assembly," Lenstativ declares, receiving yet another glare from Talsk. "Your Highness, do you have any other witnesses you can bring forward?"

Talsk's hands are wrapped into fists, his shoulders tense until they nearly reach his ears, his jaw so tight that his whole face has turned red.

"If His Highness would allow," Kstoren, from his seat near the front, has his hands out in a nearly placating gesture. "I could summon one of the men that I lent the Hunter." The Grand Officer turns to the Assembly. "Since the soldiers are still ultimately under my command, they have no motivation to take sides between the Hunter or Lady Arhys. They could offer a less biased account."

On the surface, Kstoren rallying to Talsk is not ideal. Yet the way his attention flits between Talsk and Grimvold hints that the Officer has noticed the tension there and is trying to resolve it.

"What does *His Excellency* say about this witness?" Talsk glowers at Svarik.

Svarik sits down for the first time since I was dragged into the hall. "I would be glad to hear what orders this soldier was given about imprisoning my friend," is his terse reply.

Kstoren immediately turns towards me and the soldiers that hold my chains. When his eyes happen to meet mine, he flinches and averts them quickly. "You, Dovtralin, you were there for the arrest, were you not? Come forward."

One of my guards shifts uneasily. But he relinquishes his chain lead to Tyron and walks hesitantly to the center of the raised platform.

"State your name and rank," Lenstativ orders.

"Ensign Dovtralin, sir." The man seems more afraid of the crowd than he ever was of me.

"Per the rules of the Assembly, the party which has called the witness has the right to first questioning," Lenstativ goes on. "When the first questions have concluded, it is open to anyone within the Assembly. Grand Va' Kied Talsk, you may proceed."

Talsk doesn't look at Lenstativ at all. His full attention is on the poor soldier. "Well, Ensign, spit it out. Tell them what you saw."

If the soldier is nervous in front of the Assembly, he is doubly so in front of the Grand Va' Kied. "Um, you mean, when we captured her? It was, um, it was a good snow squall so it was a little hard to see everything." The visible blossoming of Talsk's temper causes the ensign to clear his throat and quickly continue. "We had brought some of those machines that the Hunter had designed—the ones that catapult iron nets. I couldn't see anything through all the snow, but the Hunter told us where to fire. Then we saw the net fall from the sky with something gold wrapped up in it. When we got closer, I-I think it was a Dragon."

"You think?" Talsk repeats in exasperation.

"I mean, begging your pardon, Your Highness—I've never seen one before," the ensign stammers.

Huffing, Talsk waves a hand for the man to continue.

"The Hunter had already warned us that he would be using his Gifting, so we all took up the chain leads and tried to stay back." The soldier hesitates. "Then the Dragon, uh, changed. Into her." He points directly at me.

"There you have it." Talsk faces the crowd as if daring anyone to contradict the ensign. "Will you believe him, or do I need to drag all those other soldiers up here to say the exact same thing?"

There are several baffled looks my way, but no replies to Talsk.

It's Lenstativ who asks, "Does that conclude your questions, Your Highness?"

Talsk's expression is smug when he nods.

"Are there any others who wish to question the witness?" Before Lenstativ has even finished asking, Svarik is on his feet. Lenstativ acknowledges him with a nod and says, "Count Ihail, you may proceed."

"Ensign Dovtralin, what were your orders the day that you captured Lady Arhys?" Svarik's question is calm and clear, carrying through the entire hall.

The ensign glances to Kstoren, who gives a nod. "To capture the Myrandi intruder," the soldier answers.

"And who did these orders come from?" Svarik persists.

He wants to link it directly back to Talsk. But what does he plan to use to incriminate him? Assuming he has a plan, that is....

"Um," Now the ensign looks to Tyron, still disguised as the Hunter. "The Hunter, sir. But it was my understanding that the order came from the Grand Va' Kied himself."

"And what was your plan that day? I presume that you didn't simply wander off into a squall looking for Dragons." Svarik's voice turns dry.

The ensign shakes his head. "Of course not. The Hunter had information that she would be on the plains to the south of the city. We set up in advance then released prey to lure her in."

Ah, that's what Svarik's doing.

"Prey? What prey?"

"Gryphons, your Excellency."

Talsk's smugness has evaporated and left only his former irritation. One hand rubs the curved handle of his ceremonial sword.

"Gryphons," Svarik repeats. "How interesting. Those are the very creatures that attacked my sleigh on the day Lady Arhys was abducted." He turns in place, facing towards the Assembly. "We had been travelling back from a visit with Archduke Grimvold—a trip which took us across the Sltod plains the day of Ensign Dovtralin's testimony—when the attack occurred. My driver was killed, my sleigh torn to pieces, one of my horses lost. And Lady Arhys was nowhere to be found."

I see Talsk's gaze flick out across the crowd. I also notice Kstoren's furrowed brow, as if this information is new to him.

Svarik goes on. "Initially, we went to the city guard for help. All they found was the body of the driver and the remnants of my sleigh. We feared the worst. That was, until one of the guardsmen passed on a rumor he'd heard from the palace about the arrest of a foreign lady."

"Enough of this drivel," Talsk barges in. "Yes, I authorized the release of several gryphons—to draw out an enemy *spy!*"

"Except you have yet to offer any real proof," Svarik's voice is cutting as he turns back towards the platform. "By your soldier's own testimony, he was told to stay back when this 'Dragon' was captured. How, then, can he verify whether or not it was an illusion cast by your Hunter? This Hunter already looks like enough of a fraud, claiming he can 'reveal' Lady Arhys and yet failing to do so."

Perhaps it's petty, but I find an odd measure of satisfaction in watching Talsk stammer.

Svarik bangs his cane against the marble floor. "Let the Assembly and its Speaker take note of my formal complaint: the Grand Va' Kied, Udeneran Talsk, has broken many of our laws. He has illegally abducted, held, and harmed a dignitary of a foreign nation with which we have trade treaties. This is considered an act of war on a treated nation—something which may not be sanctioned without the approval of an Assembly. He has also brought harm to another foreign dignitary, the prince of Litash, who is still unwell after the attack on our sleigh. He has intentionally endangered the life of a member of the Assembly and, perhaps worst of all, he is responsible for the unnecessary death of one of his own citizens."

I half wonder if Svarik knows what I am, or if Tyron masquerading as the Hunter was not a plan he shared with the count.

"And what restitution do you seek?" Lenstativ asks, practically reciting the formality.

"I demand that the Lady Arhys of Beclian be released immediately, with a full and formal apology drafted to both her and to her father, the Lord Saen." Svarik speaks with a sureness I have never heard before. "Another formal apology is to be made to Prince Tyron, for the harm he suffered in the gryphon attack. For myself, I ask only that the equivalent of my lost property, both horse and sleigh, to be remitted to me." His voice drops slightly. "On behalf of the driver, whose name was Vitr Osn, I request an allowance be given his widow and children— enough for them to live on in their father's absence."

"Anything else?" Talsk sneers.

Svarik gives no reaction. "Yes. A public apology for the use of such military tactics on Arvenish citizens, and the promise that such an event will never be repeated."

Talsk begins to laugh, a sound that is overlayed with the thudding of Lenstativ's staff.

"The complaint of an Assembly-member requires two other members to second it before it may be officially brought before the Grand Va' Kied," the Speaker says. "Are there two such members?"

Duke Sohlv and Duchess Oskoristiv are on their feet immediately.

"Count Ihail, your complaints have been acknowledged. As a member of the Assembly, it is your right that the Grand Va' Kied hear and respond." Lenstativ folds his hands and leans them on the stand that he sits behind. "And since His

Highness has graced us with his presence at today's Assembly, does he wish to give response now?"

"I do," Talsk snarls. "And I hereby reject every last one of his requests."

Kstoren steps forward in a hush. "Your Highness, perhaps some sort of compromise—"

"—No." Talsk turns on the Grand Officer in a rage. "I will not compromise with this blind buffoon of a coward, not with his Myrandi puppet master." He jabs a finger in my direction. "And not even with the so-called Litashian that has probably sneaked in here with his little tricks of Gifting. The three of them are trying to sabotage Arvenir and I will never—*never*—let it happen!"

I watch Svarik take a deep breath and square his shoulders. "If you will not put aside all of this ridiculous conspiracy and release Lady Arhys, then you leave me no choice." He clears his throat. "Let the Assembly and its Speaker take note: In light of the illegal and dangerous dealings of the Grand Va' Kied, Udeneran Talsk, I demand that he renounce his crown and step down from his throne. Furthermore, I assert my claim to the throne of Arvenir, as is my right, handed down to me from my father, the Grand Va' Kied Ordrin Ihail."

The stunned silence does not last long. The ensuing clamor is enough to make my teeth rattle and I find myself hoping it doesn't distract Tyron too much from his Gifted façade.

"Silence!" Lenstativ beats his staff against the floor until I begin to fear he'll break it. "Silence!"

The roar of calls and quarrels are wrestled down into a hundred whispered snatches of conversation.

"For the Grand Va' Kied to be removed, another must first step forward with a claim." Lenstativ visibly strains to make himself heard. "Since Count Ihail is the firstborn of the late Grand Va' Kied Ihail, his claim is automatically considered valid by the Assembly. Do any contest his ability to lay claim?"

The murmuring continues, but none stand.

"You can't be serious," Talsk scoffs. "How could someone like *Svarik* manage a nation? He can't even manage a set of steps by himself!"

Irritating as they are, the fact that Talsk has reverted to mere personal insults displays his full desperation.

Lenstativ ignores him. "Then the vote will commence. In order for a Grand Va' Kied to be removed and for Count Ihail's claim to be upheld, a majority must be reached. If all Assembly-members would take their seats, the vote begins now."

The hall falls quiet, save for the sound of Svarik's cane sliding across the stone. I see Tirzah stand to follow then sit back down after a subtle wave from Svarik. In sure, even steps, the count crosses alone to the platform and climbs the few stairs. Then he turns so that he is facing back towards the Assembly. Next to the still seething Talsk, Svarik stands as a striking contrast of calm.

Perhaps he's better at this than I thought.

"I stand with Svarik Ihail." Duke Sohlv is the first to rise.

Another lord, one I recognize from our last ball, rises next. "I stand with Svarik Ihail."

The declaration repeats from different voices, working its way through the crowd. Yet for each person that stands, five more glance at each other and try to gauge what the others will do. They know Talsk is in the wrong. They also know that, should he win the majority, he is capable of executing whom he pleases. The only ones brave enough to stand now are those who have already personally suffered under Talsk.

And they are too few. As the pledges of support begin to slow, the nervousness of the room builds and the pace slows even further. *No, no, no! We're too close!* I search the Assembly, trying to establish eye contact with any of the many members we visited or spoke with at events. None of them will look at me.

Except for Archduke Grimvold. He meets my gaze and holds it, then frowns and shakes his head ruefully as he gathers himself. He gets up from his chair and announces, "I stand with Svarik Ihail."

Talsk's jaw nearly drops in shock. Nearby, Kstoren appears equally stunned.

As quickly as the pledges had faded out, they now redouble. A baron to Grimvold's right, a countess in the back, an elderly duke right in the front, all repeating the same words:

"I stand with Svarik Ihail."

Lenstativ scribbles away from behind his stand. Though his expression has never wavered from its fixed composure, I notice beads of sweat on his forehead.

"Traitors! Fools!" Talsk roars. "You have no idea what you're doing!"

More Assembly-members stand.

"Every person who casts their vote will pay—mark my words!" Talsk shakes a fist in empty air.

"The majority has been reached!" Relief is clear in Lenstativ's every word. "Udeneran Talsk, on behalf of the Assembly of Arvenir, I hereby order you to surrender your crown and relinquish all authority which you previously held as Grand Va' Kied. Under the laws of the Assembly, you may no longer—"

"—I have heard enough of this mockery." Talsk's face is purple with his fury. "Officer Kstoren, arrest this treasonous leech, along with every person here who joined him." He gestures out across the entire Assembly. "And as for you, *Cousin*," Talsk takes a menacing step towards Svarik. "You will wish you had stayed in your little hole back in Tulstead."

I see Tirzah look to me, waiting for a signal. I give the slightest shake of my head. *Not yet.* We have one card that may yet play out: Kstoren. The Grand Officer stands frozen at the foot of the platform.

"Well?" Talsk turns on him. "What are you waiting for?"

Kstoren looks from Talsk, to Grimvold, to Svarik. His posture gives away the strain of his torn loyalties. "Your Highness, be reasonable. By the laws of Arvenir—"

"—I write the law! I *am* Arvenir! If you are loyal to either, then you will do as I command!"

The guards that ring the room—even the ones still holding my chains—look to Kstoren.

"Udeneran, please." Poor Kstoren has been reduced to trying the personal route. "There may still be some form of recourse, but not if you do this. Trust the law; step down and we'll figure out another way."

As Talsk reaches for his sword, Tirzah moves closer to the platform. Tyron and I are too far away even if we could move.

"I won't let this happen." Talsk is like a man possessed as he draws his ceremonial blade and points it at Svarik. "I won't let you do this!"

There are various cries of "Stop him!" and "Guards!" but the soldiers are too far away. I feel the hum of Tyron's Gifting increase as if he is trying to intervene. But Tirzah is faster. As Talsk steps forward and raises the blade, she dives for the platform and slams into his legs. Both go tumbling.

Tirzah recovers quickly, snatching Talsk's sword from his now slackened grip. He tries to take it back but the guards have reached him. He is seized by both arms and hauled up onto his knees. The satisfying click of manacles reaches my ears.

"Cowards! Traitors!" Talsk pulls against his restraints. "You've doomed us all! You'll see—the Myrandi will come and slaughter you without mercy."

Svarik does not react to Talsk's tantrum, instructing one of the guards, "Have him taken to the cells."

"Fine, follow the blind." Talsk is tugged to his feet. "He can't save you any more than his father could save himself."

I see Svarik stop in his tracks.

Oh no....

Talsk grins as he leans forward. "Oh yes, that's right: *I was there*. I know how it all happened. You want to know how?"

Svarik's hands are wrapped in fists around his cane. No, no, if he lashes out now in front of the whole Assembly, there's no telling what would happen.

"Because I'm the one that killed him." Talsk's smile only grows. "Your father was as weak as you are. I couldn't leave Arvenir in his hands, could I? You should have heard the way he—"

"Enough." Svarik snaps. For one wavering moment, he stands there with his cane half raised. Then he spits, "Take him away. His fate will be decided according to the law when the time is right." He turns away and his cane returns to the floor.

Still shouting and sputtering, Talsk is dragged from the hall.

"Release Lady Arhys and detain the Hunter," Svarik orders.

I look back at Tyron. He takes this as his cue and vanishes with one last swell of Gifting.

"Spread out! Find him!" Kstoren orders above the gasps of the crowd.

One of the soldiers stops to help me, picking up the key Tyron dropped and unlocking my shackles. I pretend to be unsteady as he helps me to my feet.

"It's alright, my lady, you're safe now," he assures.

I give a weak smile in thanks, stealing a glance back towards Svarik. He's still standing on the platform with shoulders drooped as if he just remembered how to relax them.

I wonder if he's thinking the same thing I am: I can't believe this worked.

Tyron

First thing first: I return to the cell where the Hunter is still out cold. I untie his hands, return his borrowed garb, and double check that both pieces of red-bronze are still secure. Now I'm back in my servant's uniform and can exit the cell quietly. Somehow, my mop and pail are still in the corridor where I left them. I scoop these up and rush towards the dungeon exit.

"Hey, what's going on?" The soldier at the door peers through the bars.

"I-I went to clean that back cell since the prisoner was out of it," I pant, keeping my eyes wide. "There was someone in there—hiding, in the back corner."

The soldier's expression scrunches up in confusion. Then he freezes as both of us hear the same sound: guards calling to each other, "Quick! They saw him go this way!"

Perfect. Tirzah has done her part.

The soldier now nearly falls over himself in his hurry to unlock the door. "You know the protocol. Get out of here!"

I spare no time in obeying, glancing back just long enough to watch the guard draw his sword and enter the dungeon hallway. Hopefully, he reaches the Hunter before the man wakes. But the footfalls of oncoming guards tell me that I don't have enough time to wait and make sure. I hasten towards my exit.

Abandoning my borrowed mop and pail in a small closet, I Gift myself back to the still waiting carriage. I knock twice on the roof to signal the driver and I hear him cluck to the horses in response. We roll out of the palace courtyard without even a second glance from the guards.

As soon as we arrive at Svarik's borrowed manor, I head directly to my room. I change, wash my face, and practically collapse on my bed. I'm asleep before my head hits the pillow.

I sleep for a full day and a half.

The servants shake me awake after that, telling me that Svarik is now Va' Kied and I am to be his guest at the palace. They help me pack and get me into the waiting royal carriage. At the palace, I am helped in and greeted by staff. I remember asking them about Rhioa and being reassured that 'Lady Arhys' was being well looked after. I also vaguely recall them mentioning a meal and telling me that, after I was settled in my room, a physician would be in to check on me. I don't think I stay awake long enough for that.

I sleep for another day straight.

By the time I wake, I feel nearly back to rights—minus the ravenous hunger. Yet that, too, is easily remedied and soon all the energy that my Gifting depleted has been restored. Unfortunately, the palace physician does not see it my way. Not after he apparently tried to rouse me. Since he was been told that I was injured in the gryphon attack and have not been able to leave my room since, he goes into a fit about "probable cranial injury" and confines me to my room for strict monitoring. He doesn't even allow me any update on Rhioa or Svarik, citing stress as an exasperating factor for concussions.

Luckily, I am able to coax scraps of news from the servants who take turns watching me. They are at least able to tell me that Svarik is solidly in control and that there has been no real resistance from any quarter. But none of them have any word on Rhioa. Two days of that needling uncertainty and my own maddening boredom has me plotting my escape just to keep my mind busy. The sole thing keeping me from carrying out the plan is the knowledge that my 'illness' is my only alibi for the day of the Assembly.

By day three, even that bit of restraint is wearing thin. I'm not sure if it's by good fortune or the physician's intuition that I'm finally allowed a visitor.

"I hear you've been giving the poor physician quite the headache," Svarik says as he enters the room, cane tapping as he goes.

"Svarik," I can't help my utter relief, practically leaping out of my chair. "It's good to see you. How are you? How is Arhys? How is *everything*? No one will tell me any details."

The servant who had been watching me quietly bows and exits the room.

Chuckling, Svarik sits down and waits for the door to click shut before replying. "I am well. Tired, but well. Arhys is fine—she simply seems to have done too well with convincing others of her mistreatment, as she has also been confined to bedrest. But the physician says she is in good shape and should be able to attend the coronation in two days."

I take a deep breath for the first time in days, sitting back down across from him. "I am glad to hear it."

"As for 'everything,' Ilske has been a very busy place," Svarik continues. "Between all the inquiry from nobles who are concerned with how things will proceed from here, I've been working with both Lenstativ and Kstoren to get things stable. And to start undoing Talsk's mess. We started with freeing the men of Tulstead. Then it was returning the confiscated crops to the town of Jysvirun. Then clearing Baron Etdok of all allegations of treason." He crosses one leg over the other and I finally notice his new wardrobe. The deep green dress coat, decked with silver buttons and ornate epaulettes, befits his new station. "After cleaning up our mess, that is. I had to deal with that one guard you left locked up in one of the prison cells."

Oh. How had I forgotten to warn Svarik about that? "Ah, him. My apologies on that one."

With a smile, Svarik replies, "It all worked out. Fortunately, he wasn't able to identify you. So I privately debriefed him about a secret mission that had been run in an attempt to save Lady Arhys, swore him to secrecy, and—as a 'reward'—

have had him restationed up north to be nearer to his family." He sits back in his chair looking nearly smug.

I almost laugh. Perhaps Rhioa and I have rubbed off on him a bit too much. "That takes care of that, then. What about the Hunter? I'm sure he knew me."

"Oh yes, but no one believes a word the man says after the Assembly debacle. Everyone even bought the explanation that he tried to hide in that cell but passed out with the effort of Gifting himself there." Svarik's expression remains quite satisfied. "He certainly doesn't help his case, rambling on for hours like a possessed man. He makes you sound lethal enough to wipe out Ilske with nothing but a snap of your fingers."

This time, I laugh aloud. "Well then, I suppose we should all be glad I keep such power to myself."

"If only your powers were a little more useful," Svarik returns in jest. "Something like reading minds would come in handy about now. It seems that Talsk didn't believe in documenting all of his illegal schemes. It's made it very difficult to find enough information to really make reparations."

"Hence why you're keeping Lenstativ around," I guess.

Svarik's voice is wry. "Correct. He has made himself nearly indispensable. It remains to be seen if he will stay that way." He shakes his head. "Until then, he will be monitored very closely. I will not allow him the same influence or position that he wielded under Talsk, but perhaps he should be given his chance to help however much he can." He drums his fingers on the arm of his chair. "Either way, I plan on learning from his case. I hope to discard the law requiring land ownership for Assembly-member status. Maybe then we can keep others from falling into the trap that Lenstativ did: thinking that moral compromise is the only way to make a true difference."

A fair judgement. And a wise policy. Both, I think, will be a good way to show that Svarik does not plan on ruling in the same manner as his cousin. "How about Kstoren? How is he handling the change?" I ask.

"He is...adjusting." Svarik leans back in his seat. "He is really quite level-headed. But his straightforward, logical way of thinking seems to make it harder for him to grasp that others don't always function the same way. He never suspected the full of Talsk's warped and twisted actions—especially not those against my father."

I remember Talsk's final claim about how he murdered Svarik's father. I also remember the look on Svarik's face as every fear and misgiving he'd had was proved right in an instant. My voice is low when I pose the question: "What are you going to do with him?"

Svarik sucks in a long breath, rolling his cane in one hand. It stills when he replies, "For now, nothing. At least nothing until we have dredged up every aspect of his dealings from the past ten years. When that is complete, and when I can trust myself to keep my head, then he will face trial."

As solemn as the moment is, I nearly smile. Arvenir is in good hands. "That is a wise decision. I think your people will see and take heart."

Svarik sighs, murmuring, "They might not do so if they knew how hard it was for me to do it."

"I disagree," I say quietly. "For as hard as the decision was, you made it anyway. I have seen many leaders, Svarik, and few of them could have done the same. You will do well by your countrymen."

For several seconds, the room holds only the snapping of flames in the hearth and the muted howl of wind against the massive window pane. It is nearly enough to drown out Svarik's gravelly voice when he says, "Thank you. For all of it." He smiles a bit when he adds, "Even for showing up unannounced to my manor. I do not know what it really was that brought you to Tulstead, and you do not have to tell me, but I am thankful all the same. Without your encouragement, I would never have taken that first step."

A sense of warmth grows with his words. "Perhaps not right away, but I think you would have found your way in time."

"Perhaps, perhaps not. Who knows how many more might have suffered in the meantime." Svarik inclines his head. "Either way, I am still grateful. It has been a long time since I have been able to trust someone enough to call them a friend."

I cannot help but feel honored. "I have never managed to keep many friends," I admit. "But I hope I have lived up to that trust. I know I have not always been able to tell you everything, but that has been for your safety—not out of doubt."

"I understand. And I appreciate that you have always watched out for me." Svarik resumes tapping a finger on his cane. "That being said, our situation has changed. I now find myself in a slightly awkward position concerning this treaty my cousin broke. Am I correct to presume that I could bring up this issue to our mutual friend?"

So he *has* put it together. I'm sure Rhioa has already caught on to this, so I reply, "You are correct. Though I'm sure I don't need to remind you of the, er, confidentiality that such a conversation would require."

Svariks nods. "Of course." Then he grins. "So after all of that...my cousin was actually correct."

I rock my head back and forth. "Well, yes, but no one knows."

This only seems to amuse Svarik further. "Imagine the reaction if they found out."

"They can't prove you knew, though," I point out. I allow some humor in my tone when I add, "You could just blame me."

"Seeing as you actually are the one who started this, I would do so gladly." Svarik chuckles.

I smile, taking the joke. But there's one more matter I don't want to set aside yet. "Svarik, just to be sure you know, Rhy truly does care about you and your situation. It wasn't all simply—"

"Tyron, it's alright," he interrupts quietly. "I know. You would not think so highly of someone who was simply using me."

Think so highly.... Does everyone but Rhioa know? I hold in my sigh. "Thank you. If you can convince your physician to let me out, I'd be happy to be there when you bring it up."

"Is this your way of trying to escape?" Svarik doesn't hide his amusement.

So neither do I. "That depends...is it working?"

Smiling once more, Svarik taps his cane on the floor. "I make no promises, but I'll see what I can do." Then his humor dims. "I shouldn't stay for too much longer, but if you don't mind, I did have a favor to ask." He pulls a letter from his coat and hesitates. "All nobles of Assembly rank were sent an invitation to the coronation, as is standard practice. But my mother wrote back. Would you read it for me?" He holds out the parchment.

I take it, somber when I reply, "Of course." I unfold the letter and recite, "To the Grand Va' Kied Ihail: I am writing to express my gratitude for your kind invitation." I wish I could stop reading there. With a last glance at Svarik, I continue. "I regret that I must decline, for matters at my estate do not currently permit me to travel. Please accept my warmest congratulations and my well wishes for the day of your ceremony. I hope that the accompanying gift may make up for my absence. Signed, Baroness Ihail of Dolsni Manor."

Svarik sits very still, his mouth pressed into a narrow line.

"I-I think she might have begun to write a post-script," I say, unsure if I am correct or if it was simply a stray drop of ink. "I can't quite tell."

Svarik seems to process this. "I..." He opens his mouth, then closes it and lets out a long breath. "I suppose it doesn't matter."

He holds his hand out for the letter and I lay it in his palm. He tucks it back into his coat, gets to his feet, and squares his shoulders. "I should get back to work. But I'll speak to the physician on my way out and see if he'll allow your discharge. Let me know if there is anything you need in the meantime."

I pause, wishing to apologize on behalf of his mother—or at least to give some expression of sympathy. But I do not think now is the time. "Thank you," I say instead. Then another thought crosses my mind. "Actually, there is one thing...."

CHAPTER 21

Rhioa

"You're worse than Tyron," Tirzah grumbles in Pershizarian.

"That's because Tyron was actually sick," I mutter back. "I've been sitting here for days with not a thing wrong with me."

Tirzah raises an eyebrow. "In case you haven't noticed, I've been doing the same thing."

I get up from my chair and cross to the window of our little sitting room, looking out at the snowy courtyard below. "Yes, well, you don't *have* to. You could leave anytime you wanted."

"Oh yes, how silly of me," Tirzah's monotone continues behind me. "How could I forget all the *thrilling* things to go do by myself? I could go for a *stroll*, or have a nice *chat* with the staff, or maybe take a lovely *tour* of the palace." I can practically hear her rolling her eyes. "Maybe if I did all of that, I'd be sick enough that Tyron would send me flowers too."

I am very glad that I picked this moment to look out the window so that she can't see me blush. Even still, I have to keep myself from looking towards the lovely, blue bouquet to my left. "If you really want flowers so much, I'll order you some," I reply dryly. "But I was thinking you could stay occupied with more practical things. Maybe finding us a carriage to the port or packing our luggage." I turn away from the view and walk back towards my seat.

Tirzah's sarcasm has dissipated, leaving tension in its place. "How soon do we need to leave?"

I know she's been thinking of the same thing I have—or, more accurately, trying *not* to think of it. "As soon as we're sure Svarik's position is moderately stable." I sit down, smoothing out my skirts. I know someone else will be sent to monitor the situation once we're gone. "Hopefully that is within the next week. Because of the Assembly, we've drawn far more attention than we usually do.

There's too much risk of someone discovering us for us to stay any longer than necessary."

Looking down at her hand, Tirzah rolls her puzzle ring around her finger as she seems to roll her words around in her mouth. But before she can let them out, a knock comes at the door.

"Pardon my interruption, my lady, madam," A maid curtsies to us both. "But the Grand Va' Kied and his friend are here to see you."

Svarik and Tyron? "Thank you. Please show them in."

The maids curtsies again and ducks out of the room, leaving Tirzah and I to share a quick glance. Then the door reopens and Svarik walks in.

"Lady Arhys, how are you feeling?" he asks.

I'm distracted a moment by Tyron entering behind him, pausing only to close the door.

I'm still not sure how much Svarik knows, so I reply, "Much better, thanks to your physician." I add a touch of humor just to be safe. "And thanks to you, *Your Highness.*"

"Is this where I am supposed to, as you say, roll my eyes?" Svarik shakes his head, using his cane to find a chair and take his seat. "To be quite honest, I have no idea what motion is being described there. But I take it that it is sufficiently indecorous."

I suppose I never really thought about how Svarik must interpret the saying. Come to think of it, it is a rather odd description....

"Indecorous?" Tyron repeats, looking a little lost as he, too, takes his seat across from us.

Oh, right, I forget Arvenish is still comparatively new for him. I quickly translate in the trade language.

"Ah." His voice turns mischievous as he turns to Svarik. "Well, if it is so 'indecorous,' then it certainly isn't fit for an esteemed ruler such as yourself."

Svarik gives an overdone sigh. "So this is how it's going to be, is it? Nothing but jests about my rank from here on out?"

"If you don't like it," Tirzah joins in her usual dry manner. "You could always order us to stop."

Tyron laughs as Svarik's mouth hangs briefly open.

"You, too, Tahra?" Svarik collects himself, giving a frown to hide his smile. He gestures vaguely in Tyron's direction. "I shouldn't have convinced the physician to let you out today. At least then I wouldn't have been so sorely outnumbered."

Is *that* why Tyron is out when I am still confined to my room for monitoring? I narrow my eyes at him, but this only makes him grin. Somehow, this makes me remember the flowers he sent. I feel my cheeks go warm and I look away.

"Humor aside, I am very glad to hear you are well." Svarik's voice holds more sincerity now. "You gave us quite the scare after the gryphon attack, and then again when we heard of your capture. I am truly sorry for any distress you endured for helping me."

Tirzah had filled me in on her and Tyron's sparse description of my capture, so I know to tread carefully. Still, I am earnest when I reply, "You have nothing to apologize for. All of that was Talsk's doing and, as I have heard, you have already begun the steps to undo his wrongs."

Svarik dips his head. "I am trying. It is admittedly difficult when I don't yet know all of his dealings, but I am trying." One finger begins to tap on his cane. "There is one matter in particular that I find rather pressing. One concerning a broken treaty."

So he knows. I look to Tyron, who nods in silent confirmation. Something in my stomach tightens as my gaze turns to Tirzah. She has gone rigid, watching me for any sign of what to do next.

"Is this a matter which I can take up with you both?" Svarik asks.

I swallow, take a deep breath, and answer for Tirzah and myself. "We do not have the authority to repair the treaty. But we can pass on the information that you are willing to do so. Someone else will be sent to settle the details."

"Understood. If you pass that on, then, I would be grateful." Svarik speaks quite calmly, as if this is like any other conversation I've had with him and not me admitting to lying to him about my very identity.

"Of course," I murmur. Somehow, his composure only adds to my guilt. How long as he known? Why did he never question or reject us?

Svarik clears his throat. "Perhaps this is a touch too personal, but would I be allowed to know your names?"

The request catches me off guard. Tirzah's furrowed brow tells me that she has had the same reaction. Tyron, on the other hand, gives a sort of reassuring smile.

"It would be safer for you if you did not." I keep my answer low. "If anyone was to find out that you knew we were involved, it would be very dangerous for you." I hesitate, then add, "I'm sorry. And I'm sorry that we did not tell you of...this."

Svarik tilts his head. "If you told me not to apologize for the actions of my cousin, perhaps you should not apologize for the actions of those who sent you. I understand the nature of your situation, Arhys. And you as well, Tahra. I appreciate that you both have been careful not to jeopardize my safety, even at the risk of your own."

I...I don't even know what to say. Of all the reactions I'd have expected, this would have never crossed my mind. I almost want to argue with him—to tell him that he's wrong and that he doesn't understand what we are. But in the same stroke, I want him to be right about us. I *want* to believe that we only ever lied to keep him safe. I want to forget what might have happened if our orders had been different.

"Thank you," is the only thing I can think to say.

Svarik simply nods. Then he squares his shoulders. "There, now that business is out of the way, I thought we might all have tea together—for old times' sake."

"Old times? Are you referring to two months ago as 'old times'?" Tyron raises an eyebrow. He's already on his feet, heading for the door to call the maid.

"Fine, simpler times then," Svarik calls back to him. "I suppose you simply wouldn't understand how complicated life as a ruler can be."

...Is he...smirking?

"And here I thought that making fun of rank had been outlawed," I comment wryly.

"Ah, but I never said that *I* couldn't do it," Svarik replies.

Tirzah gives a rather unladylike snort. "It's been a week and the power's already gone to his head; He thinks himself above his own laws."

"Tahra's right," Tyron cuts in as he rejoins the conversation. "I say we humble him with a game of chess—for Arvenir's sake, of course."

Svarik chuckles. I don't think I've ever seen him so relaxed. "Fine, but only one game. I have a meeting with Elsze this afternoon."

Tyron returns to the circle of chairs, grinning unabashedly.

Tirzah and I look at each other and make a face.

"If you three are done making fun of me when you think I can't tell," Svarik taps on his cane on the floor. "Let's get this game set up. And let's pick who will watch Tyron to make sure he doesn't cheat."

"Why does everyone accuse me of cheating?" Tyron complains, kneeling beside the small game table and rummaging for boards.

Now it's my turn to smile. "That's what you get for winning so often."

"Isn't winning the whole point?" Tyron begins to pull out pieces. "What if I'm simply just good at it?"

"He's definitely cheating. I'll watch him." Tirzah's smug statement earns her a mock glare from Tyron.

"Perfect." Svarik taps his cane on the rug. "Tahra and I will be a team, and Arhys and Tyron, you two can be the other."

I lean forward to help Tyron set up. "Alright, *Your Highness*, you have yourself a match."

Tyron

A week and a day after Svarik's victory in the Assembly, I stand in the royal palace ballroom. I take in the sound of music and conversation, kept in rhythm by the swishing of dancers' skirts. The visual follows with the beat, mirrored in doubles by the polished floor and the gilded ceiling overhead. The wafting spices from the nearby tables mingle with the sweeter scent of flowers arranged on stands throughout the hall.

And now I get to just stand and enjoy it all. No more planned conversations, no more careful first impressions: just a celebration. It feels all the more fitting that it should be held here in the very room where Svarik was first reintroduced.

What a contrast tonight is from that first ball. I can see Svarik from across the way, his crown gleaming in the light of the chandeliers. He has worn it only a few hours and already it seems natural to him. Though, if I were to ask, I think he would be more pleased with that which is on his arm than is on his head. Elszebet Sohlv has not left his side since the moment Svarik's coronation ended.

Nearby are Elsze's parents. Not far from them, I spot Duchess Oskoristiv and Count Tskei. Lord Runim is laughing along with Viscount Postorik while Grand Officer Kstoren relays some tale. Even Archduke Grimvold looks like he's almost enjoying himself. Perhaps I am biased, but it feels as though everyone has let out a long sigh of relief. I hope that same relief spreads from Ilske to every corner of Arvenir.

"Oh, here you are." The exclamation makes me jump and I turn to find Rhioa asking, "Where have you been hiding?"

She is dressed in a gown of pale blue, embroidered with flourishes of gold that match her upswept hair. But it's her smile and warm, brown eyes that rob me of any reply.

Thankfully, Tirzah fills in with, "I'm pretty sure he's the tallest person in the room. I don't think he could hide if he wanted to."

I recover myself enough to say, "Indeed. Though that does not seem to be a problem that you two share. I do believe I missed your announcement." I gesture to the staircase that I'd been watching in the hopes of spotting them.

"We found a quieter way in." Rhioa's smile turns mischievous as she tips her head towards one of the hall's back doors. "Now that we are palace guests, the staff was all too happy to show us."

I can't help but think of the first ball again. Rhioa's entrance has been as carefully planned as everything else she'd done that evening. But now that she isn't under orders, she's wearing her favorite color and sneaking in unannounced. I've never seen her look so genuinely happy.

"Very clever," I reply, adding a dry, "I should have thought of that." Then I give a look to where Svarik is still standing and chatting with some of the noblemen. "We'll just have to make sure that Svarik knows you're here."

Rhioa follows my gaze over. "True. But not right now—he looks busy." Then she seems to notice something else. She scans the room as she asks, "Did his mother not come?"

I shake my head. "She has made her choice."

Rhioa's look grows solemn and, I think, understanding.

So I try to brighten the mood again, pointing out, "But look who *is* with him."

I watch Rhioa and Tirzah spot Elsze at the same time and give a simultaneous eye roll.

"You and your matchmaking." Rhioa shakes her head.

"I told you that all they needed was a little nudge," I say smugly.

"Which I helped with," Rhioa insists. "Remember what I told you about the concert?"

I feign a moment of deliberation. "I suppose you did contribute to some extent." I put a hand to my chin. "Although you don't quite make a full matchmaker. You're more of, hm, a meddler."

"A meddler?" Rhioa looks properly indignant.

"Please, you two, we're still in public," Tirzah reminds in monotone. "And one would think that you two could do something other than argue after being allowed out for the first time in a week."

"Actually, I've been out for a whole day now," I remind her. "Rhy is the one who just escaped the physician."

Rhioa's smile twists in rueful fashion. "Yes, it seems that I was a bit too convincing last week. I didn't think it would earn me that many days of bedrest." Then she pauses, clearing her throat. "Thank you, um, for the flowers you sent."

Oh, uh, "I thought they might brighten up the room a bit. Perhaps even keep you from plotting your escape too soon." I have to curb the sudden urge to run my hand through my hair. "I am glad you're feeling better."

She gives a little nod before a wry expression slips across her face. "Yes. Much better. Just like your arm, I see."

"Here we go again." Tirzah's back to rolling her eyes. "Back to the arguing. Could you at least go dance or something so that I don't have to stand here like a good little companion?"

Rhioa shoots her sister a glare.

But I seize the opportunity. "Perhaps Madam Tahra deserves a reprieve. Shall we take this dance for her?" I hold out my hand.

I catch the way Rhioa's eyes widen slightly as if caught off guard. She opens her mouth as if to argue, then pauses. She recovers with a narrowed look at her sister. "Fine, *Madam Tahra*, you may be dismissed for a turn or two."

She lays her gloved hand in mine and we turn towards the dancers. It's by the last glance over my shoulder that I notice Tirzah's face. Is that a smile on her lips? Perhaps I've given the title of 'meddler' to the wrong person....

We reach the floor and I turn to face Rhioa. With one hand holding hers and the other at her waist, I step into the beat and she follows.

"I'm surprised you can even dance," Rhioa says dryly. "Seeing as you slept for four days straight."

I shake my head in time to the music. "Your source has failed you—it was for *two* days straight. I got up for about an hour before I slept for one more day, and I've been fine ever since."

Rhioa gives her signature unimpressed expression. "Right. Only three days total. Such an improvement."

"I think that my efforts were rather merited, given the circumstances." I raise an eyebrow. "If you disagree with my methods, perhaps you should try staying out of prison cells."

Even as she lets go of my shoulder to step back and twirl, I can see her roll her eyes. "Oh yes, you've never spent time in one of those before."

I pull her back in, perfectly in sync with the couples around us. "I don't think a few hours in the brig of a ship counts."

"Oh? How about the little mop closet that they made you sleep in for several days after?" Rhioa picks up her chin in playful humor as she makes her point.

"The door didn't lock, therefore, it doesn't count," I reply, trying to coax out the smile she's fighting.

"Really? The door didn't lock. That's what makes a prison?" Her lips curve at the corners. "I feel like there are other requirements."

I guide our steps past a cluster of dancers, maneuvering to make sure Rhy won't get bumped into by anyone. "I suppose it all boils down to not being able to walk out whenever you please—which is what I could do with that closet." I assume an overly thoughtful frown. "Although, by that definition, Svarik's tailor would qualify. He made me stand for over an hour while he worked this time. And there was no escape without getting stabbed by all his pins."

Rhioa's smile breaks through. "You are ridiculous." She shakes her head as we swing to the side and back. "And that still doesn't count. That was for your own good."

"My own good?" I pause as I hold an arm above her head, letting her twirl. "I doubt that anyone threatening to stab me has my interest in mind."

Now Rhioa's tone turns to that of a mother scolding a child. "That poor tailor, always putting up with your antics. Whether you like it or not, he has good taste and has managed to make you look quite handsome."

As soon as the words leave her mouth, Rhioa seems to realize what they all mean. At least that's what I gather from her entire face turning scarlet.

Before her embarrassment can set in, I remark, "On the contrary, I think it looks hideous." Then I clear my throat and add, "But come, we'll have plenty of time to argue later. For now, I rather like this tune and am inclined to enjoy it while I can."

Rhioa seems to catch that this a good way for her to get out of having to explain herself. Still blushing heartily, she concedes with a final mock glare. Then she surprises me by closing her eyes. No checking exits, no scanning the crowds, no studying me for some double meaning. She responds to my cues without hesitation, her hand keeping the same light, steady contact with mine.

And for one, single moment, I have everything. The trouble of my family is behind me, the friends I've made since are all safe. Svarik has won back his crown and stands proudly beside Elsze. Tirzah is on the side of the dance floor, watching with a self-satisfied smirk. And Rhioa is in my arms, stepping and spinning with the music that weaves around us. I can't take my eyes off of her. The closed eyes, the soft smile—the peaceful expression that I've never seen her wear before. I wish it would never fade.

Then the music finishes. The soft tapping of dancing shoes around us pauses, replaced by genteel applause. Rhioa stops, too, opening her eyes to look up at me. That's when I realize my mistake: I've tasted what it is to have everything, and now I don't want to let it go.

"Is everything alright?" Rhioa's brow furrows.

Those deep, brown eyes make my breath catch. There's a rustling around us as couples bow and curtsy in turn, moving to clear the floor. We're supposed to be doing the same. But how can I bring myself to let go?

On sudden, stupid impulse, I bring Rhioa's gloved hand to my lips before I release it. She looks as shocked by the gesture as I am.

Still breathless, I hear myself say, "I think I need some air." I turn and walk way before she can even reply. I don't trust myself for even that much longer.

Idiot.

.

CHAPTER 22

Rhioa

Confused, flustered, I watch Tyron head for one of the side doors. Should I follow him? He seemed.... I don't even know. Upset feels like the wrong word.

Someone brushing past me reminds me that I'm still in the middle of the dance floor. Self-conscious, I head for the edge. How many people saw that? I spot Tirzah among the crowd. Guessing by the way she's craning her head towards the side doors, she saw every bit of it.

I reach Tirzah and her puzzled expression asks what she does not.

"I don't know what happened," I answer, keeping my voice low enough that others won't overhear. "I didn't even say anything."

Tirzah glances back to the doors. "Shouldn't you go check on him then?"

Still unsure of myself after, well, whatever it was that just happened, I reply slowly. "I'm not sure. If he just needs a moment, or maybe some fresh air, then—"

Tirzah's eyes dart to something behind me and I cut myself off.

"Oh, Lady Arhys, I'm so glad to see you out and about!"

I turn around and curtsy in greeting to the Viscountess Postorik. "How lovely to see you again, Viscountess." I don't think I've seen Elsze's friend since that first ball.

Returning the gesture, the noblewoman quickly continues, "We were all horrified to hear of what happened to you. It must have been so frightening—I can't believe you're out so soon after such an ordeal."

"I owe that to the new Grand Va' Kied," I reply, keeping my tone warm. "Without his intervention and the kindliness of his physician, I don't know where I would be."

The effervescent woman gives a sympathetic shake of her head. "Well, I'm glad it all came right in the end." She looks across the room to where Svarik is talking with a few of the lords. "He has surprised us all."

"All except for one," I counter.

The viscountess smiles and I watch her gaze drift towards Elsze. "You're right. She always did hold out for him, didn't she? I always thought that that stubbornness did her a disservice. But it seems to have finally won out." She turns back to me. "I think they will make a marvelous couple."

I am struck by how genuine the statement is. I have been in enough royal courts to know how deeply greed and jealousy runs through them. It makes me glad that Svarik and Elsze will have some true supporters after we leave. "Yes, I think you are right."

Viscountess Postorik's smile turns sly. "Speaking of, where is that handsome dancing partner of yours?"

Handsome. The reminder of my earlier blunder makes my cheeks go warm, as does the implication that the viscountess saw us dancing. Perhaps this is a good time to exit the conversation.... "I was actually just about to go find him. He managed to wander off after the last tune."

Now the noblewoman looks triumphant, as if I have confirmed some guess of hers. "Then don't let me hold you up. I was just about to go say hello to Elsze anyway."

With a farewell and a wave, we part ways. I head straight for the side doors if only to escape any further small talk. And maybe to escape Tirzah's sideways glances.

"Not a word," I grumble. "Cover for me. And come find me when Svarik's about to start his speech. I'm sure Tyron won't want to miss it."

With Tirzah's nod, I slip out the door.

The hallway is empty. I pause, glance up and down the different corridors, then pick the one that leads directly away from the ballroom. The muted noise of the party follows me as I go, audible even as I peer down the lantern-lit side passages. I don't know where any of them lead and I can't see around any of the corners. Maybe it's better just to go back to the ballroom and wait for Tyron to return. Just as I am about to follow through on that idea, I catch the low hum of Gifting.

I follow it further, down the hall and around the bend until I find myself in another long corridor. The passageway is unlit except for the floor-to-ceiling window at its end. The glowing snowscape outside, illuminated as it is by the moon, fills the hall with a pale light. All except for the silhouette that stands framed in the center of the window.

I draw a little closer, wanting to be certain its him before I call his name. He must hear my footsteps for he turns right before I speak.

"A little macabre, don't you think?"

I'm close enough to make out his face in the dim lighting, but I still have no idea what Tyron is talking about. "What do you mean?"

He nods towards the wall. "All the animals. Talsk's trophies, I presume. Do you think Svarik knows they're up there?"

...Is he talking about the taxidermy? "Actually, it's a common Arvenish custom," I explain, barely glancing at the wall. "Many of those are likely from Svarik's father and grandfather and so on."

Tyron wrinkles his nose in apparent distaste.

"Of all the things you've dealt with, are you really going to tell me that taxidermy is what bothers you the most?" I can't help my own amusement, even if I know he's just trying to avoid a different topic.

"In my defense," Tyron looks up at the wall again as I reach him. "I come from a land of shape-shifters. When most of the people you know can shift into animals, it's a little unsettling to see animal carcasses being used for décor."

"I suppose that's fair," I concede. I hesitate before adding, "Though I presume that that's not what's bothering you."

Now Tyron looks out the window, hands folded neatly behind his back. "It was just a bit stuffy in there," he says evenly. He manages a touch of sheepishness when he adds, "Perhaps I'm not as recovered as I thought. But it's much cooler out here and I feel fine now."

It is certainly much cooler in the hall—cold even. I can feel the chill emanating from the window pane a few feet away. But I still don't buy the excuse.

It makes me recall that day when Talsk had invited Tyron on the hunt. Specifically, the way Tyron had so seamlessly hidden the letter and given his own explanation for why he should go. He did the same thing the night that the Hunter beat him up, and then again when he claimed he could heal himself without too much harm. It's a pattern: He deflects the issue, brings up a lesser matter, and then gives reassurance over that.

Before I can even think it through, I find myself commenting, "I never quite realized how good you are at hiding what you're really thinking."

Tyron keeps his gaze fixed on the window, but his shoulders droop slightly. "Not as good as I ought to be, it would seem," he murmurs.

"What does that mean?" I press on.

Finally he looks at me, the moonlight casting shadows over the conflict in his features. "Please," he says softly. "Do not ask me. Not now."

I'm only further confused. "If not now, when? Why wait if it is troubling you so?"

The deep breath he lets out sounds strained, as if he has to consciously remember to breathe. "It's hard to explain. I will do so when the time is right."

Something about Tyron's refusal stings. I try to think through our dance, sifting through each step for something that I could have done wrong. "Is it something I said?"

"No, no, you didn't do anything." Tyron shakes his head.

My mind catches on the way he kissed my hand, then the viscountess and her comments. "Is it because everyone thinks we're courting?"

Tyron's calm posture cracks as he runs a hand through his hair. "Please, Rhy, let it go."

It's that, isn't it? Embarrassment flares and I look away. Why did he insist on dancing if he didn't want people drawing such conclusions? "I didn't realize that it bothered you so much," I say stiffly. "In that case, I will head back before anyone notices we're both gone."

"Wait, Rhy," he reaches out a hand as I turn from the window. "That's not what I meant."

I feel so foolish for all my earlier guesses. How could I have misread him so badly? My cheeks burn at the very thought that someone like him could ever want me. "It's alright. I understand: I know what I am and what I've done. I do not blame you."

Tyron looks baffled. "What?"

I stop in my tracks, wishing he wouldn't make me say it. "If I were you, I would not want to be associated with someone like me either." I swallow. "As I said, I understand."

Tyron looks at me for so long that I nearly give up and just walk away. I almost do. But then he calls my name in such a soft voice that I can't carry through.

"Rhioa," He sounds nearly heartbroken. "Do you really have no idea how dear you are to me?"

I stare at him, speechless.

"I have been drawn you since the very first moment I saw you, and every day since has only made you more precious to me." His words come in a torrent. "I didn't understand it at first. I tried ignore it, to stifle it as much as I could. But everything about you—your strength, your grace, your brilliance, the way you care so *deeply*—how could I pretend not to see it? I am certain now of what I suspected that day you found me: I have never known anyone like you. And I love you more than I ever knew was possible."

The declaration leaves me stunned. Perhaps even scared. Even with all my earlier guesses, I somehow feel blindsided. I'm nearly out of breath as I ask the one question that comes to mind: "Why have you never said anything?"

Tyron is back to raking a hand through his hair. "Because I also knew it could never be. If the differences in age weren't enough, I have nothing to offer you. No safety, no home—nothing." He lets out a frustrated sort of sigh. "Besides, I knew you did not feel the same way. I didn't want you to feel as though you had to reciprocate in order to earn whatever help I could give you." His eyes meet mine, his expression pained. "I hope, at least, that you know me well enough by now to know that I would never want that."

My mind feels completely numb. At least I have enough of my senses left to nod.

"I'm sorry. I shouldn't have said anything." He turns back to the window. "I had resolved not to say anything. Especially not tonight, when you were enjoying yourself." His quiet laugh is bitter. "So much for that."

I step up beside him and, for several minutes, we stand watching the wind pick up snowflakes and send them tumbling against the glass in a soundless rhythm. They scatter and fall away as quickly as my thoughts do.

"You know, I am considered the same age to my race as you are to yours." My voice sounds foreign to my own ears.

Tyron looks at me, brow furrowed deeply as if he can't understand why I would offer him hope.

I'm not sure why either. Yet, somehow, I'm still talking. "And what would it matter what you could offer? I have nothing to give in return." *What are you saying? Do you even hear yourself?*

Tyron has collected himself, hands folded behind his back once more. But his demeanor is still troubled. He draws breath to reply.

A voice interrupts. "Rhy? Tyron?" I look over my shoulder as Tirzah's voice echoes down the corridor. "Svarik is about to begin his speech."

I glance up towards Tyron. He closes his eyes a moment, sets his shoulders, then turns away from the window. "I suppose we should get back, then."

I look down at the arm he holds out to me. Just like that? He said all of that, and he's willing to set it aside so easily? Part of me tells myself that I should be glad for such a providential escape from this conversation. The other part of me wants to tell Tirzah to go back without us.

Still numb, I take Tyron's arm and nod. "I suppose so."

Together, we walk back towards Tirzah and then on to the ballroom. But somehow the beauty of the night has dimmed. The warm flickering of chandeliers and lanterns feels overbright after the pale moonlight, the singing of instruments oversweet compared to the deep stillness of snowfall. Even as Svarik gives his speech and the crowd raises their goblets in a toast, my drink tastes sour. Or perhaps that's just the regret I'm tasting.

I steal a glance towards Tyron, who keeps his eyes carefully fixed on Svarik.

Yes, I think it's the regret.

Tyron

You are an idiot.

After a whole week, I still can't believe I said what I did. I replay the conversation over and over each night as I stare at the ceiling. *What a fool!* How could I have made it so far and then blown it so suddenly? Maybe I really was more tired than I had realized. Or maybe it had been seeing Rhioa actually, truly enjoying herself. Or maybe it was letting myself get carried away with that dance.

No matter the reason, I cannot take it back. Nor can I forget Rhioa's reaction. She had been so still, completely silent as I poured out my feelings. And then she had given that delayed response: *You know, I am considered the same age to my race as you are to yours.* Had she meant to give me hope? Or was she just trying to spare me the humiliation of my situation? The uncertainty is more torturous than even a blunt refusal would have been.

But this time, I will not ask. Rhioa knows how I feel; if she wishes to bring up the subject, then it is better to let her do so when she is ready. I am determined to respect whatever she chooses to do. I can't say that it's easy, not when I spend so much of the day with her and Tirzah.

Both have been unusually quiet since the coronation. Whether it's because of me or because of what lies ahead, I'm not sure. Neither speaks of going home, only of various packing details and arranging a carriage back to the coast. It seems that they do not stay around for long after their mission is complete. It makes sense. With investigations into Talsk and the Hunters, any questions raised about 'Arhys' could become difficult to navigate.

That being said, I understand why poor Svarik is taken aback when he hears we plan to leave so soon. He tries to coax us into staying longer, all the way up to the day we're meant to leave. In fact, all the way up until we're all standing in the palace courtyard with our luggage loaded on the carriage.

"Are you certain you can't stay for a few more days?" he asks, gloved fingers tapping on the end of his cane. "It's been barely a week since the coronation."

"I'm sorry," I say sincerely. I glance towards Rhioa and Tirzah, speaking to Elsze a few feet away. I keep my explanation veiled when I say, "I really wish we could. But Arhys has already extended her stay far more than she was supposed to. She doesn't want to leave anyone worrying for any longer than necessary."

Svarik sighs. "I understand." He inclines his head as he adds, "Though, I'll admit, your help will be sorely missed."

I smile. "Missed, perhaps, but I don't think needed. You have established yourself very well for such a short amount of time—and all without me." He really does look every inch a ruler, from his crown to his dress coat to his confident bearing. He has come a long way from the count of Tulstead. "Besides, any who still suspect you of relying on me or Arhys will have no basis for such suspicion once we're gone."

"I think even those with suspicions don't mind so long as Talsk stays locked away," Svarik says dryly. "Even more so if I give them all a chance to testify while in trial."

"True," I concede. I look back at the three ladies. "And perhaps by the time you have to precede over that case, you will have someone to help you in your decision."

Svarik's face reddens a touch, but he can't seem to hold back his smile. "Perhaps. And perhaps the travel ahead will give you an opportunity to, shall we say, procure the same help."

For once, I am very glad that Svarik cannot see my face. I swallow my reaction as quickly as I can before replying, "Perhaps."

Rhioa, Tirzah, and Elsze choose that moment to join us.

"We should let them get going," Elsze says as she puts a hand on Svarik's arm. "They will want to reach the exchange station by nightfall."

Svarik lays his hand over hers, a gesture that makes Elsze appear suddenly self-conscious. "You're right." He straightens his shoulders. "All your luggage is secure? And you have the letter I gave you?"

"Completely secure," I affirm.

"And I have the letter here," Rhioa replies, holding up the sealed parchment.

"Good. Make sure to present that at any inn you stay at." Svarik is back to twirling his cane. "And at the port, too, should you find an Arvenish vessel."

I catch the way Elsze squeezes his arm slightly, as if reminding him that he has given this same instruction twice within the last hour.

"Yes, yes, sorry, I just want to make sure everything is in place for them," Svarik mumbles.

"You have been more than thorough." It is Rhioa who reassures him. "I'm sure we will have very smooth travels, thanks to you."

"It is the least I could do for such friends as you." Svarik bows his head. "You have done so much more for me than I could ever repay. I hope that you will at least visit again someday so that I might continue to try. All of you will always be welcome in Arvenir."

Rhioa looks sincerely touched as she bows her head in return. "Thank you."

And thus we come to the final farewell. We all stand there, reluctant to say it.

It is Svarik who clears his throat first. "Then I suppose this is goodbye. Be well, be safe, and do not be strangers." His voice holds humor when he adds, "And maybe try to stay out of trouble. At least for a few weeks."

I chuckle. "I'm afraid that last point might be too much to promise, but we'll do our best with the first three."

"This is Tyron we're talking about," Rhioa chimes in. "I bet we won't even make it to the coast without him getting wrapped up in something."

Svarik laughs. "Maybe I should have another letter made for you—just in case."

Taking a page from Rhioa's book, I roll my eyes. "Alright, very funny. If you two want to make fun of me, I think I'll go wait in the carriage."

I give a final bow of my head to Elsze and she, smiling in a nearly sympathetic manner, returns the gesture. With that, I turn and climb into the waiting coach.

It's a few moments more before Rhioa and Tirzah climb in after me. But then the footman closes the door, the driver calls to the horses, and the whole carriage lurches forward. I look out the window to take in my last view of the palace. Svarik and Elsze still stand in the courtyard, two steadfast figures, arm in arm as they watch us go.

"They will do very well," I comment as the carriage turns out of the front gate and cuts off my view.

"I think you are right," Rhioa murmurs.

Tirzah leans one arm against the side of the coach, still looking out the window. "It's sort of nice to be the heroes."

The candid remark takes me by surprise. Before I can say anything, Tirzah turns away from the rolling city view and back to me and Rhy.

"So what's next?"

Rhioa's expression closes off. Funny how I've forgotten that that's how it always used to be. Very quietly, she replies, "We go home."

Tirzah's gaze darts to me before settling on her sister. "Home? To Iruscaed? Are you sure?"

"What other option do we have?" Rhioa swallows. "Ovok surely knows of Tyron by now. If we go to our next meeting point, whoever they send to meet us will likely have orders to kill him. And if we run, it's only a matter of time before we're caught. He would still be executed."

Now Tirzah has also reverted to her old bearing: that stone-faced, stiff-shouldered posture. "Going home will just be getting it over with," she mutters. "Ovok has never been one for mercy. We'd be better off running and making the most of whatever time we get."

Rhioa looks away.

I decide that it's time I speak up. "I know that this matter is very personal for you both, but please remember that it is my own choices which have put me in this position. I understood as much when I followed you here from Krysophera." I keep my voice calm and even. "So if going back to your home is the only option where we all have a chance at walking away from this, then I am willing to go. And should it go awry, the responsibility is my own—not either of yours."

At first, the only sound is the frozen cobblestones rattling away beneath the carriage wheels. Rhioa and Tirzah have become twin statues, each fixated on some distant object.

It is Rhioa who moves first. She squares her shoulders to say, "We won't let that happen." Her voice is nearly brusque. "We will figure something out."

"Rhy..." Tirzah murmurs.

"There has to be something," Rhioa charges on, now addressing me. "Something to make you valuable enough that Ovok won't want to just have you killed."

"But if he's valuable, Ovok will just have him locked up," Tirzah points out. "Or worse—made into a slave or into someone like us."

Rhioa is gripping the window sill beside her as she insists, "We will figure something out. There has to be a way."

I break in to add, "We have several weeks to come up with a plan and a backup or two. Considering that we've rarely had more than a few days for planning, and seeing how it's worked out before, I'm sure we'll manage."

Judging by the way both of them are still visibly gritting their teeth, my attempt at encouragement falls short.

All the same, Rhioa gives a terse nod. "Exactly. If there is any way, we'll find it." She looks to her sister.

Tirzah's gaze remains glued to the empty seat across from her.

After all that Rhioa told me, and after all I have seen these sisters go through, I cannot blame either of them for such a reaction. But a new worry crosses my mind for the first time: If we face their father and it goes badly, will I have left them both in a worse state than when I found them? I will need to make backup plans of my own to make sure that even that possibility works in their favor.

"Fine." Tirzah pushes the word through her teeth. "We go home." She finally looks at her sister. "But this is the end of it all. No more missions, no more killing, no more watching and doing nothing. If Ovok will not let us go, then...."

The way she trails off confirms my fears.

It only worsens when Rhioa swallows and says, "I understand."

"While I hope it does not come to that, I also hope that neither of you will give up on each other simply because of me. You have fought too long and made it too far to stop now." My words come quickly, urgently. "Like I said, we still have plenty of time to plan this out. We will make sure there is a plan for even the worst imaginable outcome. But promise me: no rash decisions and no giving up. Alright?"

With a stiff sigh, Tirzah dips her head in what I decide is a nod.

I turn to Rhioa, but she will not look at me. "We'll figure something out," she mumbles again. "There has to be something."

For all our sakes, I hope that she's right.

CHAPTER 23

Rhioa

We reach the northern coast of Arvenir and follow our usual end-of-mission sequence. This begins with finding a busy inn where we will not be notable and sorting all of our belongings. All letters of introduction, along with Svarik's letter of passage, are carefully burned. Any trappings that would signify noble status are sold piecemeal throughout the city—the exception being Tyron's signet ring, which he sews back into his coat lining. Whatever practical clothing we lack is then purchased from a variety of vendors. This also allows us to get rid of any coinage large enough to attract attention.

With each letter we burn and each ballgown we quietly sell, the world feels a little colder. I hadn't realized how much I'd let myself pretend. I'd let myself forget about home, about Father, about what I am. For a moment, we'd been as Tirzah said, "the heroes," champions of a noble cause. Our victory brought justice to those who had been denied it, peace where there might have been war, and security to an entire country. The daydream had been so real that I had nearly let myself believe it.

But there is no more time for pretending. Every time we leave the inn, I find myself checking over my shoulder. Each night there, I lie awake listening for footsteps in the hall or tapping at the window. As soon as we've boarded our boat, Tirzah and I spend the first day discreetly checking the crew and other passengers to confirm they're not working for Ovok. Only then can I let myself relax.

However, the close quarters leave me with a different issue: Tyron. He is as kind and courteous as ever, but I do not miss the new quietness he wears. He never mentions that night in the moonlit hallway, nor anything he said then, yet I know that he is still thinking of it. It's the only reason I don't put it off as another part of my foolish daydreams. His features bear that same sadness as when he'd asked me that question: *Do you really have no idea how dear you are to me?*

How could he have said such a thing? And then to go on as if *he* is the reason there can't be anything between us? He knows what I am. He is smart enough to guess at the things I have done. Even now, his life is in danger simply because he knows this. Someone as good as Tyron should not be bound to someone like me. So why can't I bring myself to tell him that?

Perhaps some of it is the worry of what lies ahead. Tyron doesn't seem bothered about the threat to his life, taking up his usual habit of helping the sailors in his spare time. Occasionally, he even tries to coax Tirzah and me to go above deck. Sometimes we indulge him. Most of the time we stay in our allotted cabin, still trying to come up with some kind of plan.

"What of your brother?" Tirzah asks, still laying back in her hammock. "Isn't one of them a king? What if we used that? Even Ovok would rather not anger Litash."

Tyron, sitting in the one chair that our room has, shakes his head. "I'm afraid few Litashians would ever risk crossing the Forest of Riddles—much less an army of them. Besides, if Ovok knows anything of Judican, he'll know how little spine he has. Litash would be an empty threat."

I try to think of some workaround. There has to be something. "What of your other sibling? From what you've said of Euracia, he would be more difficult to dismiss."

Expression darkening, Tyron shakes his head again. "Even if Euracia had that kind of power, and even if he would be willing to provide such a backing, I would be worse off with him than with Ovok." He seems to realize how stiffly he is holding himself and lets out a pent-up breath. "Besides, there is still the matter of the Forest. How would we even get word out in time?"

This is beginning to feel more and more futile. That old helplessness creeps back in and with it comes the need to do *something*. I get to my feet and cross to the port hole, looking out across the green-grey waves.

"What if we told Ovok about everything that went down in Arvenir?" Tirzah's voice comes from behind me. "You know him and how he never wants to 'waste talent.' If we told him everything Tyron did, then—"

"—Then he would just force him to become one of us," I cut her off before she can hope any further. "Whatever we give as a reason, it has to be something that truly matters to Ovok."

Tirzah scoffs. "Good luck finding that."

I turn around. "Everyone has something they care about—even if it is in a warped sense." That's always the first thing I have to find out about a target. "We know Ovok still considers himself one of the Guards, keeping the world in balance."

"I don't think threatening to take over Eatris would help," Tirzah mutters, folding her arms behind her head.

"He is also very serious about his duty as Lord of the Myrandi," I press on.

"Very serious," Tirzah rolls her eyes. "Funny how we don't get taken into that consideration."

"Are you sure?" Tyron's question is asked quietly.

Tirzah sits up in her hammock, looking at him as if trying to see if he's joking. "Haven't you seen the danger he puts us in? He doesn't care about our safety." She shakes her head. "Rhioa was the only one he ever loved, and look what he makes her go through."

I flinch, looking down at my hands.

"I have seen, and that's why I hope you both get away from him," Tyron replies, tone gentle. "But from what I understand, he endangers your lives because he believes it is the best way to protect the rest of your people. It is possible that he still loves you, even if in a flawed way?"

Tirzah's lips press together in a hard line. Instead of contradicting him, she lies back down. "Either way, what he does is wrong. And it certainly isn't love."

Tyron does not reply.

Does my father love me? I've never dared to ask myself. I've always been too afraid that the answer was no. I've always cherished those few fond memories I have of him, the ones where my mother wasn't there to taint it all. But that was a very long time ago. The closest thing to love I have seen on his face since then is that faint trace of regret when he sends us off.

I love you more than I ever knew was possible. The memory of Tyron's words leaps up unbidden. I turn back to the window just to keep my expression from betraying me. What twisted irony that the one who loves me is in danger from the one who should.

Suddenly, something clicks.

"What if we found a way that appeals to both?" I ask, thinking aloud as I turn back to them.

Tyron looks at me quizzically as Tirzah sits back up. "What would manage that?" she asks.

"We know Ovok always holds to tradition, to the sanctity of the Myrandi, correct?" I go on. "Everything has to be done in its proper order."

Tyron and Tirzah exchange their confusion in a glance.

It's Tirzah who gestures for me to keep going. "What are you getting at?"

"Marriage—the Myrandi marry for life. Ovok himself must approve each match. He says he does so because our lifespan is so long that such oaths have far more weight. For the same reason, those who have married in secret—without his approval—are never forced to separate. If we pretended that...." My voice trails off at the look on Tyron's face. It's full of the same pain as that night in the hallway, but it's somehow even worse to see it in daylight.

"Go on," he says simply.

I swallow. "If we pretended to be married, killing you would go against his duty both as a father and as Lord of the Myrandi," I finish dully.

The creaking of the boat around us seems suddenly conspicuous in the silence that follows. Tirzah sits very still, eyes darting between me and Tyron. He remains in his chair, jaw taut, looking as if he is struggling to keep his expression neutral.

"Well, it's a better start than anything else we've come up with." His voice is soft and strained. "Let's keep thinking and see what else we can put together. We still have some time before we make any final decisions." He stands up, straightening his overcoat. "For now, I think a break is in order. I offered my assistance to the ship carpenter for the afternoon and I should go see if he's ready to start."

I give a mute nod and he exits the room.

The room goes back to its silence.

"Don't you think that was a bit cruel?" Tirzah is still sitting in her hammock, swaying with the motion of the ship.

I close my eyes. "If it saves his life, then it will be worth it in the end."

I hear Tirzah lie back down. "Let's try and figure out an escape plan, then."

"Yes, let's."

The weeks of sailing seem to crawl by at the slowest possible pace. In one way, it is a blessing that makes home and my father seem eons away. And yet it is also a curse, a slow torture where the inevitable hangs over my head until I wish I could just get it over with. To make it all worse, none of us come up with any better plan than faking a marriage between me and Tyron. He accepts this without a word. But that graciousness only leaves me feeling more guilty.

I keep my mouth shut all the way to Pershizar. There's too much to do and too much at stake to waste time on my stinging conscience. When we reach the southern coast, we take another boat west for two more days. Then it's into the city to trade away whatever heavy gear we didn't offload during our brief stop in Krysophera. As soon as we've purchased mounts, we leave. I dare not stay the night.

We ride northwest into the desert, away from the coast and towards home. Funny how much I hated the cold of Arvenir and now I'm tired of the heat of Pershizar. Within two days, the dunes turn to bare, stone outcroppings. After three, I can see the mountains in the distance: the southern extension of the Rheritarus range and the border between Pershizar and Myranduil.

"Once we reach the mountains, we'll release the horses and fly the rest of the way," I say, sitting down on my sleeping mat. "One of us will carry you. Likely Tirzah." I tip my head to where she is dusting off the packs and pulling out the evening rations. "Her Dragon form is larger than mine. You'll also have to hold onto some red-bronze until we get clear of the border. Though we likely won't see them, there are guards posted throughout the mountain range. I don't want to risk them sensing your Gifting."

Tyron nods as he sets down the brush and dry wood he'd been gathering. "If I might ask, why didn't we follow the coast into Myranduil? Didn't you say that Iruscaed is a port city?" He begins to stack the brush and branches together.

"Myranduil ports are very strictly controlled. No foreigners are allowed beyond the port unless they have been given a diplomatic pass and guard. Even with such a pass, someone with your Gifting wouldn't be allowed onshore without a locked red-bronze cuff," I reply, watching him and wondering why he's building a fire. "We'll enter the city via the northern gate, which is more lax since only Myrandi use it. We'll give you some red-bronze to hold on to just until we get clear of the guards."

The subtle hum of his Gifting swells briefly and flame comes to life at Tyron's fingertips. It doesn't take long to spread through the dry pile of tinder.

"And from there?" he asks, adding a few more branches.

My throat goes tight. "We head straight for the capital manor. There may be some wait if Ovok is in conference, otherwise we will be admitted directly."

"Unless he decides to split us up," Tirzah interjects in monotone as she sits down on her mat. "He likes to do that when we've disobeyed orders."

Tyron glances at her and then to me.

"He does tend to verify our stories separately," I murmur, dusting a bit of sand from my skirts. "It's how he sifts them for any inconsistencies."

Tirzah huffs. "And sends the slaves to spy on whichever one of us is left waiting outside."

Brow furrowed, Tyron repeats, "Slaves?"

I reach for my water skin and pull the cap, taking a sip of water. It does not ease my queasy stomach. "Yes. When any of us are sent to...deal with situations such as the one in Arvenir, they do not always close up so neatly. If the aggravator is not locked up like Talsk, we offer them two choices: elimination, or a life of servitude in Myranduil." I dare not look up and see Tyron's reaction. "My father calls it a second chance."

Tyron's voice is not much louder than the crackling of the fire. "What do you call it?"

"I..." I shudder. "I don't know. I always wanted to believe it was a kindness to those who didn't deserve it."

"It's nothing but cruelty. We should know—we're barely any more than slaves ourselves," Tirzah spits. "I don't understand why you keep defending Ovok after all these years. Especially when he's probably about to kill the only person who's cared about us in the last century."

Before I can reply, she gets to her feet and swipes up her waterskin. "I'm going to go top off my water." Then she strides off in the direction of the small creek nearby.

I close my eyes and try to resist the urge to put my head in my hands.

"She is just worried about what is to come," Tyron says. "Her anger is not at you."

With a deep breath, I open my eyes to find him watching me with concern. I force myself to nod. "I know." My gaze falls to the fire, a warm light in the settling dusk. "She never could forgive our father for what he let our mother do."

"Can you?" Tyron asks softly.

I realize that I've been fiddling with my puzzle ring and force myself to stop. "I suppose I'm not sure," I admit. "I-I want to. I don't know if that makes any sense, but I *want* to forgive him."

Tyron's green eyes study me closely, his expression somber and empathetic. "It makes perfect sense. What child doesn't wish to love and be loved by their parent?"

How can he be so understanding? Tirzah's angry words still ring in my head: *He's probably about to kill the only person who's cared about us in the last century.* That's all Tyron knows of Ovok, and yet he does not blame me for my attachment. Something compels me to try and explain.

"He was very kind when we were children. Always serious, but always gentle with us." I wrap my arms around myself. "Tirzah and I used to sneak into his meetings and hide under the table. We weren't so good at the hiding part—we were too prone to giggling." I shake my head at the memory. "But he would pretend not to notice. And of course, no one else in his hall would question him. He would wait until they all left and then make a big show of trying to find us. Once he did, he'd carry us out to the gardens or up to the stargazing tower or..." I swallow, finally stopping myself. "Sorry, I don't know why I'm telling you all this. I—"

"—Rhy, it's alright," Tyron interrupts. He starts to reach out a hand, then seems to think better of it. "You have nothing to be ashamed of."

In this one respect, he is wrong: I have everything to be ashamed of. But my outburst has given me enough motivation to keep quiet this time.

Tyron continues anyway, prodding the fire as he does so. "To be able to love and forgive someone who has wronged you so deeply—that takes far more strength than hate does. You should never feel guilty for doing so."

His reassurance only makes me feel worse. Here we are, mere days away from what might be his death, and he is comforting me. I can't help but wish that he never had the misfortune of meeting me.

We sit in quiet, watching the fire turn to embers and the purple dusk fade to black velvet skies. Just as I begin to worry over Tirzah, footsteps interrupt the whispering of sand over the rocks. She trudges into sight, dripping waterskin in one hand, and sits back down on her mat. She doesn't look at either of us.

"So," Tyron clears his throat, pulling something metallic from his pocket. "If we will all be spoken to separately, we'd best get our story straight. When did we get married?"

"The boat," I reply dully. "That's the only place we can be certain there weren't any spies."

Tyron tosses the item into the fire and I realize it's a coin. I hadn't realized he had anything left from Litash. Why did he—

"Alright. I presume the other details of us meeting will remain the same, then?" He uses a stick to prod the coals.

I nod.

"Are there any particular details of a Myrandi ceremony which I should know?" he asks.

Feeling worse and worse, I explain. Tyron listens carefully, as always, but I catch the increased hum of his Gifting. I watch as the coin turns to a puddle hovering above the embers. It slowly raises itself into a small orb, then separates into two. These flatten, then hollow, until two rings hover in the flames. These drift out of the flames and settle on the stone ledge as I finish my explanation.

"Alright." Tyron's Gifting ebbs. He looks to Tirzah when he says, "If he asks, I asked for your blessing before speaking to Rhy."

Tirzah nods, but my throat goes tight and I have to look away.

There is the sound of metal against metal, then Tyron's voice. "Here."

I look back to see him holding out one of the rings. The delicate band, sitting in his palm, glows gold with the light of the fire.

"It's a Human tradition," he says. "Thought it might help sell the act."

Silently, I accept the ring and slide it on. It fits perfectly.

Tyron moves on. "What else should we go over?"

I'm still staring at the ring. Had he...had he been saving his last coin for this?

"We should go over the city layout in case we have to make a quick exit," Tirzah says.

This rouses me enough to nod. "Yes, good idea. First, let's start with the layout of the manor." But no matter how much I try to focus on the task, my attention keeps wandering back to the slender, golden band around my finger.

I hope this works.

PART III

MYRANDUIL

Tyron

If I die today, I must say, flying is a worthwhile last venture. I don't even care how cold and wind chapped my face is—the exhilaration of racing through the sky is unmatched. No wonder Rhioa and Tirzah were always sneaking off in Arvenir to go fly. I wish I could spread my arms and glide as easily as they do, soaring over the rolling hills and green valleys. Instead I stay low against Tirzah's silver feathers as instructed so that I won't unbalance her.

We've been flying for most of the day by the time Iruscaed appears in the distance. We've crossed over several small towns, but the capital of Myranduil is just as Rhioa described: gleaming white walls stretching as far as the eye can see, rising up where the green of the landscape meets the blue of the sea. As we get closer, more details emerge. I spot the teeming harbor on the south side, the vast fields outside the eastern walls, the massive forests to the north.

It's not until we're about to land that I realize what the giant patches of color on the city walls are: Myrandi. The Dragon-formed guards are posted all along the battlements, their metallic feathers reflecting the sun in vibrant hues. I catch glimpses of them throughout the city itself, too, but not a single one is flying. Rhy had mentioned this. It's the reason we land a ways from the gate before entering the city.

"You have that red-bronze I gave you?" Rhioa, back in Human form, asks as she shoulders one of the packs she had been carrying in her claws.

Ah, yes, the red-bronze—that's what's making me feel so tired. Nodding as I pick up the other pack, I assure, "Already in hand." But she should be able to hear the difference. She must be very nervous.

Rhioa swallows and looks to her sister. "Ready?"

"Let's get it over with," Tirzah grumbles.

With that, we head for the gate.

Only once we've reached the base of the walls can I really fathom how massive they are. The white stone looms over us until it blocks out the sun.

"Halt—declare yourself." The gravelly voice that comes from above sounds more like a roar than an order. A large, copper-colored Dragon appears on the arch above the gate, poised and ready to strike.

"Rhioa and Tirzah, daughters of Lord Ovok." Rhioa's reply is given with authority. "The Human is with us. Let us in."

The Dragon turns its inspection on me, blinking black eyes as it tilts its head. Then it flicks its tail. "Let them in," it growls.

As if moving of their own accord, the polished, metal gates swing outward. I follow Rhioa through and hear Tirzah right behind me.

I have never seen a city such as the one before me. The stone buildings are taller than even the highest turrets of the palace in Litash, many covered in all sorts of balconies and platforms. Arches and high walkways abound, often covered in greenery, connecting many of the structures. But beyond that, I can find nothing in common between them all. One house we pass is practically covered in strange metal piping and discs, emitting a soft ticking sound as the discs all turn in slight, synchronized motions. Another house looks practically Arvenish, down to the carved cresting and polished dome. The one next to it seems to be made up of mirrors, all cut at hard, right angles.

The longer we walk, the more fascinating differences and details emerge. I also realize that I am not the only one staring. Myrandi are everywhere in the wide, white streets, both in Human and Dragon form. And most of them are staring right back. I catch many eyes flit from Rhioa to Tirzah to me, then quickly turn away.

The further we go and the busier the streets become, the more this phenomenon grows. Conversations go quiet, crowds part to make room, parents pull their children behind them. Rhioa and Tirzah look straight ahead and act as if they don't even notice. But I know better. It makes me angry to see them treated such by their own people—the very people their father is sacrificing them to protect.

Perhaps it's foolish, but it's the only idea that comes to mind; I reach for Rhioa's hand and take it firmly in mine. She glances to me in surprise, yet does not pull away. I remind myself that it is likely because it helps the ruse of our pretended marriage.

As casually as I can, I point out what looks to be a small shop. "What building is that?"

Rhioa looks lost. "An artist's studio. Why?"

"I was curious about all the painted patterns on the exterior," I reply simply. "What about that one?"

I keep up the questions for the next half hour. I'm sure Rhioa knows I'm just trying to distract her but, if it's working, then I don't care. Besides, that hush no longer falls over every person we walk past. Fear of Rhioa and Tirzah is replaced by nearly open curiosity towards me.

This works all the way until we reach a wide square. The empty space, bathed in the last warm rays of the late afternoon, reaches all the way up to the steps of a stone manor. In comparison to everything else we've passed, this building seems nearly simplistic. Yet it is that very austerity that makes it feel imposing. Rhioa doesn't have to tell me that we're here.

We climb the steps and Rhioa nods to the guard who opens one side of the double doors for us. Cool air rushes to greet us, an instant relief to the heat of the outdoors, but that is the only welcoming feature of the otherwise lifeless vestibule we enter.

"You can give me the red-bronze now," Rhioa murmurs, letting go of my hand to take the bit of metal.

The moment I let go of the red-bronze, a wave of energy washes over me.

"Lady Rhioa, Lady Tirzah," A figure clad in scarlet steps into the vestibule and bows. "Your father has been expecting you." The man nods to me. "And you as well, Prince Tyron. Please, follow me."

It would seem Ovok has already done his research. I see the way Rhioa's shoulders stiffen even as she waves for the man to lead the way.

Down the many halls we go, our footsteps the only sound in the whole manor. Somehow the man in front of us makes no noise at all. The unnerving effect is compounded when we begin to pass other silent, scarlet-robed staff and I realize what they are: slaves. Of all different races and ages, they go about their work without even looking up as we pass. It's not until we stop before another set of doors that I place why their uniform color is so familiar—it's the same shade of red that Rhioa wore to the first ball in Arvenir.

"I will go announce you," the slave says as he stops. "Please wait here." He motions to the bench in the corridor and then slips through the doors.

Neither Rhioa nor Tirzah move to sit.

"It will be alright," I say softly. "We're almost there."

Tirzah's gaze flicks towards me then back to the doors. Rhioa gives a terse nod but doesn't look at me at all. Both stand as still and soundless as the manor around us.

Then the door opens and the slave reappears. "He will see you, Lady Rhioa. You may leave your pack in the corridor."

Rhioa steps forward, but I cut in first. "Tell Lord Ovok that whatever he wishes to discuss with Rhioa, he can also discuss with me. I will not let my wife go in there alone."

The slave freezes, then purses his lips. He watches Rhioa as if waiting for some kind of signal. When she steps back, he dips his head. "I will relay your message," he mumbles.

We wait again, this time longer than the first. The slave seems flustered when he returns.

"He will see you both." He steps to the side and holds the door open.

Now it's my turn to be surprised when Rhioa takes my hand. I hold it fast, trying to pretend it's more than just part of an act. But I'll admit that, either way, it makes me feel a bit better as we step forward to meet our fate.

The hall we step into feels cavernous. The stone interior, the sparse decoration, the ceiling far overhead, and then that ominous echo that rings for long seconds after the door closes behind us. The entirety of the space leads down to a dais, drawing all attention to the single throne that sits upon it. And there, leaning one elbow on the arm of his carven chair, is Lord Ovok.

He says nothing as we approach, not to us nor the bodyguard that stands to his left. Even after we reach the foot of the dais and I let go of Rhioa's hand to copy her bow, Ovok remains silent. He watches us closely with cold, brown eyes that seem to dig up every thought and secret. Steeling myself, I return his scrutiny. Ovok is tall, well-built, dressed well but without any extravagance. A sword of dark and twisted metal is sheathed and buckled at his side. By Human standards, the only thing that hints at his extended age is the grey that dusts his otherwise black hair. And yet, without having said a word, there is something unmistakably and unimaginably ancient in his bearing.

"Leave us." Ovok flicks one hands towards his bodyguard, the order breaking the dreadful hush.

Appearing nearly disgruntled, the man does so.

Once the door latch sounds, Ovok turns to Rhioa. "Please tell me that this is some farce to get him an audience with me?" He gestures loosely in my direction.

"It is no farce, my lord," Rhioa's reply is quiet, strained. "We were married several weeks ago on the boat to Pershizar."

Ovok's lips form a thin line. Then he gives a weary sort of sigh. "Oh, Rhy." He gets to his feet, slowly descending the steps of the dais. "This is rash—even for you. If you can't tell me this is a ruse, then at least tell me it's not simply for some desperate ploy to keep him alive."

Rhioa shakes her head. I notice the way she keeps her gaze lowered. "I would not take such vows so lightly. I know that even if I did, they would not be honored."

For a moment, Ovok looks like any worry-worn father. Then he turns to me and the chill returns to the room. "Isn't it customary in Litash to procure a blessing from the lady's parents before marrying her?" His voice is unnaturally even.

"Not quite," I answer. "The custom is to ask whoever is charged with protecting and caring for the lady. Usually, that is her parents. In Rhioa's case, it was her sister." Out of the corner of my eye, I catch how Rhioa freezes. "I asked for Tirzah's blessing and received it."

Ovok gives no reaction. Those cold eyes bore relentlessly into mine even as he addresses Rhioa. "I think I ought to use this opportunity to get to know my new son-in-law. Rhy, wait outside."

Rhioa blanches. "Wait, Father, please—"

She tries to step forward, but I catch her wrist. "Woah, woah, Rhy, it's alright."

She spins to face me, her brown eyes—brown, just like her father's—wide in fear.

"Listen to me," I take both of her trembling hands in mine. "No matter what happens, it will be alright. We promised, remember?"

Her terror is palpable as she looks from me to her father. Ovok still shows no reaction. He watches closely, carefully. But that seems to be enough for Rhioa to regather herself. Swallowing hard, she nods.

"Go wait with Tirzah. I'm sure she'll be glad for the company." I squeeze her hands gently, bring them to lips, then release them as I hope that this isn't goodbye.

With one last hesitation and one more pleading glance towards her father, Rhioa heads for the doors. Her footsteps echo against the stone until the thud of the closing door cuts them off.

Now it's just me and Ovok.

I've thought through this conversation so many times in the past few weeks, trying to parse out every possible response and outcome. But I hadn't quite accounted for the sheer anger that overtakes me now that Rhioa isn't here for me to stay calm for. It crowds out the quiet awe that hangs in the room, growing with the thought of every horror and abuse that this man has inflicted on his daughters. I want nothing more than to let this rage loose. And yet, I am not here for me: I am here for Rhioa and Tirzah.

I take a deep breath. "Before we begin, I do have one request."

"Oh?" Ovok raises an eyebrow, his expression that of thinning patience.

"Should you kill me or lock me up, I simply ask that you do not let your daughters know of it," I say calmly. "Tell them we struck some sort of deal, or that I ran off—whatever you need to say to convince them."

Ovok tilts his head, pausing before asking in a skeptical tone, "You are asking to die or rot away in a cell...and have no one know?"

I fold my hands behind my back. "Yes. While some lie about my abandonment would hurt your daughters, I think they would rely on each other and move past it. If you lock me up, they would either throw away any hope of freedom to keep you from harming me, or they would risk their own lives trying to break me out." I keep my gaze leveled to meet his. "I'm not sure if you realize how close they are to breaking but, if you kill me, it would shatter them entirely. I would prefer my death to mean nothing over it being the tool of their demise."

Ovok does not reply right away. He returns to that silent watching, hard eyes giving nothing away as he seems to sift my every word. "You are very blunt," comes his dry comment.

"So I'm told." I incline my head.

Turning back to the dais and climbing the stairs, Ovok sits down on his throne. He leans back and rests one elbow on the arm of the chair as he says, "Fine. Should I kill you or imprison you for the rest of your life, I will make sure my daughters never know. But I presume that wasn't your sole strategy when you walked in here?" I can't quite discern if that is sarcasm in his tone.

"No. If you seemed to truly care for your daughters, I was planning to appeal to that. If not, my tactic would be to focus on your self-interest." I can't tell if it is my anger or my intuition that prompts such candid speech. "Either way, my end goal is to see them released from their forced service."

"Well then, what have you decided?" Ovok's gaze narrows. "Do I care for my daughters or not?"

I regard him closely. "I'm not sure yet. Your daughters don't seem to know, either." I set my shoulders. "To be honest, when I first heard of what you make them do, I thought it impossible that you could care. But the situation didn't quite add up. When they speak of their mother, Rhioa and Tirzah are equally forthright about how heartless she was. Yet they don't speak that way of you." I'm not sure if it's just my own wishful thinking or if something really shifts in Ovok's expression. Either way, I continue.

"When Tirzah mentions you, it is always brusque and with pain. She cares enough that the thought of you hurts her. And Rhioa," I let out a quiet sigh. "She refuses to speak ill of you. She even defends you, making excuses for what you do to them. She still loves you and she clings to the hope that maybe you could do the same."

If Ovok's features have changed, then they are no more readable than before. "Your strategy has a flaw," he says. "If I do love them both, and yet still endanger their lives, then I must have a reason that surpasses even a father's love for his children. How does your plan get around that?"

"By convincing you that if you continue to use them as you have, it will ultimately harm your goal. This reason you speak of, it has to do with protecting your people, does it not?" I don't really wait for an answer. "Those people are the very same ones that won't even walk on the same side of the street as your daughters. When your daughters break, they will be left with the ability to topple empires and a resentment towards a particular nation. How do you think that will go?" I shake my head. "Even if they do not act in bitterness, they will not be able to carry out their current roles. If that happens out in the field, it will cost you their mission and them their lives. How would either benefit the Myrandi?"

Ovok is so still that he seems to be made of the same pale stone as the hall. I refuse to let the silence unnerve me: I remain standing, feet steady and squared, meeting his gaze without flinching.

Then he straightens. "Your logic is intriguing. I will think on it. For now, one of the staff will show you to a room for the night." He gives a wave of dismissal. "Please send in Tirzah on your way out."

...that's it? After everything I said, this is his response? I'd imagined many ways that this could end, and a simple dismissal was not one of them. I bow, turn to leave, then hesitate. "Just be careful with her," I say.

Ovok does not reply.

I walk back down the length of the hall, unsure if I should be relieved or not. Did I get through to him? Will he take action? Or will I be dead before morning?

I pause at the door and look back. Ovok is standing, unbuckling the dark blade from his belt. He sets the still-sheathed weapon so that it leans against his throne before he sits back down. Is that a good sign? Or some kind of warning? I don't even know. Feeling strangely lost, I turn the door handle and let myself out.

CHAPTER 24

Rhioa

I sit on the familiar stone bench, waiting, straining, listening for any sound. The only reason I don't stand by the door is that I fear I wouldn't be able to stop myself from going in. The bench keeps me grounded, its hard edge providing something to wrap my hands around so that they don't shake so badly. The way Tirzah sits rigidly next to me tells me that she is doing the same exact thing.

Somehow I'd forgotten how much I hate this silence. It fills the whole manor, overtaking every room and person and thing until everything shrivels up beneath the dreadful hush. Now the weight of it makes me feel claustrophobic; I try to take deep breaths just to remind myself that I can. But how can I when Tyron is still in there?

Just when I am ready to jump up and burst through the doors, I hear footsteps from the other side. I'm on my feet before the handle even begins to turn. Then Tyron walks through and relief makes my knees feel weak.

"You're alright," I breathe.

He nods, brow furrowed.

"What is it?" I ask immediately, fears revived. "What did he say?"

Tyron's reply is nearly puzzled. "He...he said he'll think on it. He said that we would be staying for the night."

The night? Would he give his answer in the morning? Or is it simply enough time for him to spring some trap? Anxiety pricks like needles across my skin.

"He also said he wanted to speak with you," Tyron says, looking to Tirzah. "Do you want someone to come with you?"

Tirzah presses her lips together then shakes her head. "I'll be alright. Go." She nods to the waiting slave. "If they let me, I'll come find you afterwards."

I clasp her hand for one brief moment. "Be careful."

She doesn't speak, but she returns my grip. Then she heads for the doors.

Drus, the slave who had brought us in earlier, takes this as his cue. "Allow me to take your things."

"It's alright, thank you. I've got them." Tyron bends to pick up both of our packs, slinging one over a shoulder and motioning with his free hand. "Lead the way."

I falter. It feels wrong to leave without Tirzah. Tyron puts his hand on my arm, wordlessly coaxing me forward. I watch Tirzah enter the hall before I give in and follow Drus.

Down through the familiar hallways we go. Somehow the coolness, which would normally be a welcome break from the heat of Myranduil, makes me shiver. I want nothing more than to ask Tyron what happened in there, but I dare not do so until we're alone. The thought so distracts me that I don't even notice we're headed away from my room. No until Drus stops at the door of one of the many guest chambers.

"You will be in here," he says, opening it for us and stepping back.

Tyron lets me go in first, thanking Drus before joining me. He receives no reply except for the sound of the lock clicking behind us.

"That means we are to stay put for the evening," I murmur. My stomach twists as I realize what else it means: "We will probably not hear from Tirzah until morning."

Tyron glances back at the now locked door. "Alright. Then we wait it out, I suppose." He looks around the room then crosses to the single bed and sets the packs down.

I do my usual check of the room and its adjacent sitting area before returning to him. "There may be someone listening in," I warn in a low voice. "But what did he say? What happened?"

Brow furrowed, Tyron gives a slight shrug. "To be honest, I'm not entirely sure. I was very straightforward: I told him that what he was doing was wrong, that it was hurting you both, and that he needed to let you go. He was quiet for a bit, then said he would think about it for the night." Tyron runs a hand through his hair. "That was it."

That was it? I try to process. Is it some scheme? Does Father mean to strike while we're asleep? Or will he use Tirzah against us? My blood runs cold. What if that's why he called her in next and separated us?

"We should take the chance to get cleaned up and rest a bit," Tyron's gentle voice breaks through my spiraling thoughts. "Here: I'll go in the other room and wait. Let me know when you're done and then we can switch off."

I manage a nod and he heads into the sitting area, closing the partition behind him.

My hands are still shaking as I pull a clean set of clothes from my pack. It's so bad that I nearly drop the pitcher of water when I try to pour some into the basin. But I manage to return the pitcher to its stand, trading it for a cloth.

The normalcy of cleaning up and getting changed makes me feel a little steadier by the time I've finished. I trade off with Tyron to let him do the same. He looks like a different person by the time he rejoins me, clean shaven and without the layers of road dust, but his behavior is unchanged. It baffles me how he can act so calm and curious as he looks around the room and out the windows. He even comments on the balcony having no railing, and how that must make it easier for Dragon forms. Eventually, he discovers the small shelf of books and settles down with one in the nearby chair.

I remain in my seat, watching the sky grow darker and darker. At some point, lanterns light themselves in the small courtyard below and throughout the room. Still I sit, fiddling with the ring Tyron gave me and mentally counting just to assure myself that time is passing. I should be used to this waiting. If I'm not working, I'm waiting: waiting for orders, waiting to reach the next destination, waiting for the target to get into position. So why am I so bad at it now? Why does my throat go tight with panic at every slight noise or perceived movement?

I almost wish that we could have just gotten everything over with right there in my father's hall. At least then I wouldn't be left in this agonizing uncertainty.

A knock at the door startles me and I jump up in both fear and hope. Tyron gets up too, closing his book and walking with me to the door. My hands are shaking again when I reach to open it. But it is neither my father nor my sister, not even one of my father's henchmen as I had feared. Instead a slave, bearing a dinner tray, bows her head.

"Supper, my lady," Csures says, eyes still on the floor. She has not looked me in the eyes in the twenty years since I brought her here.

Tyron is the one who takes the tray, giving a quiet "Thank you."

Csures nods, I close the door, and we return to the sitting area.

"You should try to eat something," Tyron says, setting the tray down on one of the side tables.

I shake my head as I take my seat. The choking sensation already makes it hard to swallow; I don't think I could manage food.

"At least some water, then." Tyron picks up one of the full glasses and holds it out to me.

I take it in both hands, but can't bring myself to drink. "How are you so calm?" I whisper.

"Because I already weighed out my options and made my decision," he replies simply. "I would gain nothing from second-guessing what is already done. All that is left is to see it through."

How can he be so accepting when it might be his very life in the balance? Does he think so little of himself that he could throw it all away so easily? I look down at the glass I'm still holding, watching tremors ripple across the water's surface.

"Tirzah was right," I barely hear myself say. "We should have run for it."

Tyron kneels by my chair. "Don't say that—don't taunt yourself with these doubts. We all made this choice together, remember?" He lays one hand over my mine and the water goes still. "Rhy, whatever happens, I am still glad we chose this. And if things don't go as hoped, then you may still be closer to freedom than before. If your father has any regrets over having me—"

I feel something snap, making me recoil from both his touch and his words. I don't remember dropping the glass, nor getting to my feet, but somehow I'm left standing as I watch the cup shatter on the stone floor.

"Stop," I gasp. "How can you say that? How can you...." *I can't breathe, I can't breathe.* I turn away, gulping for air.

"Woah, Rhy, it's alright." Tyron is by my side again and trying to calm me.

My hands are at my neck, trying to loosen the invisible noose that has tightened around my throat. "I wish you'd never met me. I wish you'd gotten away in Krysophera and never looked back."

"Rhy, listen to me." Tyron is suddenly gripping my shoulders. "Try to take deep breaths."

I shake my head wildly as I try to pull away. "I ruin everything around me. You should have left, you should have—"

"—Rhioa, *listen.*" He shakes me gently, the motion distracting me from my own terror. "For the first time in my life, I have no regrets. None. If I could go back to when you first found me and do this all over again, I wouldn't change a single thing." His green eyes are fixed on mine, his grip still firm on my shoulders as if anchoring me to the floor. "This is not your fault."

My heartbeat drums in my ears and fear still makes my blood feel like ice. "It doesn't matter whose fault it is; you'll still be gone. I-I can't...." Tears well up and threaten to spill over. "Getting away means nothing if I don't have you."

Tyron's expression goes blank and his grasp loosens.

His shock only adds to my guilt. "I'm sorry I said nothing after that night at the window. It took me off guard and I-I didn't know what to say or how to say it. And now I've waited so long and it's too late and—"

My stammering is cut off when Tyron steps forward and wraps his arms around me. "Oh, Rhy," he murmurs.

I lean into him, his warmth and tenderness undoing whatever resistance I'd had left. "I'm so sorry," I whisper as tears slip down my cheeks. "I'm so sorry."

"Don't apologize. You have nothing to be sorry for." With my head against his chest, his voice seems to fill the whole room.

I wish I could believe him. I wish Tyron was right and that I could just stand here and let him hold me. But I know better. I can't even meet his eyes when I step back. "You know that's not true." I swallow. "You know all the things I've done. I don't understand how you could know and still love me."

Tyron brushes a strand of hair out of my face, drawing my gaze to his. The gentleness in his features only makes it harder to look at him. "One day, I hope that you look at yourself and see what I see," he says. "That you are not what your mother tried to make you. You are not even what your father uses you as. You are far more—you are meant to be loved and cherished and protected. Your parents were wrong to treat you any differently." He takes both of my hands in his, his face full of such wonderful sincerity. "I know what you were forced to do, and I know you did not want to do it. That's how I know that you can leave all of that behind. You are so very precious, Rhioa. You have so much to give. Please, if you cannot see that just yet, then trust me until the day that you can."

As much as I desperately want to believe him, a lifetime of experience makes me reject the very thought. How could I possibly be of such value? How could my life possibly be worth risking his? I don't understand. But now that my fears have quieted, the adrenaline is gone and all of my energy with it; I have no more strength to argue. And I don't want to waste any more of what might be limited time.

"I cannot see it," I finally admit. "But I trust you."

Tyron squeezes my hands. "Thank you." Then he hesitates. "Just promise me that, no matter what happens, you'll remember this."

My stomach tightens and tears threaten once more. I want to refuse. I open my mouth to do so, then close it when I realize how closely he's watching me. *He's scared.* For all his calm words and steady warmth, he's scared too. I have no way left to protect him, only this one reassurance. So although it makes me feel sick, I give the raspy promise: "I will never forget."

Relief spreads through Tyron's shoulders. For a moment, I think he's going to embrace me again. Instead he says, "Come, you should rest. You've not slept enough these past three days."

Exhausted as I am, I don't dare sleep. What happens if they come to take him and I'm not even awake? "No, no, I want to stay up."

Tyron frowns in visible concern. "At least lie down on the settee, then."

If only to make him feel better, I give in and let him lead me back towards the seating area. I sit down and he heads into the bedroom, returning with a blanket. I pull this around my shoulders as he kneels to scoop up the remnants of my broken glass. He carefully deposits these on the edge of the dinner tray before using one of the cloth napkins to soak up the spilt water.

"There. All clean." Tyron sets the soaked napkin beside the shards of glass. "Now try and rest. I'll be right here."

Still reluctant, I pull my legs up onto the settee and rest my head against the pillows. "Get me if you hear anything," I tell him. "And don't answer the door without me."

He nods. "Alright." He lays one hand briefly over mine then gets to his feet. I hear a scraping sound as he pulls a chair closer and sits down. Then there is a rustling as he picks up his book and flips through to find his place.

The room falls quiet after that. But the silence is not so fraught as before, now marked at intervals by a page being turned. The fears that had threatened to choke me mere minutes ago have been reduced to a hum that drones on in the back of my mind. I am too drained to pay it any more attention.

With Tyron's steady presence beside me, I relax more than I should. My heavy eyelids droop, then open, then close. The last thing I remember is Tyron's words echoing in my mind: *You are so very precious, Rhioa.*

Tyron

I keep up my pretense of reading until I hear Rhioa's breathing even out. I double check that she is soundly asleep, then set my book on the table and lean back. I find myself fiddling with my fake marriage ring as I watch the candles on the banister cast their dancing shadows around the room. I let out a long, deep breath, wishing I could let out some of my tangled thoughts out with it. The feelings knotted up in my chest are too complicated for my mind to sort out.

After weeks of travel and humdrum, this past day has felt like a whirlwind. Knowing my life was in jeopardy hadn't fazed me—I am quite accustomed to such risk. I had spent far more time dreading the pretended marriage to Rhioa. To have to act out the very thing I want most, all while knowing that it was beyond my reach, seemed like some cruel joke. To learn that such hope is not impossible fills me with both dizzying elation and sharp anxiety. It seems that losing everything, whether through death or imprisonment, is far more daunting now that I have something to lose.

I sigh, running a hand through my hair and trying to rein in my fumbling thoughts. If I survive all of this, there will be time to think it through later. And if I don't, there will be no need. Besides, Rhioa is under an immense amount of stress. It is hard to tell whether that has brought out her true feelings or heightened ones that are not fully there. There is no way to know until this situation has passed. Until then, I resolve not to hold her to anything nor to let my hopes grow too high.

I look back at where she lays curled up on the settee, the blanket tucked in around her. Golden hair escapes its tousled braid to fall around her face in wispy patterns. Yet even in sleep, her features do not relax. She looks both utterly drained and rigidly ready to spring up in an instant. Sorrow tugs at me as I think of how long she has lived like this. Does she remember what it is to feel safe? Has she ever lived with any measure of peace?

I don't know if we'll make it out of this. If we do, I don't know what will happen next. But as long as Rhioa and Tirzah get a chance to live—to really live—I can accept whatever comes.

I doze on and off for the rest of the night, never able to stay asleep for long. I blame the chair as much as I do my own restless thoughts. It would seem that Myrandi don't believe in having too much padding in their furniture. I give up around dawn and take to walking circles in an attempt to stretch out my stiff legs, being careful not to make any noise that could wake Rhioa. Thankfully, she has slept the whole night through.

The sky is just beginning to color when a knock comes from the other room. I freeze, looking from the door to Rhioa's sleeping form. She'd been so insistent about me waking her. But if this is someone come to take me away, then perhaps it's better that she not see.... The knock comes again and I realize that it's patterned: two slow, two fast. Could it be Tirzah? I cross to the door and open it.

"Tirzah—you're alright." My relief is instantaneous.

Tirzah gives a sharp nod, looking up and down the hallway before stepping in. "Where's Rhy?"

"Asleep in the other room," I answer, now noticing the shadow over Tirzah's expression. Something is wrong. "What happened?"

She purses her lips. "Let's wait until she's up. Then I'll explain." She looks around the room, gaze halting on the bed. "We need to make it look like you've both slept there."

Ah, good point. With her help, I rearrange the blankets and pack down the pillows to make everything look used. I try to take it as a good thing that we're still keeping up the pretense of marriage—it means that Ovok is still playing along to some extent.

"Tirzah?" Rhioa's voice comes from the sitting area, muddled slightly by sleep. I turn to see her in the opening between the rooms. "What happened? Are you alright?"

The glance that Tirzah casts my way seems nearly nervous. "I'm fine," she replies. "I just came from speaking with Ovok."

All of Rhioa's sleepiness is dispelled in an instant. She joins us near the end of the bed, asking in an undertone, "What did he say?"

Tirzah swallows, doubling my uneasiness. "He's not going to harm Tyron. He is willing to let both of you go."

I know that Rhioa catches the omission as quickly as I do. She doesn't even have time for relief before she's questioning, "Wait, what about you?"

Tirzah's hesitation confirms my fears.

"Oh, Tirzah," I sigh.

Tirzah does not look at either of us as she speaks. "In return for your freedom, I will remain here."

"*What*?" Horror is as evident in Rhioa's voice as it is on her face. "No—no, no, absolutely not. I am *not* leaving you here."

"Rhy, be reasonable: This is the only way that all of us make it out alive." Tirzah's attempt to sound calm sounds strained instead.

"We haven't all 'made it out' if you're still trapped here," Rhy snaps. Her hands are beginning to tremble, a sign of the same panic that had overwhelmed her last night. "Did you make a deal with him? Did you—"

I lay a hand on her arm and she cuts herself off, eyes flicking towards me. Her angry expression cracks to reveal the pain beneath.

"Let's all take a deep breath and figure this out," I say, looking between the sisters. "Rhioa is right on one account: It's not a solution unless all of us get out." Yet, considering my own words to Ovok, I cannot blame Tirzah for what she did.

She stands with that statue-like rigidity that she always has when stressed. "No one gets to change terms after they have made a deal with Ovok."

I feel Rhioa tense. "Then we run. We leave right now and we get as far away as we can."

Maybe this isn't a good conversation to risk someone overhearing. I release Rhioa's arm and pull at my Gifting, working quickly to create a thin barrier around us. Hopefully, it will muffle our voices without muting them entirely. I watch both sisters to make sure it isn't too much Gifting for them.

"Where could we go that would be out of his reach?" Tirzah seems too caught up in the conversation to even notice what I'm doing. "You said yourself that running would only be delaying the inevitable. We would be found, and Tyron would be killed."

Rhioa flinches as if struck. "There has to be somewhere. Some place we don't know about that has evaded his grasp."

Tirzah scoffs. "If there is such a place, it's beyond the world of Eatris."

Rhioa opens her mouth to reply then shuts it. Her eyes widen in apparent realization and she turns to me. "You made it so we will not be heard, correct?" She barely waits for my nod before looking back to her sister. "If there's no place on Eatris, then we go elsewhere."

Tirzah appears confused, but far less than I feel. What other places are there?

"But the Maze has been closed for centuries," she says. "How would we ever get in? And how would we navigate it to get to one of the other worlds?"

"Father has some way in. Back during the debacle in Nythril, I caught a glimpse of that report on Elescar—it talked about an entrance to the Maze and some sort of relic that could let him in." Rhioa's words come more and more rapidly. It's even harder to follow considering that I'm still stuck three sentences ago. "I mean, it only makes sense. We know that both Kassander and Xyrilcylduin had ways to get through."

I finally interrupt. "My apologies, could we back up a moment? Did you say other worlds?"

Tirzah nods as Rhioa answers. "Yes, Eatris is one of three. You've seen the others at a distance—they're the two moons. Baeno is the ringed one, Kryso is the other."

Oh. I...I suppose that makes sense.

"Eons ago, they interacted freely through the fourth realm, which we call the Maze," Rhioa continues her rushed explanation. "After a series of wars, the Maze was closed off and almost all interaction with it. The only ones who move through it now are those charged with guarding the various worlds."

Bits of ancient history come to mind and, all at once, so many of their strange incongruities click into place. But the ramifications of multiple *worlds* leaves me reeling. "The Iron Door..." Realization dawns. "That is one of these entrances to the Maze, isn't it?"

Rhioa nods. "Yes. It was a direct gate to Baeno. But it's closed now—has been for centuries. The reason my father wants access to Arvenir is so that he can figure out how to reopen it."

I have to wrestle aside the thousands of questions that pop into my head so that I can ask, "But if your father gains that access, then would going to one of these other worlds make any difference?"

"It's not his territory," Tirzah murmurs. "He is Lord of the Myrandi, and Guard of Eatris, but that's where his jurisdiction ends."

Rhioa looks nearly hopeful. "Baeno was Kassander's charge; with him gone, it wouldn't be safe for us. But Xyrilcylduin is Guard of Kryso and he would not allow my father to interfere there."

I give up on trying to wrap my mind around these worlds and make myself focus on the technical details of this fledgling plan. "But we still have the problem of getting there. You said there is some relic that could get us in?"

"I believe there are several." Rhioa falters. "But I don't know where any of them are, nor how to use them."

"Which means we have no way to do this quickly," Tirzah points out, crossing her arms. "Meaning that we can't run now, and I can't put off my end of the deal." Her shoulders droop. "He'll be suspicious if you don't leave. Especially if he catches wind of you looking for the Maze."

Rhioa's hope dims visibly.

"Then maybe we do exactly what he expects," I say slowly.

Both sisters look at me.

"It would mean less scrutiny, yes? Tirzah stays here, Rhioa and I go to Litash." I see Rhioa begin to react and quickly add, "The palace in Litash has what they call the Vault of the Untoward—it's where they keep any relic or article of Gifting that they consider too dangerous to be used, and record any they deem acceptable. They've been collecting and recording such items for centuries. If there is anything in Litash that could get us in to the Maze, it would be there."

Now the sisters look at each other, deep thought mirrored on their faces.

"So we split up, you two go find something to open the Maze, and I stay here and figure out how we get to the right world." For the first time in the entire conversation, Tirzah's shoulders relax. "With the Forest of Riddles, Ovok has always had a harder time monitoring Litash. This could actually work."

"But how would we know when to meet?" Rhioa asks, anxiety showing in her pressed lips. "And what if something happens to you and I don't even know? I can't just leave you here."

I'm the one who proposes, "We could set a day and place. If the one side doesn't show within a certain amount of time, that's how the other would know to go looking for them."

"But what do we do if we haven't found what we need yet?" Tirzah asks.

I look to Rhioa. "Then we meet anyway. And we make our run for it."

Lips still drawn into a thin line, she nods.

"So all that's left is to set the time and place." Tirzah lets out a pent-up breath. "How long do you think it would take you to get into the vault and find a relic?"

I run a hand through my hair. "I'm not sure. My status within the palace is...complicated. I will either have to go through legal channels or through old friends to gain access to the records. It could take time. But once we take a relic, we will have to get out of Litash as fast as we can."

"We could meet in Alarune." Rhioa's suggestion is quietly made. "If we cross the Forest of Riddles through the eastern side, it would be a straight shot to the port. We could meet in the northernmost inn."

Tirzah dips her head. "As for time, I don't know how often I will be kept on missions. I may not have many windows to look for answers here." She frowns in thought. "Three years should be safe enough."

Three *years*? I suppose such a span is not as much to them as it is to me, yet the thought still takes me aback.

"Two," Rhioa returns. "Three years leaves too much time for things to go wrong."

Judging by the set of her jaw, Tirzah does not quite agree. But she gives in anyway. "Alright. Two."

"And then we leave together—no matter what." Rhioa's voice is thick.

"No matter what," Tirzah promises.

I nearly take Rhioa's hand, then think better of it. I wish I had some comfort for them both. The possibility of them having to be separated never even crossed my mind. I should have planned for the possibility. I wish I had spoken to Tirzah beforehand, or truly convinced Ovok, or...just...*something*. Anything would have been better than being left here helpless, watching them be torn apart.

"Then it's settled." The last word cracks and Rhioa has to clear her throat to say, "I'm going to go get ready for the day and then we can talk through other parts of the plan."

Understanding her need for space, I don't try to stop her. I drop the barrier that had muffled our voices and watch as she heads for the sitting area. She draws the screen partition shut behind her.

I look to Tirzah, who stands with eyes fixed on the partition. Her usual stony countenance is on the verge of cracking.

"Are you certain about this?" I ask in a hushed tone.

She squares her shoulders and nods. "It's the best way." She sounds more like she's trying to convince herself than me. "Perhaps the only way."

I can't help but mentally run through different scenarios, trying in vain to think of some other solution. I'd never quite expected to convince Ovok he was in the wrong—not when he had been functioning this way for over a hundred years. And yet the familiar weight of failure is hard to ignore.

"I am so sorry," is all I can say.

Tirzah shakes her head. "You shouldn't be. You're the only reason we have any hope of escaping this place. Just..." she trails off, her expression crumpling. "Promise me that you'll protect her."

I don't hesitate. "With my life—I swear it."

Tirzah looks down, folding her arms around herself. "You said once that you would ask for my blessing before asking her." She speaks with quiet gravity. "If that is true, then you have it."

Wait. My chest constricts, taking my breath with it. Does she mean....

My shocked silence is apparently enough to draw her attention back up. Tirzah nearly smiles at the look on my face. "Yes, that's what I mean."

I try to speak, but what can I say? I end up with my mouth hanging open like a proper fool.

"It's alright. You don't have to say anything." Tirzah looks back towards the other room. "Just keep her safe."

"I will," I promise again. "And I will bring her back to you."

Tirzah lets out a deep breath. "Two years," I hear her whisper under her breath. "Two years."

And then, no matter the stakes, they will be reunited. And they will be free.

CHAPTER 25

Rhioa

I spend the next three days running over every possible situation that Tirzah might run into while operating on her own. She was never the strategist—that was always my role—and I'm terrified of something going wrong when I'm not there to find a way out. I drill so many different scenarios with her that I begin to think Tirzah is looking forward to my leaving.

And leave we must. In these three days, I do not see my father even once. We receive no summons, no note, nothing. Even still, I know that our every word and movement is being watched and reported back to him. We cannot risk this monitoring bringing my pretended marriage to light. The longer we wait, the higher that risk becomes. Somehow knowing this does not make what I have to do any easier.

Most of the time I simply feel numb, unable to process the surreal concept of leaving Tirzah behind. But when the panic hits, it is incapacitating. I lose count of how many times Tyron has to calm me down just so I can breathe again. His presence is so constant and reliable that I can no longer recall a time without it. He takes care of the smaller details, reminding me to eat and sleep, organizing supplies and getting packs ready, and finally, sending word to my father that we are leaving.

The dreaded moment arrives on the fourth day. There are no more plans to make, no more bags to pack, no more stalling for time. We stand in the vestibule of my father's manor with nothing left to do but say our goodbyes.

"Take good care of yourself," Tyron tells Tirzah, clasping her arm. "And be careful."

I stand silently beside my father, watching and waiting my turn.

Tirzah returns the gesture with a dry reply. "I'd tell you to do the same, but I know you won't listen. I'll trust Rhy to keep you in line."

Tyron smiles faintly. "A wise decision." Then he lets go and steps back, looking towards me.

My mouth goes dry: It's my turn. I glance up at my father in near desperation, hoping to see some kind of regret or sorrow that might indicate a change of heart. But, as always, his face is utterly impassive. I swallow hard and step forward.

"Tirzah, I..." *I can't do this.* Every intention I'd had about keeping a brave face is suddenly gone. This is my sister, my twin, the person who has lived through the same hurt and horror that I have and yet still does all she can to protect me. She has been with me as long as I can remember. How can I just leave her behind?

Just when I think I'm going to break down all over again, Tirzah leans forward and wraps me in a fierce hug. "It's okay, Rhy, it's okay. Just go."

I hug her back, clinging to her with everything I have. My throat is too tight for me to get any words past it.

"I'll be alright," Tirzah's voice is raspy. She pulls away and I realize she's crying as hard as I am. "We both will be."

I clutch her hands. "This isn't forever," I manage to scrape out. "I will see you again." *In two years.* The number rings in my head like a funeral bell.

"Of course you will. Until then," Tirzah holds up my hand, tapping my puzzle ring and then holding up her matching one. "I'm right here with you. Just like always."

I bite back a sob and try my best to nod. "Just like always," I whisper back.

I can't stop myself from hugging her again. This time I don't let go until I feel Tyron's hand on my shoulder. I do my best to compose myself as I step back.

Then I hear my father clear his throat. "You will keep my daughter safe?" His calm question is levelled at Tyron.

"With my very life," Tyron answers. I look up to see his dark expression as he asks, "Will you do the same for her sister?"

My father's eyes narrow slightly and, instinctually, I brace myself. I see Tirzah do the same.

"You underestimate what a father would do for his daughters," he says coolly.

Tyron doesn't waver. "I am more concerned with what a leader would sacrifice for his people."

Hearing him challenge Ovok so openly scares me as much now as it did last time. Yet just as before, my father barely reacts. If anything, his features almost seem to soften.

"She will be safe," is his solemn reply.

Tyron accepts this with a bow of his head.

My father regathers himself and looks at me, posture and countenance as unreadable as ever. "This is for you." I look down and realize he's holding out a small box. "It will help keep you from being overwhelmed by the Gifts of Litash and perhaps offer some protection."

Tentatively, I take the gift from his outstretched hand. I open the lid to find a small, teardrop-shaped pendant. It looks nearly like silver, if silver could be refined to the purity and clarity of glass. I have seen the metal often enough to recognize it as Ithynian Gasper—the same rare material that my father's blade is crafted from. The cost of even a small piece like this is staggering.

My voice is still wobbly when I say, "Thank you, Father," and close the lid.

He inclines his head in acknowledgement. "Goodbye, Rhioa. I hope this new life serves you well." Then he hesitates. I have never seen him look this close to uncertain in my life. "Should you ever choose, Iruscaed will always be open to you. I hope by then that you will find the city and your sister improved."

I don't know what he means. Improved? Does he mean that she will be trained to provide the skills I provide? What does he expect me to say to that? The safest response seems to be another quiet, "Thank you."

His gaze stays on mine for what seems like minutes. Just when I think he's going to say something more, he turns away. "Come, Tirzah, there is work to do."

Tirzah straightens her shoulders. With one last glance my way and a mouthed 'goodbye,' she follows Father down the corridor.

I feel Tyron's arm around my shoulders. "Come on, Rhy," he says gently. "We have to go."

I am half aware of him picking up both of our packs, and then of him leading me towards the door. All I can register is the pain in my chest, the fading sound of my sister's footsteps, and then the final thud as the great doors of the manor shut behind us.

I don't really remember our ride through the city. I do remember looking back for a final view of Iruscaed from the crest of a hill. The white walls are bathed in the light of the morning sun, as brilliant and bold as ever. They show no signs of the sorrows that have just transpired within them. I turn my horse to join Tyron.

With my mind so numb and my chest aching so sharply, perhaps it is a good thing I could not carry both Tyron and our packs by myself. Riding allows me to simply follow along behind. It requires no thought, no planning, no focus. The whole day wears away to the steady pulse of hoofbeats against packed soil.

Tyron stops at dusk and picks out a campsite for the night, laying out my bedroll first. "Sit," he tells me. "Let me take care of things tonight."

I think I nod in response.

I sit there, hollowed out by grief and exhaustion, watching him care for the horses and then build a fire. Once he has a good blaze going, he turns to our packs and pulls out the two heavy earthenware cups. He fills these with water and nestles them on the edge of the fire. He adds some of our packed vegetables, a bit of salt, and then bits of dried meat. He leaves this to simmer as he sets out his own bedroll on the opposite side of the fire.

The evening deepens around us, heralded by the chirping of insects and accompanied by the crackling campfire. I try to take comfort in the familiar sensations of home: the warm breeze with a tang of salt, the faint smell of tropical flowers, the distant gurgling of water running towards the ocean. But it all feels empty.

"I'm so sorry, Rhy." Tyron's apology is barely audible. I look up to see his green eyes fixed on me, the fire casting golden light over the regret on his face. "I never dreamed you two would be separated."

His apparent guilt is enough to rouse me from my silence. "It is only for a short time," I mumble. "And it is not your fault."

Tyron sighs, running his hand through his hair. "I know. And yet, I wish I had done more."

"You have done more for us than anyone ever has," I remind him. "Besides, we have a plan set. Freedom is finally within our reach; we need only wait for the right timing."

He does not reply, gaze dropping to the fire as he takes up a stick to prod at it.

I watch him quietly as I try to think of what to say. I know it is my pain that leaves Tyron feeling like he has failed. But he was not the one who separated us: Tirzah made the deal, and my father exacted it from her. Tyron is the one who came up with a plan to get us all out anyway—he is the reason that I know this pain is temporary.

I take a deep breath. "You told me before we went to Iruscaed that your choices were your own. If that is true for you, then it is true of Tirzah and my father. You cannot fault yourself for their decisions."

Tyron raises an eyebrow, setting his stick aside and using his Gifting to draw the earthen cups out of the coals. "Using my own words against me, I see." He shakes his head ruefully and sets both cups on a flat rock to cool. "I suppose I can't argue with that."

"Not when your words were correct," I agree. I look down at my folded hands and the puzzle ring around my finger. I twist it slowly, as the number echoes in my head again: *two years*. "And you were correct about another thing: We're going to be alright. All of us. It may not be easy for a little while, but we'll be alright."

Tyron studies me for a long time. Then his shoulders relax and he sighs again. "That is all I have ever wanted for you. To be alright."

The statement is so simple, so soft. I feel silly for the way it makes my eyes well.

"Here," Tyron clears his throat, reaching for his pack. He pulls out one of the flatbreads and breaks it in half, holding out a piece to me along with my cup of soup. "Try and eat."

I accept both with quiet thanks.

We both fall silent, eating together by the fireside. It's strange how, though nothing has changed, the world feels a little more bearable. The ache in my chest is still there but it is not so bad as before. For the first time today, I can actually breathe.

We finish our supper and Tyron collects the dishes, wiping them out before wrapping them to put back in our packs. He pulls out one of the light blankets and hands it to me. But when I reach to take it, he doesn't let go.

"Oh, my apologies," He appears nearly embarrassed as he looks down at my hands. "I forgot to take the ring back. You don't have to keep it on."

Oh. I'd forgotten I was wearing the little marriage band. I pause, unsure, then pull it off and start to exchange it for the blanket. "Just...."

Tyron's hand freezes on top of mine.

"Just don't melt it back down," I finish. "Hold on to it. I-I'm not ready for it yet, but I think I will be."

Tyron seems to soak this in slowly. His hand folds around mine briefly, then he takes the ring from my palm. "Alright," he says. "I will hold on to it for as long as you need."

As he sets down the blanket and returns to his bedroll, I realize that I can finally believe my own words: *We're going to be alright.*

EPILOGUE

Rhioa

Eight months later

I have toppled nations in a night, silenced kings and ruined emperors, I have reshaped entire societies and erased countless more...so why in the three worlds can't I manage something as simple as baking a single pie without reducing the entire thing to a flame-broiled brick? Grumbling and growling and coughing on smoke, I give up on trying to put out the flames. I seize the dish and bolt for the back door. *Of course,* the rickety latch is jammed. I elbow it twice to no avail. Out of options, I kick the stupid thing open and fling the still-smoking attempt of a pie through the opening.

As if on cue, I hear someone humming a tune from the front of the house. The wooden door opens as Tyron steps in. "Rhy, I'm—" He halts in the entryway, brows raised. "Everything alright?"

I think my irritation might be as hot as the ruined pie. "Splendid," I huff. "As long as you wanted to build a house with our dinner instead of eat it."

Tyron joins me at the back entryway, glancing down at the smoldering lump that's still sizzling in the grass. He shrugs lightly. "At least it didn't explode this time. You're improving."

"Coating the entire oven in meat filling is hardly a high bar," I mutter under my breath. "How can I be so bad at such mundane things?"

Undeterred, Tyron pushes my frazzled hair out of my face and kisses my forehead. "Everyone has their strengths, even in 'mundane' areas." He points out the door. "Just look at your garden. Look how well you've managed that."

My gaze follows his gesture towards what used to be bare ground. Now it is rows of flowers and budding stalks, vine-covered stakes that droop with young squash and bushes that bloom with the promise of berries. Yes, it's a mundane thing, but there is something thrilling about being able to bring life instead of take it.

"I always did want a garden," I admit.

Tyron's smile dampens the last simmerings of my frustration. "Now you have it." He turns back inside as he says, "And as it happens, Luros sent me home with a meal in thanks for healing her son's leg." He holds up a basket I hadn't noticed before.

With one last reproachful glare at the charred pie, I close the door and follow him to the table.

"What is the letter?" I nod to the parchment in his hand as I help him unpack the basket.

"Success," Tyron's smile widens and he holds the letter up. "I've heard back from my contact in Silbyr."

"Really? What did they say?" I remember the letter we'd drafted together over a month ago. After uncovering rumors that there was a push to identify all artifacts kept in the Vault of the Untoward, we'd written under the pretense of an elderly scholar from the town of Cerdris. We'd offered our assistance and claimed age as a reason we could not travel as far as Silbyr.

Tyron fetches the pitcher of water and sets it on the table, replying, "He accepted and will be sending a fully detailed catalogue of descriptions and any known functions for each item, along with when and where they were discovered."

I can't help my smile: Finally, some real progress. I'd been beginning to worry about our timeline. "Perfect. From that, I should be able to identify a Maze relic and all that's left is to figure out how to get it from the Vault."

Tyron nods as he retrieves wooden plates from a cupboard. "And to plan a route to Alarune."

Alarune. And Tirzah. I find myself toying with my puzzle ring, as I do so often now. "Think she'll be mad that she missed the wedding?" I ask, only half in jest.

'Tirzah?" Tyron sets the plates down, chuckling. "Miss out on having to witness pledges of love? I doubt she'll mind." He's more serious when he adds, "I don't think she would have wanted us to wait."

He's right, of course. Still, I can't help but wish she had been there.

As if sensing my longing, Tyron reaches over the table to take my hand. "You'll see her soon," he reassures.

I regather myself and squeeze his hand in return. "I know."

We both let go and sit down to our shared meal.

We divvy up the bread and cheese and fruit preserves but, as soon as I take my first bite, there's a knock at the door. Tyron looks apologetic as he gets to his feet. I shoo him off, already starting to pack up his food. Such interruptions come with him being the only Gifted healer for miles around. I am used to it. At least this time it's just supper and not the dead of night.

I hear the door latch, then the creaking of the hinges, but no greeting from Tyron. Instead, there is a pause before a deep voice says, "Prince Tyron. It's been a while."

I spin around to see Tyron standing there frozen, staring at the man in the doorway. The stranger is garbed in the royal purple of Litash, the emblem tree of seven branches and seven blossoms stamped into the hardened leather of his chest plate. Behind him, dressed much the same, stands a woman. I feel for the dagger beneath my skirts.

"May we come in?" The stranger asks, casting a dubious look around our house before his eyes settle on me.

I can see Tyron clenching his jaw. But he stands back, nodding. He waits until both have entered before shutting the door and returning to my side.

"Rhioa, meet Ethian Perras and Ethian Faelie, of the Ethian Council of Litash." His voice contains a forced steadiness. "Perras, Faelie, this is my wife, Rhioa."

Perras is tall, not as tall as Tyron but more solidly built. His narrowed eyes dart around the room, pausing at each potential exit point as if planning ahead.

His wife, nearly the same height as him, stands with a relaxed posture and seems more distracted by the unfinished meal on our table than she does the back door. But upon Tyron's introduction, both inspect me openly—Perras rather skeptically and Faelie with surprise. Both bow their heads while the latter says, "It is good to meet you, Rhioa."

I return the gesture but not the greeting; I do not think that anything about this will be good.

"I presume Judican sent you?" Tyron gets right to the point.

"You presume correctly," Perras nods.

"Then what does he want?"

Faelie starts to retrieve a rolled piece of parchment from her knapsack, but Perras waves her off. "He's summoning you back to Silbyr. If you really feel like arguing, I can read you the full pronouncement."

Tyron is back to visibly gritting his teeth. The only thing he asks is "When?"

Perras looks almost sympathetic when he replies, "Now. Pack what you can carry. A cart will arrive tomorrow morning to bring whatever else you have."

"And if we refuse?" Tyron's question is a touch too calm.

I reach for his hand.

"We're supposed to bring you in either way," Faelie says quietly.

Tyron's grip tightens.

He looks at me, switching to Arvenish when he asks, "*What do you think?*"

"*I think we have little choice.*" I try to adopt that same tone he has used to comfort me so many times. "*But I think it could work to our advantage. We'd be right there inside the palace—getting the relic would be that much easier.*"

Tyron's shoulders remain taut, his features tense. His green eyes hold worry—no, fear. He's thinking of his brothers.

So I lift my chin slightly and say, "*Don't you worry about me; I am more than capable of taking care of myself. You know that better than anyone.*"

Running his free hand through his hair, Tyron lets out a sharp breath. *"Alright."* He nods more to himself than to me. *"Alright."* He switches back to the trade language as he addresses the Ethians. "Give us two hours. We will need to pack and to settle a few matters in the village."

Perras and Faelie both accept this with a bow of their heads.

"Done," Perras says, the single word sealing our fate.

But Tyron doesn't move. He looks back at me, that anxiety still evident in his countenance. I have never seen him paralyzed by fear before. But I have felt it so many times, and he has helped me through it enough that I know what to do.

"Come on," I tug at his hand. *"Let's go pack."*

He hesitates, then swallows, then gives in. *"Alright. Let's go."*

Tales of Redemeré: Book II

ADVESPERATE

n. To draw towards evening.

Armed with a plan, Rhioa and Tyron escape to Litash and begin their search. It isn't long before they are thrown right into the heart of Litashian politics—a position they can use to their advantage...

...so they think.

When plans go horribly wrong, it triggers a chain of events that neither of them could have predicted. Friends turn without warning. Family betrays in an instant.

But once Tyron has started, he will never give up.

About the Author

Rebecca Schmid is an author and pianist from upstate New York. She credits her parents for fostering her love of books and writing. With their encouragement, she has been writing since she was a teenager (though she cringes at the thought of those early drafts) along with her best friend and sister-in-law, Niamh Schmid. Together, they co-authored the series, *A Daughter's Ransom,* debuting their first book in 2020. Both have continued to explore the TetraWorlds in solo works as well as joint projects.

While books and music take up most of her time, Rebecca enjoys dabbling in many other hobbies such as painting, horse riding, history, archery, hiking, martial arts, and more. If anyone asks her why she needs so many past times, her excuse is simple: "I'm researching...for my book, of course."

For more information about the books or author, visit
ScharaReevesPress.com

Made in the USA
Middletown, DE
18 October 2022